W9-CNZ-702

PRAISE FOR

BOUND, BRANDED, & BRAZEN

"Burton is a master at sexual tension." —*Romantic Times*

"As always, Jaci Burton delivers a hot read." —*Fresh Fiction*

"Spy the name Jaci Burton on the spine of a novel, and you're guaranteed not just a sexy, get-the-body-humming read, but also one that melds the sensual with the all-important building of intimacy and relational dynamics between partners. —*Romance: B(u)y the Book*

RIDING ON INSTINCT

"Kudos and beyond for Ms. Burton's best book yet! I cannot wait to see what comes next!" —*Fallen Angels Reviews*

"Everything about *Riding on Instinct* is picture-perfect and I stayed up half the night, unable to put it down until finishing the very last word." —*Romance Junkies*

"Another smokin'-hot Wild Riders story you will love reading." —*Fresh Fiction*

"Jaci Burton's *Riding on Instinct* took me on the ride of my life." —*Wild on Books*

"Thank you for giving us a love story where there is room for compromise and the good guys not only win, they take down the bad guys with a minimum of bloodshed and loss of innocent life." —*Night Owl Romance*

continued . . .

RIDING TEMPTATION

"Full of intrigue, sexual tension, and exhilarating release. Definitely a must-read." —*Fresh Fiction*

"*Riding Temptation* has it all—action, suspense, romance, and sensuality all wrapped up in a story that will keep you on the edge of your seat and have you clamoring for the next story in the Wild Riders series!" —*Wild on Books*

"Kudos to Ms. Burton for creating this exciting new series!" —*Romance Junkies*

RIDING WILD

"A wild ride is exactly what you will get with this steamy romantic caper. This sexy and sizzling-hot story will leave you breathless and wanting more." —*Fresh Fiction*

"A nonstop thrill ride from the first page to the last! Grab a copy of *Riding Wild* and take your own ride on the wild side of life!" —*Romance Junkies*

"What an exciting and wonderful book!" —*The Romance Studio*

"*Riding Wild* is a must-read for anyone who loves sexy romances filled with plenty of action and suspense." —*Kwips and Kritiques*

WILD, WICKED, & WANTON

"*Wild, Wicked, & Wanton* starts off with a bang and never lets up!"

—*Just Erotic Reviews*

"This is the best erotic novel I have ever read! I absolutely loved it!"

—*Fresh Fiction*

"Jaci Burton's *Wild, Wicked, & Wanton* is an invitation to every woman's wildest fantasies. And it's an invitation that can't be ignored."

—*Romance Junkies*

FURTHER PRAISE FOR THE WORK OF
JACI BURTON

"Burton delivers it all in this hot story—strong characters, an exhilarating plot, and scorching sex—and it all moves at a breakneck pace. Forget about a cool glass of water; break out the ice! You'll be drawn so fully into her characters' world that you won't want to return to your own."

—*Romantic Times*

"Realistic dialogue, spicy bedroom scenes, and a spitfire heroine make this one to pick up and savor."

—*Publishers Weekly*

"Jaci Burton delivers."

—Cherry Adair, *New York Times* bestselling author

"Lively and funny . . . The sex is both intense and loving; you can feel the connection that both the hero and heroine want to deny in every word and touch between them. I cannot say enough good things about this book."

—*The Road to Romance*

The PERFECT Play

JACI BURTON

HEAT | NEW YORK

THE BERKLEY PUBLISHING GROUP
Published by the Penguin Group
Penguin Group (USA) Inc.
375 Hudson Street, New York, New York 10014, USA
Penguin Group (Canada), 90 Eglinton Avenue East, Suite 700, Toronto, Ontario M4P 2Y3, Canada
(a division of Pearson Penguin Canada Inc.)
Penguin Books Ltd., 80 Strand, London WC2R 0RL, England
Penguin Group Ireland, 25 St. Stephen's Green, Dublin 2, Ireland (a division of Penguin Books Ltd.)
Penguin Group (Australia), 250 Camberwell Road, Camberwell, Victoria 3124, Australia
(a division of Pearson Australia Group Pty. Ltd.)
Penguin Books India Pvt. Ltd., 11 Community Centre, Panchsheel Park, New Delhi—110 017, India
Penguin Group (NZ), 67 Apollo Drive, Rosedale, North Shore 0632, New Zealand
(a division of Pearson New Zealand Ltd.)
Penguin Books (South Africa) (Pty.) Ltd., 24 Sturdee Avenue, Rosebank, Johannesburg 2196,
South Africa

Penguin Books Ltd., Registered Offices: 80 Strand, London WC2R 0RL, England

This book is an original publication of The Berkley Publishing Group.

This is a work of fiction. Names, characters, places, and incidents either are the product of the author's imagination or are used fictitiously, and any resemblance to actual persons, living or dead, business establishments, events, or locales is entirely coincidental. The publisher does not have any control over and does not assume any responsibility for author or third-party websites or their content.

Copyright © 2011 by Jaci Burton
Excerpt from *Changing the Game* copyright © by Jaci Burton.
Cover photograph by Claudio Marinesco.
Cover design by Rita Frangie.
Text design by Kristin del Rosario.

All rights reserved.
No part of this book may be reproduced, scanned, or distributed in any printed or electronic form without permission. Please do not participate in or encourage piracy of copyrighted materials in violation of the author's rights. Purchase only authorized editions.
HEAT and the HEAT design are trademarks of Penguin Group (USA) Inc.

ISBN: 978-1-61129-177-3

PRINTED IN THE UNITED STATES OF AMERICA

This book is dedicated to
Rita Frangie and the Berkley Art Department.

Thank you for the best cover I've ever had!

ACKNOWLEDGMENTS

A big thank-you to Azteclady and Renée for all your help.

To Shannon Stacey: Thank you for reading the book, and for your awesome suggestions—especially the first chapter. Have I told you lately how brilliant you are?

To Maya Banks, first for your friendship, which I find so valuable, and second for your idea for this series. I owe you big-time.

And as always, a big thank-you to my husband, Charlie, who has to give up many weekends while I'm working away on deadline. Thank you for the sacrifices and for your patience. They're noted and always appreciated.

ONE

SWEAT DRIPPED DOWN MICK RILEY'S FACE AND ARMS. The field workout he'd just endured had kicked his ever-lovin' ass. He leaned against the wall of the locker room, the cool brick and ice-cold water in his hands not helping at all to lower his temperature. He was hot and sweaty, and he'd been knocked on the ground so many times he'd probably eaten half the dirt on the field.

He was exhausted and not in the damn mood for a party tonight. What he'd really like to do is take a cold shower, go home, and order a pizza. Instead, he had to put on a tux and a smile, and hang out in a ballroom with the rest of his team, the San Francisco Sabers of the National Football League. There'd be photographers, television cameras, and probably a horde of women who wanted to hang on him.

Years ago that would have been the highlight of his night.

Not anymore.

When had he gotten so tired of it all? Hell, when had he gotten old?

He stripped off his practice jersey and tossed it to the ground, pulled off his pads and breathed a sigh of relief, then grabbed a towel and wiped the sweat from his face. He unlaced his pants, drained the water from his jug, and went to the fountain to refill it.

That's when he heard a voice outside the locker room. A woman's voice.

What was a woman doing down here? He popped the door open and saw a gorgeous blonde standing a few feet down the hall, twirling around in circles and mumbling to herself. Man, she was a sight with her business skirt that skimmed her knees, her high heels showcasing her gorgeous legs, and her crisp white blouse and pulled-up hair. All prim and proper, and she made him think dirty thoughts about getting her crisp white shirt all mussed up.

"I should have taken a left. I know it was a left. You dummy, now you're going to be lost in this cavern forever, and you're going to get fired."

He leaned against the doorway as she stared down the long hall, tapped her high-heeled shoe, and mumbled some more.

"Where the hell is the office, anyway? It can't be in the friggin' basement of this place."

"No, it's not down here."

She whirled, seemingly embarrassed to be caught talking to herself. Her eyes widened for a fraction of a second, then she headed in his direction. "Oh. Thank God. A living human being. Can you help me? I'm so lost."

"Sure. You need the office?"

"Yes."

She stopped in front of him, and she smelled so damn good—like spring and cookies or something—that he was embarrassed, because he sure as hell didn't smell like anything appealing.

"Take a right turn, then at the first hallway go left. You'll find the elevators. Punch the button for the top floor. When you get off, turn left again and go to the end of the hall. The main office is there."

She studied him, then gave him a wide smile. "You're my hero. I was afraid I was going to be lost down here forever and I'd never get these contracts signed. I have to run. Thank you!"

She turned and practically sprinted down the hall, though how she could run on those shoes was something he'd never understand about women.

She sure was beautiful, but not in the way he was used to. She wasn't overly made up, so her beauty was natural. She wasn't the kind of woman he usually went for. Maybe that's what he liked about her.

And he hadn't even bothered to introduce himself. Or get her name.

Too bad, because he could have sworn there'd been a spark between them.

Then again, it might have just been his imagination. He could just need a slap of cold water to lower his body temperature. Too much heat today.

He went back inside, grabbed the towel, and headed for the shower.

AS KICK-ASS EVENTS WENT, TARA LINCOLN THOUGHT this one might be the best she'd ever put together. And it damn well better be, because it could generate more work for her, and The Right Touch needed all the business it could get.

Event planning the team summer party for the San Francisco Sabers had been a stroke of luck. The owner's assistant had gotten her card from the usual team planner, who was booked solid on the date they wanted to have the party.

It had taken four months of nearly nonstop work, but as Tara took another turn around the ballroom, she nodded in satisfaction. They'd pulled it off. From the glittery yet understated NFL team decorations to the amazing food to the bar setup to the incredible band, it was perfect, and everyone seemed to be having a great time.

Tara mingled, earpiece tucked unobtrusively in her ear so she was only seconds away from hearing about a disaster, answering any questions, or getting help if someone needed it. So far, all the crises had been minor ones. She monitored bar stock, checked with catering to be sure the food was hot and plentiful, and meandered in and around the crowds. No one complained, and the smiling faces all around her told her everyone was focused on what they should be focused on—football and having a good time—which meant she could take a step back and simply observe.

The band was kicking, the crowd was thick on the dance floor, media was in attendance taking pictures of the star players, coaches were giving interviews, and for the first time that night, Tara exhaled as she leaned against the floor-to-ceiling glass windows that showcased the beautiful city.

"Why aren't you out there dancing?"

She lifted her gaze to the six and a half foot hunk of gorgeous man in a tux who'd stepped up in front of her. Black hair, striking blue eyes: she knew exactly who he was—Mick Riley, San Francisco's star quarterback, and her savior from earlier today. She'd been so rattled after having gotten lost in the basement of the team's practice facility that it hadn't even registered who he was until the elevator had taken her to the top floor. Okay, not just rattled, but a little tongue-tied. Who wouldn't be when faced with a shirtless, sweaty, gorgeous hunk of muscle? God's gift to women. Good Lord, he'd looked sexy. Unfortunately, all she could do at the time was ask for directions.

Idiot.

But then her synapses had fired, and she'd realized who she'd been talking to.

Mick Riley. *The* Mick Riley. Everyone who lived here knew who he was. Everyone who watched football knew him, too, no matter where they lived. His endorsement contracts put him on every television in America, and probably overseas, too, hawking a variety of products from deodorant to power tools. He was an icon, the all-American success story. And damn fine looking, too.

"We met earlier today," he said.

"Yes, we did. And thank you again for the directions to the office."

"You're welcome. So, you're a guest here tonight?"

She offered up a smile. "No. I'm not a guest."

He arched a brow. "Party crasher, huh?"

She laughed. "No, I'm the event planner."

"Is that right? You did a good job."

Oh, man, she was getting warm all over. "Thank you. I'm glad you think so."

"Not that I know a damn thing about throwing a fancy party, but I like to eat, and the food was good. There's plenty of name-brand booze behind the bar, and the band is kick-ass."

Okay, her cheeks hurt from smiling so much. "Thank you again."

Now if he would only say all those things to Irvin Stokes, the owner of the team. That would go a long way toward cementing her future.

"How late do you have to work?"

She tilted her head back and frowned. Was he hitting on her? She scanned the crowd, going blind from all the stunning female beauty in the room, many of whom had their gazes trained on Mick. Surely Tara was just misjudging his politeness for something else.

"I stay until the last person goes home."

He laughed, and the dark husky tone skittered down her spine.

"Honey, you could be up all night, then. These guys know how to close down a party."

That's what she expected, why she'd told the hotel they'd want the room for the entire night and guaranteed overtime for the band and extra staff for catering and the bar. "I do what needs to be done."

"And you look fine doing it. How come you're not wearing one of those butler outfits or a white apron?"

"I'm just the event planner. Everyone else does the real work."

"So you get to dress up, supervise, make sure every play goes off without a fumble."

"Something like that."

"And look good in case someone wants to talk to you about booking a party."

"Perceptive, aren't you."

"And they say football players are dumb."

She liked this guy. He was funny and smart, but she still didn't understand why he was talking to the help when the cream of the crop was here.

"I should probably move on," she said.

"Someone beeping you in your earpiece or screaming for help?"

"Well . . . no."

He scanned the ballroom. "Something on fire somewhere or some high-strung chef in need of a Valium?"

Her lips quirked. "No."

He moved toward her and took her hand, then slipped her arm in his. "Then you don't really have to move on, do you?"

"I guess not."

"Good. I'm Mick Riley."

"Tara Lincoln."

"Nice to meet you, Tara Lincoln." He walked her away from the crowd, outside the ballroom.

"I really should . . ."

"You have communication central in your ear. If something comes up, someone will holler. And your job is to make sure your guests are happy, right?"

"Yes."

"I'm a guest, and I'd like to get the hell out of this ballroom and talk to you. Which means you're doing your job in making sure I'm happy."

True enough, though for some reason she felt like she'd just been blindsided by a lineman.

And now who was thinking in football terms?

He sat her down on one of the cushioned benches in the outer lobby area beyond the ballroom. She had to admit it was blissfully quiet away from the noise of the party. And oh, what she wouldn't give to be able to slip out of her heels for just a few minutes. But looking fashionable was required, even if it hurt. "Why aren't you inside partying it up with your teammates?"

He shrugged. "Needed a break."

"You needed a break from that awesome party I put together?"

"Your party is fine," he said, leaning back and resting his arm over the back of the bench. "I'm just not a party kind of guy. Standing around making small talk just isn't my thing."

"And yet I see you in magazines at nearly every big event in New York and Los Angeles and here in San Francisco. Right in the center of it all, usually with some gorgeous woman right next to you."

His lips quirked in a devastatingly sexy smile that made her belly quiver. "That's just PR, honey."

"Uh-huh. That's not what the tabloids say."

She felt his arm brush against her back. Very disconcerting.

"Don't tell me you buy into those rags."

"Don't tell me all those women you've been hanging out with for the past ten years have been just arm candy and nothing more."

"Okay, you've got me there. But I've never been seriously involved with any of them."

"So you're saying you're a man whore?"

He choked out a laugh. "Wow. You don't hold back, do you?"

She smiled at him. "Just call them as I see them."

"Don't believe everything you see on TV and read in the magazines. That's not who I am."

"Really. And who are you?"

"Hang out with me after this is over, and you can find out."

He was definitely hitting on her. No doubt about it. And she had no clue why. But admittedly, it felt good. Star quarterback, fine-looking, and it had been a long time since a man paid attention to her. Plus there were some stunning women inside that ballroom, and for some reason he'd chosen her. Her ego had just climbed a few rungs up the ladder. Okay, maybe it had climbed to the top of the ladder.

Nothing was going to come of it, of course, but she was going to bask in his attention for just a few moments longer.

"I don't get it, Mick. Why me?"

"Because you're real."

"And all those women inside the ballroom aren't?"

He grinned. "Pretty much, yeah. But it'll be time for me to get back to some serious work soon. And what better way to end my time off than with a woman who's honest and not a game player."

"You had a great last season. Congratulations. But I can't imagine you wouldn't enjoy your off season by basking in the glory of a beautiful actress or model or someone to help you relax."

"Thanks. We did have a kick-ass season. And I have a top-notch agent who likes to toss these cover models and whoever's the current hot actress at me. Good for my image, ya know."

She leaned back to study him. "Yes, I can see how that would put you front and center in the entertainment news. And maybe get more people coming to your games."

"Exactly. But it's tiresome. And maybe once I'd just like to be with someone who isn't—"

"Famous? Connected? Isn't going to drag you onto the cover of the tabloids?"

He laughed. "Something like that. Someone I can just talk to, have a real conversation with. Be with because she just wants to be with me, not because it's good for her career."

She'd always envied people like Mick Riley and the women on his arm. Maybe she shouldn't have. "It doesn't sound like you're having much fun."

"Oh, on the field I have a lot of fun. Off the field . . ."

"Oh, come on. It can't be that much of a hardship having to be with all those beautiful women."

His chest rose when he inhaled, and Tara wished he wasn't wearing that tux. She watched all of the Sabers games. In his uniform, Mick was something to behold. He had an amazing athlete's body. This afternoon when she'd run into him in the locker room? Wow. She didn't know they made bodies that sculpted. She had to admit she wouldn't mind a closer inspection. Did that make her shallow?

Probably.

"Most people don't understand why I'd complain about dating the model who was on the cover of *Sports Illustrated*, or a popular actress without a single flaw. Sometimes I wonder about it myself."

"It's not always about looks. Granted, physical attraction is what gets you in the door. But there has to be something beyond that to want to keep you there."

He cocked his head to the side. "You understand."

"Of course. I like a good-looking man as much as any woman does. But there has to be some substance beyond just his great looks. Something that keeps me coming back for more. Otherwise you're left feeling empty."

"I don't have these kinds of conversations with the women I meet."

"Have you tried?"

"You mean do I try to talk to them beyond just having sex with them?"

"Yes."

"Yeah, I do. We don't get very far. They're more interested in talking about themselves and their careers. It isn't too long before I'm bored and out the door."

She smiled at him. "Maybe you're just not meeting the right woman."

"Probably because I've never looked for her." He stood, held out his hand. "Let's go dance."

A rush of panic hit her. "Oh, I can't."

"Why not?"

"Again, because I'm working."

"Bullshit." He tugged her along, and she went helplessly as he opened the door and led her back into the ballroom, through the crowds, and onto the dance floor. He pulled her against him, slid his arm around her back, and drew her close.

How timely. A slow song. The lights had dimmed, and couples were pressed intimately against each other. She cringed, certain she was the center of attention, but when she took a quick glance around, no one seemed to be looking at them. Maybe it wasn't unusual for Mick to grab random women and dance with them. She prayed the media was off interviewing someone else or taking pictures of Katrina Strauss, the latest Hollywood It Girl. Maybe she was safe from the cameras at least.

But Tara was certain any moment someone from management was going to drag her off the dance floor and fire her. She tried to search the ballroom for Mr. Stokes or his assistant or anyone else on his staff, but the dance floor was too crowded.

"Hey, would you relax?"

She snapped her gaze to Mick. "What? Oh, sorry. I'm feeling kind of guilty."

"For dancing?"

"You're here to celebrate. I'm here to work."

He slid his hand up her back and she wished she hadn't worn such a revealing dress. The feel of his warm hand against the bare skin of her back made thinking clearly a near impossibility.

"You are working. You're keeping the guests happy."

"Ha. I'm keeping one guest happy."

"The rest of the guests don't seem miserable. Relax." He pulled her close and swayed with her around the dance floor. He had decent rhythm for someone so big. She expected a football player to be clumsier, but he glided around like he knew what he was doing.

"You dance really well."

"I took ballet lessons."

She tilted her head back to search his face, certain he was joking. "You did not."

"I did. Several of us on the team did. Good for coordination."

Resisting the laugh that bubbled up in her throat, she said, "Somehow I can't picture you in tights and a tutu."

But he did laugh. "We made sure no one with a camera got within miles of the studio."

The more time she spent with him, the more she liked him. Dammit. Why couldn't he be an arrogant son of a bitch, full of himself and talking of nothing but his career and his stats? It would be so much easier to walk away from him if he was self-absorbed. But not only was he gorgeous, he was also funny and was interested in her and her career, and she liked spending time with him.

And how long had it been since she'd danced with a guy? She couldn't recall. That meant it had been too long. It felt good to feel his warm hand at her back, to clasp her other hand in his, to feel the pressure of his thighs against hers as he expertly managed the steps and moved her around the dance floor. He smelled good, like pine trees and outdoors. She leaned in a little and inhaled, amazed at the sheer size of him.

And when he dipped her at the end of the dance, her lips parted and she let out a small gasp. "Bet you didn't learn that in ballet class."

He brought her upright, a wicked gleam in his eyes. "Don't tell anyone, but my mom is a dance teacher. I might have learned a few things watching her classes."

"Your mother is a dance teacher? Like ballroom dancing for adults?"

He slipped her hand in the crook of his arm and led her to his table, then pulled out a chair for her, and she sat. "No, the teach-all-the-little-kids-how-to-dance kind of teacher."

She saw the pride in his eyes, and her heart melted just a little bit. "What a wonderful profession. I'm sure she loves it."

"She does. Though she was disappointed to have two sons who would rather be outside playing football and baseball than becoming the next Baryshnikov."

"How sad for her."

"She made up for it by having our little sister, who was forced to endure all the dance lessons."

Tara laughed. "She didn't want them either?"

"Oh, she put up with them as a kid, but she would have rather been outside being tackled by my brother and me. She's pretty tough."

Tara leaned forward and laid her elbows on the table. "Sounds like you have an amazing family."

"I do. What about yours?"

Now there was a topic she didn't want to get into. "Oh, nothing at all like yours."

"Tell me about them."

Yeah, that would send him running in a hurry. "My family just isn't hearth and home like yours seems to be."

He laughed and placed his hand over hers. "Not everyone's is, honey. Doesn't mean I don't want to know about your life."

Really, he didn't want to know about her life and the screwed-up mess that was her family. Fortunately, the caterer took that moment to beep in with a problem. She placed her hand at her ear and stood. "I need to go."

"Some emergency?"

"Yes. Thank you for the dance. It was a lovely break."

"Come back after you see to whatever crisis you have to deal with."

"Surely by then you'll have found some other female to hang out with."

He leaned back in his chair and picked up a glass of water, the look he gave her sending goose bumps down her arms. "No, I won't. I'll wait for you."

She hurried off, warmed to her toes by Mick Riley. He would be a dangerous man to get to know better. But he intrigued her, and it had been a long time since any man had done that.

Unfortunately, it was hours later before she freed herself again. The caterers had run out of one of the meats, the head bartender had a meltdown about a waitress who decided at the last minute to have a fight with her boyfriend via text message and storm out in tears, and Tara had to make a couple frantic phone calls to get every ruffled feather smoothed. By the time all that had been dealt with, she'd had to make a once-around again to make sure no other brush fires had erupted.

The party had mellowed out by then. Many people had left, and only a few diehards remained. But Mr. Stokes's personal assistant had stopped her and told her that Mr. Stokes was very pleased with the party, and he would likely use her company again. She resisted the squeal that hovered at the back of her throat, calmly thanked him, and said she'd be happy to provide event services at any time. Hopefully he'd recommend her to others. She needed her business to grow.

Another couple hours, and everyone was out the door. Tara made sure the band packed up, and she thanked them, as well as the bar staff and the caterers, for doing such a great job.

Once everyone left, she looked around the empty ballroom, unable to resist a smile. She'd done it. Her first major event, and she'd pulled it off perfectly.

Her feet were aching. She fell into the nearest chair, kicked off her shoes, and twisted open the top on the mineral water she'd snatched from the bar before they'd closed up. She took a long drink and sighed.

"I thought they'd never leave."

She jerked upright in her chair, half turning to see Mick walking past the rows of empty tables. "I thought you'd left hours ago."

He pulled out a chair across from her and sat, surprising the hell out of her by grabbing her legs and propping her feet on his lap. "Me and a couple of the offensive linemen ended up in coach's room for a couple hours, rehashing the last season."

"Oh. And how did that go?"

He lifted one of her feet and began rubbing the arch. She bit her lip to keep from moaning at how damn good it felt.

"We ended up blaming the division championship loss on the defense."

She laughed. "How convenient."

He shrugged. "The defense was probably in the defensive coordinator's room blaming it on us, so why not?"

She wanted to tell him she'd missed him, that she'd sort of casually looked for him while she was wandering around the ballroom, but she couldn't bring herself to admit that out loud. It sounded too desperate. She barely knew him.

Then again, her feet were in his lap and he was giving her a delicious foot rub that made her nipples tingle and her panties dampen. What did that say about her?

What it said was that California wasn't the only place that had been in a drought for the past several years. And she was alone in a massive ballroom with one very sexy man with amazing hands. She wondered what else he could do with those amazing hands.

"You don't have to rub my feet."

"I saw you wince when you kicked your shoes off. And heard you sigh."

"It's been a long night on very high heels," she said with a laugh. "I freely admit I'm more of a blue jeans and flats kind of girl."

He cocked his head to the side. "I could definitely see you that way. I'm more of the same way myself."

"Blue jeans and flats?"

He laughed. "Uh, no. But this tux is killing me." He loosened the bow tie and unbuttoned the top two buttons, then shrugged out of his jacket. "That's a little better."

"If you're going to start stripping, maybe you should head on home," she teased.

"Why? Never seen a man naked before?"

She choked out a laugh. "No, that's not it. But I don't think this oversized mausoleum of a ballroom is going to offer you the privacy to take off everything you want to take off."

"And how do you know how much I want to take off?"

She dropped her chin to her chest and shook her head. "I'm digging the hole deeper and deeper, aren't I?"

"Is there someplace you have to be right now?"

Her head shot up, her gaze meeting his. "No. Why?"

"Come with me." He laid her feet on the ground, bent over and retrieved her shoes, then grabbed his coat and slung it over his arm.

Tara followed him out of the ballroom. "Where are we going? And shouldn't I put my shoes on?"

"Nah. We're not leaving the hotel." He pushed the elevator button.

"You have a room here?"

"Everyone does. The team didn't want the guys driving tonight after the party. You know, in case there was overindulgence of all that great alcohol you provided."

She stepped in while he held the door open for her. "I don't recall seeing you drink anything but water."

He shrugged and pushed the button. "Not much of a drinker at events like this. Too much of an opportunity to make a total ass of yourself in public. And the media loves getting shots of players partying a little too hard."

She turned to him. "You prefer to do it in private, then?"

"Ha-ha." The elevator doors opened, and he led the way down the hall, retrieving the key card from his pocket. "I prefer not to do it at all. Got all that out of my system when I was younger."

He opened the door for her and held it while she walked in. Since they held the party at one of San Francisco's premier hotels, the room was nice. Really nice. A suite, actually, with an outer room and a hallway that must lead to the bedroom. Tara walked to the window and stared at the killer view of the city skyline, rubbing her arms as she did.

"Cold?"

She half turned to face him. "A little."

He put his jacket over her. "Slip into this. I'll adjust the temp in here."

She slid her arms into his jacket, which was miles too big for her but instantly warmed her. His scent surrounded her again as she pulled his jacket around her. She turned to face him. "Thank you."

"You're welcome." His fingers lingered over the lapels of his jacket, his knuckles resting on the swells of her breasts. Even though the fabric separated his hands from her skin, she still felt the pressure of his hands there, and that warmed her more than his jacket ever could. Her heart kicked up a fast beat, and she became aware that she was in his room—alone. She didn't do this, didn't blindly follow men she didn't know to their rooms. And she wasn't easily captivated by fame, so who he was meant nothing to her.

Where had her common sense gone?

MICK HAD BEEN WITH PLENTY OF WOMEN IN HIS LIFE-time. From college to the pros, women had gravitated to him like he was an irresistible magnet. And he'd never been one to turn down a beautiful woman who wanted to crawl into bed with him.

So he'd never had to pursue a woman. Until tonight, until he'd seen Tara leaning against the wall of the ballroom, not participating, just watching, the sparkles on her champagne-colored dress lifting the light from the chandeliers and all the candles shining around her as if she were the main event in the ballroom.

She'd captivated him from the first moment he'd seen her in the locker room area today. He'd hated missing the opportunity to meet her then, and finding her at the ballroom tonight had seemed like it was meant to be.

She'd been polite but hadn't fallen all over him when he'd introduced himself. And oh man, had he liked that. A lot. Surprisingly, a lot. Especially when she'd walked away from him. Women tended to latch onto him like he was the Holy Grail, and once they did, they never let go. That, he didn't like. But Tara actually seemed more interested in doing her job than in being with him. It was damned refreshing.

So he'd stood back and watched. She was good at her work. Efficient. He'd noticed she had a couple assistants working with her, and she treated them like equals. No browbeating, no talking down to them like they were ants under her feet. But when she gave instructions, people moved and moved fast. And she seemed more than willing to get in there to do whatever needed to be handled to get the job done. She'd opened bottles of wine with efficiency, folded table napkins, directed a new waitress on what tables were hers, and calmed down a very agitated bartender with quiet words and more patience than Mick could have ever come up with.

He liked to watch her move in her high heels, her swishing skirt giving him glimpses of what must be spectacular thighs. She was slender, but not too much. She looked like she actually ate three meals a day, unlike a lot of the women he'd been forced to spend time with. She curved in all the right places, and he was fascinated by her neck, which was nicely visible, since her blonde hair was pulled up in a fancy hairstyle that didn't suit her at all. He'd bet she usually wore her hair down or in a ponytail or in one of those messy hair clip things. She didn't seem the type of woman who messed with her hair so that it had to be perfect. She had full lips and a narrow face and the prettiest brown eyes he'd ever seen.

But what he'd liked best about tonight was talking to her. She was a real person, not interested in furthering her career by being seen on his arm, but an actual, honest-to-God real woman. Funny and warm, with her own career. She hadn't once searched out the media so they could take pictures of Mick and her. In fact, she'd done her best to avoid having the media see the two of them together.

It felt good to just be in this room with her. He wasn't in any hurry, had no place to be for the rest of the weekend. It had been a long time since he'd really wanted to be with a woman—hell, had he ever really wanted to be in the company of a particular woman? He couldn't think of any. As a release, yeah. To kill time, definitely. Someone thrust on his arm by Elizabeth for PR—all the damn time. But no woman had captured him enough for him to really want to be with her. They'd all been in and out of his life like some damn revolving door. Faces and names all blurred together, and he couldn't remember a single one of them other than he'd met them and fucked some of them. He'd forgotten them as easily as they'd forgotten him.

Now Tara, he'd definitely remember.

There was something about her that made him want to do more than just fuck her.

Except right now he really wanted to kiss her and touch her and get her naked so he could explore the rest of her skin and see if it was as soft as the parts he'd already touched.

Easy, man. Not too fast. He didn't want to scare her away. She wasn't like any other woman he'd ever met. And for the first time in his life, he didn't want to run the clock down too fast. He wanted this night to go into overtime.

MICK HADN'T SAID MUCH FOR THE PAST FEW MINUTES, just seemed content to stare out the window with her. Tara waited for discomfort to set in, but it hadn't. There was something special about him, something she'd noticed from the start, and it had nothing to do with his career and everything to do with who he was as a man. She liked Mick, liked him more than she had any other man in a very long time. Since she had the entire weekend to herself, why not indulge?

"Would you like some champagne?" He motioned to the bucket sitting on ice. "They delivered it earlier. I think we all got one as a thanks from the owners."

"I'd love a glass."

He popped the top and poured some into a glass, handed it to her. She took a sip, the bubbles tickling her nose. "It's very good. Aren't you going to have any?"

"I'm more of a beer kind of guy."

She laughed. "Me, too."

"Yeah? You're dressed like a champagne kind of woman. Your sparkly dress even matches."

She looked down at her cocktail dress. Admittedly, she loved it. Tiny straps hung on her shoulders, the bodice dipped across the swell of her breasts, hugging them tight. It fit her well and was her favorite. "Only when I work events like this. Believe me, there's no champagne stocked in my refrigerator at home. Only beer and soda."

"Chips and hot dogs?"

She laughed. "Two of my favorites. I'm sorry to say the elegance only comes out as part of my job. You'll typically find me barefoot, wearing jeans, with my hair up in a ponytail."

He examined her near-perfect updo. "So that doo-dah hairstyle isn't the norm for you?"

"Hardly. It'll be hell getting all these pins out."

"Want me to help?"

Heat swirled around her. "And shatter my Cinderella image? I don't think so."

"Okay, Cinderella. Your secret is safe with me."

She sipped her champagne and tried not to openly stare at him, but it was damned difficult, considering it was just the two of them in this room with the lovely view of the city. She stared out the window, still wondering what the hell she was doing here with Mick Riley.

He came up behind her. "You're a beautiful woman, Tara."

She turned to face him, wishing he knew the real her. But he never would, because the real Tara was light-years away from his world. "I usually don't follow strange men up to their hotel rooms."

He smiled down at her. "You don't? Damn, and I thought I'd found a sure thing in you."

Everything he said either made her laugh or made her hot. Why hadn't some woman grabbed him by the hair and dragged him back to her cave by now? There had to be some chink in this knight's armor. "Sorry. You should have gone for one of the actresses or models."

"Not interested in them. They have agendas."

"What makes you think I don't?"

"Because I came to you. You didn't come to me."

"Maybe that's part of my evil plan."

"Honey, I don't think there's a damn thing evil about you."

"I'm hardly innocent, Mick."

He took her glass and set it on the table, then grasped the lapels of the jacket and pulled her closer. "Is that right?"

Liquid heat rushed through her veins, opening her up to desires and emotions she hadn't felt in far too long. She normally closed herself off to men. Too busy. Too many other priorities. Right now there was no other priority but the feel of him against her. She leaned into him and tilted her head back, giving him the green light. "That's right."

He shifted his fingers, and the fire he'd stoked began to burn even brighter. There was a sizzle of magic between them. She'd be a fool to walk away from that, even if it was only for one night. And that's all it could ever be—just one night—so why not go for it when she had the chance? Who knew when something this good would come along again? With the way her life was structured, probably never. And she'd have this one hot night to look back on and remember forever.

"I didn't bring you here to seduce you, Tara. I just wanted to spend more time with you."

She covered his hands with hers. "Maybe I'm seducing you. You wouldn't want to hurt my feelings by rejecting me, would you?"

His lips quirked. "I'd never do that."

"Then kiss me."

She saw the spark ignite in his eyes as he gathered her against him and pressed his lips to hers.

Ahh, contact. An explosion of heat and liquid fire melted her from the inside out. Oh wow, it was everything she imagined—and so much more. Tenderness as his lips brushed hers, and then the power of his mouth as he deepened the kiss. His tongue slid between her teeth to capture and slide and lick as his hands pressed in along the curves of her body.

Tara suddenly couldn't breathe. It was like being kissed for the very first time, when her head and her emotions tangled with everything her body felt. Only she wasn't a kid and neither was Mick. This was a man's hands on her body, and a woman's desires coursing through her. And what they were doing wasn't going to stop with a kiss. She already knew this, already knew where she wanted this night to go.

Cinderella wasn't going to make it home before she turned back into the dour scullery maid with bare feet and blue jeans.

And she didn't care.

TWO

MICK HADN'T BEEN LYING ABOUT HIS REASONS FOR bringing Tara up to his room; he'd really wanted to spend some more time talking to her. But she obviously wanted more than that—or needed more than that—and he was damn happy to oblige. She tasted like champagne and mint, and sliding his tongue inside the heat of her mouth had tightened his balls into a painful knot.

She was as ramped up as he was, her mouth moving under his, her body one ball of energy as she reached up to undo the buttons of his shirt. His heart pounded against his chest. He wondered if she could feel it, if she'd laugh that he was so caught up in this. It wasn't like this was a first for him. Women threw themselves at him. He should be kind of jaded about the whole thing. But she was so different from the other women he'd been with. Fresh and exciting and . . . normal.

She lifted her lips from his. "Your heart is racing." She laid her palm flat against his chest. "I thought it was just me who was supposed to be excited about this."

He arched a brow. "You think I'm not affected by you kissing me?"

She shrugged. "Women probably kiss you every day."

He laughed, then pulled her onto the sofa with him. "Not every day. And you aren't just any woman."

She slid her legs over his lap. "Oh, right. I'm special."

"You are."

"Really. In what way?"

"You're not famous."

She tilted her head back and laughed, then hitched her dress up, revealing her thighs as she straddled him. Just as he imagined, she had killer thighs.

"Gee, you sure know how to compliment a woman."

She wound her arms around his neck and leaned in, her breasts brushing his chest.

He'd really wanted to spend more time talking to her, to show her that he wasn't primarily interested in getting in her panties.

But with her body full-on against his, he inhaled the scent of her shampoo—something sweet that made him want to lick her skin, and he figured, screw it. He really did want to get in her panties. He swept his hand down her back, mapping his way through a mix of skin and the sparkly dress. He tucked his hand inside, definitely preferring the skin part.

Tara moaned and got closer, as if she wanted to crawl inside him.

Oh, yeah. This was the warm-up. He was ready to get in the game now. He reached up and started pulling pins from her hair. She tilted her head back and lifted her lips.

"Determined to destroy my Cinderella image, aren't you?"

He dragged a pin from a golden strand and let it fall to the floor, then dove into the softness of her hair for another. "You get any more beautiful and I might drop dead."

She arched her brows. "You're very good at that."

"My sister liked having her hair put up."

"No, not that. The lines."

He shook his head. "No line. Promise. You're gorgeous."

She looked like she didn't believe him. Obviously no one had told her lately how stunning she really was. A damn shame, since the naked honesty in her eyes could make a man do anything she wanted. He pulled the last pin out of her hair and shook it loose, letting it tumble across her neck and cheeks.

"Amazing. Soft." He inhaled. "Peaches."

She giggled, and the sound vibrated against his chest.

"I don't know any women who smell like peaches."

"The shampoo was on sale at Walmart."

Yeah, he could seriously like this woman.

TARA DRAGGED IN BREATHS AND LET THEM OUT IN rapid succession. Hyperventilating and passing out would be the most embarrassing thing she could do right now, but Mick's face was buried in her neck, and it was a serious erogenous zone. If he licked her there, she'd rob a bank for him.

When she felt his tongue glide across her throat, she quivered all over. Mick tightened his hold on her, and then the bastard did it again. Goose bumps popped out along her flesh, desire roaring to an inferno inside her. Her nipples beaded, aching for his mouth to do to them what it was doing to her neck right now. She could already imagine him sweeping his tongue across her nipples while she watched. She'd lift her dress and slide her hand inside her panties and rub her throbbing clit until the orgasm she so desperately needed made her scream.

Damn, she'd been alone with her vibrator and late-night Cinemax for too long. But she wasn't going to get herself off tonight. Tonight, Mick was going to make her come, and if she got her wish, it wasn't going to be just once.

She almost laughed at her bold audacity. It just wasn't her at all. But dammit, she wanted Mick, and she refused to apologize for being a woman in the prime of her sexual life who hadn't been getting any for a very long time. And she was being held and kissed by one of the best specimens of male humanity she'd ever seen—a guy who for some reason seemed to really want her. No way was she going to second-guess herself or pass up this opportunity.

Mick held his hand in her hair, massaging her scalp in a way that wasn't at all medicinal. It was sensual, designed to drive her half mad with lust. And oh, did she have the lust thing going in a big way.

His other hand rested at the small of her back, his fingers tapping along the top of her butt. Tara felt his erection as she shifted on his lap, and her panties dampened as if this were the first time she'd ever been close to a cock before.

It felt the like the first time—the first in a long, long time. She'd thought denying herself was a wise idea, all things considered. Right now it didn't feel wise at all. It felt stupid, because she'd forgotten how utterly awesome it was to be close, to be kissed, to be touched by a man.

She held on to his shoulders and leaned back, searching his face, wanting to memorize how utterly beautiful he was. His eyes were a mesmerizing shade of blue, like some faraway ocean she'd likely never visit. No wonder women fell all over themselves to get close to him. He had rugged features and full soft lips that didn't seem to belong on such a masculine face. His nose was a little crooked, making his impossibly faultless face just a little less perfect. She liked that. Too flawless and she'd feel inadequate.

"You're staring."

His breathing was hard. Just like his cock. She liked that, too. "Can't help it. It's the eyes. The face. The body. Hell, it's the whole package, Mick. You're gorgeous."

He cocked his head to the side, frowning. "Men aren't gorgeous. Women are. You are."

She knew she wasn't, but hey, she'd go along with the fantasy tonight. Especially when he stood, sliding his hands under her butt to lift her. She wrapped her legs around him, her dress inching higher up her thighs. The room got a few degrees warmer as he walked her down the hall, not once taking his gaze from hers.

He made her feel special, and no one had done that for her in a while.

He shoved the door open with his shoulder, and Tara got a glimpse of wide windows and cloudless night sky before Mick placed her in the center of one incredibly large, soft, king-sized bed. He moved on top of her, his hands positioned on either side of her shoulders, holding himself off her by just the barest of inches, making her lift to brush her breasts against his chest.

"Tease."

"You're the one teasing. Get down here and kiss me," she said, needing to feel his body crushed against hers.

"I'm too big to be on top of you."

Big. On top. Didn't that conjure up images that made her wet. She palmed the back of his neck and drew his head down. "I think I can take it."

Mick uttered a low growl and dropped down on top of her, his body pressed against hers. She realized the sheer size of him as he lay full on her, but she knew from the tension in his body that he held his weight from her. Still, the pressure of a man's body on top of hers felt so damn good she could cry. His cock rubbed her thigh, and a rush of heat enveloped her, making her lift against him, arch toward what she wanted more than anything.

"You sure about this?"

She loved that he asked and framed his face with her hands. "Definitely, positively, absolutely sure."

His lips covered hers, and all reluctance was gone as he took possession, his tongue diving inside. He groaned with a seeming desperation that surprised her. Surely he did this all the time. She was the one who should be desperate, because she sure as hell *didn't* do this all the time.

His mouth was an amazing piece of artwork, full and soft and devastating to her senses. He slid his lips back and forth across hers as his tongue turned her brain to mush. And his hands were the devil's own soldiers as they moved over her, gently pressing in to sail across each of her curves from her sides to her hips, sliding underneath to cup her butt.

Tara resisted the urge to climb all over him and strip him naked in order to lick him and have her way with him in about ten seconds flat. She realized there had to be a certain finesse to this, but God Almighty, she wanted this man in a hurry. And he seemed to be taking his time moving his lips over hers, his hands roaming over her body as if he intended to thoroughly map every square inch of her with his fingertips. And oh, it felt so damn good. Her body quaked in response, throbbing and moistening in all the right places, but she was finding it hard to breathe.

"You okay?" he asked when he pulled his lips from hers.

"Yes. Fine. Why?"

"You're breathing kind of heavy." He laid his palm on her, his fingers resting just under her breast.

"You touching me there isn't going to make my breathing any easier."

He arched a brow, leaned up on his elbow, and covered her breast with his hand. "I get the idea it's been a while for you. Want me to slow things down?"

"Yes, it's been a while. How kind of you to notice. And God, no, I don't want you to slow down. I'd like us both to be naked right now."

His lips quirked. "So you're saying things are moving too slow."

"You're killing me here, Mick."

"Let me see if I can't speed things up a little for you." He pushed her up on the bed so her head was on the pillows, then spread her legs and crawled between them.

That's exactly what she needed. Maybe they wouldn't even bother with taking their clothes off. She just needed him inside her. Now.

But he didn't unbutton his pants or crawl up her body. Instead, he slid his magical fingers up her dress and teased her thighs, lifting her dress as his lips traced the trail his fingers had blazed.

Dear God. He really was trying to kill her, wasn't he? Up her dress went, to the tops of her thighs, baring the panties she'd carefully selected to match her dress, even though she'd laughed at the thought that no one would ever know.

Now she was glad she had, because Mick lifted his head and smiled as he regarded the skimpy golden lace and silk, the only barrier between his mouth and her pussy.

"Now this is pretty." He laid his hand over her sex and rubbed back and forth.

Throbbing sparks of pleasure spread from her clit to her pussy and throughout every nerve ending in her body. She began to tremble as she realized how close she was. Tara lifted up on her elbows and arched her pelvis against his hand. "I could come from you doing that."

His hand stilled, but his palm against her sex made her wet.

"That fast, huh?"

She met his gaze head-on. "That fast."

"I'd like you to come in my mouth, Tara. Try to hold off." He jerked the material to the side and planted his mouth over her pussy. Suddenly she was overwhelmed with his lips and his tongue sliding over her sex, licking at her juices, tucking inside her and lapping around her clit.

A roll of mindless pleasure seized her, melting her to the mattress.

She reached down to wind her fingers in his hair, lost in an earth-quake of sensation that she couldn't hold back.

"Mick," she whispered, then bit down on her lip as she made good on her promise. Hot waves of orgasm rushed over her, and she cried out as she flooded his face with her come. She fell back against the pillows and rode out a mind-numbing orgasm that flashed through her in relentless waves. Mick held on to her hips and continued to lick her, suck her clit and pussy until she couldn't stand it any longer. Then he moved away and kissed her thighs while she enjoyed some amazing aftershocks and caught her breath.

"Wow," she said when she could find her voice. "That was really incredible."

"Now that you got that first one out of the way, let's take our time for the second."

"What?"

Mick ignored her question. He reached for the strings holding her panties on her hips and dragged them over her butt and down her legs. Once off, he used his shoulders to nudge her legs apart.

"You have a pretty pussy, Tara. Pink and wet, and your sweet taste makes my dick hard."

And just like that, she was ramped up and ready to go for round two. Just seeing him down there between her legs made her quiver with anticipation. He was right. She'd sailed right into that orgasm without having the time to thoroughly enjoy the kind of magic he'd performed on her. She'd like the opportunity for that, wanted to watch him and feel his tongue on her.

His warm breath flowed across her aching flesh. A tease, an anticipation. She tensed, waiting for his tongue to touch her, and when it did, she shuddered. Hot and wet, he slid his tongue across her swollen flesh, lashing her clit until he took the bud in his mouth and sucked.

Tension built fast again. It had been so long, and pleasuring herself was nothing like having a man between her legs, licking her pussy and bringing all her hot fantasies to life. Mick was one seriously hot fantasy. Her dress rode up above her hips and she was naked from the waist down and oh, damn, this was just so mind-blowing and erotic she couldn't stand it.

Mick's tongue and lips danced over her sex. He added his fingers to the mix, tucking one inside her pussy.

God, that felt good. She dropped her head back and just allowed herself to feel as he fucked her slow and easy with his fingers while he took her clit in his mouth and rolled his tongue over it.

"Yes, like that," she whispered, tightening her hold on his hair as the sensations peaked, taking her close to the edge. "I'm going to come."

He laid his tongue against her clit and began to fuck her hard with his finger. She splintered, crying out and bucking against him, this orgasm just as strong as the first one, as wave after wave crashed over her.

When she fell to the mattress she was spent, utterly amazed, and profoundly grateful. When Mick crawled up and smiled at her, she swiped her fingers across his chin and licked her fingertips.

"You taste like me."

His nostrils flared and his eyes went dark. "You taste yourself often?"

She shrugged and wrapped her fingers around the nape of his neck. "Sometimes when I'm fingering myself."

She couldn't believe the things she said to him, the bold way she let herself go. But this was one night and it was her fantasy and she was going to have it the way she wanted it. And she wanted it to be perfect and no holds barred.

So when Mick rolled off the bed and started unbuttoning his shirt, Tara rose up on her knees to watch, not wanting to miss a moment of the unveiling. He shrugged out of the shirt, and he didn't disappoint. His chest was wide, his pecs absolutely spectacular. His abs were flat and chiseled with that proverbial six-pack she saw on models and on TV but didn't think existed. She reached out and laid her hands on his stomach, shocked at the rock-hard feel of his abs. "Wow, these six-pack things do exist."

He laughed and unbuttoned his pants, let them fall to the floor. Tara licked her lips at the outline of his erection pressing insistently against his boxer briefs.

"Let me." She pulled her dress off and cast it aside, then unhooked her bra, not at all self-conscious when Mick's gaze roamed appreciatively over her body. She'd never been one to focus on how she looked, but right now she felt like a goddess. There was nothing like a man's hungry gaze to make a woman feel desired.

She shimmied to the side of the bed to grab his briefs and roll them over his hips, releasing his cock. His briefs fell to the floor, and he kicked them off, giving Tara free rein to map those magnificent abs with the palms of her hands, then reach around to grab a handful of his tight ass. Wow. Talk about a work of art. She'd like to lay him down and run her hands over him for a couple hours. And then taste him.

Tara circled his cock with her hands, needing to touch him, to taste him, before he fucked her. He'd made her feel so good, she wanted to do the same to him.

She stroked the length of him, slipped one hand underneath to gently squeeze his ball sac, rewarded by his rough growl. And when she leaned over and took the smooth crest of his cock between her lips, his growl grew more pronounced. Mick slid his fingers in her hair and pulled her head toward his shaft. She gladly took him in, winding her tongue around the heated length of him.

"That's good, Tara. I like your mouth."

He tasted salty and powerful. She drank in the sight of him standing over her, her nipples tightening as she sucked him. He swept his hand over her hair in a tender gesture, and she knew he held back as he eased his cock along her tongue. She opened her mouth and let him watch, then curled her tongue over the crest and licked the salty fluid that escaped there.

"Jesus, woman, you're going to make me come."

She teased him with a slow lick of his cock head, then wrapped her fingers around his shaft and stroked him. "Isn't that the idea?"

He moved away, then pushed her onto the bed. "Yeah. When I'm inside you and your pussy is squeezing the come out of me."

He reached into his pants and pulled out a foil packet. Tara sighed in relief that he was prepared. He put the condom on and moved over her, spreading her legs, sliding his hands up her thighs, her belly, over her breasts. She arched and he filled his hands with them, then leaned over her and fit one aching bud in his mouth.

For someone so big she expected him to be rough. He surprised her with a gentle pull of her nipple between his lips, drawing it inside to glide his tongue over the bud. A slow warmth began to build as he sucked and licked one nipple, then the other, drawing out the anticipation as he rode his cock between her legs, not entering her yet, making her wait for it.

"Please," she whispered, pulling his head up. "Please."

He pressed his lips to hers, a soft brush of mouth against mouth. So tender and just what she needed. She reached up and caressed his face as he settled between her legs and slid his cock inside her.

She gasped at his entry. It was everything she'd expected and wanted. He fit her perfectly and knew just what to do to give her the kind of pleasure she craved. He slipped one hand underneath her and tilted her up, drawing them closer, taking her mouth in a hard, deep kiss, obliterating the gentleness of a few moments ago. But gentle wasn't what she needed now. Now she wanted passion, and oh, did he give it to her. She wrapped her legs around his hips and dug her heels into him, bringing him deeper inside her.

Mick met her gaze and gripped her butt, thrusting deep.

"Yes," she whispered as he rolled his hips over her, rocking against her clit. His hands added warmth and sensual pleasure as they glided over her body, stroking her sides, her breasts, tunneling into her hair to capture her and hold her steady while he kissed her, his mouth and tongue taking hers in a frenzy of passion and need that made her senseless.

She swept her hands over his back, memorizing the feel of his muscles as they moved, the steel of them working within the confines of his flesh, the heat and sweat of his skin as he powered against her.

She couldn't recall making love with a man this . . . intimately before, feeling this connection. She brushed it aside, figuring she was out of practice. It was just sex, and it had been a while, so for her, this was monumental. To him, it was likely just good fucking.

But the way he held her, caressed her, and kissed her, the way he lifted and then thrust, slow and easy, taking his time, seemingly in no hurry to race to the finish line, made her heart do flip-flops even as her body sizzled with the kind of pleasure a woman knew didn't come around very often. She let herself be seduced by the magic of this moment, by the way he ground against her and took her up again. She let herself feel every quake and tremor as her body reawakened to the pleasure of lovemaking.

Tension filled her, coiling around her middle as Mick licked her nipples while he continued to move inside her. The sensation rocketed to her pussy, bringing her ever closer to orgasm.

"Harder," she asked, and he complied, grabbing her knee and bending her leg, his gaze focused on hers as he thrust deeper, then rolled his pelvis against hers.

She gasped. "That's going to make me come, Mick."

"Oh yeah. Squeeze me with your pussy. Come for me."

He reached between them, holding his hips off hers so he could rub her clit while he fucked her, keeping his gaze trained on her face.

"Let me see it," he said, using his thumb to find the most tortured part of her, sweeping gently against the nub while continuing to rock inside her.

She trained her gaze on him as she let go, as her climax hit, the intensity of the physical pleasure combining with the emotional contact of him watching her, at the way his face contorted as he came with her, making her spiral out of control with a riot of emotions and sensations.

And then he kissed her, and she held tight to him as she continued to come, rolling over the edge again because he continued to move inside her, refusing to let go.

She didn't want him to let go. Not until they were both spent, and Mick rolled off and left her only for a moment. Then he was back, pulling her against him and dragging the covers over them both.

Tara felt so small wrapped up in his embrace. Small and cherished as he kissed the back of her neck, held her tight and played with her breast in a lazy way that made her hot and made her smile at the same time.

"I guess I won't be sleeping much tonight, will I?"

"Sleep's overrated. You can sleep later." He nipped at the back of her neck, and she shivered from the chills that skittered along her nerve endings. She turned to him, pushing him onto his back so she could climb on top of him. She felt his cock hardening underneath her.

"You're right. I'll sleep later." She bent and kissed him.

THREE

MICK ROLLED OVER, CURSING THE BRIGHT SUNLIGHT that poured into his room. He dragged the covers over his head, but the pounding wouldn't stop.

It couldn't be a hangover. He knew better. He cracked one eye open and listened.

Someone was at the door.

Oh, yeah. Hotel room. He threw the covers off, expecting to find Tara in bed with him.

But she wasn't. As he rounded the corner to the bathroom, he noticed she wasn't there either.

"Housekeeping." The pounding intensified.

"I'm not dressed. Come back later."

"Checkout was an hour ago, sir," the person outside the door said with an obvious sigh of frustration that Mick had no trouble understanding.

Mick dragged his fingers through his hair. "Oh. Sorry. I'll be out shortly."

He went to the bathroom and took a fast shower, then packed up his things, trying not to think about the woman he'd shared a bed with last night. He wasn't one to worry about women he slept with, since he was usually the one to get them out of his room before he went to sleep. The last thing he wanted was to face the morning after and the possibility that a woman would want a next day with him. He didn't do next days or next dates or next anythings with women.

But with Tara, it had been different. He was disappointed as hell to find her gone when he woke up.

Where the hell was she? The last thing he remembered was passing out with her curled up next to him. It had to have been near dawn when they finally fell asleep, because he remembered them laughing about the sky outside lightening by the time they'd finally gotten their fill of each other.

Not that he had been even close to getting his fill. Exhaustion had finally set in, but Mick hadn't come close to getting enough of Tara.

He wanted a next day with her. And he had no idea how to reach her, didn't get her number. But he knew how to find out.

After he checked out and climbed into his car, he pulled out his phone and dialed Elizabeth's number. If anyone could find someone, it was his agent.

"Shouldn't you be working out with your trainer or in bed with some hot woman? And if you are in bed with some hot model or actress, let me know when and where so I can send a photographer to get a pic, 'kay?"

He laughed. "No. I need you to find a woman for me."

"I'm appalled you think of me as your pimp, Mick. It's sort of true, but I'm appalled. Who is she?"

"Tara Lincoln. She was the event organizer for last night's team party."

"Why do you want to find her?"

"None of your business. Just get me her info."

"Planning a little soiree of your own?"

Mick snickered. "Yeah, you know me. Just a wild party guy."

"Please. If you were, my job would be a lot easier. I'll get her info and get back to you."

Mick clicked off and headed home to his condo in the East Bay. He pulled into the garage, closed the door, and grabbed his overnight bag. His cell vibrated before he got to the kitchen.

"That was fast," he said, grabbing for the orange juice and hitting the speaker on his cell.

He knew Liz was grinning. "I'm just that good, Mick. Tara Lincoln, owner of The Right Touch. The business is located in Concord. Grab a pen and I'll give you her phone number and address. This is her business address and office phone number. If you want her personal info, it might take me all of an hour."

"You scare me, Liz." He grabbed a pen and the pad of paper on the kitchen counter. "The business information is good enough. I don't need you digging up her ancestry."

"I might if you're thinking of dating this woman. I'd need to know more about her."

"Not even my mother knows as much about the women I date as you do."

"Your mother isn't as invested in your career as I am. One misstep and you're fucked."

"And all that money you make off me goes down the tubes."

"I'm crushed, Mick. You know how much I adore you."

Mick shook his head and smiled. Where would he be without Elizabeth Darnell in his life? A hot redhead who looked more like one of those fashion models he dated, no one looking at her would think she was a sports agent with the killer instinct of a hungry shark. She was the main reason he and his brother were multimillionaires. "Yeah, yeah. I'm touched by your sincerity. Just give me what you've got."

After he hung up with Liz, he changed and took a run in the park first, needing to clear his head and draw some oxygen into his lungs. It was mid-June and warm in the East Bay, especially since he'd gotten a late start. He was usually up at dawn and running early. Now it was afternoon, and the sun beat down on him as he rounded the turn on the jogging trail, ignoring the sweat that streamed down his back, concentrating only on his breathing and his time.

Thirty years old was getting up there in years for an NFL athlete. But he was far from being done with this sport he loved. He was in great shape physically, and he intended to stay that way. He was nowhere near ready to retire yet.

After five miles he took it down to a walk and headed back to his condo. An hour later he'd showered and was in his car again, this time heading into Concord to the address of Tara's business. It was Saturday, so chances were she might not even be there. They might not be open. Then again, he could get a feel for her place, if nothing else.

Yeah, and you have no idea what the fuck you're doing. You could have just called, moron.

He didn't chase after women, ever. It wasn't ego talking, it was just that Liz threw women at him all the time. And the ones Liz didn't toss his way came to him on their own. He usually had to fend them off, so he'd never had to go after any. This was new territory for him.

He found the center where her business was located, parked, and went to the big window where THE RIGHT TOUCH was etched in white scrolled letters. There were lights on and a few people inside. He didn't see Tara right away, so he stepped through the door.

Definitely a woman's kind of place. Lots of fabric and paper thing-
ies spread on tables and tacked to the walls. Some looked like invitations. And there were champagne glasses and giant books loaded
with . . . stuff.

"May I help you?"

He turned and smiled down at a petite redhead with tortoise-
shell glasses perched on the bridge of her nose. "I'm looking for
Tara."

The redhead's eyes widened and she took a step back, obviously
recognizing him. "Oh. Sure. She's in the back. I'll get her for you."

The redhead walked away, and Mick decided to wander around
Tara's place, though with all the breakable gizmos in here and as big
as he was, the "bull in a china shop" saying definitely applied. Maybe
he should just stay put.

"Mick."

He turned and smiled at Tara. "Hey."

She wore a skinny black skirt that went to her knees and a yellow
sleeveless blouse that looked feminine and silky, and he wanted to
pull her into his arms and kiss her. But she wasn't smiling and didn't
look happy to see him.

"What are you doing here? How did you find me?"

"My agent found you. You left without waking me this morning."

Tara looked around the shop, and it was then that Mick saw three
women staring at them and whispering to each other. He heard his
name mentioned.

He loved female football fans. He dazzled them with a big smile.
"Hi, ladies."

Tara dragged him by the arm. "Come into my office."

He followed her, winking at the three women who gaped at him
as he walked by.

Tara's office was a tiny little room in the back of her shop. He felt
like a giant standing in this small space.

Her desk was clean and tidy, with a laptop in the center and neat piles on each end.

She shut the door and went around to the desk, clearly using the furniture as a defense. "Why are you here?"

He arched a brow. "Isn't it obvious? I wanted to see you again."

"Oh." Her lips lifted for a second, then she frowned. "That's not a good idea."

He crossed his arms over his chest. "Why isn't it a good idea?"

"Um, you and me . . . well, let's just say I'm very busy with my career."

"So the sex was bad?"

Her eyes widened. "Oh my God, no. It was wonderful." She came around her desk and laid her hand on his arm. "Mick, I had a great time last night. Surely you know that."

"I had a great time, too. I want to see you again."

She shook her head. "I can't."

"Why not?" Then it hit him. "Oh, shit. You're married." He did not do married women. Ever.

"No! Of course I'm not married. What kind of woman do you think I am?"

"I have no idea. That's what I want to find out. Let's go to dinner tonight."

"I can't. Please, let's just leave it at one great night together."

"So you had fun last night."

"Yes."

"With me. You enjoyed being with me."

"I did."

"But you don't want to see me again. Ever."

She rubbed the side of her head. "I know, it doesn't make sense. But I just can't." She looked at the clock. "I'm sorry, but I have an appointment. I really have to go."

"Okay." He didn't need to have a shoe shoved up his ass to know he was getting the brush-off. Feeling like a moron, he turned and headed for the door. "See you later."

She looked as miserable as he felt. He didn't get it.

"Good-bye, Mick."

He heard the regret in her voice and stopped, turned, and marched over to her, pulled her into his arms and kissed her, covering her gasp with his lips. It took her all of point two seconds to respond, leaning into him, wrapping her arms around him, and making all kinds of moaning noises.

Mick slid an arm around her waist and pulled her against him, deepening the kiss, sliding his tongue inside, tasting the sweetness of her. It was Tara who broke the kiss, who stepped back, her eyes glassy with passion, her nipples peaking through her blouse.

Yeah, she felt it, too. Whatever was between them wasn't one-sided. And her brush-off wasn't because she didn't want to be with him.

"See you later," he said, and walked out the door, leaving her standing there heaving deep gulps of air.

She had a great time, he had a great time, but she didn't want to see him again? Something was wrong. And he was going to find out what it was.

He might have lost that down, but Mick always got up for the next play.

DAMN.

It took Tara a full ten minutes to pull her act together before she could walk out of her office. By then her client had arrived, and she spent the next hour going through the motions of showing the prospective client everything there was to know about her company and the services they offered.

Or at least she thought that's what she'd done. She had no recollection of that client meeting. For all she knew, she might have recited the Burger King menu to the poor woman. Then again, the client signed an agreement for services, so she must have done something right.

"Tara, do you have any idea who that was?"

"Mrs. Stenson?"

Maggie, her assistant, rolled her eyes. "No. That hot dude who rolled in here before Mrs. Stenson did."

"Oh. You mean Mick."

Maggie looked stunned. "You're on a first-name basis with Mick Riley, quarterback of the San Francisco Sabers. Just what exactly happened at the party last night?"

"I don't want to talk about it." Tara headed back to her office, but Maggie's heels clipped on the tile floor, along with those of Tara's other two employees, Ellen and Karie.

Deciding to ignore them, Tara sat at her desk and opened her appointment book on her laptop.

"Tara, you have to give us the scoop," Ellen said.

"No scoop to tell. Sorry."

"When you walked out of your office, your cheeks were red and you looked like you'd been kissed. Really, seriously kissed. Did he kiss you?"

Tara looked up at Maggie. "None of your business."

Maggie grinned. "So he did kiss you. Oh. My. God."

Tara blew out a breath. "There's nothing going on between me and Mick Riley, so hold off on calling the gossip magazines, okay?"

"Did he or did he not come in here to ask you out?" Maggie tapped her foot.

Tara felt like she was the defendant in an inquisition as three sets of very determined eyes stared her down.

"Maybe."

"And you said yes, right?" Ellen asked.

"I said no."

Karie threw her hands in the air. "Tara, he's gorgeous. Talented. Rich. Is it possible your standards are just a little high?"

She stared down at her employees—really, her best friends, the trio of blonde, brunette, and redhead, all gorgeous, single women who would never turn down a guy like Mick. But they didn't have the life—the complicated life—she had. They didn't understand.

"I'm not looking for a guy."

"Why the hell not?" Maggie asked. "You're young, beautiful, and single. Why shouldn't you be looking for a guy?"

"You know what my life is like. I'm busy here and at home. There's no room in my life for a man."

"Worst excuse ever." Ellen shook her head, her short blonde curls swaying back and forth. "You're not getting any younger, you know."

"Gee, thanks."

"And guys like Mick Riley only come around once in a lifetime. If ever," Karie added, flipping her dark ponytail over her shoulder.

"And no one says you have to marry the guy. But come on, Tara. Why wouldn't you go out with him?" Maggie asked.

For one reason only. One very good reason.

FOUR

MICK HADN'T BECOME THE NFL'S LEADING QUARTER-
back by lying back and playing dead. He stayed in the pocket no
matter the pressure on him, and he got pass completions, both on
the field and off. If that meant he had to take some heat to get the
job done, that's just what he'd do.

So he waited until Tara left her office on Monday, then strolled
in, knowing the women there might be his best offensive line.

The cute redhead hurried over. "Mick Riley."

He held out his hand. "Yes, ma'am. And you are?"

She pushed her glasses up the bridge of her nose while shaking
his hand. "I'm Maggie, Tara's assistant. And this is Ellen and Karie."

"Hi, ladies." He shook their hands, too, his confidence growing
after seeing their wide grins. Great. That meant at least one of them
might be willing to help him out.

"I'm sorry, but you missed Tara," Maggie said. "She just left for
an appointment."

"Actually, I was hoping you would help me. Tara thinks it's not a good idea for us to see each other, and I think it is."

"Oh. I see." Maggie all but smirked in triumph. "Well, Tara doesn't always make the best decisions."

"So I was hoping maybe you could help me."

The three women's eyes all but sparkled.

Women made the best matchmakers, especially if it involved one of their friends.

"What can we do to help you?" Maggie asked, looking for all the world like Cinderella's fairy godmother.

Score!

TARA WAS THRILLED AT THE POSSIBILITY OF ANOTHER new client, even though that meant she'd be working her butt off all weekend. Thank God it was a free weekend for her, otherwise it would be a nightmare. If Nathan didn't already have plans for the weekend, she'd be in a bind, though he was usually busy on the weekends anyway these days. Still, she didn't like leaving him.

She pulled into the restaurant parking lot and got out. Nice place in Sausalito, high on a hilltop with a view back toward the city.

She went inside and gave her name. The hostess led her to a private dining area that was closed off from the restaurant. The view was spectacular, four windows showcasing San Francisco at night.

One table was set up in the corner with a white linen tablecloth centered with a vase of a half-dozen bloodred roses, gleaming white china, and perfectly placed silverware. The crystal was expensive and was the kind of place setting she'd choose for a client if money were no object.

Who was this potential client anyway? She hoped whoever it was had money to spend on an event.

And why all the secrecy? Either Maggie had failed to write down all the information, or this potential client was some kind of freakin' oddball.

Not that it mattered. She'd take oddball as long as the client had enough money to book an event. Growing her business was everything.

"Have a seat. He'll be here shortly," the hostess said.

"Thank you."

Tara sipped her water, trying to tamp down her nerves. When she heard the door open, she stood and turned around, plastering on her brightest smile.

Her smile turned to a frown as Mick shut the door.

"Mick. What are you doing here?"

He came over and lifted her hand, pressed a kiss to the back, and folded it between his extra large ones. "Hi, Tara."

She tried to look around him, certain her prospective client was going to walk in at any moment. "You have to leave. I'm expecting someone."

"No, you're not."

Then she understood. Her hope for new business died, and in its place irritation grew. "You set this up."

He smiled. "Yes."

"But Maggie said . . ." Then it dawned on her. Maggie. Of course. The little matchmaker. "Oh, I see. You talked to Maggie."

"Your friends like me."

She rolled her eyes and jerked her hand away. "Obviously all women find you irresistible." She went to grab her purse.

"Except, apparently, you?"

His smirk indicated he wasn't at all offended by her impending exit.

"I'm leaving. I don't like being set up."

He held the door open for her, which only irritated her further, as if he was going to just let her walk right out. She pushed it closed and laid her purse on the table by the door, then advanced on him. "Look, Mick. I had a great time with you. But it was a one and out, okay?"

"Why?"

"What?"

"Why was it a one and out? Didn't we get along?"

"Of course we got along. You were there."

"Yeah, I was there. We had great chemistry, in and out of bed."

She opened her mouth to object, but really, what could she say? He was right. They did have great chemistry. And she'd enjoyed the hell out of that night. "I'm just not in dating mode right now."

"Because of your career."

"Yes."

"Because it takes up every single minute of your time."

She crossed her arms. "When you're playing football, doesn't it take up every single minute of your time?"

That smirk again. "No. I don't let my career run my life. I like to actually have a life. You should try having one, too. And you managed to have one for a night with me, didn't you?"

"That was different."

"So is this. You do have to stop and eat now and then while you're busy becoming rich and famous, so we're going to eat."

"I don't appreciate your lying to get a date with me."

He held out the chair for her. "Then stop turning me down."

This was ridiculous. She should just walk out. Then again, she was hungry. And if he wanted to pay for her to eat an expensive dinner, then it was fine with her. He certainly owed her after setting up this ruse.

She took a seat. "Fine. But this is the last time."

"If you say so." He sat across from her, and the waiter came in bearing menus and a wine list.

"Would you like some wine?"

Tara looked up from her menu at Mick, who deferred to her.

"A Sauvignon Blanc would be nice."

The waiter left while they looked at their menus.

Mick took a long swallow from his glass of water. "So, business is good?"

"It would be if you had been an actual client."

He smiled over the rim of his glass. "How do you know I'm not?"

She arched a brow. "You have an event to plan?"

"Okay, not really. But I am interested in finding out more about you. What made you decide to become an event planner?"

"I fell into it, actually. I got a job working for a catering company while I was putting myself through college, and discovered I enjoyed the work."

"Catering is a lot different than event planning, isn't it?"

"Yes, it is. But the woman I worked for wanted to be a wedding planner. She and I got to be friends and she told me her idea. It was so exciting. The thought of running an entire show like that, being in charge of everything from catering to entertainment to décor—it just clicked with me."

"It's a lot of responsibility, planning someone's wedding."

"It is, especially if you're doing big weddings. But it can be so rewarding to take the bare bones and build it up, see it grow from nothing to something spectacular. Anyway, I helped her with the start-up, then went to work for her when she got it off the ground. It was fun, and her company really grew. But I knew even then I wanted something more than just doing weddings. I wanted to plan other events, too, and that's when I got the idea to be an event planner. So I saved my money, started making contacts in the industry, and when I could, I started my own business."

"Scary."

Tara nodded. "Like the standing-on-the-edge-of-a-cliff kind of scary. I thought about it for months before making the decision, but

I knew it was a now or never kind of thing. If I didn't make the leap I knew I'd always regret it. So I did."

"Good for you. How long have you been doing this?"

"I started The Right Touch two years ago. First year it was just me and one other person. It was all I could afford. We were very small, but Maggie and I worked our tails off building the business. This past year I managed to bring in enough business to add more staff. It's going well enough that I'm scarily optimistic."

"I take it you get a lot of business from word of mouth."

"I take it you know more than football."

He laughed. "I did more in college than just throw the ball around. I did manage to get a degree."

"In business, I'm guessing?"

"Yes. You surprised it wasn't in something like parks and recreation, or PE?"

She snorted. "I didn't say that."

"You didn't have to."

"I'm impressed. A hotshot football player, and you're smart, too. No wonder women flock to you."

"They don't flock to me because I'm smart. They flock to me because my agent is a PR wizard. She's like a pimp for beautiful actresses and models. If they want to be seen and photographed, Elizabeth finds them and attaches them to me."

Tara picked up a slice of bread and buttered it. "How nice for you."

"It puts me on the cover of a lot of magazines, and that sells game tickets, which is good for the team."

"It helps that you're also a stellar quarterback. Your stats are amazing."

He leaned back in his chair. "You're a fan."

She shrugged, took a sip of wine. "I like football."

"Do you like it in the way of, 'Hey, I know it's on Sunday and

Monday and Thursday,' or do you like it like you can't live without it and you know everything there is to know about the game?"

She laughed. "I know a hell of a lot about football. Why, are you going to quiz me?"

"Greatest quarterback of all time?"

"I think that's a subjective question."

"Give me your subjective answer, then."

"Joe Montana."

"You just say that because you live here."

"No, I say that because he's the greatest quarterback to ever play the game. Four Super Bowl titles, three Super Bowl MVP Awards, and I dare you to match any quarterback, past or present, to his pass rating, not to mention his cool factor in clutch situations."

"He wasn't even a first-round draft pick. And what about Johnny Unitas or Terry Bradshaw, Tom Brady or Peyton Manning?"

She narrowed her gaze at him. Was he serious? "You're saying that you think those quarterbacks are better than Joe Montana?"

He paused. "I didn't say that."

"Aha! You agree with me, don't you?"

His lips lifted. "Actually, I do. And not just because he and I played in the same city. Nobody played the game better than Joe."

She nodded. "Exactly. He was a master at come-from-behind victories. And nothing could match his ninety-two-yard drive in the final minutes of Super Bowl Twenty-three for the win against the Bengals. Best. Game. Ever."

His lips lifted. "So you might know something about football."

"Told you."

He grinned. "I'm glad. Most of the women draped over my arm couldn't tell the difference between a run and a pass, let alone a draw play from a sweep. They can tell you which actor was the biggest box office draw last weekend or who the top hot designer is. But football? Forget it."

"Then why do you date them?" She waved her hand. "Never mind, I already know. Your agent."

"Elizabeth knows what she's doing."

"Your pimp, you mean."

"She's very good at her job and only has my best interests in mind."

Tara leaned back, wineglass in hand, and regarded him. "If you say so. But I would think your agent, who has your best interests in mind, would let you choose your own women."

The waiter delivered their food. Tara dug in and started eating. It took her a while to realize Mick hadn't said anything, so she cast glances at him above her lashes, but he seemed content enough. Had she said something to offend him? Not that she cared—much.

When he was finished, he pushed his plate aside, took a long gulp of water, and said, "I'm trying to choose my own woman. But she's being damned difficult about letting me."

Tara blinked, then emptied her wineglass in two giant gulps.

No man had ever pursued her like this. No famous, gorgeous, could-have-any-woman-he-wants-so-why-does-he-want-me man had ever given her the time of day. She had no idea what to do about Mick Riley. He was utterly and completely out of her league, and couldn't have come into her life at a worse time.

Then again, was there ever a good time?

Probably not. But this time was definitely not a good time. No matter how much her toes curled at the thought of being sought after by a man like Mick, she had Nathan to think about. This was not a good time.

And she knew just how to shut him down and get him to run like hell from the restaurant faster than he could run a hundred-yard dash. She hated bringing it up, but there was no choice now.

"I have a fourteen-year-old son, Mick."

*   *   *

MICK STARED ACROSS THE TABLE AT TARA. A KID, HUH? He hadn't expected that. She didn't look old enough to have a fourteen-year-old son. "You must have had him when you were pretty young."

"I was sixteen."

"That explains it."

"Explains what?"

"You don't look old enough to have a teenager."

"Trust me, I'm old enough." She laid her napkin on the table. "You'd probably like to leave now."

Oh, now he understood. "You think I want to cut and run because you told me you have a kid."

"I'm not exactly the kind of woman who's in your dating pool."

"No, you're not."

She stood. So did he, coming around to her side of the table.

"Thanks for dinner."

"Sit down." He took her shoulders and gently pressed her back in the chair, then kneeled in front of her. "If that was your version of a Hail Mary pass to finish things with me, sorry—I happen to like kids."

She stared down at him, a confused look on her face. "The women you date are young and single, and I'm sure they don't have teenagers."

He shrugged. "I don't have any idea what they have at home. Most of them have those annoying little yippy dogs."

Tara laughed. "I don't have any dogs, though Nathan would love one. A big one, like a Lab or a retriever or a German shepherd."

"Smart kid. Nathan, huh?"

"Yes."

Mick returned to his chair now that he was fairly sure Tara wasn't going to bolt. "Tell me about him."

"He's fourteen—almost fifteen, really. His birthday is next month. He just finished up his freshman year in high school, and he's cocky as hell. He—you really don't want to hear about my kid, do you?"

"Why wouldn't I? I told you, I like kids."

"You have any of your own?"

"No. I'd like to someday. And in case you're wondering, no, I haven't fathered any that I'm paying child support for. I'm very careful with women."

"I didn't ask."

"But you thought it."

"Okay, I did think that, you being a superstud with women and all."

He snorted. "Yeah, right. I don't believe in getting a woman pregnant and leaving her. Not my style and not the way I was brought up."

"Well, aren't you just a saint."

He leveled his gaze at her, wanting her to know just what he was. And what he wasn't. "I never said I was a saint, Tara. Just that I'm responsible."

She looked down at her lap. "Sorry. I'm being a bitch."

"No, you're not. I handled this badly. I'm pushy, I know. I backed you into a corner."

She lifted her gaze to his. "No, you didn't. If you want to date me, or whatever it is you want to do with me, then you needed to know about Nathan. I'm not trying to hide him. I'm not ashamed of him. It's just that most men don't want the baggage. And we haven't really even dated, so I understand if you want to head out."

What kind of assholes did she go out with? "You must pick some real losers if they bail as soon as they find out you have a kid."

Her lips curled. "You haven't met Nathan. He's . . . challenging."

Mick laughed. "He's a boy. And a teenager. We're all challenging at that age. I was."

She studied him. "I can only imagine."

"I need to keep you away from my mother. She has stories about me and my brother that will send you running away screaming. We kept her busy when we were kids."

There was a look on her face that Mick didn't understand. Kind of a sadness that didn't make sense when he mentioned his mother and his brother. "Hey, we were good kids. Honest."

"I'm sure you were. Anyway, thank you for dinner. I really need to get home."

"What's wrong?"

"Nothing." She plastered on a smile, but there was no light in her eyes. "I had a great time tonight, but I have some paperwork to do."

He knew an end around when he saw one. Mick signaled for the waiter. "Put it on my account, Tim."

The waiter nodded, and Mick led Tara outside, but not to her car, to his instead.

"Where are we going?"

"For a ride. I'll bring you back to your car. I'd like to spend a little more time with you."

He opened the door on the passenger side and held her hand while she climbed in, admiring the way she hiked up her skirt to climb in. She turned to him. "Somehow you struck me as a sports car kind of guy, not an SUV."

"I'm too big for sports cars, and the SUV has enough room for all my gear."

He went around and got in, started the car up, and drove away from the restaurant, taking a drive up into the hills. Typical for summer, the fog had rolled in, so there wasn't going to be much to see while they drove. He let her settle and drove to the top of one of his favorite hills, where it was clear and on top of the fog.

"It's like a sea of white," Tara said as he put the car in park. The lights from his car cast out over the fog.

"It's better in the daytime when the fog first starts rolling in. But I still like it up here. It's quiet. Good place for thinking and for being alone."

"And for parking?" She slanted him a quizzical look.

"Well, we are parked, but I didn't bring you up here for that."

She unbuckled her seat belt and turned to face him. "I kind of like the idea."

"Of what? Making out in my car?"

"We could start with that, and see where it goes."

"I think you're using sex to avoid having an honest conversation."

She paused. "Isn't that a woman's line?"

They looked at each other, and both of them laughed. Tara kicked her heels off and crawled over the console. Mick had to admit he liked watching her maneuver in that tight skirt as she straddled him. He pushed the button and slid the seat back as far as it would go, giving her room. She settled over his lap and laid her hands on his chest. "So we're having a role reversal. Does this mean I get to seduce you?"

He'd lost all train of thought since all the blood in his head had rushed to his dick. "Honey, you're sitting on my cock. I'm pretty sure you can do whatever you want with me."

She smoothed her palms over his chest, then leaned back, letting her hands travel down his stomach toward where his brains currently resided. His dick twitched, and he rocked upward against her. "Do you really want to do it here?"

She lifted a half-lidded gaze to his. "I really want to do it here. Oh. Provided you have protection. I didn't even think about that. I mean, I usually don't run around having sex in cars."

He opened the center console and pulled out a condom.

She grinned. "Ever prepared, aren't you?"

"I try to be."

She took the condom from his hand and laid it down, then leaned over him and pressed her lips to his. Any conversation he'd wanted to have with her drifted away with the first taste of her mouth. He caught the scent of wine on her lips, but it was *her* flavor he was mainly interested in. More intoxicating than any alcohol, she drifted into his senses until he was lost. He dove his hand under her blouse so he could feel her skin.

She moaned against his lips when his hands moved up her back and found her bra. With practiced skill he undid the clasp, then traveled around to the front to slide his hand under the cup, finding her nipple.

Her breasts were small, but her nipples were sensitive, and he could tell she liked when he touched them, because her breath caught when he slid the pad of his thumb over one. The swell of her nipple against his thumb made his cock jerk against his zipper.

Tara drew back, her eyes already gone in that sexy way that seemed to turn them to amber glass.

She leaned back and shrugged out of her jacket, then began to unbutton her blouse. Silk seemed to fit her. She was classy, from the long column of her throat to the way her hair curled at the nape of her neck. She'd worn her hair up again, and he liked taking it down, pulling the clip out, and shaking the curls with his hand, transforming her from buttoned-up businesswoman to sex goddess before his eyes.

Her blouse unbuttoned, her bra opened, and he pulled it over her breasts.

"This is the way I like you," he said, reaching for her breasts, sliding his fingers over her nipples. "All out of sorts. Your nipples hard, you rocking your pussy against my dick."

She reached for her skirt and hiked it up over her thighs, revealing sexy pink panties that matched the satin bra. She let her hand drift down and palmed his cock. "This is the way I like you," she said, her voice dark and breathless. "Hard and ready for me."

She reached for his zipper and tugged it down, freeing his cock. They maneuvered so he could pull his slacks down over his hips. Tara grabbed the condom, taking a few seconds to stroke him, sliding her thumb over the crest, capturing the fluid that spilled there and licking her fingers after.

"Christ. You're going to make me come before I get inside you if you keep teasing me."

"Then let's not tease anymore, because I need you to fuck me."

She tore open the condom package and fit it over his shaft, then pulled her panties aside and straddled him. He watched his cock disappear inside her, holding her hips as she settled on him.

Now, that was a sight to make his balls tighten.

When she was fully seated on him, she dug her nails into his shoulders and focused on his eyes, her pussy pulsing around him. She didn't move at all, just looked at him.

"Feel that?"

He nodded.

"Oh, God, Mick, that feels so good. I could stay here just like this and feel you inside me."

He squeezed her flesh. "I'm not going anywhere, honey."

He liked that she wasn't in any hurry to show him her great prowess in the sack. Every woman that ever took him to bed seemed to want to impress him with how good they were, but there'd always been a remoteness about them, like fucking was a performance or an audition.

With Tara, she was in it with him, sharing it with him. He liked that she made eye contact with him. She wasn't pleasuring just him; she pleasured herself, too. She dragged her clit against him and paused, her eyes drifting closed, her lips opening as she let out a low moan.

There was nothing that turned him on more than a woman out for her own pleasure. Because she wasn't here trying to score points in her own game to land him. In fact, he was pretty damn sure that was the last thing on Tara's mind.

She dug her nails into his arms and lifted, then slid down on him again, every slow inch an agony of sweet sensation. He didn't know where to look—down at where they were joined or at her face, her ragged pleasure there for him to see.

He reached down and stroked her clit, felt how wet she was, knew this wasn't a performance for her at all, knew it from the way her pussy squeezed his cock every time she moved, knew it from the way her eyes got hazy and her lids half closed, knew it from the sounds she made and the way the car smelled like sex. No, she was in it to win the game for herself, and he was part of the team.

He lifted into her, stroked her with both his cock and his fingers, needing to feel her come apart around him. Her nipples dangled just out of reach of his mouth. He rectified that by pulling her toward him, flicking his tongue over one, then the other, before taking one between his lips and sucking.

Tara pressed herself further into his mouth. "Yes, Mick, yes. Suck it. Harder."

He did, and she pushed against him, lifting and dropping down on him, then rocking toward him and riding him faster.

"That's going to make me come."

Exactly where he wanted her—in the red zone and headed for the goal line. He left one nipple and went for the other, sucking it hard like she wanted. She shrieked as she came, her pussy clamping down on his dick like a vise. He held tight to her as he jettisoned a hard come into her, jamming his feet into the floorboards and shuddering while his orgasm rocked him.

Touchdown, point after, game winner. He laid his head between her breasts, feeling her heart pound.

"You made me sweat all over my good suit," she murmured.

He smiled. "Uh . . . sorry?"

She laughed and leaned back to smile down at him. "You aren't sorry at all."

"No, I'm not."

They disentangled and righted their clothing while Tara made a decent attempt to climb over into her seat. "This is not my finest moment. I can't believe we had sex in your car. I'm hardly sixteen anymore."

"So?" He buckled his pants. "There's nothing wrong with acting like it once in a while."

She wrinkled her nose. "I should know better."

"So you're supposed to act like a stuffy grown-up all the time?"

She reached down for her shoes and shrugged. "I have a kid. And yes, I should. You're a bad influence on me."

He pulled her toward him and kissed her, making sure she understood just what kind of influence he was. When he finished, her lips were swollen, her eyes dazed. "I like to think I'm a good influence on you."

They drove back to the restaurant and to Tara's car. She reached for the door handle and paused.

"Thank you again for an . . . interesting night, Mick. But I'm going to have to be up-front and tell you we can't have any kind of relationship."

He wasn't buying it. "Because you don't like me."

She looked out the window instead of at him. "That's not it."

"Because you're embarrassed to be seen with me."

"That's not it, either."

"Because you're ashamed of your son."

She snapped her gaze to his. "Of course not."

"Then I want to meet him."

"Oh, hell no."

He arched a brow. "So there's either something wrong with me or with him. Which is it?"

She rubbed her temple. "Neither. I don't know. You confuse me."

His lips quirked. "Good confuse or bad confuse?"

She blew out a breath. "I don't know. You just confuse me."

He wasn't going to give her an opportunity to walk away this time. "I'll call you."

She waved her hand and opened the car door. "Yeah, you do that."

"Good night, Tara."

She slammed the door shut and got into her car. Mick waited until she left, then followed her through the fog, making sure she made it to the highway safely.

It wasn't until he made the turn to go back to his place that he realized he only had her office number, not her personal one. And he didn't know where she lived.

He could fix that, though.

Tara was someone he wanted to know better. And she could put up whatever defensive line she wanted, but Mick wasn't the kind of guy to back down from a good defense.

It was time to shore up his offense.

FIVE

"HOW WAS FOOTBALL CAMP?"

"Fine."

"Did you learn any new plays?"

Shrug.

"Meet any new friends?"

"Mom, I'm not six years old. It was fine, okay?"

Nathan took his cereal bowl to the sink and dropped it in there.

"In the dishwasher, please. I'm not your maid."

"Whatever. I have to go get ready for practice."

He rinsed his bowl and threw it in the dishwasher, then huffed out of the kitchen and into his room, where he slammed the door shut.

Delightful.

Tara let out a long sigh. Why didn't parenthood come with a manual? There were no guidelines for dealing with a teenager, and she had no parents or siblings to go to for help.

Had she been this difficult at his age?

Probably.

Ugh. Then again, she was much nicer than her own parents had been. Point in her favor. Not that it was helping with Nathan. She could be pleasant to him or she could be surly, and neither seemed to impact him in any way. He had *attitude* down to an art form. No matter what she did or what she said, he was pissed-off about it.

He was turning fifteen in a less than a month. She should plan something fun for him, let him invite his friends over, and . . .

And what? She had no idea what he liked anymore. He had his earbuds shoved in his ears and listened to music or played games on his laptop when he was home. Otherwise he played football and hung out with his friends. The kid wasn't exactly a social butterfly. As far as she knew, girls hadn't yet entered the picture.

As far as she knew. And admittedly, she didn't know much, though she was determined to not be like her parents. Like it or not, she was going to be involved in her son's life.

She chewed on a hangnail and nursed her cup of coffee, pondering how to reach her recalcitrant child who really wasn't a child anymore.

He was almost fifteen. At fifteen she'd been partying with her friends and with boys. And she was getting pregnant, mainly because her parents were too busy with their own private demons to pay any attention to what she was doing with her life. And oh, *how* she'd screwed up her life.

Lord. She rubbed her temples and sent a silent prayer to God that history wouldn't repeat itself.

No, it wouldn't. She was on top of Nathan and what he was doing. She wouldn't let him fall through the cracks. She loved her son, paid attention to his schoolwork and his after-school activities. It was only this past freshman year in high school that he'd gone quiet and sullen on her, and she'd chalked that up to hormones and puberty. She had to give him some space, hated those parents who laid a thumb over their kids, never giving them any freedom. So far, Nathan's grades were good, and he hadn't given her any reason to think he was in any kind of trouble.

She owed him her trust—until he gave her a reason not to trust him.

And she hoped to God she could trust him, because it was summer and she had to go to work and he was too damn old for a babysitter.

But at least he had football practice that would keep him busy for part of the day, and that was part of the day she wouldn't have to worry about what he was doing or what kind of trouble he was getting into.

Which was another reason she couldn't get involved in any kind of relationship right now. Nathan was her first priority. She had to stay on her toes, and frolicking with a hot guy like Mick Riley would definitely divert her focus away from Nathan. That she refused to do.

By the time she got into the office, she'd managed to shove worry over Nathan into the corner of her brain she normally compartmentalized him into. Always there, but not overpowering her every thought. He had a cell phone and knew he could call her in case of an emergency. Her office was ten minutes from home, so she could get there in a hurry if necessary.

The day went by in a flurry of meetings about clients and events. Thank God for her job and her clients, and for Maggie and the other women, who kept her sane.

By the time four o'clock rolled around, she was astounded the day was already gone. She sipped a cup of tea and went over paperwork and entered dates into the computer.

"Have you been seeing that hot quarterback any?"

Tara looked up to find Maggie making herself at home in her office.

Actually, it had been a week since that night on top of the mountain with Mick. He hadn't called her. He said he would. Then again, he was a man. They'd had sex. He was popular and went through a ton of women, none of whom had children. Tara knew once she'd dropped that bomb on him, it would be the end of Mick Riley pursuing her.

It's what she'd wanted. Still, it stung. Just a little.

Fortunately, she'd been too damn busy all week for it to bother her too much.

"No. Not seeing him at all. I told you we weren't getting involved."

"Uh-huh. He's in the front waiting area."

Tara shot forward in her chair and spilled drops of tea all over her paperwork. "Shit."

Maggie laughed.

"Dammit, why didn't you just tell me that?

Maggie grinned and grabbed a few tissues to blot the tea stains. "More fun this way."

"Bitch." Tara smoothed her hands down the front of her flowing black-and-white checkered skirt, adjusted the wide black belt, and was just vain enough to take a quick glance at her hair in the mirror over her desk.

Her blouse was tucked in and looked fine. She looked fine.

"What is he doing here?" she asked Maggie.

Maggie shrugged. "I'm sure I don't know, but he looks good enough to eat."

Tara rolled her eyes, moving around her desk toward her door. "You need a man of your own."

Maggie sighed and followed Tara out of her office. "Don't I know it."

She was nervous as she walked to the front of the store. Mick stood there at the window, his dark hair highlighted by the sun streaming in. He was so tall, so imposing, so incredibly gorgeous. He turned when he heard her and smiled that dazzling smile that made her just a little bit weak in the knees.

"Hi," she said.

"Hi, yourself."

Maggie came up next to her, and Tara had to turn and give her a look.

"Oh. Yeah. Paperwork. Later, Mick."

Mick's lips quirked. "Later, Maggie."

"What are you doing here?"

"It's been a week since I've seen you."

"I realize that. Figured you'd moved on." She almost bit her tongue clean off. Why did she have to say that? It sounded . . . mopey and girlie and needy and all those things she'd rather not sound like.

"No, I just had some business things I had to take care of. I would have called you at night or come by your house, but you didn't give me your cell number or your home address."

She crossed her arms. "When has that ever stopped you? Couldn't your oh-so-stealthy agent scout them out for you?"

"Actually, yes, she could have." He cocked his head to the side. "I figured maybe you'd want to give them to me yourself this time. Maybe even invite me over to your house."

"Why would I want to do that?"

"Because you like me."

Telling him no was on the tip of her tongue. She'd just gotten to the point where she thought she'd never see him again.

And she'd spent the entire week missing him and feeling achy about not seeing him. How utterly pathetic, especially since she hadn't wanted to start up a relationship with him in the first place.

"I'd really like to meet your son. Does he like football?"

She sighed. "He loves football."

He moved in closer, picked up a strand of her hair, twirling the curling end between his fingers. "Invite me over for dinner. We'll have pizza."

"You don't strike me as the pizza type."

"Then there's a lot you don't know about me."

No doubt. "That's not a good idea."

He leaned in closer. God, he smelled good. Her hormones noticed.

"Invite me over for pizza."

"Would you like to come over for dinner tonight, Mick?" Damn hormones.

His smile could melt a woman straight into the floorboards.

"I'd love to. Give me your address."

She jerked a piece of paper from the pad on the table and wrote her address.

"Might as well add your cell phone number, too."

She did, then handed him the paper. "Six thirty okay?"

"Perfect."

He leaned in and brushed his lips across hers, and her stomach did flip-flops. Her utterly girlie stomach. Dammit.

"See you then."

He walked out. Tara stupidly stood at the window watching him walk across the street, his stride eating up the asphalt. He looked damn hot in a pair of cargo pants and a white T-shirt that stretched tightly over his mighty fine muscles.

Maggie's sigh over her shoulder jolted her back to reality. She whipped around to face Maggie, Ellen, and Karie.

"What?"

"You're dating the captain of the football team," Karie said with a dreamy sigh.

Tara rolled her eyes. "Go back to work. All of you. This isn't high school."

"No, but it's every girl's dream *from* high school," Ellen said with a laugh.

TARA HAD A HALF HOUR BEFORE MICK WAS DUE TO arrive, and she was a total wreck. One would think the queen was arriving instead of just a guy coming over to sit on her couch and have pizza.

Her house was a disaster, the scourge of having an unsupervised teenager running amok during the day. Empty soda cans littered the tables in the living room, the sink was filled with dishes, and said culprit had already taken off for his friend's house for the night.

The kid was going to be toast. She'd have him on housecleaning duty the rest of the week.

She picked up, ran the vacuum, tossed the dishes into the dishwasher, then dashed upstairs to change clothes, deciding Mick was either going to have to deal with her life and the state of her house or he'd leave, preferring the jet-set lifestyle of caviar, maid service, and supermodels.

Tara was neither caviar nor supermodelish, and she sure as hell didn't have maid service. She was pizza on a Friday night, and the way she looked now, which was tank top, blue jeans, and flip-flops, with her hair wound into a messy ponytail thingy. He was going to have to take it or leave it.

She let out a low shriek when the doorbell rang, then hurried downstairs toward the door, shooting a glance at the clock as she took the stairs two at a time.

She was out of breath by the time she flung the door open, and Mick frowned.

"Asthma attack?"

"More like a panic attack. I was picking up the house and trying to make myself presentable."

He walked in with a bouquet of flowers in his hand. "You look pretty presentable to me. These are for you."

Wildflowers. Not a dozen roses, but daisies and bellflowers and lilies and freesia and baby's breath. "They're beautiful. Thank you."

He followed her into the kitchen. "You didn't strike me as a roses kind of woman."

"I'm not a roses kind of woman. I love these." She grabbed a vase and filled it with water, then arranged the flowers in it and put it on her dining room table.

"Where's Nathan?"

"Not home." She wasn't about to tell him that Nathan was spending Friday night at a friend's house. She wasn't ready for Mick to meet him yet. It was too soon, and she wasn't sure where she and Mick were headed. Hell, she wasn't sure about anything. No way was she going to involve her son.

"I see." He grabbed her around he waist and jerked her against him, then planted his lips on hers, giving her one seriously hot kiss that melted her feet to her kitchen floor. Tara sank into the kiss, forgetting all about where she was until Mick pulled away.

"Wow."

He grinned. "Figured we wouldn't get any alone time for that tonight, so wanted to get it in now."

She blinked to clear her head. "Okay then."

He looked around. "So show me your house."

"It's just a condo, Mick. Nothing fancy."

He turned to her. "I live in a condo. Nothing fancy, either. So show me yours, and when you come to my place I'll show you mine."

His words evoked images of *you show me yours and I'll show you mine* that had nothing to do with living space. She tried to suppress the tingle that rolled down her spine, but as she led him from room to room, she felt his eyes on her and wondered if he was really looking at her place or at *her*.

"You have a nice place, Tara."

She shrugged. "I try to make a home for Nathan. And he's a slob, so if you find stinky tennis shoes anywhere, blame him."

He laughed. "You forget who you're talking to. And I'm glad we're not at my condo right now, because you probably *would* find smelly tennis shoes somewhere. So relax. The fact you have a teenage boy and he actually lives here isn't going to send me running out the door. I *was* a teenage boy once. I get how they live."

"Fine. I'll try not to panic." She took him through the living room and dining room.

"I don't think you want to see the upstairs."

"Sure I do. I want to see your whole house."

She sighed. "Fine."

They took the stairs, and again she felt his gaze on her. It wasn't making her uncomfortable, exactly, just aware that she was alone in her house with a man. When was she ever alone in her house with a man?

Uh . . . never? She never brought guys over, never wanted to parade a stream of men in and out of Nathan's life. She figured if she'd ever thought about having a permanent relationship with a guy, she'd let him meet Nathan.

So why had she invited Mick over? They weren't even really dating.

"There are three bedrooms up here. Nathan's room, my room, and the third I use for an office. I should probably warn you about Nathan's room . . ."

"You can skip it. That's his private domain, and I don't want to violate it."

She stood outside her bedroom door. "Oh, but you'd be fine with violating my private domain?"

He leaned over her and turned the door handle. "Honey, I've already violated your domain."

There went that flutter again, her sex and her nipples all too aware they were entering her bedroom.

She stood back and let him look, figuring he'd take a cursory glance and they'd be on their way back downstairs.

"It looks like you."

She stared at her bedroom, at the cream and brown comforter, the pictures on the walls, the photos of Nathan. She turned to Mick "Really? How?"

"Colorful. The art on the walls isn't just some mishmash of crap. The textures of the two pictures over the bed bring out the colors in the bedspread. I like Mondine's art, by the way. She's trendy, but doesn't paint that weird shit where you can't figure out what the hell it is. The black-and-white photos of your son seem to capture his personality. He looks like he's trying damn hard to be serious as hell and all grown-up, but he's just a big goof and probably feels dorky a lot of the time. Curse of being almost fifteen. Cute kid, by the way."

"Thank you." Her voice caught because he'd so perfectly described her son's early awkward teenage years.

"I can tell you put thought into each piece. Same thing with the knickknacks that you have spread throughout the house. It's not overkill, just subtle touches. It's not fussy; it's simple. I don't feel like I have to watch where I walk or where I would set a glass down. And I imagine your son is comfortable living here. Your place looks lived-in. It's inviting."

She stared at him for the longest time, until he laughed.

"What?" he asked.

"Who *are* you?"

"Huh?"

"No football player knows art and décor. And you know who Mondine is."

"Oh. Well, blame Liz for that."

"Liz?"

"My agent. She makes me go to gallery openings and museums and charity events for the arts—the kinds of things no football player should have to endure. You soak enough of it up, some of it sticks. Like this sculpture here," he said, picking up the entwined lovers. "It says something about who you are as well as the artist."

"What does it say about me?"

"That you know good art. I saw this at a gallery opening a few months back. It also says you're a romantic."

She sat on the end of her bed and looked at him. "There are sides to you that boggle me, Mick Riley."

He sat next to her. "Is that a good thing or a bad thing?"

She rubbed her temple. "I haven't decided yet." She knew he'd wowed her because he was way more complex than she'd given him credit for.

He pulled her onto his lap. "When you decide, let me know. In the meantime, I want to tell you how much I missed you this week."

Just being close to him set her nerve endings firing, waking up all the female parts of her that had missed him, that craved his touch. The logical part of her, on the other hand, just knew this was a bad idea, especially since they were sitting on her bed. But she couldn't get her damn body to listen to the signals from her brain that told her to get up. Instead, she wound her arms around his neck and snaked her fingers into the thick softness of his hair. "You missed me?"

"Yeah. If I'd had your number, I'd have called you."

"I'm glad I gave you my number, then."

"I missed being able to talk to you."

"I like talking to you, too." That was the truth. He made her laugh. He was smart and wicked funny. He was interested in her, in who she was as a person, not just as someone to have sex with. Men like him were so rare.

He rolled her onto the bed. "I thought a lot about kissing you."

"Is that right?"

"That's right." He pressed his lips to hers, his tongue diving inside and taking her breath away, making her forget everything except his taste, his scent, the feel of his hard body next to hers. She slung her leg around his hip and brought him closer, already wet and needy as a hey-I-missed-you kind of kiss became something deeper, more passionate. She pulled his shirt out of his pants and slid her hand inside, pressing her palm against his hot abdomen, needing to touch his skin, to feel his pulse beating against her hand.

Mick rolled her over onto her back, his body on top of hers as he moved his lips from her mouth to her jaw, his tongue sliding to her neck. She shivered as he applied suction there.

"That makes my nipples hard."

He pulled her tank top up. "Does it? Let's see."

He jerked her bra up over her breasts, smiled up at her, and covered one nipple with his mouth. She arched against the wet heat and the way he gently sucked her nipples.

Yeah, she'd missed him a lot. And now that he was here, she had a sudden quaking need to feel him inside her.

"Mick, please. Fuck me."

Instead, he popped the button of her jeans and unzipped them, then kissed his way down her belly.

Tara gripped the comforter with both hands, her entire body taut with tension and need as he dragged her jeans and panties down her legs. He spread her legs and crawled between them, draping them over his shoulders and planting his mouth over her sex.

"Did you touch yourself this week?" he asked, looking up at her.

"No."

"Why not?"

"Too busy."

"You should never be too busy to come, Tara."

"I need to come now." She reached down and slid her fingers into the softness of his hair.

"I like that you haven't come since you were with me." He kissed her thigh, then put his mouth on her.

"Ohhhh" was all she could manage as he licked the length of her sex, his tongue and lips finding her clit. She was so ready for an orgasm she arched against him, leaning forward to touch him, to watch as he licked her, sucked her, slid his tongue inside her, and did every possible thing he could to take her right over the edge. He swirled his tongue over the most sensitive spot, relentless in taking her right there only to ease off until she was panting and begging to come.

And when she tugged at his hair, he fit his mouth around her and rolled his tongue flat and gave her just what she needed.

"Yes. I'm coming." She pushed her pussy against his face and he held her hips while she came in hot, sweet waves that rolled over and over, stopping her breath. And when she fell to the mattress he was right there, climbing up her body to kiss her, to let her taste the sweetness of her own pleasure. She wrapped her arms around him and licked his lips and chin, taking one hand down his body to palm his cock.

"Now fuck me. Hurry."

He pulled a condom out and flipped her over the edge of the bed onto her stomach. He entered her hard and fast, and she gasped, chills breaking out on her skin.

She rose up, and Mick smoothed his hands down her back as he eased out and thrust inside her again. He leaned over and swept her hair to the side, pressing his lips to the nape of her neck.

"You're wet. Do you know how wet and tight and hot you are?"

She didn't think his question required a response. She was too busy gasping as he moved inside her, so she couldn't have answered him. Her only reply was moving back, giving him more access to her.

Mick grabbed her hips to draw her against him. He leaned over to cup her breasts, pounding inside her with hard thrusts now. Tara fisted the comforter and braced herself against the edge of the bed as he pushed deep, then retreated, each time faster than before, each time taking her higher, his shaft seeming to swell inside her, brushing all her sensitive tissues.

She wanted to come with him inside her. She moved her hand between her legs and rubbed her clit, so filled with him that just touching herself made her climax draw closer.

Mick slowed down and took it easy then, wrapping one arm around her waist and rocking against her in an easy rhythm, seeming to know what she needed. She felt the pulses, felt her pussy grip him in a tight vise as she rolled over the edge with him.

He groaned and tightened as he thrust over and over again. Tara cried out with her orgasm until they were both spent, her facedown on the bed and Mick lying on top of her back.

She breathed in and out, enjoying the feel of him against her. She felt dizzy, elated, took her time to get her bearings as she opened her eyes just as her phone rang.

"You going to answer that?"

"I should. It might be Nathan."

She grabbed her jeans and fished her cell phone out. It was Nathan. She blushed as she answered, even though Nathan couldn't know Mick was here.

"Hey."

"Hey, Mom. I forgot my key, so I just wanted to make sure you were home."

She shot off the bed. "Your key? Why?"

"I need to get a game I left there. Be home in about ten minutes."

"Uh, okay."

"Shit!" she said, grabbing her panties and jeans as she clicked off the phone.

"What?"

"It's Nathan. He's coming home."

Mick's lips lifted. "Oh. Sooner than you thought?"

"No. He wasn't supposed to be here at all. He was spending the night at his friend's house."

"So. You got me over here with false pretenses, huh?"

"Oh, shut up and get your clothes on."

She dashed into the bathroom and turned on the faucet, threw a washcloth at Mick, who grinned as he walked by her. How dare he look so relaxed and at ease?

She cleaned up in record time, put her wild, sex-crazed hair back in a ponytail, and splashed cold water on her flushed face, then practically dragged Mick out of her bedroom and down the stairs.

"Okay, kitchen," she said, out of breath as she dashed into the kitchen and started making tea.

"Would you relax? He's not here yet, is he?"

"No. But my God, he could have walked in. What were we thinking?" She shook her head as she filled the pot with water.

He came up behind her and wrapped his arms around her. "I don't know about you, but I was thinking how good it felt to be inside you."

She shoved him with her hip. "Stop that."

"Mom! I'm home!"

She jerked around and plastered on a smile. "In here."

If only her heart would stop frantically slamming against her chest, she might not drop into a dead faint.

Nathan came into the kitchen, took one look at her and then at Mick, and his eyes widened.

"Holy shit."

"Nathan, watch your language."

"You're Mick Riley."

Mick smiled and went to shake Nathan's hand. "I am. And you're Nathan. Nice to meet you."

Nathan swallowed, and Tara was sure she'd never seen her son so incredibly starstruck before.

"I take it you know who Mick is?"

He didn't even glance at her, just kept his stunned gaze focused on Mick. "Duh, Mom. I'm not a moron."

Mick pulled out a chair and sat. Nathan sat in the chair next to his. "Your mom says you play football."

"Yeah. Junior varsity since I'm just a freshman. Well, I'll be a sophomore in the fall."

"I played JV as a freshman, too. Didn't make the varsity team until I was a junior."

They started gabbing away about football, which gave Tara a minute to get her heart rate under control. Okay, disaster averted. Her son hadn't found her and Mick in the middle of wild monkey sex. Good Lord, where had her common sense gone? She never brought a man over to the house, let alone had sex with him there.

Mick was a very bad influence on her.

"So where did you two meet?"

"Your mom planned an event for our team a couple weeks ago." Nathan shifted his wide-eyed gaze to her. "You did?"

Tara brought tea to the table. "I did."

"I didn't know that."

"I believe I mentioned it. More than once, as a matter of fact. You might try listening when I talk about my job."

Nathan shrugged. "Your job is mostly boring."

"Evidently not," Mick said, "or you wouldn't have missed the part about her catering an event for my team. She might have even finagled you an invitation if you'd been paying attention." Mick elbowed Nathan. Nathan had the decency to bow his head and blush.

Nice move, Mick.

"Yeah, okay, so maybe I should have been listening. Anything else good coming up, Mom?"

"Sadly, no. Unless you want to accompany me to a luncheon for the city council. Or maybe a garden party for the Daughters of the American Revolution?"

Nathan shook his head. "No, thanks. I'd rather have my legs waxed."

Mick laughed. "Can't say as I blame you, buddy."

Tara ordered pizza, and Nathan somehow managed to finagle invitations for a "couple" of his best friends to come over. Tara balked at that, but Mick said he didn't mind. Before she knew it, five teenagers were hanging on Mick's every word and devouring the ten pizzas she'd ordered, which Mick had insisted on paying for. Once the ravenous horde of teens and one very hungry adult male had been satiated, Mick sat in the living room with Nathan and his friends crowded around him, and they talked nonstop football.

Tara leaned against the wall and listened. Mick seemed so at ease with the kids, didn't mind answering the barrage of questions, and she hadn't heard her son talk this much since he was six years old. Of course, it wasn't like she routinely talked football with him, either. After all, she was his mother. And a girl. So many points against her, whereas Mick was made of hero. He was a football star, and he never had to do the dirty work like tell her son to do his homework or ground him for not making his curfew.

So unfair.

"And what about Gavin? Is he as awesome as he seems?" Nathan asked.

Tara mentally ran through the list of all of San Francisco's players and came up blank. She thought she knew them all. "Who's Gavin?"

Nathan shot her a look that said she was a complete idiot. "Gavin Riley, Mom."

"Uhhhh . . ."

Tara shifted her gaze from Mick, who looked amused, to Nathan, who looked appalled.

"Mom, Gavin Riley is not only Mick's younger brother, he's also a professional baseball player. First base? Plays for Saint Louis, which, by the way, is also Mick and Gavin's hometown? What planet are you living on, anyway?"

"Mars, apparently," Tara said, shooting a helpless look to Mick, who laughed.

"I don't think she's required to know every player in every sport, Nathan. And your mom and I just recently started going out, so she doesn't know my bio as well as you do."

"Yeah, but if she's going out with you, she sure as hell should know who your brother is."

"Language, Nathan," Tara shot back.

Nathan just shrugged.

"We've mainly been just talking about each other, not getting into family history, Nate," Mick said with a smile that was directed at Tara.

The guys ooohed and ahhed in a very adult way. Nathan cast a curious look at Tara that made her want to slink out of the room.

"That is gross. So anyway, about that game with Green Bay . . ."

Saved by football. Tara slipped out of the room before any other embarrassing topics about her and Mick came up. Tara let Mick enjoy the adoration of teen boys for a while longer, until he found her in the kitchen doing dishes. At least she hoped the guy sliding his arms around her was Mick. She turned around when he kissed her neck.

"You don't have to hide in here," he said.

She dried her hands on the kitchen towel and backed away. "I didn't want to get in the middle of such hero worship."

"Good kids. But like all boys, they tend to want to be the center of attention. I'm dating you, not them. And you have a right to assert yourself."

"I didn't mind. Where are they now?"

"I sent the fan club home. Nathan is upstairs working out some plays for tomorrow's practice with his buddy, then they're taking off. He said he has practice tomorrow, so I told him he should be asleep by eleven."

Tara heard the heavy stomping of feet down the stairs. Nathan and Devon appeared in the kitchen.

Her son was smiling. Grinning, even.

"We're outta here. Bye, Mom. See ya, Mick."

"See ya, Nathan," Mick said. "Don't forget to get some sleep."

Nathan saluted. "You got it."

After he left, Tara snorted. "Lights out at eleven? Yeah, right. Like that's going to happen."

"It will. He promised me."

She arched a brow. "You're serious. He's actually going to sleep at eleven."

Mick shrugged. "I gave my speech about growing boys and athletes needing sleep and how much football practice takes out of a body every day, especially in the summer. I can guarantee at eleven p.m., he and his friend will go to sleep."

Tara leaned back. "I'm . . . stunned. I can't tell you how often I fight with him about going to bed at a decent hour."

"I was a teenage boy once. I know how hideous we are and I apologize for my gender."

She couldn't help but laugh. "Apology accepted."

"Good. Now come sit down with me and relax."

He dragged her into the living room, turned on the television, and flopped down on the couch, then expected her to snuggle up with him.

She hesitated.

"What's wrong?"

"I don't bring guys over here."

He propped his feet up. "Why not?"

She sat on the chair instead of the couch with him. "I don't know. I just . . . don't."

"So you think it's wrong for your son to know you have a guy over watching television with you?"

She stared at him. "Mick. I don't know. I don't . . . date."

"He's fourteen, Tara."

She chewed her bottom lip. "His birthday is next month."

"So you're telling me that he'll be fifteen next month, and you've never brought a guy over? In how long?"

"What do you mean?"

"What about his dad?"

She hesitated. "He's not part of Nathan's life now."

He studied her. "How long has his dad been out of the picture?"

"Oh." She looked down at her hands for a few seconds.

"I'm prying. Sorry."

"His dad's never been in the picture."

"Ever?"

"No."

"Bastard."

She shuddered an inhale and lifted her gaze to his. "Long story."

"Wanna talk about it?"

"Not tonight."

"Okay. But still, you've got a right to have a life."

She shrugged. "I've been busy, first when Nathan was little, and then with my education, and now trying to get my career going."

"Again, you need to have a life. And it's okay to bring a date over now and then."

When he put it like that, it sounded ridiculous and provincial.

"I just never wanted to be the kind of single parent who paraded a bunch of guys in and out of his life."

"And you haven't, have you?"

"No."

"Then come over here and let's watch a movie. I promise not to ravish you."

"Well, where's the fun in that?"

OH, MAN. MICK WAS IN BIG TROUBLE.

He liked this woman. Really liked her. And he liked her kid, too. She was a good mother; he could tell. She wasn't out for her own pleasure. She took care of her son and his needs, obviously didn't party to the detriment of Nathan's welfare, and was actually one of those women who put her kid first.

And this was so far out of his element he had no idea what he was doing.

An hour and a half into the movie and she was zonked out on his shoulder, lightly snoring, which he found incredibly—real. No woman Liz would fix him up with would be caught dead with her mouth open and snoring on his shoulder, let alone her hair sticking out the sides of her ponytail.

He adjusted and laid Tara's head in his lap. God, she was cute. Not drop-dead gorgeous in the sense that he was used to. He'd had plenty of stunning women on his arm before. But he liked that Tara was just . . . normal and pretty. And she snored. Yeah, he really liked that about her.

She snorted once and then rolled over onto her side, drawing her knees up toward her chest. Mick grabbed the blanket from the top of the couch and covered her with it.

She didn't wake up, was probably exhausted. He wondered how long she'd been doing everything alone. Raising a kid by herself?

Man, there couldn't be anything easy about that, and she didn't say anything about her family.

Nathan seemed like a nice kid, too. So did his friends. Which meant she was doing everything right. Alone.

As if he didn't like a lot about her already, he had to go and start admiring her, too.

Yeah, he was in big trouble with this woman.

SIX

"SO HOW LONG HAS THIS BEEN GOING ON?"

Tara nearly jumped out of her skin as Nathan's voice shattered the silence of her normal Saturday afternoon laundry folding activities. She'd gone to work early that morning, and he'd been gone by the time she got home. As was often the case, they were like two ships passing each other in the night.

She laid the towel down on the top of the dryer. "You scared me. When did you get in?"

"I dunno. A while ago."

"I didn't hear you over the dryer. How long has what been going on?"

"You and Mick Riley."

"Oh. There's nothing going on."

Nathan cocked his head to the side and gave her the same look she gave him when the answer wasn't good enough. She resisted smiling.

"Come on, Mom. No guy comes over to have dinner with your kid if he doesn't really like you."

"You think so?"

"Guh. You have it bad for him." He turned and walked out of the laundry room.

Tara followed him into the kitchen and lifted the lid over the pot cooking on the stove. She stirred the sauce while Nathan fixed himself a glass of chocolate milk.

"So, does it bother you?" she asked.

"Does what bother me?"

"Me seeing someone."

"He's not just someone, Mom. He's the freakin' quarterback of an NFL football team."

"If he wasn't, would it bother you?"

"Mom, I don't care if you're dating the guy who picks up our garbage, as long as he's nice to you." Nathan stopped in front of her and looked her straight in the eye. "Is he nice to you?"

His question shocked her. "Yes. He is."

"Then go for it. But it's pretty darn cool that you're dating Mick Riley. Don't expect me to keep a lid on that one." Nathan kissed her cheek and walked out of the room, milk and a handful of cookies in hand.

She was too choked up and teary eyed to jump on him about eating junk food before dinner.

MICK WAS PHYSICALLY DRAINED, DRIPPING SWEAT, AND cussing his trainer, which made Ben laugh at him and call it a good workout.

Mick wiped the sweat from his eyes and drained his bottle of water. "You're a son of a bitch," he said, panting.

Ben sat next to him on the weight bench. "You pay me to be a son of a bitch. If you hate me at the end of a workout, then I've done my job."

"Uh-huh. I'm dying here."

Ben slapped him on the back, his bald head gleaming in the overhead lights. "Quit whining like a pussy and get on the treadmill for twenty to cool down. Then you can hit the shower."

"You enjoy this." Mick dragged his sore body to a standing position.

"It caters to my sadistic tendencies. And I get paid for it. What's not to love about it?"

Mick shook his head and dragged himself over to the treadmill, hit twenty minutes and a reasonable yet not pathetically slow walk, and started up. By then Ben was off to torture some other poor bastard. Mick focused on the television and hoped this twenty minutes would go by fast.

"Man, you must be getting old. Ben's workouts are damn near killing you."

Mick grinned as Randy Lasalle, his best wide receiver, hopped onto the treadmill and started up a brisk pace. Randy was twenty-two and in the second year of his contract. Mick was glad to have him. The kid had come from a state school in Louisiana, drafted high because he had the best damn hands and the quickest stride Mick had ever seen.

"You here to work out with Ben?"

"Yeah. Gotta stay in shape for the ladies, don'tcha know."

Mick snorted. "What you mean is you've gotta keep those fine legs in shape for me."

Randy laughed. "Just don't tell the ladies, okay?"

Ben came by, leaned over Randy's treadmill, and punched in some numbers. "Not quite fast enough, pretty boy. You want to keep making the big money on fast legs, then less talking, more running."

After Ben walked away, Randy said, "It's like being back in school again. I'm too old for this shit."

"I don't hear you sweating enough, Randy," Ben said from across the room.

Randy rolled his eyes, and Mick laughed.

Mick showered, dressed, and headed toward the front of the gym, when he saw a gorgeous redhead wearing a power suit that was almost but not quite too short to be considered appropriate. Her hair was stylishly swept up, her eyes a witchy green, her heels sinfully high. She looked like sex incarnate—and smiled like she knew exactly how she looked as she leaned against the front counter while she talked on the phone, one hip cocked to the side, seemingly oblivious to the drooling masses of sweaty gym guys who were oh so obviously repeatedly walking by to catch a glimpse of her.

But Mick knew she was anything but oblivious.

Mick's agent, Elizabeth Darnell, was nothing if not a traffic stopper. She let her shocking good looks get her in the door and reel you in. And then she went in for the kill while your tongue was dragging the floor.

She finished her phone conversation when she saw him heading in her direction, and turned her dazzling smile on him.

"Mick, I didn't know you were here."

"Liz, I doubt there's very little you don't know."

She slid her arm in his. "True. Take me to lunch, and let's chat."

"Sure."

They hit a restaurant a few blocks away. Mick was starving after his flogging from Ben, so he loaded up on protein and carbs, while Liz nibbled at a grilled chicken salad.

"You need a cheeseburger," he said, waving his fork at her pitiful attempts at eating.

"Honey, if I get fat, general managers won't ogle my legs and my tits. Then who'll get guys like you multimillion-dollar contracts?"

Mick took a long drink of water. "I'd rather see you eat a cheese-burger."

She arched a brow, dabbed her oh-so-pretty mouth with her napkin, then pushed her plate to the side. "There's a Hollywood premiere this week I'd like you to go to."

"Not interested."

"You always say that. And then you always go."

"Still not interested."

Liz inhaled deeply, as if she were a parent exasperated with a difficult child. He knew she wasn't trying to impress him with the hint of cleavage on display. Mick didn't fuck people he did business with, which worked out really well for Liz, too, because she didn't mix her business with her pleasure either. To Mick, Liz was like a sister—a sometimes extremely annoying sister—who made him a lot of money.

"Mick, it's summer blockbuster season. People are paying attention to television and magazines and to who's showing up at these big movie premieres. This would be a great time to make an appearance at one of these huge, moneymaking movies. Cynthia Beaudreaux's new film releases Wednesday."

"What kind of movie is it?"

"Romantic comedy."

Mick bit into a piece of bread. "I like action flicks."

"But wouldn't you love to attend the premiere of her movie?"

He'd rather have a root canal. But maybe Tara liked romantic comedies. "Let me check my schedule, and I'll get back to you."

Liz arched a brow. "Honey, I'm your schedule. I know every move you make."

"No, you don't."

"Yes, I do."

"You don't own me, Liz. Don't make the mistake of thinking you do. You want to manage my career, fine. Don't think you manage my life. I'll check my schedule and get back to you."

She picked up her glass of sparkling water, not at all offended. Her life consisted of dealing with athletes with huge egos. He knew it would take a steamroller to stop her.

"Can't you do that right now?"

"My phone's in the car."

"Can't you go get it?"

"No."

And Mick had to admit that he enjoyed pissing her off.

She sighed. "You try my patience, Mick."

"Yeah, but I make you a hell of a lot of money, so you're willing to put up with me. I'll call you later tonight, Liz. And then I'll tell you whether to grab me some tickets for that premiere."

"I meant for you to take Cynthia Beaudreaux to the premiere of her movie."

"Doesn't she already have a date?"

"I don't know. Maybe she does. I don't care. I'll arrange for you to be her date."

"There you go again, arranging people's lives for them."

"For their benefit. For *your* benefit."

"If I go to this premiere, it won't be with Cynthia."

Liz's eyes flashed with irritation. "Who will it be with?"

"I'll bring my own date."

"That event planner?"

He shrugged. "Maybe."

"She's a nobody."

"But the point of me going to the premiere is for me to be seen and photographed, right?"

She tapped her fingernails on the table. "Yes. But—"

"But nothing. You've introduced me to these women for years

now, Liz. And the PR has been great. Now and then I'd like to choose my own date, okay?"

She opened her mouth to say something, but the look he gave her made her think twice.

Smart woman. She knew when not to argue. "Call me and let me know what you decide."

"I'll do that."

NATHAN WAS SPENDING THE WEEK AT A FOOTBALL camp. Both teams—JV and varsity—were attending. He'd never been away from her for so long. A few days for school excursions yes, but not all week long. Tara had put him on the bus at five a.m. this morning and tried not to let him see the tears that threatened to fall, knowing he'd be embarrassed. Plus she wanted him to grow up strong and independent, and he certainly was that and more. He'd been so excited about this camp, and she'd scrimped and saved to be able to afford this. She was happy to be able to do it for him. He'd earned it with good grades and doing chores, and if his attitude over the past year hadn't been spectacular, she'd understood it wasn't easy being a teenager and starting high school. There were so many pressures on kids these days. She tried to cut him some slack as long as things didn't get too out of hand. And those pesky hormones accounted for at least some of his Jekyll and Hyde behavior.

But now she had an entire week of quiet nights at home. She didn't know what she was going to do with herself. Days she kept busy with work. She had a luncheon on Wednesday, so today and Tuesday she and the other women would be busy enough prepping for that.

But what was she going to do at night? She supposed she'd better start preparing herself for those lonely times, since eventually he'd get his driver's license, start dating, go off to college. He wasn't going to be around all that much anymore.

She caught herself staring out the kitchen window, zapping back to reality at the sound of her cell phone ringing. She grabbed it and answered.

"Hey, beautiful."

Mick. She smiled at the sound of his voice. "Hey yourself, handsome."

"What are you up to?"

"Feeling sorry for myself because my son has abandoned me for a week."

"Oh yeah? Where's he off to?"

"Football camp."

"I remember those. He'll have a good time."

"I'm sure he will. But it's the first time we've been apart this long."

"Geez, Mom, time to cut the apron strings."

Now it was her turn to laugh. "You're right. I'm going a little overboard, aren't I?"

"Definitely. So what are you doing Wednesday night?"

"I have a luncheon to do Wednesday."

"But Wednesday night? Are you free?"

"Um, I guess so."

"What time is your luncheon over with?"

"We should finish up about two o'clock, including cleanup."

"Would you like to see a movie with me Wednesday night?"

She smiled. That would be the perfect way to relax after doing the event Wednesday. "I'd love to."

"Great. If you give me the location of the event you're doing, I'll have a limo pick you up there around two."

"A limo?"

"Yeah. They'll bring you to the airport."

"Airport? To see a movie?" She felt like she'd missed a part of the conversation somewhere.

"We're flying to L.A. to see the premiere of *I Dream of You*."

She fell into the chair. "Are you kidding me? I've been dying to see that movie."

"Yeah? Great."

"Are you serious? A premiere?"

"Serious."

"Oh my God, Mick."

"Does that mean yes?"

"Um, yes. Of course yes. I'd love to."

"Good. I'll have the limo pick you up at two. We'll fly down there, stay in a hotel there overnight, if that's okay with you."

"Yes. Perfect. Oh, God, I have to find something to wear to a premiere. Good Lord, I don't have much time, do I?"

"I'll take you shopping tomorrow."

"I don't need you to take me shopping. And I don't have time to shop. I'll be busy all day tomorrow finishing up plans for this luncheon."

"Fine. I'll have Liz send something over."

"No. I can shop for my own clothes. I'll make time."

"Tara, I didn't invite you to the premiere so you'd panic. And I'll make sure you have something premiere-worthy to wear. That's my responsibility, so don't sweat it, okay? Besides, my agent has people who work for her who don't have nearly enough to do."

She laughed. "Okay, if you insist. And Mick?"

"Yeah?"

"Thank you for inviting me. I'm very excited."

"Me, too."

THE NEXT TWO DAYS PASSED IN A FLURRY OF ACTIVITY. When she told the girls about the invite to the premiere, she wasn't sure who was more thrilled about it—her or them. Even though she had a million last-minute things to do for the luncheon, Maggie insisted Tara get a manicure and pedicure, despite Tara's vehement protests that she had zero time for it. But Ellen and Karie said everything was covered for the luncheon, and Tara was worrying needlessly.

But that was her job. If she didn't worry about every small detail, who would?

At least the luncheon kept her mind off going to some fancy movie premiere with Mick. Otherwise she'd have been an utter basket case worrying about what she was going to wear and how she'd put her hair up and what jewelry she'd choose.

But those things, apparently, were out of her control, at least according to one Lisa Montgomery, who showed up bright and early Tuesday morning. Lisa worked for Elizabeth Darnell, Mick's agent. She burst into the store right when they opened, took Tara's measurements, asked about Tara's preferences on dress colors, shoes, hairstyles, makeup, and even jewelry. Maggie, Ellen, and Karie giggled and got into the spirit of it while Tara mostly just sat there shocked through it all until Lisa thanked her, told her everything would be taken care of, all Tara had to do was show up in L.A. on Wednesday, and breezed out the door.

By the time the luncheon—which went off perfectly—was over, Tara was physically and mentally drained. Yet when the limo service showed up, she couldn't help but feel a renewed sense of excitement, more because she'd get to see Mick again than over the premiere. But Maggie shooed her out the door and told her they'd finish overseeing the last of the cleanup.

So she climbed into the black stretch limo, feeling way more important than she was, and tried to relax as they made their way to the San Francisco airport. She was surprised to find they were taking a small private jet rather than a commercial airline. She climbed on board the luxurious jet. Mick was seated at the back in one very comfortable looking chair. He stood when she walked in, came over to her, folded her in his arms, and kissed her soundly.

She melted in his arms, all the stress of the week floating away as his lips moved over hers, his tongue sliding inside to lick against hers. She sighed, leaning against him, loving the feel of his hard muscles as she held on to him.

It was hard not to want to continue kissing him, touching him, but they weren't alone. She broke the kiss, and he touched his forehead to hers.

"I missed you."

She smiled, loving that he said the words that she felt. "I missed you, too."

"How did your luncheon go?" He motioned her to a white leather sofa.

This plane didn't look like a plane. It looked like a hotel suite with lush carpet and oversized chairs that swiveled. And the sofa. She'd never seen anything like it.

She sat, and he sat next to her.

"It went really well."

"Great. I hope you get more business from it."

"Me, too."

The flight attendant on board served her a glass of champagne. She grinned, feeling a little decadent, but gladly accepted it, then turned to Mick, who sipped a glass of what looked like club soda. "No champagne for you?"

"It's summer and I'm in training. My personal trainer would kick my ass if he found out I was sweating out alcohol."

She laughed. "Working you hard, is he?"

"Sometimes I cry a little after a workout. But don't let it be heard I said that. It'll just pump up his ego."

"I can't even imagine, as in shape as you are, what it takes to get you like that."

He shrugged. "I'm getting older. It's harder to get me this way, so I have to work at it."

"Football is a brutal sport. You have to be built like the side of a mountain to take the kind of hits you do."

He leaned back and played with the ends of her hair. "It's easier on me than a lot of the other guys. I just stand back there and throw."

"Uh-huh. I've seen the games. You take your share of hits."

"So, you're a fan. Want an autograph?"

"Why, yes, I do. You can autograph your tongue on my—"

"We'll be ready for takeoff shortly, Mr. Riley."

"Thanks, Amanda," he said, not once taking his eyes off Tara. Once Amanda left for the front of the plane, Mick leaned forward and brushed his lips across hers.

Tara swallowed, her body engulfed in an inferno of need.

"Tattoo with my tongue, huh?"

She should be embarrassed that Amanda the flight attendant had probably overhead what she said, but at this point, her only concern was Mick. "Yes."

"I'll keep that in mind. Time to buckle up."

They moved to separate seats until after takeoff, at which time Amanda brought them fresh drinks, grilled shrimp appetizers, and a salad.

"I figured you'd need something to eat," Mick said. "Once we touch down there won't be any time to eat until after the premiere."

"What's the agenda?"

"Liz said she arranged for someone to do your hair and makeup, and she has your dress and shoes and all that jewelry stuff ready in L.A."

"Mick, you've gone to an awful lot of trouble on my behalf. You didn't have to do that."

He picked up her hand and kissed her wrist. "I want this to be a fun night for you."

"Obviously this is some event your agent wanted you to attend for exposure?"

"Of course."

"And she didn't exactly expect you to bring me as your date."

"I don't do everything Elizabeth tells me to do." He'd held her hand and licked the inside of her wrist. She shuddered.

"How long do we have before the flight lands?"

Mick picked up his cell phone to glance at the time. "About forty minutes. Why? You have something in mind?"

Her gaze panned the confines of the plane. "Not much privacy here."

"More than you think." He stood and took her by the hand, leading her through the door at the back of the plane. She gasped when she realized it was a bedroom.

"Holy shit. Who owns this thing? Some sultan?"

Mick laughed, coming up behind her and wrapping his arms around her. "It's Irvin Stokes's plane."

"Oh my God. I had no idea. He must really like you."

"Well, yeah. But he really likes Elizabeth, too. She schmoozes him, has lunch with his wife all the time. I think he thinks of her as his oh-so-successful daughter."

She turned and wrapped her arms around him. "I think he really likes *you*. I can't believe this airplane."

"Enough talk of airplanes." Mick reached behind him and locked the door, pushing Tara against the wall. "Care to join the mile-high club?"

"I thought you'd never ask." She pressed her lips to his, her nipples already tingling at the thought of having sex with Mick on this plane. She was having so many wild experiences with him, but this one was insane and all too exciting. She was wet and ready and wished she could be instantly naked so he could fuck her.

Then again, why did she have to be naked at all? His mouth was on hers, his hard body pressed to hers, and she was wearing a sundress. His cock was hard against her hip. She adjusted her body, putting his hard-on in direct contact with her sex, then rubbed against him.

He dropped his gaze to hers with a smoldering look that made her melt inside.

"Something you want?"

"Yes. Your cock inside me. Now."

He lifted her dress, fisting it in his hand as he pushed it over her hips, then reached for her panties and dragged them down. She wiggled, letting them drop to the floor. Mick unzipped his pants and took out his cock, reaching into his pocket for a condom, tearing it open, and sheathing himself in record time.

Mick pushed her against the wall and lifted her leg over his hip, shoving inside her with one hard thrust that would have made her scream if she wasn't cognizant of not being alone on this plane. Instead, she gasped as he pulled out and drove into her again. She felt the pulse of her pussy, demanding more of the sinful pleasure he gave her.

He dragged the straps of her dress off her shoulders and bared her breasts, then bent to latch onto one of her nipples and sucked, hard. Tara shivered, banged her head back against the wall of the plane, the roar of the engines equaling the roar of her blood as it pounded in her ears. She pulled on Mick's shirt, and he lifted his arms, allowing her pull it off him.

Oh, she liked this, having him slam her against the wall of the plane, her dress nothing but a wad in his hands as he held on to it while he pummeled her with deep upward thrusts, the frenzy of their lovemaking taking her out of her mind to a place where she felt crazy and free. She knew nothing but this man and this moment and the center of her being where desire coiled like a snake, fierce and unhindered. She scored his shoulders with her nails and demanded more.

"Shit," he said, rocking his pelvis harder against her, giving her the more she'd wanted, sliding his hand between them to massage her clit, separating enough to let them both watch as he fucked his cock inside her and used his fingers on her clit.

"I'm going to come, Mick. Keep fucking me like that."

She felt her pussy clamp down around his cock, a wild spiral of sensation taking over, and she came with a wild cry.

Mick slammed his mouth over hers, sucking on her tongue as he rocked against her, shoving deep inside her with a groan as he hit his climax and wrapped his arms around her, lifting her off the ground while thrusting hard and deep inside her.

Out of breath, her legs tingling, she went with him when he carried her to the bed and fell on it, her on top of him, both of them panting and damp with sweat.

Tara didn't speak for a few minutes, content to just feel Mick's heartbeat against her while he stroked her back.

"I think I wrinkled your dress," he finally said.

She laughed. "I don't think I care. But we might be sweating on Mr. Stokes's bedspread."

"I don't care, and I'm sure he doesn't."

They cleaned up in the very nice and not at all typical airline bathroom. Tara smoothed her hair and dress to the best of her ability, but it was quite obvious from her pink cheeks and slightly puffy lips that she had a just-fucked look about her.

"I definitely look like I just had sex. How will I ever face the flight crew?"

"The flight crew is paid very well not to notice anything. Let's go have a drink before we land. You made me thirsty."

She laughed and took his hand, suddenly very thirsty herself.

THE ONE THING TARA LEARNED VERY QUICKLY UPON arrival in Los Angeles was that Mick's agent was one hell of a planner. A limo met them at the plane and whisked them off to an incredibly ritzy hotel, where she was pulled away from Mick by an entire team of makeup and hair people. She was tossed into the shower, and afterward was buffed, puffed, and polished to within an inch of her life. She'd had her makeup professionally applied, her hair done, and she even had a woman come in and dress her.

She wondered if this was the lifestyle movie stars grew accustomed to. It certainly was nice to be pampered and all, though it was a bit overwhelming. By the time she stood in front of the mirror dressed in some shockingly expensive designer gown and adorned with jewelry she didn't even want to know the cost of, she had to admit they'd done wonders on her, because she didn't even look like herself. Airbrushing did magical things to a person's complexion. The scar over her eyebrow she had gotten as a child when she fell off her swing set had been expertly obliterated. Her eyes looked huge and . . . beautiful, and her eyelashes—whoa. No amount of standing in front of the mirror with a mascara wand could ever hope to replicate the magic of false eyelashes.

The copper-colored strapless gown cinched in at her bust, waist, and hips, then fell in magical waves to the floor, and was the most beautiful thing Tara had ever worn. And the shoes—God, the shoes. Strappy and stiletto with a cute bow over the toes. They matched the dress, and she wanted to sleep with them until she died.

"Thank you all—so much. I feel like Cinderella tonight. You all worked so hard to make me look pretty, and I can't tell you how much I appreciate this."

The staff of makeup and hair and dressers all grinned back at her, hugged and kissed her, then left the suite. Tara inhaled, let it out, then turned once more to the mirror.

"Holy shit, woman."

She whirled at the sound of Mick's voice.

He stood at the entryway to the bedroom. Again, she was struck by how utterly amazing the man looked wearing a tux. His broad shoulders filled the jacket so well, and he was tall enough to carry the elegance of the outfit, his black hair combed perfectly, his blue eyes even more striking against the solid black of the tux. He strolled in and walked around her as she stood in the center of the room, then came to her, lifted her hand, and pressed a kiss to her fingers.

"You are the most beautiful woman I've ever seen."

She felt herself warm. "I am not. But I sure feel that way tonight. Thank you for this."

"You *are* the most beautiful woman I've ever seen, because you appreciate this in ways no woman I've ever been with before can appreciate it."

She felt the sting of tears. "Don't make me cry, or you'll have to call that entire horde of people back to fix me."

He held out his arm. "Ready to go have some fun?"

"Yes."

SEVEN

TARA DIDN'T KNOW WHAT TO EXPECT, HAVING NEVER been to a movie premiere before. The flashbulbs going off in her face and the seemingly thousands of questions asked about who she was and what her relationship was to Mick were overwhelming and kind of surprising. She'd expected the movie stars to be blasted by the media. But her? She was a nobody.

Then again, Mick was famous. The media would want to know who his companion was.

Mick seemed very comfortable, smiling and waving to fans and posing for the cameras. And when asked about Tara, he seemed fine with introducing her—to everyone, including national reporters, magazines, even entertainment television.

Oh. My. God.

Tara wanted to crawl back in the limo, go back to the suite, and watch other people on TV. She did not want to see herself on television, though she was certain the cameras were way more interested in the movie and TV stars and models in attendance, and not her. She was not news. And fortunately, all the media people figured that out soon enough and ran off after the real celebrities so Tara could breathe.

What she did enjoy was ogling the cream of the crop of Hollywood, who stood just feet from her, giving interviews and smiling for the cameras. So when she wasn't having cameras popping off in her face, she wished she'd thought to bring her own camera and take some pictures for Maggie and Ellen and Karie to see. Though she supposed it might have been inappropriate for her to rush up to the stars of the movie and take a candid shot of them with her mini camera.

When they finally got inside, Mick led them to their seats, and oh, the movie was wonderful. And the time spent with Mick was great. He held her hand or put his arm around her, and they both laughed at the movie, which was funny and so romantic. It was a perfect night, and Tara felt like she really was Cinderella. Mick even leaned over a few times during the movie and kissed her. She couldn't have asked for a better date, and she'd remember this night forever.

When the movie was over, everyone shuffled out and headed for their limos.

Tara leaned against Mick, her arm entwined with his, as they slid into their car.

"I had a wonderful time, Mick. Thank you."

He grinned at her. "You're welcome. But it's not over."

"It's not?"

"No, there are premiere after-parties. Unless you don't want to go."

"Oh, no. That sounds fun."

They went to another incredibly swanky hotel where there was a party in the amazing and huge ballroom filled with balloons and movie posters and champagne fountains and—thankfully—food.

"Oh, thank God. I'm starving," she said as she and Mick found a table.

"Me, too. I'm so glad you like to eat."

She laughed. "Why wouldn't I?"

He gave her a look. "You'd be amazed by the number of women I dated who didn't eat. You wouldn't believe the look of horror on their faces when I suggested real food. There's nothing more depressing than watching a woman nibble on a piece of celery."

She laughed. "No fear of that from me. Lead me to the nearest cheeseburger."

There were photographers and media present here, too, but it didn't seem to be as much of a frenzy as there had been on the red carpet. Still, Tara was mindful that Mick had an image to uphold, so she tried not to shovel food in her mouth, even though at the moment she could have eaten a photographer's right arm.

The media seemed content to pick on the actors and actresses in attendance and leave them to themselves.

"You're probably sorry you didn't bring someone more famous with you," she said, finally able to speak after her stomach was full.

Mick took a drink of soda, then arched a brow. "Why would you say that?"

"Because we're pretty much being ignored by the media. If you'd brought some hot actress with you, you'd have gotten more—what do they call it?—face time?"

He laughed. "Honey, I didn't come here so I could get photographed. God knows I get more photo opportunities than I need. I wanted to bring you so you could have a good time."

"Oh." She looked down at her lap, feeling stupid for saying what she'd said. "I'm sorry."

He tipped her chin with his fingers. "Don't be sorry. But don't misinterpret why we're here. I'm not using you for a photo op for myself, Tara. I brought you here tonight because I wanted to show you a good time. No ulterior motive."

She slid her hand around the nape of his neck. "Thank you, Mick. It's truly been the best night of my life."

He brushed his lips across hers, the kiss soft and gentle, the kind of kiss that made her heart want to do dangerous things—like fall in love.

The flash of a camera made her jump. Tara blinked and looked into the face of a photographer.

"Send me some copies of that one, will you, Jimmy?" Mick asked.

The photographer laughed. "Sure thing, Mick."

Tara lifted a brow at Mick after the camera guy moved away. "First-name basis with the paparazzi?"

"They shove a camera in your face often enough, you learn who they are. Jimmy's a nice guy. He's a freelancer. And I really do want a copy of that picture."

"Me, too."

"So, you ready to meet some movie stars?"

Her heart stuttered. "Seriously?"

"Sure." He stood and held out his hand. "No point in bringing you to one of these fancy things if you can't say you met some of the big names in Hollywood, right?"

She might just faint on the spot.

MICK SUCKED DOWN A BOTTLE OF WATER AND PUT THE cap back on, staring down at Tara, who'd fallen asleep in the limo on the ride back from the after party.

He'd loved bringing her to the premiere, had enjoyed seeing

it through her eyes. He'd been to so many of these things over the years he'd become jaded about the whole experience. And the women accompanying him had been after only one thing—career exposure and as many photo and media opportunities as they could get. Which meant cameras in his face all night and nothing but interviews, with a smile plastered on his face the entire time. These events had become a painful experience.

Until Tara. She'd been wide-eyed and enthusiastic about everything, damn near petrified of the cameras, and had done her best to avoid them. And then she'd gone and apologized for the lack of camera time for him.

Amazing. And refreshing to be with a woman who wasn't out for herself, but who cared about him. He didn't really know what to make of her.

But he liked her. Really liked her. A lot. What wasn't to like? She was beautiful, fun, and sexy, and their chemistry together was explosive. She was sweet and caring, and if he wasn't careful, he could fall madly in love with her.

If he was ready to fall in love.

Was he?

"You're staring at me."

He looked down. Her eyes were sleepy and half-lidded and sexy as hell.

"I am. You're beautiful when you sleep."

She shifted, sitting up and smoothing her hand over her gown. "I am not. Sorry I sort of just dropped off there. I think the excitement of the day and night just took its toll on me."

"It's okay. You've had a long day. You were entitled to take a nap."

When they arrived at the hotel, Mick took Tara's hand and escorted her out of the limo. He liked being seen with her, not because she was a star, but because she was beautiful in a natural sort of way that turned people's heads when she walked by. Another thing he really liked about her was that she had no idea how pretty she really was.

In the elevator she laid her head on his shoulder, her fingers tightly clasped in his. Mick swallowed, a giant lump in his throat.

Keep this light and easy and quit thinking about how big this could get between the two of you.

He slipped the key inside the lock and pushed the door open, holding it for her as she walked inside, her full skirt making all kinds of sexy noises as she glided into the living area of the suite.

She turned to face him, the skirt billowing around her. She looked like a freakin' princess, and that lump in his throat sank to his chest.

He moved to her and laid his hands on her waist. "Have I told you how incredibly beautiful you look tonight?"

He liked that she actually blushed. She placed her hands on his shoulders. "Have I told you what an amazing time I had tonight?"

And just like that, he started moving with her in his arms, their feet in perfect rhythm as he heard this idiotic song in his head. She was a princess tonight, and they needed to dance together.

"Mick."

"Yeah."

"Do you realize we're dancing?"

"Yeah."

"I have to say again how good a dancer you are."

"You can thank my mother for that. She insisted on ballroom." He raised his hand, and she slipped hers in his. He began to glide around the marble floor of the living room.

"I'd love to thank your mother for this. You're amazing."

"Don't tell the people at *Dancing with the Stars*. You know they love to get football players on that show."

She laughed. "I can't see you wanting to do something like that."

"No. So for the love of God, don't put *that* bug in Elizabeth's ear, either. That would be right up her alley."

"Your secret is safe with me."

That was the thing. He could well imagine any of his secrets being safe with her. But not the biggest secret. It was too soon to tell her everything.

He danced her to the balcony, slid the door open, and led her outside. The night was warm, the lights of the city bright and glowing. She looked over the city, and Mick wrapped his arms around her, breathing in her scent.

"It's been a perfect night, Mick. Thank you again."

"You're welcome. I'm glad you had a good time."

"Your life is amazing. The opportunities afforded to you because of your fame are incredible."

"They are. I've enjoyed them while I have them, appreciate them for what they are. Fame is fleeting, especially for someone in sports. We don't tend to have a long shelf life."

She turned to face him. "That's a very reasonable outlook. So what will you do when your football career is over?"

"I've invested well, haven't lived beyond my means. I'll have plenty of money when I retire from football."

"But you won't just do nothing, will you?"

"No. I run a few charities, so I'll oversee those. Maybe get into coaching. There are a few other options I'm exploring. Haven't really decided yet what I want to do. It depends on how long I play."

She stared at him, didn't say anything.

"What?" he asked.

"You're just a little too good to be true. You're educated, wealthy, you don't piss away your money on drugs or partying. You give to charity, and you're actually planning for the future. Don't you have any skeletons in your closet, Mick? Isn't there a bad boy lurking in there, something that makes you less than perfect?"

If only she knew. "No one's perfect, Tara. Not even me."

She sighed. "I don't know. You sure seem that way."

"Would it make you happy if I was bad?"

She frowned. "No, not at all. I'm just afraid I can't even begin to live up to . . ."

"To what?"

She shook her head. "Nothing. Never mind. I'm being ridiculous." She leaned up and pressed a kiss to his lips. "This has been a wonderful night, and I'm giddy and exhausted. But not so exhausted that I can't show you how utterly happy I am to be in your company. Now come help me out of this expensive jewelry and sinfully expensive dress. It's time for Cinderella to turn back into a pumpkin."

He laughed and let her lead him into the bedroom. He helped her remove the jewelry, unzipped her dress, held his breath when she stepped out of it, revealing the sexy-as-hell strapless bra and matching barely-there panties she wore with those stiletto heels.

"I like the pumpkin more than Cinderella. Can you keep that outfit on? With the shoes?"

She laughed, untied his bow tie, pushed his jacket off his shoulders, and then took her damn sweet time undoing the buttons on his shirt.

"Seems it wasn't that long ago we were getting you out of a tux."

"Our first night together," he said, remembering it as clearly as if it were yesterday.

She lifted her gaze to him while she jerked his shirt out of his pants. "Yes. I loved watching you undress. Tonight I'm going to undress you."

He shuddered when she reached for the clasp at his pants, damn near lost it when her knuckles brushed against his zipper. His cock strained against the fabric of his slacks, hard and throbbing and ready for her touch. She drew his pants down, then his boxer briefs.

He kicked his shoes off, and she knelt to remove his socks, leaving him naked and standing in front of her.

Tara sat on her heels, staring up at his cock. "Sit on that chair, Mick."

He'd stand on his head if she'd continue to look at him like that. He moved to the chair and sat, spreading his legs as she moved between them to kneel. He shuddered when her breasts brushed against his thighs, then his stomach, as she leaned forward to kiss him.

He cupped her face between his hands and kissed her with a hunger he hadn't known he possessed. Though he tried not to care, he felt something for Tara, and it was getting harder and harder to pretend that what was between them was something casual. And when she kissed him with a soft moan and a need that matched his own, his cock lurched against the softness of her belly, and all he could think of was being inside her, of how safe he felt, how right it felt, and he suddenly wanted her to know everything about him.

Whoa. Time to slow the hell down. He took a deep breath and concentrated on the physical, on the way her flavor burst in his mouth whenever she kissed him, on how damn difficult it was going to be to hold off and let her play this game of seduction.

She pulled her mouth from his and dragged her lips over his jaw, his neck, her fingers playing with his nipples. He drew in a breath, realizing how much he liked her hands on him. She kissed his nipples, licked them. He liked seeing her mouth on him, liked watching her flatten her tongue across his chest and snake it down across his abs, knowing what she was doing, anticipating every movement. He shuddered as she slid lower across his stomach, resting her face on his thigh as she looked at his cock, then back at him.

She smiled up at him before grabbing his cock with both hands. He hissed out a breath. His patience was hanging on by a thread. It cost him to let her do this when all he wanted was to throw her down on the carpet and sink inside her. But this was her game, and he was going to let her play it her way.

"I like you touching me, Tara."

She licked her lips and rose up between his legs. He leaned over her to undo the clasp of her bra, letting it fall so he could see her breasts, the rosy tips hard as she stroked his shaft, rolling it hand over hand. She seemed to be mesmerized by it as she played with it, taking her time, squeezing it hard, then lightening her touch.

He could watch her touch his cock for hours, the heat and softness of her hand nothing at all like when he jacked himself off. There was a finesse to her movements unlike his hurry-up-and-get-it-over-with style. She was all grace and softness, and when she put her mouth over the head of his cock and swirled her tongue over it like a goddamned ice cream cone, he almost lost it, almost shot his come into her mouth right then as if he were a fifteen-year-old boy with no control.

She licked the length of him, her little pink tongue riding his shaft like she couldn't get enough of him.

"Jesus Christ, Tara, that's so fucking good." He reached for her hair, started pulling all those careful pins out of it, needed it loose so he could tangle his fingers in it. And when it was finally free, he fisted her hair in his hand and gave it a tug. Her gaze snapped to his, and she smiled, then took his cock deep, seeming to know exactly what he needed.

She let him thrust his cock deep in her mouth, let him fuck his shaft between her sweet lips hard and fast until he was panting, until he could feel his balls tighten up.

"Yeah. Suck my cock hard."

She took him deep, swallowing his cock head, squeezing him, making the sweat roll down between his shoulder blades. Tension pulled at his spine, and he fought the urge to let go, wanted to savor her sweet lips on him for a few minutes longer. She was a goddess with a perfect mouth and doing things to him that made him grit his teeth and dig his heels into the carpet. He could hold on a little longer.

She swept her thumb over that place between his balls and his ass, and oh fuck, that felt good, to be teased there while she sucked him. He craved more. She was like a drug. He shoved his cock deep and he knew this ride was going to be over soon, because he wanted to come in her mouth so damn badly he could already imagine what it would be like to feel it spurt on her tongue, to feel her draining him until there was nothing left.

"I'm going to come in your mouth, Tara, so if you don't want me to, you'd better tell me now."

But she only hummed around his shaft and tickled his asshole with her fingers, and goddamn if that didn't make him shoot right then and there, hard and fast and all the way down her sweet throat. He came with a loud shout, his ass bucking up off the chair, his orgasm coming from somewhere deep inside him. He felt light-headed, climaxing from his spine, his brain, from every part of him, leaving him shaking and sweaty and utterly spent.

He fell back against the chair, and Tara went with him, her mouth still on him, licking every last drop of what he gave her until she finally let go of his cock and laid her head on his thigh.

It took Mick a minute or so before he felt coherent again. He pulled Tara onto his lap, and she looked so fucking sexy wearing only her panties and those shoes. He kissed her deeply, tasting himself on her tongue, amazed by what she'd done for him.

She pulled away, licked her lips, and smiled at him. "You tasted good."

He shuddered. "Christ, you damn near gave me a stroke."

She giggled. "Good."

"I'll give you good." He lifted her and put her on her feet, then pulled her panties off, leaving those shoes on that drove him half crazy. Then he sat her in the chair and spread her legs. "Your turn."

He kissed her first, wanted to taste her mouth, lick her lips, slide his tongue in her mouth and suck on her tongue. It made his cock come to life again, even though she'd taken everything he had.

He kissed her neck, and she shuddered. He knew her neck was sensitive, and he gave it extra attention, dragging his tongue over the side of her throat before sliding down between her breasts, then licking her nipples, sucking each hard berry until she arched her back to feed them to him. He cupped her breasts in his hands and rolled the buds between his teeth, tugged on them, heard her ragged cry and drank it in because it made his dick hard.

He swept his hands over her belly, kissed it, then shouldered her legs apart, moved his hands down her sweet legs and lifted them, kissing her feet.

"Those are some rockin'-hot shoes, Miss Lincoln."

She laughed. "I might wear them every day if I get this kind of reaction."

"Feel free to dig those spikes into my back if you like what I do to you."

She leveled her pretty brown eyes on him and swallowed when he draped her legs over his shoulders. He moved between her legs, inhaling the scent of her sex. She was so wet, so sweet and enticing, it made him go rock hard.

He swept his tongue over her pussy lips. She whimpered and laid her hand over his head as he licked the length of her, put his mouth on her clit and sucked.

"Oh, damn, Mick. Yes. Lick me right there."

She made his dick pound when she talked to him, when she told him what she liked, when she lifted her ass and rocked her pussy against his face. He liked her turned on and out of control like she was now, moaning and talking to him, her pussy so wet his tongue slid easily all over her. And when he sucked on her clit and slid two fingers inside her, she lifted her butt off the chair and came, hard, crying out and yanking on his hair, bucking against his face like she was in the rodeo and he was the bronco she rode to the grand prize.

He didn't even wait for her to come down off the waves of her orgasm. He grabbed a condom, sheathed his cock, and shoved inside her still-spasming pussy with one hard thrust. She let out a loud moan, scored his arms with her nails, and rocked against him.

"Yes!" she cried. "Fuck me."

He drove into her, pulling her hips down so he could piston his cock deep inside her. He wanted Tara to come again. He dropped on top of her, her breasts against his chest, so he could roll against her clit.

"Mick, that's so good." She grabbed his head and kissed him, hard, her teeth mashing to his, her tongue sliding against his. She whimpered, her eyes filled with unshed tears. This is how he wanted her, because this is what he felt, his heart mixing with his body as he rode this incredible wave with this amazing woman.

He held back, his balls tightening as her pussy squeezed him in a tight vise. Her eyes widened.

"I'm going to come, Mick. Come with me. Come in me."

He held tight to her as the ragged edges of control tore away. "I'm coming with you. Give it to me."

She held his gaze as she went out of control and he let go, shouting out as his orgasm roared through him. He dug his fingers into her flesh, pulled her tight against him, and buried his face in her neck, licking her as she screamed her orgasm this time, rocking against him and crying out his name.

It took a while for the calm after the raging storm, as he held her and stroked her and felt her wild heartbeat pulse against his chest.

He picked her up and took them both into the shower, Tara laughing that it would take an hour to wash all the makeup off, then both of them laughing as one of her false eyelashes ended up on her cheek. Once they cleaned up, they dried off and climbed into bed. Tara was asleep in minutes, her head on Mick's shoulder.

He held her like that for a while, content and just a little bit worried about what all this meant.

And hell, wasn't it the woman who was supposed to be all concerned about what the whole "relationship" thing meant, anyway? They had fun together. God knew the sex together was great. Maybe he should just stop thinking about it and enjoy the ride. It was too soon to start thinking about the important things, anyway.

EIGHT

TARA OF ALL PEOPLE KNEW BETTER THAN TO START thinking of her and Mick as having a relationship. They were going out, sure. And they were having a good time together. But as sure as hell as she started thinking something good was going to happen between them, it would all end.

Everything good ended. She had plenty of experience with that.

Fortunately, after their whirlwind trip to Los Angeles, Mick had to drop her off and work out with his trainer, then attend a team meeting, and she had to dive back into her own work for the next few days. She'd needed some distance anyway after being with him. He overwhelmed her a little bit, and not in a bad way, but with everything good. She needed time to think, to rehash the night in her mind to make sure it hadn't all been a dream.

And the reality of work and bills to pay and waiting in the high school parking lot for her kid to come back from camp certainly gave her a dose of reality.

Though Tara had noticed two things when she met Nathan at the bus to pick him up from camp. One, he was happy to see her, which was kind of surprising. And two, apparently her cool factor with her son had suddenly jumped several notches. Not because of anything she'd done but because of the man she was dating.

At this point, she'd take anything as long as he had more than grunting, one-word conversations with her. He seemed animated and happy, and his friends surrounded her and asked her a hundred questions about Mick and football as if she'd suddenly become his agent instead of the woman he was dating.

She'd had to back them off and explain she knew nothing about the upcoming season or what free agents San Francisco might sign, and no, she wasn't hosting a giant get-together for Nathan's entire team and inviting Mick's team.

Good Lord, was this what Mick went through with the media? She could barely handle Nathan's friends and teammates, let alone hounding journalists.

"So when's he coming over again, Mom?" Nathan asked her for the fiftieth time as she sorted through his foul-smelling laundry.

"I have no idea."

"Did he call you today?"

"No, he did not."

"Does he call you every day?"

She rolled her eyes. "No, he doesn't."

"Well, why not? Did you piss him off?"

She turned on the washing machine and backed her son out of the room. "Nathan, give it a rest."

Her cell phone rang, and Nathan hollered, "I'll get it," before she even had a chance to close the door to the laundry room.

She didn't even bother to yell at him. What was the point? It would probably be Maggie, and he'd toss the phone at her in disgust.

"It was great. Yeah, we did workouts in the morning, then drills in the afternoon. Coaches taught us new plays from playbooks, stuff we never did before, so it was cool. And the drills were like the real deal, NFL stuff, ya know?"

Had to be Mick. Nathan would not be discussing football camp with Maggie. She went into the living room where Nathan had flopped onto the sofa, making himself at home with her cell phone. And her man.

Not that Mick was her man or anything.

"Yeah, the food sucked, but we didn't mind. The lake was awesome. Going to bed early wasn't too bad because they worked the shit out of us the whole day, so we were pretty wiped by the end of the day anyway."

"Nathan, language."

Nathan rolled his eyes, listened, then laughed. "Yeah, she gets on me about that sh—I mean about that stuff all the time. Yeah, you're probably right. Okay, sure. Here she is."

He begrudgingly handed her the phone. "It's Mick."

She smiled up at him. "Oh, really? I thought it might be Maggie."

"Funny, Mom. Real funny."

Nathan stood and watched her. Tara cradled the phone against her chest.

"Do you mind?"

"You listened while I was talking to him."

"You're not dating him."

Nathan rolled his eyes. "What-ever." He left the room and headed upstairs.

"Hi."

Mick laughed. "Hi, yourself. Sounds like he had a good time at football camp."

"I suppose he did. I was mauled by the players when he got off the bus. Apparently he told them I was dating you, so now I'm very cool."

"How nice for you. So now they want to go out with you?"

Now she laughed. "Uh, no. Now they all want to come over for dinner when you're here. They want nothing to do with me."

"I'll try to hit one of their practices, if you don't think Nathan's coach would mind."

"I think Nathan's coach would probably fall all over you in gratitude."

"What have you been up to?"

"Working. You?"

"Same. I was wondering if you and Nathan were free this week-end."

"I've got nothing on the calendar. I can check with Nathan, but I'm sure he doesn't. Why?"

"I'd like to fly you to Saint Louis."

"Saint Louis. Why?"

"It's my hometown and where my family lives. No big thing, but it's my brother Gavin's birthday. There's a party. He has a home game Saturday afternoon, then there's a party at my parents' bar that night. Thought you both might like to come."

As usual, Mick's lifestyle made her head spin. "Um, wow. Let me think about this for a minute."

"It's okay if you can't make it. I understand it's last minute, but they like to throw these things together at the drop of a hat. So if you don't want to come—"

"No, it's not that at all. Let me call you back, okay?"

"Sure."

She hung up, her pulse jacked up and her heart rate accelerating. Meeting his parents and his brother? With her son along? This was all moving so fast. And maybe it didn't mean anything at all. Maybe he brought women to meet his family all the time, and it was no big deal to him, so she was blowing this out of proportion. And it was a Major League Baseball game. Nathan would enjoy the chance to fly out to Saint Louis and see the game and meet Gavin. Why deny him that opportunity just because she thought the whole deal had ramifications that it probably didn't?

"Hey, Nathan? Can you come down here?"

He opened his door and leaned over the railing. "What?"

"Come down here. I need to ask you a question."

"What did I do now?"

She sighed. Why did everything with teenagers have to be so difficult?

You know why. You were one once.

"You didn't do anything."

He came down the stairs and lingered there.

"Mick asked if we'd like to fly to Saint Louis for the weekend. It's his brother's birthday. His family is having a party for him after his game Saturday afternoon."

Nathan's eyes widened. "Are you shi—are you kidding me?"

"No, I'm not kidding you. Would you like to go? We'd go to Gavin's game Saturday, too."

"Oh, man. That is just so cool. You said yes, right?"

"No. I wanted to talk to you first to make sure you'd want to go."

Nathan slumped his shoulders, then rolled his eyes. "Dude. Mom. Call him back. Say yes. Now, before he changes his mind."

MICK WAS BRINGING A WOMAN HOME TO MEET HIS FAMily. And not just a woman, but a woman and her son.

He'd never done it before, and he wasn't sure why he was doing it now, other than when his sister Jenna called him about the party for Gavin, his first thought had been to bring Tara and Nathan with him. He'd never wanted to do that before. He'd always gone home alone, because his parents were always after him to settle down and find a woman to share his life with. If he brought a woman with him, there'd be constant questions about whether she was "the one." He never wanted to deal with that.

Christ. What was he thinking? This was going to be pure hell.

And yet he liked the idea of having them with him.

He had to be out of his goddamned mind.

"So you grew up here?" Nathan asked as Mick headed south on the highway from the Saint Louis airport.

"Yes. Spent my entire life here until college."

"Then you went to University of Texas, where San Francisco drafted you number six."

Mick laughed. "You do follow your football players, don't you?"

"I know a lot about the players I like in the sports I follow. Which means I know a lot about you and your brother."

"I'm honored. Gavin will be, too."

"Tell me about your brother," Tara asked.

"Not much to tell. He's two years younger than me, decided he liked baseball better than football. He's a giant pain in my a—uh—butt."

Nathan snorted. "She'll make you put money in the cuss jar if you don't watch your language."

Mick skirted his gaze to Tara. "A cuss jar, huh?"

Tara looked over her shoulder at Nathan. "A quarter for every cuss word. The jar is getting very full."

"You've put some quarters in there, too, haven't you, Mom?"

She looked straight ahead instead of at Nathan or Mick. "I guess I have."

Mick laughed. "Well, we're going to have to have a quarter-free weekend, because my family is Irish, and you're going to hear a lot of cussing at the family bar. Cover your ears, Nathan."

"I'll do my best not to hear anything I'm not supposed to."

Tara snorted. "Yeah, right."

"It's pretty here. I like it. Everything's green."

"It's supposed to be green in the summer."

"Where we live the hills are all brown."

Nathan was right, Tara thought. It was beautiful here. Lush and green and summery. And it was hot and humid here, but Tara loved it. She loved the feel of the city as they drove down the highway. It felt homey, like a small city within a large metropolis.

"This is really beautiful," she said as Mick turned off the highway into a residential neighborhood of thick trees and brick homes, well-manicured lawns and wide picture windows—the kind of home she'd love to own someday. Mick pulled into the long driveway of a pale brick home, two stories, with one of those picture windows in the front that she loved so much.

"This is your parents' house?"

"Yes. I grew up here."

"How wonderful your parents still live in the same home you lived in as a child. It must give you an amazing sense of security." She wanted to give that to Nathan, but they'd already moved three times because her economic status had changed. At least it had changed for the better, so she couldn't complain about that.

She stood and looked at the huge home while Mick and Nathan pulled their suitcases out of the trunk of the rental car. Her heart lodged in her throat. What if they didn't like her? How many women had he brought here before? She hoped Nathan didn't burp—or something even worse—in front of his parents.

Mick slipped his arm around her waist. "What are you doing?"

"Girding my loins."

He laughed and pressed a kiss to the top of her head. "This isn't an inquisition. My family is easy to know and very friendly. You're going to love them, and they're going to love you and Nathan. Quit worrying."

Her son obviously didn't have a shy or worried bone in his body, since he was already dragging their luggage ahead of Mick. That's what she loved about her kid. No fear and full of adventure.

She'd been fearless and adventurous once, too, and look where it had gotten her—pregnant at fifteen.

The double doors flung open, and two people came out, one a tall, slightly thicker version of Mick, with a shock of salt-and-pepper hair, and a slender, petite woman who could not have possibly given birth to Mick. Her red hair was cut short to her chin, and she was just stunning.

"Oh, you're finally here!" the woman, who must be Mrs. Riley, exclaimed, enveloping Mick in a hug. He picked her up and kissed her cheek.

"Hi, Mom."

Mr. Riley hugged him, too, and kissed him on the cheek. "Been too long since you've been home, Michael."

Mick grinned, totally comfortable and happy with his parents. Nathan was smiling, too, though obviously a bit bemused at all this affection. Tara laid her hands on her son's shoulders.

"Come in, come in," Mrs. Riley said. "It's so hot outside today. We'll do introductions inside where it's cool."

They walked inside and left their luggage in the entry. The house was definitely older, yet beautiful, all light colors, beige and brown and cream, beautifully decorated, and the rooms oversized with lots of furniture. It looked welcoming and comfortable, not artsy and stiff.

"Come on into the living room and make yourselves at home," Mrs. Riley said, hugging Tara. "I'm Kathleen, and this is my husband, James, but everyone calls him Jimmy."

Mick made the introductions. "Mom, Dad, this is Tara Lincoln and her son, Nathan."

Tara was enveloped in a hug by both of Mick's parents. Jimmy shook Nathan's hand, and Kathleen hugged him. "Welcome to our home," Jimmy said.

"Jimmy, bring out the iced tea I set in the refrigerator. I'm sure everyone's thirsty. We'll go sit down."

Mick took Tara's hand and led her to an oversized chair for two. Nathan took a seat on the sofa by the window, and Kathleen sat in a chair covered by a quilt.

"Your home is lovely, Mrs. Riley," Tara said.

"Call me Kathleen, or I'm not likely to answer you," Kathleen said.

"All right," Tara said with a laugh. "Kathleen."

"Thank you. Mick and Gavin keep trying to buy us some big new fancy house, but we love this old place and don't want to move. We had the kids in this house. It's home to us and always will be."

"Besides, it will give me something to work on when I retire," Jimmy said as he brought the tray filled with tea. Kathleen passed out glasses, and Tara took a long swallow.

"And when's that going to be, Dad? Never?"

Jimmy laughed. "Who's going to run the bar for me? Jenna?"

"She does that now, doesn't she?" Mick asked.

"She gives lip to all the customers."

"And they love every insult she hurls at them," Kathleen said.

"Jenna is my sister," Mick explained. "She bartends at Riley's, our family bar and restaurant. Mostly a bar, but we also serve sandwiches. Big sports bar, really."

"Oh, fun. So do you have multiple screens to show all the games?" Nathan asked.

Jimmy nodded. "Can't miss my boys' games while I'm workin', now can I? And it's a big draw for customers. We have the main big screen over the bar, then multiple small screens to show whatever else is on. Baseball, football, hockey, basketball, NASCAR, soccer. You name it, we'll have it on."

"Awesome." Nathan turned to Tara. "Will I be able to get in?"

Tara lifted her gaze to Jimmy. "I don't know. Can he?"

"Sure, as long as he doesn't go to the main bar because he's not twenty-one. But he can sit in the restaurant portion. There's even some video games in there for the kids."

"Rockin'," Nathan said. "Can't wait to see it. So do you have all your sports trophies from when you were in high school and college and stuff?"

"You mean the hall of fame room? Yeah, unfortunately, it's all here in the shrine."

"The shrine?" Tara asked, laughing.

"It's not a shrine," Kathleen scoffed. "What do you want us to do with the trophies and awards you and Gavin won? Box them up and throw them in the attic?"

"Actually, that's a great idea. I can take care of that while I'm here."

Kathleen waved her hand. "Don't be ridiculous." She turned to Nathan and Tara. "Would you like to see them?"

"Yeah!" Nathan said.

"I'd love to see them." Tara stood.

Mick pulled at her hand. "You don't have to go see them."

"I want to."

"Ugh."

She laughed and followed Kathleen upstairs.

Mick was right. It was like a shrine, but it was very sweet. There were trophies and pennants dating back to grade school. Everything from peewee football and T-ball all the way to the awards both the brothers had won in college, tucked away in what looked to be a room now used as an office, since there was also a desk and a computer.

The pride on Mick's parents' faces was evident as they stood by and beamed while they pointed out what each of the guys had won each particular trophy for. Mick, meanwhile, just looked damned uncomfortable, which Tara also found incredibly charming. There were also trophies for Jenna for gymnastics, dance, field hockey, and softball.

Clearly an athletic family.

"Wow. All your stuff is just bangin' awesome," Nathan said, ogling Mick's college awards. "You worked hard, huh?"

"I did."

"He also maintained a three-point-eight grade point average at the University of Texas," Kathleen said. "We were more proud of his grades than we were of all the trophies in this room."

Tara mouthed a silent thank-you to Kathleen over the top of Nathan's head. Kathleen winked.

"Yeah, but you don't really need to worry about that once you make money playing football."

Mick slung his arm over Nathan's shoulders. "Not true, my man. You gotta have the smarts to get into college in the first place. They might want to draft a decent player, but they don't want someone who's going to struggle to make the grades, because it makes their job harder. Second, do you know how many football players piss away all the money they make in the NFL, and then when their careers are over they end up dead broke?"

Tara and Mick's parents followed Mick and Nathan down the stairs. Tara listened intently to the conversation, determined to let Mick do all the talking.

"No."

"More than you think. A lot more than you think. You need to put all you effort into your grades and into using your head first, because you'll use up your body fast. And when that's done, you'll have to have something to do after. If you blow out a knee your second season, you'll be what? Twenty something years old with your whole life ahead of you. You don't want to be a dumb-a—

you don't want to be dumb and stupid with no education and no money, right?"

Nathan looked up at him. "Huh. I never thought about that."

Mick slapped him on the back. "A lot of guys don't. Always use your head, not just your muscle. The smart guys always do."

Nathan tilted his head back to look at Mick, and Tara's breath caught at the abject hero worship.

She hoped he listened to what Mick said about using his brain. Because Nathan was a smart kid. And his grades were good. She hoped and prayed they stayed that way and he didn't count on football to see him through life.

"So where's your brother?" Nathan asked.

"He has a game tonight," Mick answered. "He'll be by later, I imagine. Or at the bar." Mick lifted his gaze to his mother.

"I talked to him this morning. He'll come by for the party at the bar tomorrow night. He's busy tonight."

"Got a hot date?" Mick asked.

Kathleen laughed. "I have no idea. Neither of you are very forthcoming about your love lives. Though I'm very pleased you brought Tara and Nathan with you this weekend. A step in the right direction."

Kathleen took a seat on the sofa next to Tara. "So tell me about yourself, Tara. Are you from San Francisco?"

She swallowed, sensing the inquisition forthcoming.

"Hey kid, let me show you the workshop out back," Jimmy said. "Mick, you can come along. Nathan and I might even kick your butt in a game of hoops."

"In your dreams, old man." He turned to Tara and winked.

Tara knew it was get-to-know-his-mother time. She returned her gaze to Kathleen. "I grew up in the East Bay, outside San Francisco. Never lived in the city. Too expensive there."

"And your ex-husband?"

"I was never married. Nathan's father isn't in our lives."

"Oh, I see. Well, I'm sorry about that. So what do you do for a living?"

That was it? No probing or disapproval for being a single mother? Huh. Not what she expected. "I'm an event planner. That's actually how I met your son. I planned a party for the team."

Kathleen clapped her hands together. "How delightful. And what a fun career for you. You must enjoy that very much."

"I do, actually. I've only had the business for a couple years, so we're still growing, but it's going very well so far. I have high hopes for it."

"It takes time to grow a business. And perseverance."

"I have both. It took me a while to get to the point where I could afford to start up a company, but this is something I've always wanted to do. I'll do whatever it takes to make it succeed."

Kathleen took her hand and squeezed it. "Years ago, women couldn't do what you're doing. I admire you, being a single mother, juggling your own business, and raising that fine son of yours. It's not easy."

"Nathan's worth the sacrifices I've had to make."

"Can I ask you a personal question?"

"Sure."

"And you can feel free to tell me it's none of my business. It won't hurt my feelings at all. What about Nathan's father? Did he just not want to be part of his life?"

She could tell Kathleen she didn't want to talk about it, but surprisingly, she didn't mind. "I didn't want him in Nathan's life. I was only fifteen when I got pregnant, which was stupid, but I knew I wanted to have my baby. And the guy who got me pregnant wasn't someone I wanted in my life or in my baby's life. Drugs, theft, time in jail—he was a total loser. I made him sign away rights to my child before he got sent off to prison. He can never make a claim to Nathan now."

Kathleen nodded. "Even then you did what was necessary to protect your child. You were smart."

"I was dumb. I shouldn't have gotten pregnant. But Nathan didn't need to suffer for my stupidity. And how could I regret having him? He's everything to me."

Kathleen's eyes watered. "A good mother is willing to lay down her life for her child. You're a good mother."

Tara blinked back tears. "Thank you. I don't think anyone's ever told me that."

"Your mother?"

Tara laughed. "That's a topic for another day and another conversation. I think I've burdened you enough for our first meeting. Any more, and you'll tell your son to run as far away from me as he possibly can."

"Oh, I don't know about that, Tara. My son, like me, is a very good judge of character. I don't need to tell him what to do. If he chose you to be in his life, it's because he thinks you're good for him."

"Thank you, Kathleen. I like Mick very much. I like being with him. I like the way he makes me feel when I'm around him."

"That's all I needed to know about you. You never once said you like the things he gives you. It was all about feelings. I'm so glad you're here this weekend,.."

Her heart swelled with the feeling of family, something she hadn't felt in—ever. "Me, too, Kathleen."

MICK LEANED AGAINST THE WALL OF THE HALLWAY, feeling all kinds of guilt for listening in on the conversation Tara was having with his mother.

But he couldn't help it. He liked hearing her talk to his mom, liked how freely she opened up, talked about the guy who'd gotten her pregnant. One of the things he admired about Tara was how she'd done so much on her own from such a young age. He didn't know everything about her past, but he was getting glimpses into it little by little. And from what he was getting, he understood that it had been shitty from the start, from her parents to the guy who knocked her up. And she'd gotten where she was today all on her own.

It was time to sit down with her and get the story directly from Tara. He wanted to know more about her. And there were things he needed to tell her about himself. He wanted things to progress between them, because he was starting to care pretty damn deeply about her.

And if you cared a lot about someone, you told them your secrets. And they told you theirs.

So maybe it was time for that talk.

Uh . . . soon.

NINE

"YOU BROUGHT A WOMAN HOME."

"Yes, Mom."

"This is the first time."

"Yes, it is."

"Don't think it's going to go unnoticed or that I don't have questions."

Tara was upstairs taking a shower before they went out to the bar tonight. Mick's dad and Nathan had bonded and were off somewhere in his dad's workshop doing God only knew what. Building . . . something together. Which left Mick in the kitchen with his mother.

"So, is it serious?"

Mick leaned against the counter. "I don't know. We've just started seeing each other."

"That doesn't matter. Is it serious?"

"Maybe."

His mom crossed her arms, a smile lifting her lips. "I like her, Michael. A lot."

She always used his given name when she wanted to get his attention.

"I like her, too, Mom. But I haven't told her everything yet, so don't say anything."

She smacked his arm. "It's not my place to tell her all your secrets. That's up to you." She tsked. "As if I would."

He pulled her into his arms and hugged her. "I know. But I'm taking this slow, and I don't want to screw it up. She's special to me. She's . . . different."

His mother pulled away. "Different from the skinny little women who wear all the makeup I see you with on the covers of all those magazines?"

"I wasn't really dating any of them. Not seriously."

"Well, handle this one with care. I get the idea she's treading the waters of love very carefully."

"Yeah, I get that idea, too. I'll be careful with her, Mom. I promise."

MICK ENJOYED BASEBALL PRETTY MUCH LIKE HE EN-joyed all sports. But today was different, because he got to watch the game through Tara and Nathan's eyes.

Nathan was wide-eyed when he led them to the box seats above the dugout. Thanks to Gavin, they had a great view of the game and the players. Gavin came out during warm-ups, spotted Mick, and waved. Nathan's eyes nearly bugged out of his head.

Of course Mick had even more surprises in store for Nathan.

And Tara loved baseball, too, he discovered as she watched the game. The woman was a constant surprise to him. He figured—like with most of the women he dated—that he'd have to explain the nuances of the game to her. He didn't. She understood innings and teams and balls and strikes and outs and positions from the pitcher to the center fielder and shortstop and what their functions were—in fact, she looked downright insulted when he started to explain what each player did.

She looked at him like he'd sprouted two heads. "I love sports, Mick. I know all about baseball, just like I know football. Don't make me slap you upside the head with my hot dog."

He promptly shut the hell up and let her watch the game.

Nathan, however, talked nonstop about Gavin and the Saint Louis team. He knew their standing in their division, who the weaker players were, what Gavin's average was, and knew Gavin leaned too far inside the batter's box and that's why he walked more often, because he got hit by the ball more than the average batter, which was something Mick had told Gavin time and time again, despite Gavin telling him to fuck off and mind his own sport.

Nathan was pretty astute, and they spent a lot of the game dissecting the players and the plays as well as the other team's strengths and weaknesses.

Fortunately, the home team won, and since it was a sold-out game, it was raucous, and Tara and Nathan seemed to have fun.

"Thank you, Mick," Tara said after the game. "We had a wonderful time."

"Yeah, it was awesome," Nathan said as they watched the teams leave the field and waited for the crowds to head up toward the exits.

"Oh, it's not over yet. I have a surprise for you."

"You do?" Nathan's eyes widened. "What is it?"

"It'll take a while, though, so have a seat and be patient."

They waited about an hour, then Gavin popped up from the dugout. "Hey."

"Hey, yourself." He turned to Tara and Nathan. "Come on. Let's go down."

"Holy crap."

"Nathan," Tara whispered. "Please watch your language, for the millionth time."

Gavin put his arm around Tara. "I think he gets an excuse for excitement."

They went down to the dugout, and Mick hugged his brother. "Good game. You didn't suck."

Gavin laughed. "Bite me." He turned to Tara. "You must be the girl who's dumb enough to date my brother."

"I think I might have just been insulted, but yes, I'm Tara." She grinned and held out her hand.

Instead, Gavin grabbed her and hugged her. "Nice to meet you, Tara, but I think you've lost your mind to date this loser." He pulled away and shook Nathan's hand. "And you must be Nathan."

Nathan smiled. "Yeah. You played great today."

"Thanks. We won, so it's a good birthday present."

"Happy birthday, Gavin," Tara said.

"Thank you. So how about a tour of the place?"

Nathan's jaw dropped. "Serious?"

"Serious."

Gavin was a good host and took them all around the stadium, even to the locker room, which had been pretty much cleared out, so at least Mick didn't have to shield Tara's eyes from any naked players. And Nathan's biggest surprise came when Gavin gave him an autographed jersey.

"Wow, thanks. And it's not even my birthday yet."

"Mick told me your birthday's in a couple weeks. Fifteen, huh?"

"Yeah."

"Soon you'll be driving, and your mom won't sleep anymore."

Tara laughed. "Don't remind me."

"You look too young to have a kid who's going to be fifteen."

"Thank you. You're now my favorite person in the whole world."

Gavin winked. "I need to head out. Got a few things to do before tonight. See you at the bar later?"

"Yeah," Mick said. "Thanks, Gavin."

"Anytime. Thanks for coming to the game."

"WHO'S THE CHICKLET? ANOTHER MOVIE STAR?"

Mick laughed and leaned over the bar to press a kiss on his sister's cheek. "Not at all. She's an event planner, not an actress, not a model."

Jenna gasped. "You mean she's a normal, everyday person like you and me? Well, like me. You're a bona fide stud and star. I'm the nobody of the family."

He rolled his eyes. "You're the star of Riley's, pumpkin."

"Yeah, that's exactly what I always dreamed of being when I was a little girl."

"Well, with those tattoos and ear piercings, I'm thinking rock star, but since you haven't yet stood in line for *American Idol*, I have no idea what you're dreaming of."

She tapped her finger on his nose and winked at him. "I'm just totally fulfilled being the head bartender at my family's restaurant."

He snorted. "Yeah, I'll bet."

Jenna was gorgeous, and she really did look like a rock star with her short black hair spiked up all over the place and dyed at the ends with—purple, he supposed. She had a wild array of tattoos on various parts of her body and probably other parts that as a brother he just flat-out didn't want to know about. Her left ear was pierced within an inch of its life, and she had a tiny little diamond pierced at the side of her nose that even he thought was kind of cute. But he really had no idea what Jenna was about or what she wanted out of life, since she seemed content enough to run the bar at Riley's. Then again, at twenty-three, maybe she just hadn't figured it out yet.

"And she has a kid, too?"

Mick's gaze traveled to where Tara and Nathan hung out with his dad over at the video games.

"Yeah. Nathan is fourteen. Almost fifteen."

"Ready-made family. How utterly unlike you, Mick. What's up with that?"

He leaned against the bar. "I have no idea."

"So, will I like her?"

He turned to Jenna. "Yeah. I think you will."

TARA HAD ALREADY HAD A WONDERFUL DAY, AND SO HAD Nathan. Mick's brother was amazing. They looked very similar, though Gavin was more slender and his eyes were an emerald green like Kathleen's.

Nathan had been in heaven after the game and the tour, and getting the jersey was the icing on the cake. And now the bar tonight.

She didn't know what she had expected when she'd been told the Rileys had a family bar, but it wasn't this. Riley's was an incredible upscale sports bar and restaurant.

Tara thought she was going to be tense tonight, but so far it was going well, even if she had lost sight of Mick. But at least Nathan was in heaven. He was in an actual bar, for one thing, and it was noisy and atmospheric. There were vintage video games like Pac-Man and Donkey Kong, and he and Mick's dad had bonded in a major way. Nathan having no grandparents had been something Tara regretted, but there was nothing she could do about that. She'd cut off all contact with her parents long ago, and not a thing had changed between her and them after all these years, so there was no point in exposing Nathan to their style of parenting. Or lack thereof.

Being around Kathleen and Jimmy was good for Nathan. They

were warm and nurturing, and Nathan naturally gravitated toward an older couple that offered unconditional love with no expectations.

"You going to hide against this pillar all night?"

She lifted her gaze to Mick. "Just making sure Nathan is settled."

"My mom and dad will see he's taken care of. And if not them, I have a lot of uncles and aunts and cousins you haven't even met yet. Once Nathan's introduced to them, the kid won't stand a chance of being alone for even a second. He'll be watched like a hawk. My mother will make sure of it, since he's a minor in their bar."

She believed him. She pushed off the wooden pillar to face him. "You have a big family?"

"Just my brother and sister, but yeah, lots of extended family. You'll meet a bunch of them tonight."

She looked around the bar, which was already filling up with people waving to and hugging each other. Riley's was warm and inviting, with polished wood floors and paneling, tables and booths set up near all the TVs—and there sure were a lot of those spread throughout the place—as well as a couple pool tables and video games and a very long bar where a stunning young woman was pouring beer.

"Is that Jenna?" she asked.

"Yeah."

"She's beautiful."

"She is, but don't tell her that. She already has an overinflated ego."

Mick took her hand and led her to the bar, where Jenna was setting up glasses and pouring drafts of beer.

"Jenna, this is Tara."

Jenna leaned across the bar and held out her hand, her smile genuine. "Nice to meet you, Tara. Welcome to the insanity that is Riley's Bar and the Riley family."

"Nice to meet you, too, Jenna. Is there anything I can do to help?"

"No, but thanks for offering. You're obviously nicer than my brother."

"Hey, you don't offer to play football for me."

Jenna snorted. "I could probably throw better than you."

Mick arched a brow. "Is that a challenge?"

"Maybe. You know I've got an arm."

"In your dreams, pumpkin."

"Wuss. You're just afraid I'll show you up because I'm a star with the long pass and you're an old man now."

"You and me. Backyard. Tomorrow."

Jenna grinned and nodded. "You're on. Now go away so I can get some work done. Tara, great meeting you."

"You, too, Jenna. I'll be there to see you kick his butt."

Jenna looked up at Mick. "Oh, I like this woman."

Mick flicked his gaze to Tara. "I can't believe you'd root against me."

Tara shrugged. "Girl power, you know."

Mick laughed and put his arm around her.

"So where's the birthday boy?"

"He'll stroll in late as usual so he can make an entrance. He likes to be the center of attention. Middle child syndrome, I think."

While Jenna went off to serve some drinks, Tara looked to Mick. "You and Gavin seem to get along well."

"Heh. You should have seen us when we were kids. There was no getting along then. We competed over everything, from sports to toys to attention from our parents."

"Some boys outgrow that."

He grinned at her. "Some do."

"And what about your sister? She must have had it hard having two big brothers. Were you overprotective of her?"

He shook his head. "She never gave us a chance. She just tossed herself in the pile and mixed it up with the two of us. Or tried to, anyway. The girl has no fear."

"Obviously, if she can handle herself with the two of you, she can probably handle anything."

"Yeah, we never had to worry about her taking care of herself."

Over the next hour or so, Tara was introduced to Mick's aunts and uncles and cousins and more people than she could ever possibly remember. The good thing was, there were some kids around Nathan's age, so Mick made a point of introducing him to them. They seemed to hit it off, and Tara breathed a sigh of relief that he wouldn't be the only teenager here tonight.

At the moment he was sitting at a table with a group of about six kids ranging in age from twelve to seventeen, all of them shoveling food into their mouths, drinking soda, and laughing. God, she loved seeing her son smile and laugh. It was all too rare these days.

"He's fine. Quit worrying."

"I'm not worrying at all. I'm . . . blissful, I guess is the word." She turned to Mick. "You have an amazing family. Thank you for this weekend."

He cupped her cheeks and brought her face to his. "You're welcome. Thanks for coming with me."

He brushed his lips across hers, and Tara breathed in his scent, wishing she could do more than lightly kiss him. While this weekend had been fun and she'd loved meeting his family, they hadn't had more than a few seconds of alone time. She missed that, craved having time to do more than hold hands and steal a few short kisses.

When he pulled back, she saw the heat flare in his eyes and knew he thought the same thing.

"We're going to need to steal an hour in a closet or the basement or something."

She laughed. "I'd be down with that."

"And if I keep thinking all the dirty thoughts I'm thinking about you, I'm going to get a hard-on in front of my entire family."

She batted her lashes at him. "I'm not making you think those thoughts."

"You don't have to do anything but look at me like you want to eat me. Or fuck me."

Tara shuddered an inhale, lightly pressing her fingertips against his chest and leaned in to whisper to him. "Stop talking like that. You're making me wet."

Mick looked around the room, then back at her. "I have an idea. How about we—"

"Well, I finally get to meet this mystery woman you've been spending all your time with."

"Elizabeth."

Tara spun around to face one stunningly beautiful woman. She wore a black suit that fit her perfect curves. Her red hair was pulled up in a French twist, her nails manicured, and the shoes she wore were not at all knockoff, but designer, with killer heels made to show off her dynamite legs. Tara might be a woman, but she could appreciate another beautiful woman, and Elizabeth was sex on stilettos. And she was a sports agent? Good Lord, those poor owners never stood a chance once they locked onto her ice blue eyes.

"Hi, sweetie," she said to Tara, holding out a creamy hand. "I'm Elizabeth Darnell, Mick's agent."

Warning bells went off in Tara's head right off the bat. From the scrutinizing look in Elizabeth's eyes, she could tell the woman didn't like her. She plastered on a professional smile and shook her hand. "Nice to meet you, Miss Darnell."

"Oh, call me Liz. All the women in Mick's life do."

Zing. Clearly she wanted Tara to know that she was one in a string of many women Mick was fucking. "How nice."

"Why are you here, Liz?" Mick asked.

For some reason Tara was pleased that Mick didn't seem happy. And she was doubly pleased when he slipped his arm around her waist and tugged her next to his side, a movement that made Liz narrow her eyes.

"I had some paperwork I needed Gavin to sign, and he insisted I attend his birthday party tonight."

"Insisted, did he? You and Gavin being so close?"

Liz threw her head back and laughed. "Why, we're practically married, didn't you know?"

"Elizabeth, no man wants to be married to you. You'd eat him for breakfast."

"Mick, why would you say that? Someday I hope to settle down and raise two point two children as is expected of my gender."

Mick snorted. "No. Can't picture it, sorry. You love your career and all the money all your clients make you. Can't see you giving that up for any man. In fact, I don't think I've ever seen you dating any man. You don't have time for love in your life, Liz. You're too busy chasing money and success and trying to beat the big boys you compete with."

Liz laughed. "You're probably right. What would I do with a man other than slap a contract in his hand and hope to God he could do something with a ball or drive a race car, right?"

Tara caught a flash of something in Elizabeth's eyes, but just as quickly it was gone. It might have been regret or sadness, but she didn't know the woman all that well, so she couldn't be sure.

Liz turned back to Tara. "So, I hear you have a little boy?"

"Teenager, actually. Nathan. He's over there in the Saint Louis jersey hanging out with Mick's cousins."

"Oh, I see. Well, you must have started when you were young."

"Yes, I did, as a matter of fact. I was pregnant at fifteen."

Elizabeth arched a perfect brow. "Are you from a . . . rural area?"

"Liz, Jesus. That's enough."

"No. From a fairly large city, actually."

Elizabeth waited, no doubt thinking Tara was going to spill her guts about her background. Wrong. It was time she told Mick about it, though.

"Hey there, gorgeous. Glad you came by."

Gavin spun Liz around, and Tara's jaw could have dropped at the way Elizabeth's face changed. The haughty, holier-than-thou cemented expression disappeared and the icy chill in the air melted. The woman even sported a genuine smile. She looked about sixteen years old when she smiled at Gavin. Her eyes just melted.

Holy cow.

"Hi, there, handsome. Happy birthday." She did maintain distance and gave him what Tara would consider a professional hug, but Gavin pulled her into his arms, put his lips on her, and gave her a kiss that wasn't at all professional. When she pushed back, her cheeks were flushed. She licked her lips. And she couldn't quite tear her gaze away from Gavin's face.

Well, well, well. So the ice queen was human after all.

"Come with me," Gavin said. "Some friends of mine are here I want you to meet."

Elizabeth rolled her eyes and said, "The things I have to do to keep a client happy. Ta-ta."

Gavin took her hand and tugged her along.

"Oh. My. God," Tara said, watching Liz disappear into the thick crowd with Gavin.

Mick scratched the side of his nose. "Yeah, I know. Liz can be a real bitch sometimes. Never thinks before she speaks. Hell, you should hear the insulting things she says to me. But she's really good at her job and—"

"No, Mick. Not about that." Tara waved her hand, dismissing

his worries about Liz's nasty comments. "That didn't bother me at all." She lifted her gaze to Mick. "But did you see the two of them together?"

"The two of—" He followed her gaze. "Gavin and Liz? Oh, yeah, she represents him, too."

She shook her head. "Not what I meant. It was like as soon as he showed up, a switch went off inside her. Total personality transplant. She went warm. Melty, womanly warm. You know what I mean?"

"What?" Mick shifted his gaze to where Liz sat at the bar next to Gavin and his friends. He looked back at her. "No. No way. Liz doesn't have feelings."

"Yes she does, Mick. She has them, and she has them big. For Gavin. I mean, I don't know her at all, but I can read a woman's signals with a man, and her signals were pinging loud and clear. She's in love with him."

Mick frowned and shook his head. "Liz doesn't love anyone. Liz loves money. And her career as a sports agent. Believe me, I know. She's been my agent and Gavin's since we started out. Besides, she's older than Gavin by like . . . four years. She's like . . . thirty-two or something."

Tara laughed. "So?"

"So she doesn't have those kinds of feelings, I'm telling you. Gavin's a commodity to her. We all are. And if you thought all the stories about *me* being a man whore were true? Trust me, the ones about my brother *are* true. He goes through women like he goes through shirts. He doesn't see Liz as anything but his agent. He's sweet to her because she helps his career. There's nothing between the two of them."

Tara shrugged. "Well, there might not be anything on his end, but I can guarantee there's something on hers."

"I think you're wrong. Liz is a great actress, and you just read her wrong. She plays up to Gavin's weakness, which is a gorgeous woman with great legs."

"If you say so."

But Tara wasn't buying it for a second. If there was one thing she could spot, it was a woman with warm gooey love yearnings for a man.

And Elizabeth Darnell had it bad for Gavin Riley.

TEN

MICK HAD HAD ENOUGH OF TOSSING AND TURNING IN the bed that was too damn small for his frame. And knowing Tara was at the end of the hall was driving him crazy.

Nathan had ended up going home with one of Mick's aunts for a sleepover with her and her husband's two teenage boys, since they'd pretty much hung out nonstop at the bar anyway talking football and some online video game that they were probably going to stay up all night and play. Tara was thrilled he'd found some friends, so she'd been fine with it.

But Mick had spent the entire night at the bar watching Tara, touching her but not really touching her, breathing her in and wishing he could do what he wanted to do with her. Instead, he'd had to be content with holding her hand and the occasional kiss, and that just wasn't cutting it.

He finally threw on his shorts, grabbed a couple condoms, and as quietly as he could, opened the bedroom door. The house was quiet, no

TV noise or movement from downstairs, which meant everyone had gone to bed. He crept down the hall to Tara's room. He didn't want to knock because he didn't want to wake his parents, but he also didn't want to scare the hell out of Tara by just walking into her bedroom, either.

He decided to risk it, turned the knob, and opened the door.

"Tara?" he whispered.

"I'm awake. Come in."

Thank God. He slipped in and shut the door, locked it for good measure.

She was sitting up, the pillows propped up behind her. She had the shutters open, moonlight spilling in and shining on her as she sat there and watched him approach.

She wore his team T-shirt. It swallowed her up, but damn if she didn't look sexy as hell in it. It was worn and threadbare, one he'd gotten when he first joined the team. She'd snatched it from him and said it was soft and comfortable and she intended to sleep in it. It made him hard just thinking about her breasts brushing against it, her skin against something he owned.

It made him feel possessive of her, and a rush of heat tightened his groin.

"I couldn't sleep," she said. "I was hoping you'd find a way to come in here."

He dragged her into his arms. "I couldn't stand not touching you for one more night."

"Good, because I was only going to give you about another half hour, then I was coming to you."

His mouth came down on hers with a hunger that he'd held in for too long. He was afraid he wasn't going to be able to hold back, that he would hurt her, but she seemed as needy as he was. She climbed onto his lap and slid her fingers into his hair.

"It's been a long, dry weekend," she said, brushing her lips against his.

He kissed her, and it only made the heat explode inside him.

He lifted her T-shirt and saw she wasn't wearing panties. His cock rocketed against his shorts, his need to fuck her driving him insane.

He lifted his gaze to hers, saw the heat flare in her eyes.

"I need you, Mick. No preliminaries. All I've been able to think about is you inside me. I'm wet and I'm hot and I need you. Fuck me now."

He swept his hand over her back, over the front of his T-shirt, pressing his team logo over her breasts. He slid his thumbs over her nipples. They were hard pebbles, and he needed to fill his hands with her. He slid his hands under the shirt to massage her breasts, to feel her nipples, then grabbed her waist and flung her onto the bed, dropped his shorts, and grabbed a condom from the pocket. He put it on in record time and lifted her hips, bent over, and shoved his cock inside her.

She gasped, grabbed his arms, and held on while he fucked her, pouring everything he'd been holding back for all these days.

"I've needed you," he whispered. "I've been thinking about fucking you, about kissing you. I've missed your mouth." He leaned forward and pressed his lips to hers, needing her tongue alongside his while her pussy tightened around him.

She licked at his lips, her gaze so clear, so filled with emotion, it was almost hard to look at her. "I missed you, too, Mick. It's hard to sleep without your body next to me at night, without your hands on me, without you inside me. It's all I can think about."

To know she felt the same desperate need he did calmed him down somehow, and he slowed the pace, wanting to make sure she came, that it was good for her. He'd been ready to go off the second he slid inside her. She was hot and tight, and this was all he'd been thinking about for days. It seemed like he couldn't get enough of her.

And when he lifted and she reached down to rub her clit, it rocked him.

"Yeah. Make yourself come. Let me see it."

He leaned back, pulled his cock partway out, and eased in slowly, letting her set the pace.

"You tell me what you want, how you want me to do this. And I'll make it good for you. Because I'm ready to come in you when you're ready."

She held on to his wrist with one hand, lifted her butt, and strummed her clit faster. Her golden hair spilled over the sheets, her body naked and open to him as he pressed in and out of her while she took herself to the edge with her fingers, naked desire tightening her features.

"Come on," he said, shoving his cock deep inside her. "Come on, honey."

"I'm close, Mick. Oh, God, I'm coming right now."

He felt it as she said it, felt her pussy constrict around his dick. He shoved inside her and took her mouth and tongue in a long, searing kiss as he emptied inside her, wishing he could shout, because it was so goddamn good he felt the orgasm shoot through him until his knees went weak.

When she stopped shaking, he rolled them over on their sides and pulled Tara against him, kissing her and stroking her body.

He waited, figuring she'd fall asleep, but she rolled over to look at him, the moonlight bathing her face. She looked worried about something, had tugged her bottom lip with her teeth.

He smoothed her hair back. "What's wrong?"

"I want to tell you who I am, where I came from."

He shoved to a sitting position and took her with him, pushing the pillow up so they were comfortable. "Okay. Want me to turn the light on?"

"No, this is fine. Probably easier for me this way."

He could still see her, but if this was how she wanted it, he'd give her anything she needed. "Fine. Go ahead."

"As you've probably figured out, I don't have brothers or sisters. I was an only child and my parents both worked, so I had a lot of alone time as a kid. I walked to and from school, let myself in the house, and it was my responsibility to make sure I ate something. My mom was a waitress, and she often worked at night. My dad worked construction so I tried to make sure to fix something for him to eat, otherwise he wouldn't eat anything."

"How old were you?"

"Eight or nine, I think. I don't really remember all that well."

Jesus. She was a kid. They were supposed to be taking care of her, not the other way around.

"Anyway, I would do my homework, and the dinner dishes, and go to my room. Dad would sit in the living room and watch TV. The thing is, Mick—he drank. And when my mom got off work, she'd join him. And late at night, things between them would get loud. They'd argue a lot when they were drunk."

Shit. Shit, shit, shit. A rock plummeted into his stomach and sat there.

Her fingers were twisted so tightly together her knuckles were turning white. He slipped his hand in between and took her hand in his. "You don't have to talk about this. I can tell it hurts you."

She lifted her gaze to his. "No, it's okay. I want to. It's important to me that you know this."

"Okay." He laid her hand in the palm of his, then rubbed his thumb over the top of hers, trying to calm her as she talked. She was trembling now, and he hated that bringing all this back freaked her out so badly. He wanted to take the hurt away, to make it never have happened, but it was part of her, had made her who she was today, and she was right—he needed to hear it.

"The fights between them escalated over the years, as their

drinking escalated. It got to the point where I just didn't want to be around it."

"Did they hurt you?"

She shrugged. "They'd yell at me about stupid stuff, but mostly they just got ticked at each other. I learned to stay out of the way, holed up in my room listening to music. The louder the music and the TV, the less of them I had to hear. When I got old enough, I'd go out with my friends at night just so I wouldn't have to be around them."

He nodded. There was nothing worse than being around a surly drunk. He understood that better than anyone.

"When I was fourteen and started high school, I met some new friends. Not great friends, either. A pretty rough crowd. Big drinkers, drug users, and partiers, but they stayed out late, and anything that kept me away from drunk central was okay by me. They let me crash at their place as much as I wanted, and that suited me. All my old friends drifted by the wayside because they were the good kids, the kids that did their homework and went to bed early. But I couldn't stay at their house, couldn't face them knowing how fucked up my home life had become. The other kids—my new friends— they understood and didn't judge me.

"There was this guy—he'd dropped out of high school a couple years earlier and had his own apartment. He was nineteen and I was fifteen. We'd all hang out at his place to party. By then I was drinking, doing a few drugs, too, anything to numb the pain, you know?"

He nodded, swallowing past the lump in his throat. He knew. God, how he knew.

"Anyway, he liked me. Really liked me. And I liked anyone who would give me attention. I realize now it was because I had gotten so little love and attention at home. We started having sex pretty regularly. He used a condom, but they're not 100 percent effective. And you know, when you're drunk or on drugs, who knows if he remembered to even use one. I got pregnant. That was the end of him wanting anything to do with me. He freaked out, said the baby wasn't his. I hadn't been with anyone else, so I knew it was his baby."

"What a bastard."

She smiled. "Yeah, he pretty much was, but you know, I had to own it. I made the dumb choice to have sex with him."

He tipped her chin with his thumb. "You were fifteen, Tara. A child. He wasn't a kid. He should have known better."

She shrugged. "Anyway, that was the end of partying for me. As soon as I found out I was pregnant, I straightened up. No more drugs or alcohol. I quit hanging with that crowd, and I went home and told my parents."

"What happened?"

She laughed, tears brimming in her eyes. "They called me a whore and kicked me out of the house. Said I was irresponsible and should know better. Said they, quote, unquote, raised me better than that." She swiped at the tears. "Isn't that the funniest thing?"

The tears fell down her cheeks, and Mick's gut tore up inside. "Good God. How could they do that to you?"

"They didn't care about me, Mick. They cared about their own lives. I was just an inconvenience to them. They barely even remembered having a kid, and sure as hell didn't want to be responsible for me, let alone the child I was going to bring into the world."

"So what did you do?"

"I called Social Services. I knew at fifteen the state at least had to be responsible for me. I told them I was pregnant and my parents were kicking me out, and that they were drunk and abusive."

Mick leaned back and regarded her. "You are a rock star, Tara. I'm proud of you for not taking what they dished out."

She laughed, swiped at the tears on her cheeks. "I was pissed and afraid for my baby."

"So what happened?

"They removed me from the home and found me a nice place for unwed mothers where I got to be with other teens having babies. I got to attend school, the state paid for my prenatal care, and I had Nathan. I was always good in school, so I started studying again. They helped me with child care so I could graduate, and eventually I found an apartment and started college. And it got me out of that hellhole I lived in with my parents because I filed for emancipation and it was granted on the grounds I was self-sufficient, had no other living relatives to care for me, and the state thought it in my best interests not to be returned to that environment."

Mick couldn't believe what Tara had gone through growing up, what it must have been like for her to feel so alone, and what she'd done on behalf of Nathan.

"It must have been scary for you, just a kid being on your own."

Her gaze caught his, and he saw nothing but love in her eyes. "I'd have done anything to protect Nathan. That's why I found Damon—who'd been arrested for drug dealing—and made sure he signed off, giving up parental rights, even though he still insisted he wasn't Nathan's father. He had no problem signing that paper, and I was relieved to get him out of our lives. I wanted to make sure none of my mistakes would ever come back to haunt my son."

"How much of this does Nathan know?"

"Everything. I don't keep secrets from him."

"Has he ever wanted to see his father?"

"No. He doesn't have that curiosity. I told him about the mistakes I made, and told him someday maybe I'd marry a man who'd be a decent father to him, but Damon was a sperm donor and nothing else. And it had nothing to do with Nathan, and everything to do with the bad choices I made when I was young and stupid."

"I admire your honesty, both with yourself and with your son. Does he know about your parents?"

"Yes. He knows everything, Mick. I'll never hold anything back from him. He deserves the truth. He had to know why my parents aren't in his life."

"Thank you for telling me all this. It explains a lot about who you are, why you're so strong, so driven. I admire the hell out of you, Tara."

She bent her head. "Don't. I'm no hero, Mick. I was stupid and irresponsible, and my child had to pay for my mistakes."

He forced her chin up, made her look at him. "Are you kidding me? You're amazing. Look what you went through, what you endured. To be where you are today after the kind of childhood you had? What you could have ended up like? Instead, you have a great career, a wonderful kid, and you're one of the most remarkable women I've ever met."

"I'm not perfect."

"I never said you were. But you're one of the most hardworking women I've ever known. And you've overcome more than most women ever will. I—"

He'd almost said something. Something he wasn't sure he was ready to say.

"What?"

"I admire you."

She laughed. "Stop admiring me. I just did what I had to do. For Nathan. If I hadn't gotten pregnant with him, who knew what kind of self-destruction spiral I would have continued on. Trust me, I was doing my best to ruin my life."

"Sometimes we're our own worst enemies."

"Please. You have the perfect family and the perfect life. I doubt you've ever done anything to fuck your life up."

He pulled her against him and laid them down, the truth hovering on the tip of his tongue, ready to spill. But he didn't think tonight would be the right time, not after what Tara had told him about her past.

And maybe he was just a coward.

He had some thinking to do.

TARA WAS STILL SLEEPING WHEN MICK WENT DOWN-stairs the next morning for coffee. His parents were going to pick Nathan up after they ran some errands, so he didn't have to worry about that, which left him a nice quiet house to himself for the moment to sit and think about what she'd told him last night.

How was he ever going to tell her the truth about himself after she'd been so honest with him about her past last night? Last night would have been overkill. It had been her night. And now . . .

Well, not now. It just wasn't the time. Now he was just going to sit back and enjoy his coffee alone.

"Well, don't you look all broody and moody this morning."

Or so he thought. He lifted his gaze to Jenna, who'd slipped in through the back door. "What are you doing here? I thought you were a vampire and didn't get up till like noon or something."

"I know you guys are leaving today. Figured I'd drag my sorry ass out of bed early so I could say good-bye."

"Really." He watched as she moved around the kitchen, grabbing a cup and filling it with coffee, then adding enough cream and sugar so that it really wasn't coffee when she was finished with it. She pulled up a chair next to him.

"You don't come home all that often anymore, and we didn't get much time to talk last night."

Uh-oh. Jenna was not the warm and fuzzy sisterly type. Which meant something was up. "Something on your mind you want to talk about?"

She palmed the cup and lifted it to her lips, took a sip, and raised her gaze to his. "It's Mom and Dad."

His heart stumbled, his mind already swirling with the possibilities, none of them good. "What about them?"

"Their fortieth anniversary is coming up."

"Oh. Crap. I didn't even know."

"Of course you didn't. You're a guy, and guys pay no attention to stuff like that. Anyway, I think we should throw them a party."

"Okay. When and where?"

She took out her phone, clicked to her calendar, and slid it between them. "Their anniversary is on the fifteenth. Gavin's in town again on the weekend of the eleventh for a game series. He has a day game on Saturday the twelfth, which means we could do something that night. I pulled him aside last night and hit him up, asked him if he'd be around that Saturday night, and he said he would be."

"I can be here, for sure."

"Great. Now all we need is someone to put a big party together for them."

She pushed her phone aside and stared at him.

"What? Why can't we just do it at the bar?"

She gave him a look. "Oh, right. You know how that'll turn out. We throw a party for them at the bar, and Mom and Dad both will end up working all night long. Is that really the way we want them celebrating their anniversary?"

He laid his head in his hand. "You're right. We can't do it at the bar. So what are we going to do?"

"Don't look at me. I bartend. I'm not a party planner."

"But I am."

Mick turned to see Tara standing in the doorway to the kitchen. She walked in.

"Hey. Morning," Jenna said.

"Good morning," Tara said. "Mind if I help myself to some coffee?"

"Of course." Mick watched her grab a cup and fill it with coffee. She looked gorgeous in her sweats and tank top.

She grabbed a seat. "I didn't mean to eavesdrop on the two of you. I just happened to hear part of your conversation when I was walking down the hall. You're planning a party?"

"Yes," Jenna said. "Our parents' fortieth wedding anniversary in a few weeks."

"Oh, how lovely. I can help. It's what I do for a living."

"Of course," Jenna said, laying her hand on top of Tara's. "Would you? I mean, I know you don't live here, so maybe you only do local stuff out there in California."

"I can do anything, anywhere. I'd be happy to plan the event. Eventually I want to expand my business nationally." She turned to Mick. "Not that I want to butt in. I'm sure I could help you find someone local, which would probably be easier for you."

"Are you kidding? I can't think of anyone I'd rather have organize this party. You're serious about this? You'd coordinate everything?"

Her eyes shone with warmth. "I'd love to, Mick. Your entire family has been wonderful to me this weekend. I can't think of any event I'd love to plan more than your parents' anniversary party. So when is it?"

Jenna showed her the dates.

"Okay, that's Nathan's birthday weekend, but I'll work around it."

"No," Mick said. "You don't put your kid second."

She laid her hand over his and offered up a warm smile. "I never put Nathan second. But I imagine for game tickets, he'd love to spend his birthday out here. And he loves your family. Unless you see that as a problem."

He kissed her forehead. "Spending time with you and Nathan isn't a problem."

He caught the look Jenna gave him, but he didn't care what she thought. He was having a hard enough time wrapping his head around his feelings for Tara and what it all meant. He sure as hell wasn't going to try to explain them to Jenna.

Tara turned to Jenna. "Jenna can help me on this end, and it'll be a breeze."

Jenna nodded and picked up her coffee. "Done deal, then. We're on for the twelfth. I'll shoot a text message to Gavin and let him know."

Little by little, his life was becoming more and more entwined with Tara's. And the knot in his throat was growing.

ELEVEN

MICK DRIPPED WITH SWEAT BUT STOOD UNDER CENTER, took the snap, dropped back a few steps, ignoring the rush, fixated on his targeted receiver. Three, two, one . . . now. He threw the pass, and Rodney had the ball in his hands and sprinted away.

Not that he expected a tackle. His offensive linemen were the best and would protect him while he stayed in the pocket.

Coach Lewis blew the whistle and came off the sidelines toward him.

"Still as cold-blooded as ever, Mick."

Mick took the bottle of water handed to him and swallowed down a couple sips, then handed it off. "Thanks."

"Your off-season workouts have added some muscle. Your timing is good. Arm feel okay?"

Mick nodded, ignoring the pinch in his shoulder and the aches in just about every damn joint in his body. "Just fine."

Coach patted him on the back. "I've never seen you work drills this hard."

"Just trying to keep those hungry young quarterbacks off my back."

Coach laughed. "You know we have to recruit young talent. They're no threat to you. Not for a while anyway."

It didn't matter. Mick was always aware that he was one injury away from being replaced in the game. He was thirty years old, and his time was limited. He took a glance to the sidelines where Brad Samuelson and Coy Bowman stood with clipboards in their hands. They knew every play; they practiced every day. They stood at the ready to step in and take his place. Young kids, eager to be the next big thing in professional quarterbacks. They were good, too. A little green, but good. Which meant Mick had to stay on his game if he wanted to continue to live his dream for a few more years.

Not just yet, boys. I still have several more years to play.

As long as he stayed healthy.

They worked drills for a couple more hours, then hit the showers. When he stepped out of the locker room, Liz was there in a killer gray suit and high heels that looked like they could do some serious damage to a man's private parts. She pushed off the wall and came toward him.

"Hoping to ogle some naked man flesh?" he teased.

She rolled her eyes. "If I wanted to see all of you naked, I'd have walked in there."

True enough. Wouldn't be the first time she'd strolled into the locker room and had conversations with one of her clients while they were showering. Most of the guys had gotten used to seeing her, though the younger guys usually dropped their tongues on the floor when she came walking in. She was definitely noticeable, and she knew it and used it to her advantage. Liz didn't have a shy bone in her body.

"What's up?" he asked.

"Samuelson and Bowman looked good today in drills."

"Uh-huh." He turned and headed out the side door toward his car. Liz followed. "Your point?"

"You're thirty now, Mick. Time to focus more on the game and less on some woman and her kid."

He stopped, turned, leveled his gaze on her. "My relationship with Tara is none of your business."

"It's my business if she affects your game play."

"Did you watch me practice today?"

"Yes."

"How did I look?"

She lifted her lips. "Like the number one quarterback in the league."

He clicked the remote and opened the door to his SUV. "Then stay out of my personal life, Liz, and go bother some other client who's not the number one player in his position."

NATHAN'S POPULARITY HAD GROWN BY LEAPS AND bounds, and all because of Tara dating Mick. She tried to keep his feet on the ground and tell him that this could all end tomorrow if she and Mick decided not to see each other anymore, but Nathan brushed her off and said that he and Mick would always be—what was the word he used? Tight. That was it.

She was afraid her son was growing too attached to Mick. And not only Mick, but Mick's family. He Skyped with Ian and Steve, Mick's cousins, on a regular basis, as well as whatever the hell those kids did online in that Warcraft game. Not that she really minded, since it was another avenue that was safe and kept her kid off the streets, and Mick assured her they were good kids.

But little by little her life as well as her son's had begun to revolve around Mick. And Mick's family. Now she was even planning a party for Mick's parents' anniversary, and that meant almost daily phone calls to Jenna, who she decided was an absolute riot. She had a wicked dry sense of humor, took nothing seriously, and she fiercely loved and protected her family. Tara could see why. Mick's family was perfect. If Tara could choose a family for herself, the Rileys would be the kind of family she'd want.

But they weren't her family and likely would never be her family. Sure, she and Mick got along great, but Mick had a lifestyle totally foreign to her. She was enjoying the hell out of playing the game with him right now, but it was temporary. Once his football season started up, he'd be busy, Nathan would start school and his football season, she'd dive into moving her business to the next level, and that would be the end of things. She just hoped Nathan wouldn't be hurt over all this when Mick no longer had time for him.

Maybe it was time to start easing back a little. She was already having a little too much fun with him. And okay, that too much fun thing was engaging her heart and her emotions in a way she hadn't expected. She hadn't wanted to get involved with him at all, but he'd been insistent, and she hadn't exactly been forceful in pushing him away. After all, the sex had been phenomenal, and oh, God, had she really needed some great sex in her life after years of drought. But now? Now things were starting to get serious, at least on her side of it.

So, yeah, it was definitely time to let go.

She leaned back on the chair and picked up her notebook, jotting down some shopping supplies for the party. Nathan was out with the team tonight, so she intended to enjoy her quiet time.

Until someone knocked at the door. She sighed and set down her cup of tea and the notebook, went to door, and peeked through the peephole, smiling when she saw it was Mick.

"Hi. What are you doing here?" she asked as she opened the door.

"I gave one of the guys on the team a ride home. His car's in the shop and his wife had the other car," he said. "He lives near you, so I thought I'd drop by."

"Come in." She closed the door behind her. "A little late for practice, isn't it?"

"Offensive team meeting went a little longer than expected."

"I see. Would you like something to drink?"

"Water would be great."

"Okay." She went into the kitchen and grabbed a bottle of water, came back, and handed it to him. He was sitting on the sofa, so she went to sit next to him as he finished the bottle in a few long gulps.

She realized he had been looking at her notebook. "Am I interrupting something?"

"No. I was just working on some notes for your parents' party."

"Thank you again for doing it."

"You don't have to keep thanking me, Mick. You did insist on paying me, after all. Which is totally unnecessary."

"Hey, it takes time out of your day to put an event together. Why not get paid for it?"

"Because it's your family, and I volunteered to help because I wanted to, not because I expected money for it."

"If we'd hired another event planner, we'd have paid them, wouldn't we?"

"Yes."

"Then enough talk about the money."

"Okay."

He looked upstairs. "Nathan home?"

"No, he's out with some of the guys from the team tonight."

"Oh. Will he be home soon?"

"I have to pick him up later."

"Uh-huh."

She arched a brow. "Did you come over to see Nathan?"

"Yeah, I'm secretly only seeing you so I can be Nathan's best friend." He pulled her onto his lap. "I think you know why I came over here."

And just like that her heart started racing, her body temperature rose, and heat filled her. Lying against him like this, her thighs over his, her breast rubbing against his chest, put her libido into overdrive. The physical chemistry she shared with Mick was combustible.

She arched a brow. "So you thought you'd drop by for a booty call?"

He tilted his head back and laughed. "I assumed Nathan was home. So the answer is no."

She affected a pout. "How disappointing. And here I thought you'd just come over to admire my ass."

"You do have a great ass, Tara. I have no problem spending time worshipping it."

"Really."

His eyes went dark. "Yes. Want me to show you?"

Heat coiled low in her belly. "Oh, most definitely."

He flipped her over so fast her head spun. He pulled down her shorts, dragging them to her knees. Her panties went next, and then his lips were on the globes of her ass, warm and making her pussy quiver. She clenched her fingers in the couch cushions, needy for what Mick could give her.

He slipped his hand between her legs, sliding his fingers along her pussy lips. "Is this what you want?" He tucked two fingers inside her, her pussy already wet and ready for his invasion.

She arched against him, pushing back against his hand. "Yes."

Time without him meant time thinking about him, about being with him, about doing this with him.

"You've been thinking about me kissing your ass, huh?"

She tilted her head to look at him. "Among other things."

He pressed his lips to her buttocks while he finger-fucked her. "I'd like to know what other things you want me to do to you."

He swept his fingers over her sex, swirling them over her clit, and any thoughts she had flittered away. "I can't think when you're touching me like that."

"Really."

"Yes."

"Then just make noises if you like what I do."

She did, letting out a whimper when he rubbed her butt with one hand and her pussy with the other, especially when he trailed his finger between her butt cheeks, teasing her anus. The sensation was incredible, sparking her desire even more.

"Like that?"

"Yes."

He teased her anus and slid his fingers into her pussy, fucking her with relentless strokes until she lifted her butt in the air against him, craving more of what he gave her.

And then she felt his finger at her back entrance again, and this time it was wet, whether from his saliva or her juices, she didn't know. But he slid it past the tight muscles, and oh, God, it felt so good she cried out, arching upward to get more of the burning, pleasurable pain that seemed to make her pussy pulse, too.

He fucked her pussy with his fingers, using his thumb to swirl over her clit, while at the same time sliding his finger in and out of her ass. Her mind tried to process of all the sensations, and it overwhelmed her with the sweetest, most wicked pleasure she'd ever felt.

"I'd like to fuck your ass sometime, Tara. Would you let me?"

If it felt as good as what he did with his finger, she'd deny him nothing. "Yes. Yes, you can fuck my ass."

She'd never felt anything like this, this lightning strike of intense pleasure that made her lose her mind. She arched her back, pushing against his hand as she climaxed with a wild cry.

Mick held her, giving her more of what she needed as she rocked through the pleasure, not stopping until she was spent and panting. Only then did he withdraw, roll her over, and kiss her. He went into the kitchen for a moment while she caught her breath, returning with a cold glass of ice water. He held the glass for her while she sipped, coating her dry throat.

It was very strange to be sitting on the floor naked from the waist down. Then again, she supposed there was no point in being modest with Mick. He'd pretty much seen it all.

"Thank you," she said, leaning over to kiss him. "That was very nice."

"You're welcome." He took her glass of water and swallowed down two quick gulps. He set the glass on the coffee table and sifted his fingers through her hair. "You make me thirsty."

She climbed on his lap. "Is that right? Let's see what we can do about that."

His cock was still hard, and she surged against him, ignoring the fact he still had his pants on and she was naked. She reached for his zipper, taking her time about tugging it down, taking a quick glance up at his face to find him zeroed in on watching the movement of her hands.

She slid down on his thighs and pulled his pants down over his hips. He lifted to help her, and she freed his cock.

"Got a condom on you?"

"Pocket."

She dug in his pocket and pulled out the foil packet, waving it back and forth. "I like that you're always prepared."

"Around you? Hell, yeah. I always want you, Tara. I think about making love to you all the time."

She lifted her gaze to his and saw the heat in his eyes, glad to know he thought about her. She wrapped her fingers around his cock and stroked. He hissed, grabbed the condom packet from her fingers, and tore it open. "I need to fuck you."

He reached for her hands and pulled her toward him, holding on to her while she lifted and held his cock, settling over him, sliding onto him.

Every time he entered her it was like the first time, a shock of awareness, a thrill of excitement as he expanded and filled her. Fully seated on him, she fanned her fingers over his abdomen and closed her eyes, just let herself experience the sensations as her pussy accommodated his cock, felt the flutters and contractions and pure joy as their bodies joined.

"Good?"

She opened her eyes and met his curious gaze. "Heaven. I love the way you fit inside me."

He arched, and she gasped. "I like being inside you, Tara. I like feeling the way your pussy grips me, the sounds you make when I fuck you."

She rocked forward, dragging her clit against him, and felt the walls of her pussy grip his cock in response. Mick grabbed her hips and pulled her toward him, then back, setting the pace.

"Yeah," he said, watching where their bodies were connected. "Look down, Tara. See my dick pulling your pussy lips apart when I pump up inside you?"

She bent forward, watched his cock disappear inside her, then pull out, coated with her cream. "Yes."

"I love the way you swallow me up."

Her belly clenched, her entire body going up in flames at the way he touched her, the way he spoke to her, his touch, his voice, everything about him hot and sexy and filling her senses with fire. She leaned forward, pressing her breasts against his chest, running her fingertips across his jaw and his lips.

He cupped her face and drew her to him for a soul-shattering kiss, then grabbed her butt cheeks and lifted her up and down off his cock while his tongue dueled with hers. She gasped against his mouth, so close now she felt the stirrings of orgasm tightening inside her.

"Mick." She pulled back just enough to search his face, her nails digging into his shoulders.

"Come on, Tara. Let me feel it."

She held on for only a few seconds more, driving her clit against his body, letting the sensations take her to the ragged edge. Then she cried out and let go, latching on to his mouth as she came. Mick dug his fingers into her hair and kissed her deeply, held on to her as she shook against him with the force of her orgasm. He groaned against her lips as he thrust upward into her when he came, his fingers digging into her flesh. It was just so good to be held tightly in his embrace, to know it affected him as hard as it had her.

She blew out a breath and laid her forehead against his. "So glad you stopped by tonight."

He laughed. "Me, too."

They cleaned up and dressed, then sat on the sofa together watching TV while Tara made her notes. Her cell rang about eleven p.m., and she frowned as she went to grab it, thinking it was odd that Nathan would call early to be picked up from the party.

But it was Maggie, and her eyes widened as she listened, tried to calm Maggie down, then hung up and turned to Mick.

"What's wrong?"

"Maggie's having a meltdown."

"About what?"

She chewed her lip, wondering how much she should confide in Mick about Maggie's personal life, then decided she didn't have much of a choice. "Her brother is a mess. He gets into a lot of jams, then expects Maggie to come to his rescue. She doesn't know what to do, she's in crisis mode, and she's not clearheaded where he's concerned because he's her baby brother and she's practically raised him by herself. We've been friends a long time and seen each other through some rough spots. I'd like to help her."

"You need to go to her? I understand." Mick stood.

"There's another problem. Nathan. I was supposed to pick him up from the party at midnight."

"I'll get him. You go take care of Maggie."

"Are you sure? I can go get Nathan now, then go to Maggie's."

"And Nathan would hate that. Write down the address, and I'll pick up Nathan, bring him back here, and wait for you to come home."

"God, Mick, I hate burdening you with my personal stuff."

He put his hands on her shoulders and steadied her. "Things between us are personal, Tara. So write down the address and let me go get him, okay?"

She nodded, gave him the address and her spare garage door opener, then kissed him, thanked him, and ran out the door. As she climbed into her car, Mick stood at her open doorway, waving to her.

She waved back and a sudden pang of abject fear slammed into her.

How had he become such an important and integral person in her life?

And what was she going to do about that?

IT WASN'T HARD TO FIND THE BRIGHTLY LIT HOUSE where the party was. Mick looked for all the cars parked haphazardly in the driveway. And the noise level was jet engine loud. For this late at night, he was surprised the cops hadn't been called. These people must have really understanding neighbors. He went up to the front door and rang the bell, then figured there wasn't a chance in hell they'd hear it since the music was ear-splitting. He tried the knob, and the door opened. Great. He rolled his eyes and walked in.

Disaster, was his first thought. Discarded paper plates and plastic cups and napkins and food and drink and furniture had been shoved out of whack. It looked like a crime scene. Or a party. The first thing Mick smelled was the alcohol, which had a stronger odor than the pizza, surprising considering there were about twenty or so empty pizza boxes strewn all over the room.

He picked his way through a throng of beefy football players, several jailbait-age inappropriately dressed girls, all of whom sized him up—were they serious?

"Anyone seen Nathan?" he asked of one of the guys, who looked up at him with a half-lidded gaze that spelled either drunk or stoned.

"Nuh-uh."

Mick moved on toward the kitchen. So far he hadn't seen an adult in sight. Good thing Tara hadn't come to pick up Nathan. She'd be near fainting by now.

He found Nathan out back hanging with a group of three guys and two girls. And he was just about as shit-faced as the rest of the partygoers.

Not good.

"Mick! My man! Wazz up?"

"Let's go."

"Dude, let's stay and party." Nathan threw his arm around Mick. "Do you know who this is? This is Mick Riley, San Francisco's quarterback."

"We know, dude. Dude, you are one lucky sonbitch." One of the guys grinned. "How awesome is it that your mom is with him?"

"Like, wow, you're Mick Riley." One of the girls stumbled out of her lawn chair and fell toward him, trying her best to look provocative.

"Whose house is this, Nathan?" Mick asked.

"Tim O'Banyan."

"And where are Tim's parents?"

"Cabo," everyone said in unison, laughing as they raised their plastic cups to Tim's parents in a toast.

Oh, shit. "Come on. We're leaving. Say good night." Mick should probably call someone and put a stop to the debauchery, but his only concern was Nathan and getting him home. He couldn't be responsible for the entire team and their girlfriends.

" 'Kay. Night, peeps."

Mick led Nathan to his car and got out of there, figuring it was only a matter of time before the local cops made their appearance.

"Have a good time?"

Nathan grinned, hiccupped, then laughed. "Yup."

"Do a little drinking?"

"Nope. Did a *lot* of drinking."

"I can tell. Think that's a smart idea?"

"Yup. Very smart."

No point in trying to talk sense to him tonight. Mick drove in silence, listening to Nathan hum, then sing, burp, laugh, and rattle on nonsensically.

Unfortunately, Nathan started weaving back and forth in the seat. And Mick noticed he was getting paler by the minute.

"Nathan, you okay?"

"Not really. I think I might need to puke. Like right now."

"We're a block from the house. Can you make it?"

Nathan burped. "No."

Shit. Mick pulled over while rolling down the window. Nathan unbuckled his seat belt and heaved out the window—all over the side of Mick's truck.

Just fucking awesome. Mick sat there and waited it out while Nathan continued to vomit up whatever he'd had to drink. When he was finally done, Mick handed Nathan one of the towels he kept in his gym bag, then drove to the house and helped Nathan out of the SUV, carefully avoiding the door panel while he did so.

Nathan wasn't too steady on his feet, so Mick had to throw his shoulder under Nathan and help him walk.

"Come on, buddy, let's get you upstairs."

"That's a long fucking way up," Nathan said, tossing his head back and staring up the steps.

"Uh-huh. You can make it." God, the kid reeked. "Shower time."

"I just wanna go to bed."

"Too bad." Mick took him into the bathroom and turned on the water. "Can you handle this, or do I need to do it for you?"

Nathan blinked. Weaved. Dropped to his knees in front of the toilet and threw up again.

Mick kneeled down and kept the kid from drowning himself, then tossed him, fully clothed minus his tennis shoes, into the shower. It seemed to help him a little.

"I feel terrible," Nathan said.

"I'm sure you do."

Mick turned off the shower, helped Nathan undress and dry off, then went to his room and found him a pair of sleep pants to slide into and shoved him into his bed.

Nathan was out cold two seconds later. Mick shook his head and turned off the light, then went in and cleaned up the mess in the bathroom.

By the time Tara came home around two thirty, Mick had warred with himself over telling her or not telling her. Turned out she wasn't in the door a second before she knew something had happened.

She frowned. "You have vomit on the side of your truck. Is Nathan sick?"

"Sort of."

She got a worried look on her face. "I should go check on him."

"He's passed out upstairs. Come sit down with me, and I'll tell you what happened."

"Passed out?"

She took a seat on the couch next to him.

"There were no adults at the party tonight, Tara. It was a free-for-all. And your son was shit-faced drunk."

Tara's eyes widened. "Oh." Then her eyes narrowed. "Oh. Son of a bitch."

"Yeah."

She leaned forward and clasped her hands together. "How bad?"

"Pretty bad. I tossed him in the shower and cleaned everything up. He should sleep it off now."

She laid her hand on his. "I had no idea this was going to happen. I'm so sorry you had to deal with it. And your truck. Good Lord."

"My truck is washable. And your kid is going to be sick as hell tomorrow."

She inhaled and sighed, then stood and ran her fingers through her hair. "I can't believe Tim would have a party like that without his parents being around. Where were they?"

"Cabo, according to reports."

She wrapped her arms around herself. "Jesus. Wait till Coach finds out. And I'm sure he'll find out. Were there girls there, too?"

"Quite a few. Underage. Hell, they were all underage."

"Oh, Jesus. Thank God you got him out of there before the cops showed up. He is in so much trouble. And I was nowhere in sight." She sat on a chair, looking lost and devastated.

"It's a rite of passage, Tara. You couldn't prevent this from happening."

She shot an angry glare at him. "Rite of passage, my ass. Lots of kids make it through their teen years without getting stinking drunk. I need to pay more attention to where I let my son hang out. If I wasn't—"

She stopped herself, but he knew what she'd been about to say. "You think if you weren't with me, you'd be able to keep your thumb on Nathan's every move? Come on, Tara."

She lifted her chin. "I don't know. Maybe. Between seeing you and the hours I work at my job and Nathan, it's getting to be too much. I knew this was going to be a problem. I have to put Nathan first."

She was angry and hurt and scared, and he had to give her time to think. The last thing he wanted was to come between her and her child or argue that it wasn't his fault that her son had made a stupid decision. "I'll get out of here so you can get some sleep."

"Okay."

She walked him to the door and held it open but caught his hand before he walked out. "Thank you for being there for him tonight."

"Anytime."

He walked to his car, feeling like somehow he'd been the one who'd done something wrong tonight.

But he hadn't. Had he?

TWELVE

TARA KNEW SHE WAS BEING UNREASONABLE. AND, quite possibly, a total bitch.

But what had happened with Nathan—who was now grounded—scared the hell out of her. Drinking and hanging out at an unsupervised party at fourteen could have ended badly in ways she didn't even want to begin to think about. Unfortunately, all she'd done for the past three days was think about all the possibilities. And she had heard from Nathan's coach, who'd been apprised of the party, though he hadn't said by whom. He intended to have a long talk with Tim about it, and there would be sanctions. She almost felt sorry for Tim because she was certain Tim's parents were going to be livid when they found out the entire football team—plus girls—had been over at their house drinking.

And none of what had happened had been Mick's fault. In fact, she was grateful he'd been the one to step in and pluck Nathan out of that situation. Had she been the one to walk into that house, she'd have likely flipped out and embarrassed her son. From what Nathan told her—as much as he could remember—Mick had been calm and had taken Nathan out of there without a scene. Tara would have most definitely caused a scene. She was certain shrieking would have been involved. And she'd have probably called the parents of every kid there, which would have mortified Nathan, who probably would have never spoken to her again. She was so glad Mick had been there and acted rationally on Nathan's behalf.

But had she thanked him profusely? No. She'd basically blamed him for it. Not directly, of course, but indirectly she'd pointed the finger at Mick for all her failings as a mother.

God. She let her head rest against her arms and just shut it all out for a few minutes.

"Thinking of ending it all?"

Her head shot up, and she gaped at Maggie, who leaned in the doorway to her office. "Pondering it, especially if you're bringing me some new catastrophe. I'm full up at the moment."

"No crisis to report, but Jenna called while you were on the phone earlier, and she has final RSVPs for the anniversary party so I have your head count, plus she wanted to go over place settings and something about the caterer."

Oh, hell. The anniversary party for Mick's parents was coming up this weekend. And Nathan's birthday was this weekend, too. She laid her head in her hands and closed her eyes, wishing she could be anywhere but here.

Maggie shut the door. "Want to tell me what's wrong?"

"Everything."

"I've got time. Shoot."

Tara laid it all out for Maggie, skipping nothing. She told her about Nathan getting drunk and Mick picking him up, and Tara not being there because Tara was off counseling Maggie, even though

Maggie would probably feel guilty about that. But she and Maggie were best friends, and Maggie would understand it had nothing to do with her.

"So this is all Mick's fault."

Tara leaned forward and folded her hands together. "Of course it isn't his fault."

"Seems to me you're blaming him for everything from Nathan getting drunk to you feeling like you're not quite perfect at the job of superwoman."

That one hurt. "Screw you, Maggie."

"No, thanks. I like men. Look, Tara, wasn't it you who just a few short days ago told me I can't save my brother? That I need to let him fall on his face and I'm only enabling him by bailing his ass out every time he fucks up?"

"Yes. I did tell you that, because it's the truth."

"Well, it hurt me when you told me that. But you were right. And now I'm going to hurt you by telling you that you're trying to be everything to everybody, and in the end you have to realize you can't. It's okay to have an awesome career you love and be a mom at the same time. It's okay to try to date at the same time you're juggling said career and said kid, and it's okay to not do any of it perfectly. You're going to screw it all up now and then. You have to give yourself a break."

"Easier said than done. What happened with Nathan scared me."

"Because he got drunk? Please. Kids do that. They screw up. So did I at that age. So did you."

"I know. God, don't I know. I don't want him to make the same mistakes I did."

"But you can't follow behind him every step he takes to try to prevent it from happening, either. You'll smother him if you try. Let him fall a few times and see what happens."

She inhaled and let it out on a shaky sigh. "I'll try. No guarantees."

"And in the meantime, go apologize to your hunky boyfriend for blaming him because your idiot son got drunk."

She laughed. "Yeah, I think you're right about that one. I hurt him."

Maggie nodded. "Okay, so kiss the boo-boo and make it better."

TARA ALMOST DIDN'T MAKE THE TRIP TO SAINT LOUIS for the party. She could have handled it all long distance, but this was business and her reputation was at stake, and besides, she'd promised Nathan a baseball game for his birthday. Despite him being punished for being drunk the weekend before, it was still his birthday, and she wouldn't take this away from him.

So she'd made the trip with Mick, who was surprisingly still speaking to her, though things between them were strained and she hadn't had a moment alone with him to talk to him about it. She'd had to work nonstop before they left Friday, and then of course Nathan was with them. And even Nathan was having a hard time making conversation with Mick, no doubt because he was highly embarrassed about the prior weekend, which he rightly should be. He'd apologized to Mick for the drunken episode, and thankfully Mick hadn't brushed it aside or said it was no big deal. He'd accepted Nathan's apology but said nothing further.

So they'd sat on the airplane together and talked about . . . nothing. Fortunately, Mick had picked up the slack and talked to Nathan about his practice with the team the past couple days, working out with his trainer, meeting with his nutritionist, and the two of them had talked about a couple other guys on the team. He'd kept the conversation flowing, and Tara had opened her laptop and worked so she wouldn't have to say much other than interject a few "Oh, that's interestings" and "Reallys" and "That's greats." It had been uncomfortable, and she'd actually been glad when they arrived at Mick's parents' house.

"Tara, I'm so happy to see you again." Kathleen had folded her into a hug.

"I'm happy to be here." That much was true. She liked Mick's mother, and wished she could talk to her about the tension between her and Mick, but that would be kind of difficult.

Kathleen had hugged Nathan, too, who didn't seem to mind it at all. He'd even managed a huge smile when Jimmy rounded the corner from the other room and enveloped Nathan in a bear hug.

"Missed you, kid. No one to shoot hoops with."

"No one to kick your butt, you mean?"

"Nathan," Tara admonished.

"Hey, he just thinks he's that good," Jimmy said, slinging his arm around Nathan's shoulders. "But, like Mick and Gavin and Jenna, they soon learn they're outmatched by the master."

"In your dreams, old man," Mick said, hugging his father.

"Well, we'll see about that, won't we?"

The luggage soon forgotten in the entry, Jimmy, Nathan, and Mick had taken off for the back, where the bouncing of a basketball and shouts and insults could be heard.

"It's always like this, I'm afraid," Kathleen said from the kitchen as she fixed Tara a glass of iced tea. "Jimmy eggs them on, and none of the kids could ever resist the challenge."

Tara laughed. "I'm sure it's how your children became so good at competitive sports."

Kathleen nodded. "The Rileys do have that competitive spirit, for sure. But Jimmy uses it to keep himself fit. Most nights he drags me out there for a game or two."

Tara laid her hand over Kathleen's. "That's how you stay so fit."

She laughed. "We don't sit on our butts around here, that's for sure. And neither do you, by the looks of you, girl."

"I stay busy."

"And speaking of staying busy, thank you for planning this party. Jimmy and I are so honored."

"I'm the one who's honored to be a part of it."

"Nonsense. You're practically family."

Tara laughed and cupped her hands around the cool glass. "Hardly."

Kathleen studied her. "So you're saying you have no feelings for Mick?"

Oh, crap. How was she going to get around this one? "I have a lot of feelings for Mick. I just don't exactly know what we have together yet."

"Well, I can tell you he has never brought a woman home to meet the family, so whatever it is he feels for you, it's pretty special."

"Thank you. But I don't think it's anything permanent or long-lasting, Kathleen. I mean, we lead two very different lives."

"And what does that have to do with how you feel about each other?"

"It can make it difficult to make a relationship work."

"Why? Because he's a football player and is on the road during the season? Do you think you'd be any different than any of the other players who have relationships with their girlfriends or wives?"

"No. That's not what I meant." She was handling this badly. "But I have Nathan, and he needs some stability in his life. I've worked very hard to create that for him."

"So you're saying Mick couldn't give that to him?"

Oh, God. Where had this gone all wrong? "I don't know what I'm saying. There's nothing wrong with Mick. Nothing at all. He's wonderful, Kathleen. Any woman would be lucky to have him."

Kathleen leaned back in her chair. "But not you."

"I didn't say that."

Kathleen breathed out a sigh. "And I'm being defensive about Mick, which made you defensive. I'm sorry."

"I am, too."

"We're both mothers, so you understand what it's like to protect your children."

Tara nodded. "I do."

"I don't want anyone to hurt him. And I know you care about him."

"I do care about him, Kathleen. But give us time to figure out what we are to each other. This is still new."

Kathleen laughed. "I push, I know. I want him to be happy. I want him to have what Jimmy and I have together. And I like you. I like you and Nathan. I like the two of you with Mick, so I can't help but want to push for a family." She stood and put her glass in the sink. "It's time for me to butt out and let you and Mick figure things out for yourselves."

Tara lifted her gaze to Kathleen. "Thank you."

Kathleen came around behind her and hugged her. "But you know, I'm ready for a daughter-in-law. And I can't think of anyone I'd rather have in my son's life than you."

She straightened and headed for the back door. "Now I think I'll see if those boys have killed each other yet."

After Kathleen left, Tara had to blink away the sting of tears. How long had she craved a mother in her life? God knows her own mother had never been the kind of parent Tara had needed. She'd longed for someone whose counsel she could seek, and she'd never had that, not even when she was a child. She'd learned to rely on her own instincts, and often she'd made the wrong choices.

Kathleen was warm and kindhearted but also a straight shooter who told it like it was. She was exactly the type of woman Tara wanted and needed in her life. She'd love to be her daughter-in-law. Or her daughter. Or her friend.

But not at the sacrifice of Nathan's well-being. She wasn't about to rush headlong into something that would endanger the family she had now, which was her and Nathan. She'd sacrificed so much for him. If she had to give up more, she'd do it. If she and Mick were meant to be together, it would happen.

As she saw it right now, though, there were a lot of insurmountable obstacles to that happening. Like the fact that they hadn't even talked about how they felt about each other.

It was still too soon. She and Mick were walking on eggshells around each other right now, mostly due to her own idiocy and blindness.

So yeah, Tara could love Kathleen all she wanted, but that's not who her primary relationship was with. Maybe it was time to figure out if there was any substance to her relationship with Mick beyond just the sex. She was beginning to wonder if that's all they had. And if it was—yeah, it was pretty damn great sex, but it wasn't enough for her. There was way too much at stake to invest her heart, and Nathan's, in something that would end up burning itself out in the end.

TARA STOOD BACK AND ADMIRED HER WORK. ADMIT-tedly, she'd done a killer job. The venue was perfect and decorated in all white with summer greenery interspersed on and around the tables. Fresh flowers in crystal vases graced each table, and live trees and bushes had been brought in to give the illusion of an outside setting, so even though the anniversary party was indoors, Tara had replicated the meadow where Jimmy and Kathleen had said their vows forty years ago.

"Hey, Mom."

She wrapped her arm around her son. "Hey, yourself, birthday boy. How does it feel to be fifteen?"

He grinned. "Pretty good."

She still felt a little guilty that she was working on his birthday. "I'm sorry I didn't have the chance to give you a party or anything. And you didn't get to be with your friends on your birthday."

"Are you kidding? I got to go to the game today, and Gavin got me a ball signed by every member of the team, plus Mick took me down right after the game to hang out with the guys in the locker room. And they won. Best birthday present ever."

She leaned against him. "I'm glad. I was worried."

He shoved into her. "You worry too much."

"Probably."

"I'm going to find my friends. See you later?"

She nodded, realizing how easy he was to please, and how lucky she was to have a son like him. "Later."

She watched him walk away, realizing how fast he was growing up. Time was so fleeting. Nathan sat at a table with Mick's cousins, his laughter ringing out and so easily discernible even over this noisy crowd. God, she loved her son so much.

"It's beautiful, Tara. Breathtaking. Thank you." Kathleen came up to her and hugged her, her eyes filled with tears.

"You did good, girlie," Jimmy said, grabbing her into a bear hug. "You made Kathleen cry happy tears."

Tara laughed. "Jenna helped me out with photos of your wedding. You were such a beautiful bride, Kathleen. And you look just as lovely today."

Kathleen's cheeks turned pink. "Now don't be silly. I'm a little older."

"But still as sexy as the day I married you," Jimmy said, sweeping Kathleen up in his arms and planting one hot kiss on his wife.

Tara made a discreet exit as Jimmy took his wife out onto the dance floor. The band struck up and started playing some rocking seventies music, which got most of the crowd boogying their way onto the dance floor.

Tara made her way over to the bar where she naturally found Jenna, who seemed out of sorts standing on the other side of it. But Kathleen had insisted her daughter not work tonight and instead enjoy the festivities.

"Don't know what to do with yourself?"

"No. And she made me wear a damn dress."

"You look incredible. The dress is beautiful on you." A summery silk dress that fit Jenna's slender body so well, it was a multiple print halter that showed off some of Jenna's tattoos. She'd even worn heels.

Jenna wrinkled her nose. "I suppose it's okay to dress like a girl now and then. Hard to fend off my idiot brothers if they want to play tackle football though."

"I doubt they'll do that tonight. I think you're safe."

She laughed. "You're probably right."

"And you might want to dance."

Jenna shrugged. "Doubtful. I'd rather be flipping the tops off beers."

"So no guy has caught your eye?"

"I get my fill of these moronic, beer-swilling jocks at the bar. Don't need to dance with any of the brainless twits."

Tara could tell Jenna had no love for any of Mick's or Gavin's friends.

"Anyway," Jenna said, lifting her glass of wine to Tara. "Success. You did it."

Tara nodded. "It looks that way. And you did a lot of the work, too."

Jenna waved her hand in a dismissive gesture. "I did nothing but toss you the guest list, some pictures, and suggest a few spots that could hold this crazy crowd." Jenna turned to her. "You're really good at this."

Tara laughed. "Thanks, Jenna. I do love my job."

"Maybe there's hope for my brother yet. I was beginning to wonder, since all he ever dates are bimbos."

"I think those were mostly public relations setups."

Jenna took a sip of her wine. "Uh-huh. That what he told you?"

Tara turned to her. "Yes."

"Well," Jenna said with a wry grin. "Okay then."

Tara pondered Jenna's comments after Jenna had slipped away to talk to her mother, wondering what she'd meant by them. Had Mick's relationships with some of the women he'd been photographed with been more than just photo ops and public relations stunts?

She knew he had a reputation as a bad boy lady-killer, but assumed that was all PR, too.

Maybe not.

"Nice party. You do good work."

Elizabeth Darnell. The perfect person to ask that question of, since she was Mick's agent, but no way could she, or would she, ask.

"Thank you. You look beautiful. Not working tonight?"

Elizabeth arched a perfect brow. "Now why would you ask that?"

"You're in a dress, not a suit."

Elizabeth laughed. "I'm always working, honey, no matter what I wear. I just have to dress to suit the occasion."

And Elizabeth was dressed impeccably in a tightly fitting black strapless cocktail dress that wrapped around her incredible body, and designer shoes with shiny crystals across the straps that called attention to Elizabeth's perfectly manicured toes and exceptional legs. "So you're meeting clients, then?"

"Mick and Gavin are my clients, as well as a couple other men in attendance here."

"Gavin isn't really just a client for you, though, is he?"

Tara read the shock in Elizabeth's eyes, but she masked it right away. "I don't know what you're implying."

"Oh, I saw the way you looked at him at his birthday party. You have a thing for him."

"Gavin is my client. I treat all my clients like they're special."

"I'm sure you do. But the way you look at Gavin is different."

"I don't look at him any special way. What are you talking about?"

Her normally cool demeanor was ruffled, Tara could tell. She was wondering what it would take to knock some of the ice chips from Liz's heart. Maybe she wasn't as cold as Tara thought.

Tara shrugged. "I'm a woman. I see things."

Elizabeth crossed her arms. "What things?"

"The warmth in your eyes when you look at him. A certain yearning. It's not there when you look at other men."

Now there was fear in her eyes. If Tara didn't think Elizabeth was a giant pain in the ass, she'd almost feel sorry for her.

Almost.

"You're imagining things, Tara. Gavin is a great client who makes me a ton of money. You know what you see in my eyes when I look at him? Dollar signs. I do whatever it takes to make my players happy."

"I see. So really, nothing is ever downtime for you, is it?"

"There's always work to be done." Elizabeth slipped her arm in Tara's and led her toward the back of the ballroom. "And speaking of work, let's talk about Mick."

This should be interesting.

Elizabeth led her out the door and into the garden. The night was warm, but fortunately not hellishly so. Elizabeth walked over toward the fountain where a string of lights highlighted her red hair, which was expertly pulled up in what Tara decided had to be her trademark French twist. Pieces had been pulled down to frame her face. Elizabeth turned to Tara and smiled, but it was a calculating smile.

"Okay, Elizabeth, you got me out here. What about Mick?"

"I like Mick's off time to be put to good use."

"Which means what, exactly?"

"Charitable foundations, public events, premieres, galleries, anything where he can be seen and photographed. It's good for his image and for the team."

"And you think his relationship with me is getting in the way of that."

"I'm glad you see things my way."

"I'm not saying I agree with you, Elizabeth. I'm just saying I understand your meaning. I'm certain Mick can choose to do whatever he wants."

Elizabeth didn't frown, but Tara saw the flash of anger in her eyes. "Look, Tara. I'm sure he's having a wonderful time with you and your son, but the appeal is going to wear off eventually, and he'll move on. He'll miss the glamour, the parties, the fun and excitement that he's used to."

Tara shrugged, refusing to let Elizabeth get to her. "And if he does, then I guess he will move on. That's his choice to make when and if that happens. Or rather, it's our choice to make as far as our relationship. Or do you expect me to kick him to the curb now in order to spare myself the heartbreak later?"

"He'll leave you eventually."

Tara refused to rub the ache in her stomach where Elizabeth's words had created a hole. "So you say. And maybe he won't. Maybe I can offer him something he can't get anywhere else."

Elizabeth laughed. "Tara, you don't have enough to hold him, and he's way too much of a playboy to settle down. You carry too much baggage and he can't handle it. It's only a matter of time. You should get out now before he hurts you. You have your son to think about, after all."

What a bitch. No wonder she was so good at her job. She knew right where to stick the knife. "I think my relationship with Mick is none of your business."

Now her eyes narrowed. "You don't want me to make it my business."

"You already have. Butt out."

Elizabeth opened her mouth to speak, then shut it, the anger leaving her expression and a bright smile replacing it. Tara could guess why.

"Hey, there you are. I've been hunting you down and couldn't figure out where the hell you'd disappeared to."

Tara turned, already figuring out Mick had showed up. "Hi, there."

He cast a worried gaze between her and Elizabeth. "What are you and Liz doing out here?"

Elizabeth strolled past, a plastic smile on her face. She patted Mick's arm. "Girl talk, sweetie. I was complimenting Tara on what a wonderful job she did on your parents' anniversary party."

Mick relaxed his shoulders and cast a warm gaze at Tara. "She's wonderful, isn't she?"

Elizabeth kissed Mick on the cheek. "A peach." She winked at Tara as she walked through he door. "We'll talk again later, Tara."

Mick's gaze followed Liz, then he turned back to Tara. "What was that all about?"

Tara didn't need Mick to intervene on her behalf, and the last thing she wanted was to cause friction between him and his agent. Elizabeth didn't like her. So what? Tara could handle it. And if Elizabeth was right about Mick, then there was nothing she could do about it, was there? "Just chatting about the party and football. And you, of course."

"Was she giving you a hard time?"

"Nothing I can't handle. So, are you having fun?"

"No."

Tara frowned. "Why not?"

"Because I couldn't find you. Where've you been?"

"I'm the event planner, remember? Trying to make sure every-thing's in place, and seeing that everyone is having a good time."

His lips lifted. "My parents are having a good time, which is all that matters. Thank you."

"You're welcome."

Silence stretched between them, and she hated it. "Mick . . ."

He took her hands in his. "Let's sit down."

"Okay."

He led her to the stone bench near the fountain, then sat next to her. She half turned to face him.

"Tell me what's bothering you, Tara."

"Nothing's bothering me, other than me needing to apologize to you."

He cocked his head to the side. "For what?"

"For blaming my failures—and Nathan's—on you. I was a mess the other day when Nathan got drunk. I wasn't there when it hap-pened, and for some reason I felt I should have been."

He rubbed her hand with the pad of his thumb. "So now you're supposed to be psychic?"

She sighed. "I don't know. This parenting thing is hard. And doing it by myself all these years has been even harder. Sometimes I fail. A lot of times I fail."

"Guess what? Even two-parent families fail. No one's perfect at raising kids."

She took a glance through the doors at Mick's parents, gazing lovingly into each other's eyes as they slow danced. "Some manage to get it right without screwing up."

"You think my parents raised perfect kids?" He tilted his head back and laughed, then got serious again. "I think there are a few things you need to know about me, Tara. I'm not perfect. Never have been and never will be. I made mistakes when I was young. I messed up. Bad."

She crossed her arms. "I find that hard to believe. Look where you are now."

"Right. But you only see the finished product. You don't see what it took to get me here." He looked around. "There's something I need to talk to you about, but not here. Later, when we get back to the house. It's important, and it has to do with your idea of perfection. And Nathan, too."

She cast him a questioning look. "I don't understand."

"I know you don't, but I don't want to talk about it here where there are so many people. Can we table this conversation for later?"

"Sure."

He lifted her hand and pressed a kiss to her knuckles. "Let's go inside and dance. Show me your disco moves."

She let out a soft laugh. "Oh, Lord. I might need some dance lessons from your mother before I attempt the hustle."

He slid her hand in the crook of his arm. "Don't worry, baby. I'll teach you everything you need to know."

THIRTEEN

IT TOOK A LONG TIME FOR THE PARTY TO WIND DOWN. Mick's family and friends could party all night long, but this time the venue hadn't been booked for the duration of the evening, so they'd moved everybody out of the ballroom by midnight. As a gift to Mick's parents, the kids had gotten them a suite at a very posh resort, so they'd already packed up and headed over there for a night in the honeymoon suite. Nathan was spending the night with Mick's cousins again, which meant Tara and Mick had his parents' house to themselves for the night.

Tara ran upstairs and changed, grateful to get out of her sole-killing high heels and the tight dress. She slid into a pair of shorts and a tank top, then came back downstairs to find Mick had done the same thing. He'd shucked the suit and put on a pair of to-the-knee cotton gym shorts and a sleeveless tank.

"Better?" he asked.

She sighed in relief. "My feet were killing me, so yes, definitely better." She sank onto the sofa next to him.

"Want something to drink?" he asked.

"No, I'm good. How about you? Want a beer or something?"

There was something odd about the way he looked at her. "Have a bottled water here, so I'm fine."

"Okay."

She propped her elbow up on the back of the sofa and leaned her head in her hand.

"Tired?"

"I'm okay. How about you? You're the one who ran ragged all day taking Nathan to the ball game and keeping him entertained so I could get everything set up. And then you helped with the party."

"I didn't organize the party. You did. And Nathan is never a problem, so stop apologizing for your son."

"I wasn't—"

"You do. A lot."

She sat up. "Do I?"

"Yes. You make Nathan sound like an inconvenience to me, and he isn't. If he was, I wouldn't be with you. I knew almost from the beginning that he was a part of your life, Tara. I get that he's part of the package, so stop apologizing for his existence."

Tears sprang to her eyes. That's what she'd been doing? Oh, God, it was. She'd been apologizing for Nathan, for having him, for him being in her life. "You're right. I have been. I'm sorry."

Mick swiped at a tear that had escaped down her cheek. "You don't have to apologize to any man that you have a son. He's a great kid. You owe no one explanations or apologies for your life."

She shuddered out a sigh. "I guess you're right. I keep holding up other people's childhoods and lives as examples of the perfection that I always found lacking in my own."

"No one's life is perfect, Tara. Not yours, not mine, no one's."

"So you say. Hard to see the imperfections through all the happiness sometimes."

"You see what people want you to see, not what's necessarily there."

"You're telling me your life wasn't perfect. I find that hard to believe."

He leaned back against the sofa and shoved his fingers through his hair. "There's something I want to ask you. It has to do with Nathan."

"Okay."

"I'd like your permission to take him to a meeting with me when we get back home. I think it would be beneficial for him."

"A meeting? What kind of meeting?"

"An AA meeting."

Tara's eyes widened. "Alcoholics Anonymous? Are you serious?"

"Yes."

"Why would you want him to go to an AA meeting? Nathan's not an alcoholic. As far as I know, that was his first foray into drinking."

"Did you talk to him about that night?"

"Yes. Of course I did. He understands what he did was wrong. And he felt terrible."

Mick's lips lifted. "Of course he felt terrible. He had a hangover. But that's how it starts, Tara. One party, a lot of drinks. It's social. It's how they get accepted. Often it doesn't stop there. I'd like him to see some cold reality."

"I think that's a little harsh, Mick."

"Yeah, it is harsh. But it's real. It's not glossed over, and it's not a sit-down lecture from his mother that he probably only half paid attention to. It's never too early for them to hear what it's really like when drinking gets out of control."

"What do you know about AA?"

"Plenty."

She cocked her head to the side and frowned. The way he looked at her, cold and straightforward . . .

Then it hit her. "You don't drink alcohol."

His gaze never left her face. "No."

"It has nothing to do with training, does it?"

"No."

Her throat went dry as the realization of all these weeks together finally fell into focus. Her palms dampened, and she pulled her legs behind her, straightened herself up, and prepared herself for the truth. But she waited, not asking, knowing it had to come from Mick.

"I'm an alcoholic, Tara."

The gut punch hurt. She palmed her stomach, was glad she was sitting, because the room spun. "How long?"

"Since I was a teenager. Still think I lived a perfect life?"

She didn't know if she was angry or hurt, at him or for him. She forced back the anger because she needed to know, and because he had the guts to sit here and face her with the truth. She reached out to grasp his hand. "Tell me."

"Just like Nathan, it started at football parties." He looked up at the ceiling for a few seconds, seemingly lost in thought. "God, seeing him drunk at that party the other night—"

He dragged his gaze back to hers. "It was like seeing myself. I went back in time sixteen years, and there I was, shit-faced drunk and having the time of my life. I was invincible, cock of the block, popular as hell at fourteen. All the seniors invited me to their inner circle, and all I had to do to stay there was drink. Easy, right? Drink with the guys and you stay in the circle.

"I was desperate to stay on top, so I did whatever it took. I kept drinking. At first I hated it. It made me sick and it wore my body down. When you're in football, staying in prime physical shape is everything to a guy. The last thing you want or need is a bunch of chemicals polluting your system. I was at war between what I knew was best for my body and what I wanted most of all—acceptance from those above me on the team."

"You chose the team."

He nodded. "Yeah. I'd never had big brothers. I'm the oldest in my family. The responsible one, ya know? So when faced with someone older than me telling me what to do, I crumbled. I did what they said. I drank. And I taught my body to manage it all the way through high school and college. Because by then my body had learned to depend on it. So I gave it just enough to where I could still function at peak performance, but I could party, too. By the time I was a senior in high school I was rocking hard on the weekends, but I was the leader of the team. So I could tone it down somewhat and let the others pick up the slack, which meant I coasted by okay my senior year, enough to pick up that scholarship.

"But then college came around, and I was low man on the totem pole and it started all over again. I had to drink hard and party hard to fit in. By then I was already accustomed to doing whatever it took, so the daily drinking began. And the grades were easy to come by, so I spent a lot of time in college drunk."

Mick paused, unscrewed the top of his water, and took a long drink. Tara released the breath she'd been holding, not wanting to say a word, hurting inside for what he'd endured.

"Anyway," he said, replacing the top on his bottle of water. "By junior year of college the alcohol was starting to take its toll on my grades and my football performance. Coach started to notice it, and so did my parents. Once they started looking closer, it didn't take them long to figure out I had an alcohol problem."

"What did they do?" she asked.

He shrugged. "They told me to get help. But the thing is with an alcoholic, we're big into denial. I was certain I didn't have a drinking problem. I knew how to handle it. I could stop whenever I wanted to."

"So did you?"

"I tried because they told me I couldn't. Coach even benched me for a game, and in college that's some serious shit. I had to prove to them I could stop. The problem was, I couldn't. I went home for a weekend and tried not to drink for two days, and it damn near killed me."

Tara squeezed his hand, aching inside for him, wanting to fold him in her arms and hold him, wanting him not to have to relive this, but knowing it was important to him to tell her his story.

"I'd never been so sick. I was shaking, sweating. I couldn't sleep, I couldn't eat, couldn't think straight. I started hallucinating. God, the things I saw that weren't real. They scared the shit out of me. But the thing that scared me most was that I craved a drink more than anything. I was such a bastard to anyone around me. I screamed at them that they were killing me. And I wanted to kill anyone who got in the way of me getting a goddamn drink."

"Oh, Mick, I'm so sorry."

He shot her a straight look. "Don't be sorry for me, Tara. I did it to myself. I had no one to blame but myself for how I felt."

She nodded. She knew what it was like to be a drunk, had faced it every day she'd lived with her parents.

"I came at my dad and I hit him because he wouldn't give me the keys to my car so I could go to the liquor store. I hit my father."

Tears filled Mick's eyes, and Tara couldn't stand it. She felt the sting of her own tears but knew she had to allow him to finish.

"My dad refused, wouldn't punch me back, just let me continue to fight him. Fortunately I was too weak by that point to do much damage, and I finally gave up. I don't even remember the crying and the begging, thank God. I just remember waking up the next morning, mortified that I'd hit my father. After that I knew they were right. I was an alcoholic. I admitted it and asked for help."

"Thank God you were smart enough to realize that."

His eyes were narrow slits of anger. "I wasn't smart. If I'd been smart, I wouldn't have become an alcoholic in the first place. I was lucky people loved me enough to want to help me and push me into realizing how bad I fucked up. I went to a treatment center, dried out, and got counseling. I haven't had a drink since. It scared the hell out of me. I could have lost everything, all because I wanted to fit in and be popular. All because of one night all those years ago when I was fourteen. That started it all. So I'm sorry if you think what happened to Nathan is no big deal. To me it's a big fucking deal."

"But you don't talk about it. Nobody knows you're an alcoholic, right?"

"No. No one knows, and that was my choice. I chose not to make it public. I go to meetings and it's done quietly. But I'm willing to take Nathan to a meeting with me if you think it might prevent him from making the same mistakes I did."

"Mick, I can't ask you to do that. Not for my son."

"Isn't he worth it?"

"Dammit, that's not what I meant. Of course he's worth it. Nathan is everything to me. I'd put myself in front of a bullet for that kid." She drew her knees up to her chest and wrapped her arms around them. "But don't put me in this position. Don't ask me to risk you over my son."

"Why not?"

"You know why not. What if someone sees you going to a meeting?"

He laughed. "I've been going to meetings for ten years now, Tara. That's why they call it anonymous."

"You'd do this—for Nathan."

"And for you. Because I don't want you to ever have to go through what I put my mother through."

She laid her head on his chest.

It took him a minute, but he finally put his arms around her. She felt his tension, so she climbed onto his lap and raised her head, saw the anguish in his eyes.

"You've never told a woman about this, have you?"

"It's not easy for me to trust people with the story. In the wrong hands it could go worldwide in an instant."

She laid the palm of her hand on his face. "You can trust me."

"I worried that telling you this might end things between us."

Her eyes widened. "Why?"

"After you told me about your parents . . . I wanted to tell you that night, but I kind of chickened out. Your parents were alcoholics. I'm an alcoholic."

She palmed his jaw. "Oh, Mick. I would never judge you based on who and what they were. Look at how you changed your life for the better. They never did. Look how good you are with my son. I don't want to scare you or want you to think I'm asking anything of you for the future, because I'm not. But you've done better parenting of my son in the short time we've known each other than my parents ever did of me in all the years they had me. So no, I would never judge you or compare you to them."

He closed his eyes and breathed heavily. When he opened them, it was as if a giant weight had been lifted. And yet there was still a glimmer of uncertainty and pain there. Tara was surprised she hadn't seen it before. Maybe it would always be there.

It was so quiet in the room—in the entire house—she only heard the two of them breathing. It was a surreal moment. What he'd shared with her was so raw and painful it made her heart hurt for him, for what he'd gone through and survived. Mick was nothing like the magazines portrayed him, nothing like the PR Elizabeth laid out. She knew him now as she never thought she would know another person, and she'd never wanted to be closer to him than she did right now. She wanted him to forget the pain and the sorrow and know only pleasure.

She leaned forward and brushed her lips against his, tunneling her fingers in his hair.

He wrapped his arms around her and pulled her against him, deepening the kiss, his tongue sliding inside and taking possession of hers.

Tara sensed a need in him, and she fed on that need, wanted to give him everything tonight. And when he picked her up and laid her on the floor, coming down on top of her, she wrapped her legs and arms around him, needing the feel of his body. The hard ridge of his cock rode between her legs, and he surged against her, ratcheting up her arousal to a fevered state as he continued to plunder her mouth with deep, soul-penetrating kisses.

He pulled her arms out to her sides and locked his hands down on top of hers while he spread her legs with his knees and drove against her pussy with his cock. Even though they were still clothed, it made her whimper, made her wet, made her crave the feel of him inside her. He loomed over her, his face above her etched with need and hunger, and she arched up against him.

"Fuck me," she said in a harsh whisper. She'd planned to take things slow and easy tonight, to make it sweet and romantic, but that's not how it was coming down. There was a desperate passion between them, an intense, frantic pull toward each other that they had to fulfill. The air was fraught with tension, and if she didn't get Mick inside her soon, if he continued to rub his cock against the outside of her clothes, she was going to come—just like that.

"I like touching you this way—thinking about how good your pussy feels, knowing how desperate you are to have me fuck you, but . . . waiting."

Tara panted, licked her lips, and lifted against him again. "You're going to make me come, rubbing me with your hard cock against my clit. Keep doing that, and I'm going to come."

He smiled down at her, a wicked smile that made her belly tingle. "Yeah? Show me."

He ground against her, hard and . . . oh, God, yes, right there. She lifted her hips and he hit that spot and she cried out, climaxing, shuddering as he continued to roll his hips against her sweet spot until she fell to the floor and he went with her, taking her mouth in a kiss that stole her breath.

Then it was a frenzy of removing clothes, and there was no finesse in it. Tara was elated that Mick was in a hurry to get his shorts off, and she shimmied out of her shorts and panties, spread her legs, and waited for him to grab a condom and slide it on. He came back to her, slid his hand under her butt, and entered her, hard. She bit down on her lip as he pumped into her with several hard, exquisite thrusts that made her arch into him.

"You're tight and so fucking wet. You make me want to come hard inside you."

She loved when he lost it like this, when all he could think about was fucking her, because it's all she wanted right now—this meeting of bodies and animal passion and nothing else. Their need for each other was primal and wild. She wrapped her legs around him and pulled him into her, seeking depth and possession. Mick buried his face in her neck and licked the side of her throat, making her shudder with delight, making her rake her nails along his shoulders and down his arms. He growled against her and dug his fingers into her butt cheeks. He rolled his hips, and the action rocked his pelvis against her clit, taking her right to the edge again.

"I feel your pussy squeezing me. You gonna come for me again?"

"Yes." She groaned, so close she had to grit her teeth. "Come inside me, Mick."

"I'm going to come hard, Tara. Now."

He kissed her, letting out a groan as he thrust several times in succession while he came. That set her off, and she whimpered against his lips as the dam burst inside her and she climaxed in torrential waves of the hottest, wildest pleasure she could ever imagine. She held on while he continued to pump inside her with furious thrusts until he finally settled, until the pulses inside her stilled.

"I might have rug burn," she whispered in his ear.

He kissed her neck. "I might have a groin pull."

She laughed. "Oops."

He rolled them onto their sides, and Mick swept her hair out of her eyes. "I can't get enough of you, Tara. You bring out a side of me I've never given to another woman."

Her heart filled with emotions, things she didn't dare say out loud.

Even if she was falling in love with him, she couldn't seem to find the courage to tell him.

Loving someone gave them power over you, and she wasn't ready to do that just yet.

FOURTEEN

TARA LET MICK HAVE NATHAN FOR THE ENTIRE DAY. He had a plan that he'd cleared with Tara. She was trusting him to show Nathan the light—or at least the what-ifs and what-could-bes. He hoped he wouldn't fuck this all up.

Mick started out the day by taking Nathan to the team practice facility, something that made Nathan's eyes bug out, especially since he was supposed to be grounded. But Mick had made a big deal out of telling Nathan that he'd talked his mom into it since it was a special event. It was media day at the facility, so there were going to be a lot of extra people at the training facility today anyway. He'd already cleared it with the team to have Nathan on board to watch from the field and meet all the guys.

Of course the workout wasn't as intense as it would be on a normal day, mainly because of the interruption of the press, but that was okay, because it gave Mick an opportunity to take Nathan around and introduce him to everyone, and he even put him behind center and let him throw a few passes, which made Nathan nervous as hell. He looked so small behind Mick's offensive line. But to Nathan's credit he did okay, didn't drop a pass, and even managed to hit a receiver or two. The kid had a pretty good arm and would probably get a decent scholarship provided he pulled his head out of his ass and concentrated more on football and less on socializing, which was Mick's intention for the day.

After Nathan took a seat, Mick concentrated on his own drills, working with some of the new receivers. A couple were decent, one had serious attitude and some work to do if he had any hopes of making the team. But that was the coaches' problem to deal with, and Mick didn't envy the coaches' job dealing with kids who came into the game with a sense of entitlement. But guys like that were also good for Nathan to see—the ones who played up the media like they owned them, fresh out of college with tons of attitude, thinking they could step into their first NFL game and be a star. Sure, there were some who could make it right out the gate, but they were rare. And Mick could already tell this kid wasn't as good as he thought he was. A good safety jumping in front of the passes with a few key interceptions and this kid would get a dose of humility quickly.

After giving some interviews about his fitness, his overall plan for the year, and what he thought the team's chances were—basically typical interview fodder—Mick showered up, and he and Nathan went to dinner.

"So, what did you think of it all?"

Nathan looked up from his plate where he'd been shoveling food in his mouth. "It was awesome. All the photographers and reporters there, working out with the team, plus the new guys from the college draft. It was so cool. I can't wait to tell all the guys on my team about it."

Mick had finished eating, so he pushed back his plate and picked up his glass of water, took a sip, then leaned back in his chair. "So, hanging with me has upped your cred with your teammates?"

Nathan grinned. "Definitely. As a freshman you're pretty much dirt under everyone's cleats, at least until you can prove yourself on the field. You dating my mom has gotten everyone's attention." Nathan cocked his head to the side, a worried look on his face. "You're not dumping her or anything, are you?"

Mick's lips lifted. "Uh, no. I'm not dumping your mom."

Nathan blew out a breath. "Thank God. That would really screw with my popularity."

Teenagers. Had Mick ever been so clueless? Obviously he had, or he wouldn't have fucked up his life so badly. "Yeah, I'd hate to mess with your popularity quotient."

Nathan ducked his head and at least had the decency to look sheepish. Maybe he wasn't as clueless after all.

After dessert they climbed into the SUV. Mick glanced at the clock in the car. Perfect timing.

"So where to now?" Nathan asked.

"We're going to a meeting."

Nathan half turned to face him. "No kidding? Like some team meeting or something?"

"No. This kind of meeting is personal to me, but I wanted you to come with me because I think you can get something out of it. I hope you don't mind."

"Hey, if it has something to do with you, I don't mind at all."

Mick pulled into the parking lot of the Presbyterian church, one of the places he'd found that was having an open meeting tonight where anyone could attend. He parked and got out. Nathan followed.

"Oh, man, are we going to church?"

"Not exactly."

"Then what are we doing?"

Mick stopped and turned to Nathan. "Nathan, I need you to keep your mouth shut and just listen when we get inside, okay?"

Nathan backed up, clearly not used to hearing Mick talk to him that way. "Okay. Sure."

They walked inside, and Mick found the meeting room downstairs. Mick signed in, shook a few hands, grabbed a cup of coffee and a soda for Nathan.

"Oh, man, this is an AA meeting, Mick."

"Yes, it is."

"Why did you bring me here?"

"What did I tell you outside?"

Nathan dropped his chin to his chest. "Yeah, okay."

It was pretty crowded in there, which was good. A guy got up and went over the administrative portion of the meeting, then they all said the Serenity Prayer, which Mick had recited so many times over the past years he probably said it in his sleep.

"God, grant me the serenity to accept the things I cannot change, courage to change the things I can, and wisdom to know the difference."

Saying the prayer always brought a wave of peace over Mick, gave him the strength to continue on with his fight against alcoholism, made him realize he could never go back and change the past, but he did have control over today, tomorrow, and every day after that. And he knew that so far today he hadn't had a drink. He'd made it through another day.

People got up and started sharing stories. There were longtime alcoholics there who'd been through rough times. Some had regressed and started drinking time and time again, only to start fighting their demons and give it another try. Some had never touched alcohol after they gave it up. Others got up and shared success stories and received coins for milestones, which always made Mick smile.

When there was a lull he got up, which made Nathan's eyes go wide. But this is what he'd brought Nathan here for. He wanted him to hear the story. So he got up in front of all these strangers— though he wasn't a stranger to many of them—and told the same story he'd told Tara the other night. And he kept his gaze trained on Nathan, making sure Nathan heard every detail. Mick didn't worry about spilling this information in front of all these people, because AA was anonymous and people didn't share what they heard outside of the meeting room. Your secrets at AA were always safe.

When he was finished, when he'd stood up there and introduced himself as Michael, when he'd told them all he was an alcoholic, he hoped his message had gotten through. And maybe it had, because Nathan's eyes had filled with tears. And he didn't say a word when the meeting was over, when Mick visited with people there. No one asked for his autograph or talked football, because there Mick was just another struggling alcoholic trying day by day to fight his ad- diction. It's why he liked coming to meetings, because he could be just another person there who was fighting his demons.

They climbed into the car, and Nathan didn't buckle up, just sat there with his chin pressed to his chest.

"Nathan?"

Nathan shuddered as he inhaled, then turned his tear-filled gaze to Mick. "You think I could turn out like you. Because of what I did the other night."

"I didn't say that. I never said that. But yeah, I worry it could happen to you. Or any one of your friends who doesn't think about the consequences of drinking and partying. Think about that prac- tice you saw today, how hard those players work in the NFL. Then think about how hard they had to bust it in college making grades and getting through classes while also playing football."

"But I thought—"

"You thought what? That someone else does their classwork for them? That they can float through and professors will cut them some slack? College isn't like high school, Nathan. Colleges don't care if you're playing football or not. They still expect you to pass. And try doing that while downing a bottle of vodka a day, or a case of beer, or whatever your poison is. Mine was whiskey and beer."

"Jesus. I didn't know. I just wanted to be cool like the other guys."

"I'm sure the other guys don't know either. They have no idea, because they think they can handle it. I thought I could handle it. And for a while I was doing fine. But then everything crumbled, and even then I wouldn't listen to the people who knew what was best for me. I wouldn't listen to my parents or my coaches or the team physicians. I almost lost out on my chance to play in the NFL. I could have lost everything. I could have died. All because I wanted to drink and party. Mainly because I wanted to drink. And it all started when I was your age, because I wanted to look cool and I was desperate to fit in."

The tears fell down Nathan's cheeks now. "So what am I supposed to do? They all drink. There are parties all the time. I'm accepted now."

"You can still be accepted. You can be cool without drinking. And if they don't like you because you aren't a drunk, then what kind of friends are they? You're a great football player with a lot of potential, Nathan. Let your skills and your academics do the talking for you. I'll wager not every member of the team is a hard partier. Find those guys and hang out with them."

He slouched in the seat. "I guess so."

"Look, I'm not going to make the choices for you. You're old enough now to make your own. I just wanted to show you what could happen. Your life is entirely different than mine. It's up to you to choose."

He took Nathan home. The kid went straight up to his room, hardly saying a word to Tara. She cast a worried look at Mick.

"Didn't go well?"

Mick shrugged. "I don't know. I think I got the message across. It scared the hell out of him."

She crossed her arms and nodded. "That's a good thing. He should be scared."

"I don't know. I don't know anything about teenagers, Tara. I tried."

She went to him, put her arms around him, and kissed him. "Thank you. You did more than most people would have. He knows you care. And I appreciate it."

He just hoped it would be enough.

FIFTEEN

TARA WAS THRILLED TO HAVE THE OPPORTUNITY TO DO the AIDS charity fund-raiser at the art museum, a very high-profile annual event in San Francisco. Black tie, very ritzy, and she and her staff had been planning it for months. It was going to be incredibly well attended, with local dignitaries like the mayor planning to come. Plus, the rumor was being tossed about that some Hollywood people were planning to be in attendance.

She hadn't been able to eat, sleep, or breathe for the past week, nor had she and Mick been able to see each other, which was probably a good thing, since Mick was doing preseason game prep, and he said Elizabeth had been running him ragged with PR appearances so he'd been unavailable, too. She missed him terribly, but during a quick phone call earlier in the week they'd made plans for tomorrow.

She was looking forward to seeing him. Nathan was spending the night at a friend's house now that he was through being grounded. He'd been on his best behavior lately and had actually been hanging out with a few new friends—nice kids, actually, so Tara had checked them out, made sure the parents of the kid he was staying with tonight were going to be home, and gave her okay for him to stay over.

That left her free and clear to dive into full-on panic mode for this event. She'd arrived at the gallery three hours before the doors opened, making sure the caterers were in place, the bar was set up, and there was a clear pathway to all the silent auction items.

With a few free minutes before the gallery opened, she ducked into the ladies' room to check her appearance. She wore a black cocktail dress with tiny spaghetti straps. The bodice was form-fitting and tight enough that she could barely breathe, which was perfect. She wore sinfully high shoes that she loved and adored and—as usual—killed her feet. Her hair was piled up high on her head with cascading curls. She applied a new layer of gloss to her lips and inspected herself in the mirror. Not too bad. Stress had added some color to her cheeks, so she actually looked okay. It was important she make a good impression on the foundation and any potential new clients she might meet tonight.

"You breathing?"

She turned around and grimaced as Maggie walked in. "Hyperventilating is more like it. You look lovely."

Maggie pushed her glasses up the bridge of her nose. She had on a blue dress and wore the top of her hair up, the bottom straight and teasing her cheeks.

"Well, thanks. I just want to get through tonight without passing out. I can't believe you made me come tonight. I'm office help, not front lines."

Tara slipped her lip gloss into her clutch and went to Maggie, patting her on the arm. "Nonsense. I need your help working the auction tonight."

Maggie inhaled and blew it out. "Whatever you say, boss."

"You're the most outgoing person I know, and we need all the new clients we can get. So let's plug in and get started."

Once the doors opened, there was no time to be nervous or worry about the small details. People streamed in, likely because they'd heard there was a chance a few movie stars were going to be in attendance tonight. Tara didn't care who was there as long as the event went over well. So when Olivia McCallum, Susan Winters, and Layla Taylor arrived—all hot and upcoming Hollywood starlets, she practically fainted because this was the draw she'd been hoping for. And when movie heartthrobs Derek Davis and Malcolm Brown came in, Tara knew the night was going to be perfect.

The gallery was packed to the gills with the cream of the crop of San Francisco elite, a few of the top Hollywood singles, and enough media to ensure success. The silent auction bids were filling up, thanks to Maggie's skills at dragging people over to the bid table. Plates were kept filled with the latest haute cuisine from one of the best chefs in San Francisco—and everyone raved about the food, much to Tara's delight. Drinks were plentiful, conversations were flowing, and she couldn't be more pleased.

"If this is how all the events turn out, I can see how much you love being in the trenches," Maggie whispered as they snuck a minute together to catch up.

"Trust me," Tara said to her. "They're not always this good."

Maggie visibly vibrated with excitement. "This is glorious. Did you see Derek Davis?"

"I did."

"And Malcom Brown? I had to keep myself from screaming like an idiot fan girl."

Tara's lips twitched. "Glad you managed to subdue yourself. Now how about you check in with the bar and make sure they're still well-stocked. These people drink like fish."

Maggie giggled. "Consider it done. I'll be sure to check the bar frequently just in case Derek Davis decides to belly up there for a drink."

The possibility of that happening was slim to none, but Tara didn't want to disillusion Maggie from her celebrity hunting quest. And as long as Maggie did her job, Tara didn't care how much she ogled the celebrities. She was just glad she had a second set of eyes monitoring all the corners of the gallery.

Tara made another pass through the tables where the silent auction was going on. Pens and pads still in place, long lists of bids on-going, which should make the curators ecstatic. People with money always made charitable foundations happy, which meant all the promotion for this event had paid off.

Flashbulbs popped all over the place, and Tara did her best to avert her eyes whenever she saw a flash. She kept herself busy and hovered in the background, making sure the limelight stayed on the people it was supposed to stay on. She brought those not too popular but eager to meet celebrities to the right people so introductions could be made, happy she had just the right contacts to make that happen.

Everything was going smoothly, and she was thrilled with her choice of caterers and waitstaff for tonight's event.

She finally had a chance to stop at the bar, grab a mineral water, and take a breath before doing her next circuit through the gallery. Since things seemed to be running smoothly, maybe this time she could stop and ogle all the art.

She was admiring a great piece of metal sculpture when she heard a round of applause and commotion the next room over. She wandered in that direction and stopped dead in her tracks when she saw Mick, dressed in a very fancy dark tux, smiling for the photographers who were taking his picture.

His back was to her, but she'd know him anywhere, from the slightly shaggy look to his dark hair to the way he stood, right hand in his pocket, the casual stance like he was comfortable in any situation. She caught his profile and was about to go over and say hello when he shifted, bringing the woman on his arm to the center of attention.

A beautiful woman with short raven hair, stunning chandelier earrings that dripped in diamonds, and a multilayered black dress that showed off a considerable amount of cleavage, and oh, God, did she have killer legs, too.

Tara recognized her instantly as the actress making all the buzz in that new television drama on Tuesday nights. She was young, single, and talented. And her incredible violet eyes seemed to be planted right on Mick. She had her body cemented against Mick's, her arm wrapped around his while he smiled down at her and gave her his full attention as if she were the only woman in the room. Then the two of them turned their heads toward the camera. They looked like the perfect couple.

Tara's stomach dropped, and she stepped back.

"Hey, Tara, isn't that Mick?"

She fought back tears as she nodded at Maggie. "Yes, it is."

"With Alicia Brave. Wow. What's he doing with her?"

Tara turned and walked out of the room, her heels clicking on the marble floor. "Posing for the cameras."

Maggie hurried after her. "Aren't you going to say something to him?"

She stopped, turned. "Maggie, this isn't the time. Go check on the canapés for the auction area. They looked a little thin and might need to be restocked."

Maggie gave her a worried look but nodded. "Okay."

Tara moved off, determined to tamp down the hurt and anger.

They were exclusive, dammit. At least she thought they were. She'd met his parents—she and Nathan both had. Didn't that mean something to him? In Tara's world, it did. Maybe to him it meant nothing, which just illustrated how their worlds differed.

She'd so wanted this to work, had started to think they could somehow bridge the gap between his lifestyle and hers, but if this was the way he intended to carry on, then something was going to have to give, and it wasn't going to be her.

Dammit, this hurt, and she had no time for her heart to hurt.

She was working, and that's what she needed to concentrate on. She went to the bar and checked on things. Maurice said they were well-stocked and not to worry, so she hid out in the kitchen for a while until Stefan gave her the evil eye one too many times. The last thing she wanted to do was piss off a high-strung chef, so she hightailed it out of there and once again checked the silent auction bids, but there were quite a few people milling about, and it was nearing time for the end of bids. She was in the way, and last-minute bidding could be crucial.

"Tara. Is something wrong?"

She lifted her chin and offered a comforting smile to Evan Jervis, the manager of the fund-raiser. "Of course not, Evan. Everything is perfect. Don't you think so?"

Evan visibly relaxed and grabbed her hands. "Yes, I do. You've done a remarkable job on tonight's event. I can't thank you enough."

His compliment helped her more than she could say. "I'm so glad you think so. And the bidders are going crazy at the moment, with only ten minutes left until the cutoff. I have a feeling the charity is going to make a lot of money tonight."

"From your lips to their checkbooks, honey," Evan said. "I guess I'll go monitor the bids for the last few minutes, then get ready for the announcements of the winners. Will you be in place to help me?"

"Of course."

Tara did her last walk-through of the gallery, then settled in at the front with Evan once he pulled the bids at the conclusion of the silent auction. Evan made his announcement on the loudspeaker that the silent auction had concluded, and everyone gathered to hear the winning bids.

"I want to thank you all for being here tonight. I hope you've had a good time."

He continued on, thanking the sponsors of the event and those who donated prizes. Everyone applauded since some of the prizes were pretty magnificent, from beautiful artwork to private, in-house chefs to trips and luggage to designer jewelry.

"I also want to thank our glorious event planner for putting tonight's party together—Miss Tara Lincoln of The Right Touch."

Tara hadn't expected Evan to acknowledge her, but she was thrilled. She stepped up and gave a gracious bow to the applause, and that's when she caught Mick's eye. He looked as surprised to see her as she had been to see him. In her flurry of last-minute activity before the end of the auction, she'd almost forgotten he was here. Almost. But as his gaze met hers and she caught the beautiful Alicia Brave clinging to his side, the pain inside renewed, and she looked away, smiled at the crowd, and stepped aside so Evan could continue on with his speech, finally getting to the winners of the auction items.

One by one the highest bidder was revealed, and they had to come up, claim their prize, and pay their money. Applause and squeals of delight could be heard when the auction items were awarded.

"And now for the romantic weekend getaway to a private Caribbean island, complete with your own butler and fully stocked food and bar service for the entire weekend. This is the ultimate in decadence for two. The highest bidder is—San Francisco's own Mick Riley!"

Tara swallowed and waited for Mick to come claim his prize. She held on to the envelope, waited for him to write his check to the charity's accountant, then handed him the envelope.

"Thank you," he said, smiling at her as she handed him the envelope.

"You're welcome. Congratulations and thank you for your donation. Enjoy your prize." It was her standard speech to all the recipients. She had a smile plastered on her face, and she refused to treat him any differently than any of the other auction winners, no matter how much it pained her.

Private island in the Caribbean, huh? She wondered which of the many actresses and models that were in his little black book he was going to be taking to the island.

You're being ridiculous and petty. Stop it.

Once the prizes had been awarded, everyone was cut loose to enjoy the rest of the night. Tara moved out of the room, needing air and a cold drink. She headed for the bar and grabbed a drink, then decided to find the nearest corner and wait out the crowd until it was time to go home. She was good at blending in. She could do this, could hide out, and no one would find her.

"Tara."

Dammit. There were five hundred people here, and she'd tucked herself into a crowd. How the hell had he ferreted her out so easily? She turned and faced Mick, who was surprisingly alone. "Where's your date for the night?"

"Surrounded by her Hollywood friends for the moment. And she's not my date."

"Uh-huh. Look, Mick. I'm busy tonight, and I don't have much time for idle chitchat. So if you'll excuse me . . ."

She tried to walk away, but he grabbed her arm.

"Are you kidding me? You're angry at me because I'm here with Alicia?"

She tilted her head back to glare at him. "What did you expect? That I'd be okay with it?" She blew out a sigh. "I don't know, Mick. Am I supposed to be okay with you seeing someone else?"

"I'm not seeing anyone else."

"And I guess I'm blind. And stupid. Forget it. We're nothing to each other."

Now he had the damn nerve to look mad. "We aren't?"

"No. We aren't. Now, if you'll excuse me, I have work to do."

He threw his hands in the air. "Fine. You go back to work. And so will I."

"You do that."

She walked away, her nerve endings blasting out anger signals all over the place. She had to take deep breaths in and out so she wouldn't look pissed-off at the people she was supposed to be entertaining. *Plant a smile on your face and look happy, for the love of God. These are all potential clients, and giving them a death glare isn't going to endear you to any of them.*

By the time she reached the front of the gallery she was calmer, smiling, at least on the outside—though it would probably help to dig her fingernails out of the palms of her hands.

She even stood by and watched all of young Hollywood give interviews for the television cameras, gritting her teeth when it was Alicia Brave's turn. And there was Mick, right by her side.

Ugh.

Though she couldn't help but inch a little closer so she could hear what Alicia had to say.

"Mick was my savior tonight," Alicia said, grabbing his arm. "My fiancé, Phil, came down with the flu at the last minute so he couldn't be here with me. Mick's agent and my agent are great friends, so they got on the phone, and Mick agreed to drop everything to escort me." Alicia laid her palm across her lower stomach. "You see, with the baby on the way, I didn't want to be alone. Now who better to see to my welfare than a big strapping quarterback like Mick Riley. Anyway, Phil and I are planning to get married very soon . . ."

Flashbulbs went off, Mick kissed Alicia's hand, then stepped out of the way, letting Alicia have the limelight.

"Wow, she just dropped one hell of a bomb, didn't she?"

Dumbstruck, Tara nodded at Maggie. "I guess she did. Who's Phil?"

Maggie rolled her eyes. "Really, Tara. Don't you read the entertainment magazines? Phil Bates from the same show Alicia's on. There were rumors the two have been in love for a while now. I guess they are in love. And engaged. And having a baby together. Wow. That's some serious news."

"Sure is." But not as much news as the fact that Liz shoved Mick at Alicia as a last-minute escort for tonight's event. And nothing more. Not because he wanted to hop in bed with her.

God, she was such a flaming idiot.

She stood on her toes and tried to find Mick but couldn't see him.

There. Heading for the front door with Alicia.

Dammit. She tried to ease through the crowd, but between the reporters and the onlookers, she didn't have a chance. And this wasn't the time anyway.

She saw him through the glass, helping Alicia into the limo, then climbing in after her. The driver shut the door, and then they were gone.

Tara turned and walked back into the gallery, feeling stupid and empty and hurt.

She hadn't trusted him. And she'd said terrible things to him.

Why couldn't she believe in Mick? Why couldn't she believe in herself?

And why hadn't he just told her what he was doing here tonight?

Because you didn't give him a chance, moron. Quit trying to blame him. You know damn well who fucked this up tonight.

She nodded to herself and kept on walking.

Somehow she was going to have to fix this.

MICK PACED HIS CONDO, DRAGGING HIS FINGERS through his hair and cursing himself and Liz in the process.

Stupid move. He should have known better when Liz called, begging him earlier tonight to bail out Alicia. But Liz had sounded sincere, and Alicia even phoned him asking for his help. This AIDS charity was important to her because her uncle was afflicted, and she wanted to put in an appearance, but her fiancé was sick and she was pregnant and they really had wanted to make the announcement about her pregnancy together. But Alicia had explained she was starting to show, and they couldn't put it off much longer, so she wanted to do it tonight, and Liz had offered up Mick since he was local.

What was he supposed to say to her? No? He supposed he could have, but it was very last-minute, and it was an easy enough thing for him to do, so he'd said yes.

Alicia was a sweetheart, very much in love with her fiancé. They were planning to get married in a month or so, hopefully somewhere quick and private and out of the public eye, but she wanted to set the rumors to rest about her and Phil. The girl looked tired. She laughed and said the first trimester had been hell on her, that Phil had been her rock, but this flu had kicked his butt, and he refused to come anywhere near her while he was sick because he didn't want to infect her or the baby. Mick laughed and held her hand and told her he'd fend off any annoying paparazzi, which meant he intended to stick to her side like glue the entire night.

He hadn't made the connection that it was the same event Tara had been planning. It had just never entered his mind. He knew Tara had been worked up about some charity event, but hell, in this city there was always some charity event or other going on. And he hadn't even had time to call Tara and tell her what he was going to be doing tonight. He'd grabbed a shower, thrown on his tux, and the limo had shown up. Plus, he knew she'd be busy, and this was such a nonissue to him that he didn't think it was a big deal. He figured he'd tell her about it when he saw her tomorrow.

And then he ran into her tonight and realized he'd escorted Alicia to Tara's event. But instead of her giving him time to explain, she'd already made up her mind what was going on and had played judge, jury, and executioner. It had pissed him off that she didn't believe in him. In them.

Dammit.

Mick filled up a glass with ice, water, and a wedge of lime, then went into the living room and turned on the television, propped his feet up, and stared at the screen for a while, flipping through channels and not really seeing anything.

A knock at the door had him grabbing his cell phone to look at the time. It was one in the morning. Who the hell was at the door this late? He rolled his eyes and hoped one of the guys on the team hadn't gotten kicked out by his wife.

He took a look through the peephole, surprised to see Tara standing outside. He opened the door and pulled her in.

"What the hell are you doing out this late?"

Her eyes widened. "I came to see you."

Mick shut and locked the door. "You should have called me."

"I'm sorry. It was a spur-of-the-moment thing. Bad time?"

"No, it's not that. I just don't want you out on the streets or wandering around in this parking lot late at night by yourself."

She stepped in and slid her fingers into the pockets of her jeans, looking as uncomfortable as he felt. "Oh. Well, thanks for your concern."

"You want something to drink?"

"Whatever you're having."

"Water with lime."

"That'll suit me just fine."

He fixed her a drink and brought it out to her. She was still standing in the same spot as she was when she walked in. "You can sit down, Tara."

"I don't know if you want me to stay or not."

He handed her the drink. "Sit down."

She did, taking a seat in his oversized chair, not on the sofa with him. Okay, so it was going to be like that.

She stared at the television for a while and he let her, figuring she'd come here to say something. He sipped his water, watching her, knowing she was thinking, organizing her thoughts. She always went quiet when her brain was working, when she was thinking about what she wanted to say or working out a plan of action.

He finally gave up and found them a movie to watch.

"Mick, I'm sorry."

He muted the TV and gave her his attention. "I'm sorry, too. This thing between Alicia and me tonight was very last-minute. Liz called—"

She held up her hand. "It doesn't matter. You don't owe me an explanation."

He pushed off the sofa and came over to her, dropping to his knees in front of her chair. "Liz called and said this was very last-minute," he continued, needing her to hear him, telling her the story of how Alicia's fiancé had fallen sick and she didn't want to tell the world about her fiancé and her pregnancy without some support. "I was nothing more than a glorified bodyguard to keep the press from knocking her over."

Tara pulled her knees to her chest. "You were very nice to her. I saw how close you stayed to her. I'm sure she appreciated it."

"She's a nice kid. But she's a kid, Tara. She's twenty-two."

Tara's lips lifted. "Some of the women you've dated haven't been much older than that."

She was right about that. "I've reformed. I like more mature women now."

She snorted. "Gee, thanks."

"You know what I mean." He slid his hands over her knees.

"I should have called you and given you a heads-up. I wasn't even thinking that we were attending the same event as you. I was just operating blind here, assuming I was going to do this good deed and tell you about it tomorrow. I didn't want to call and bother you with something trivial like this when I knew you were busy with work."

Tara leaned forward and tangled her fingers in his hair. "I know. And then you ran into me, and I acted like a giant bitch about it all."

He gave her an impish grin. "I'm going to assume it just means you care about me."

"If I didn't, you wouldn't have seen me act like a giant bitch."

"So we're good?"

"We're good. And I'm really sorry. I acted petty and jealous and I don't know why. It's a very ugly side of me, and I don't like it. Did I mention I was sorry?"

"You don't need to be. Next time I'll give you a heads-up when Liz tosses some stunning, sexy young babe at me."

Tara mimicked a knife stabbing repeatedly into her heart. "You're killing me here, Mick."

He laughed and stood, pulling her into his arms. "Just kidding."

She leaned against him. "No you're not. It's likely to happen again. It's your job to do these promotional things. I need to learn to live with it."

"No, it won't happen again. No one needs to be on my arm but you."

Tara swallowed, her throat gone dry. She tried to say something, but what retort could she come up with for that statement? Instead, she reached up and cupped the back of his neck, drawing his lips to hers. Enough had been said, and they were already headed into dangerous territory. Kissing was a much better idea.

When his lips met hers, the anguish of the night dissolved and she felt settled again. Every time she was in Mick's arms she felt . . . she didn't know how she felt. She wanted to say *calm*, but that wasn't it, because whenever he touched her he riled her up and got her excited, so *calm* definitely wasn't the right word.

Perfect. It felt perfect and right to be with him, and when he wrapped his arms around her and deepened the kiss, exploring her tongue with his, she sighed, because everything was in balance again.

He broke the kiss and leaned back. "Can you find someone for Nathan to hang out with for a weekend?"

His question made her pause. "What? Why?"

"I bid on and won that private island in the Caribbean. I want to take you there."

She reached up and laid her hand across her heart. "You do?"

"Yeah. What did you think I was bidding on it for? To take my mother?"

She was in total awe of this man. "Wow. Well, uh, I guess I could ask his coach."

"Do that. We'll have to do it soon because once we get into preseason games, my weekends are shot."

"I'll ask Coach tomorrow."

He slid his hands down her back and cupped her butt in his hands. "I'd like to have you to myself for a couple days, where no one bothers us."

She shivered in his arms, already imagining what that would be like. "I'm already packing."

"Better make that phone call tomorrow, then. We can go next weekend if you're free."

"As a matter of fact, I am free next weekend."

His eyes crinkled as he gave her a devilish smile. "Then if it's okay with Nathan's coach, we're on. Start packing."

SIXTEEN

OKAY, SO PRIVATE ISLANDS AND HAVING YOUR OWN butler and wearing very little clothing was as far away from Tara's normal daily existence as she could get.

She could get used to this kind of lifestyle. She'd thought when the auction item said "private island," they meant a little slice of an island with a privacy fence.

Uh, no. They'd flown to the Virgin Islands, then taken another flight somewhere. Tara had gotten lost and had no idea where they were. Maybe that was the point. They'd taken a boat to a tiny island that was truly uninhabited by anyone other than the two of them and their butler, who served them meals, took care of their every need, and other than that made himself totally invisible. If they needed something, they picked up a phone and called him. He told them his quarters were off island, so they could be assured of their privacy. Which meant they could walk the island naked if they wanted to.

Tara couldn't imagine doing that, but it had taken Mick all of an hour to throw off his clothes and sunbathe naked on the sand. Who was she to argue with the primal urge to go native? Soon she was lying on a cozy beach chair with no clothes on, and she'd never felt more decadent in her entire life.

The island—what could she say about this island? A stretch of sand that looked out over turquoise waters with no other land in sight, making her feel totally isolated. Lazy palm trees that bent and swayed in a gentle breeze, providing shade over the sand. Their own two-story home nestled in the forest that overlooked the bay. It was heaven.

The warm breeze sailed across her skin, and she inhaled the salty air, lifting her arms to stretch and roll over. After about an hour in the sun, she'd pushed her chair under a palm tree to soak up some shade, careful not to sunburn her skin. The last thing she'd want is to miss any of this glorious tropical paradise while nursing a burn.

It was too perfect. Warmth, breeze, and utter relaxation. Her eyes drifted closed, but then she felt warm lips against her back, and she smiled as a hand followed, smoothing down her spine to rest at the spot where her lower back met her buttocks.

"Mmmmmmmm," was all she could manage.

"I like you like this," Mick said, teasing between her butt cheeks with his fingers. "Your body warm from the sun, every muscle like liquid."

"I'm pretty much at your mercy right now. You can do whatever you want with me."

"Is that right. Anything?"

Her limbs felt heavy, and so did her head. She couldn't even muster the strength to nod, but the other parts of her—the female parts—they were firing up like a roaring engine. "Anything."

He continued to massage her back with light touches, and it felt so good, especially when he kneaded the small of her back, teasing her by lightly tracing his fingertips over her butt cheeks. From hard pressure on the muscles of her back to the torturous caresses on her butt, it was driving her crazy, making her relaxed and tense at the same time. Her nipples peaked against the chair, and she wanted to rub them against the towel, anything to get some friction. Being naked meant her clit was getting some contact, too, and she felt the urge to reach between her legs and rub the throbbing ache Mick had caused.

But then he spread her legs. She felt the brush of his hair against her thighs and the swipe of his tongue across her pussy lips. She arched, lifting her butt, and his tongue slid across her clit.

Yes, that's what she wanted. She got up on her knees, and he tucked his head between her legs, licking her pussy in long, delicious swipes.

She couldn't believe they were outside, naked, right there on the beach, his head between her legs taking her so close to orgasm she was ready to scream, and no one was there to hear her if she did. She felt so free doing this with Mick, so wild and uninhibited. Never before had she given so much to one man.

His tongue was one hot slide across her tortured flesh. She shuddered as he licked around her clit, flicked his tongue there, tucked his finger inside her pussy, and began to pump in a slow, maddening rhythm that took her to the brink, only to withdraw and start over again with his tongue and fingers.

She laid her head in her hands and closed her eyes, attuned to everything he did to her. And when his tongue traveled up her pussy and across her anus, she jerked in response, lifted her head, and turned to him in question and uncertainty.

"Easy, baby. Let me taste all of you."

She relaxed into it again as he patted her, licked her, took her right to the edge again as he licked every part of her, using his tongue and fingers to drive her crazy. She pictured his head buried between her legs, the warm breeze off the ocean not at all cooling her damp skin as he brought her to the brink time and time again, licking her clit, her pussy, and finally sliding his tongue into the puckered hole in back while he used his fingers on her pussy.

"Mick. Oh, God, Mick. Yes, just like that." She never knew those kinds of sensations coupled together could make her so crazy, but she was going to come.

He pulled back. "Not yet. I don't want you to come. Not until I fuck you."

She drew in a ragged breath, so close to orgasm the pulses undulated within her.

Mick held her there on her knees, his hands on her hips as he pressed against her, his cock sliding between the seam of her buttocks.

"You're so wet here," he said, his fingers dancing along her pussy lips, dipping inside to coat her anus. "I'm going to fuck your pussy, Tara. Then I'm going to fuck your ass. And I'm going to make you come, hard."

"Yes," she said, her voice hoarse from panting. "Yes. Fuck me."

She shivered as he swept his hand along her back. He reached into the beach bag on the table. She heard the condom packet as he tore it open, then he slid inside her pussy, pressing against her as he held tight to her hips and rocked back and forth. She gripped him in welcome, pulling him closer as she balanced on the edge of orgasm.

"Not yet, Tara. Hold on for me."

She gritted her teeth and felt every sweet inch of him expand inside her. "Dammit, Mick. It's so good."

He leaned forward, kissing her sweat-soaked neck. "I know it is. It's going to get better." He withdrew and shoved in, hard, and she cried out, tossing her hair back and rocking back to meet his thrusts.

His fingers dug into her hips as he continued to power inside her, stopping short every time she drew close to climaxing. He withdrew and poured lube over her anus, using his finger to coat her, tease her opening, dipping his finger inside to open her, prepare her. The sensation was maddening. The pressure was intense, and she was so ready to come. She was past the point of reason, past the point of knowing anything but the orgasm she craved.

She felt his cock at the entrance to her ass.

"I'm going to fuck your ass now, Tara. You ready?"

"Yes. Fuck me. Now."

He slid his cock head past the tight barrier. She hissed, breathing through the burning pain.

"Relax. Push out when I push in. You'll take me in easier that way. And then I'll make you come."

She did, and he eased inside her. He held still while she waited through the intensity of feeling him there. He was so full, so big in such a small space, and it hurt. But through the hurt was a pulsing wave of such pleasure to be had. Mick leaned over and began to rub her clit in gentle circles, and soon the pain was replaced by that driving need to come again. She pushed his hand away. "Fuck me. I'll do this."

He held on to her hips, withdrawing just enough to push back inside her again.

"Oh, shit, oh, God, Mick. Yes. Fuck me like that."

She massaged her clit harder, faster, while he thrust his cock in her ass, and she spiraled out of control. She rose up, sliding her fingers into her pussy, and continued rubbing her clit with her other hand. The sensations pounded at her as she lost everything but the feel of him inside her. "I can feel it. Yes, fuck me. Faster."

"You gonna come for me, Tara?" he asked, his voice harsh and dark.

"Yes, Mick. Hurry and fuck me. I'm going to come."

Nothing was going to stop her now as she felt the blast of orgasm hit her. She rocked back against him, taking his cock fully in her ass as she splintered into a thousand pieces with her climax. She screamed, the sound echoing through the treetops. Mick dug his fingers into her hips and shoved hard against her as he came, and his orgasm only intensified hers. She cried out, she couldn't breathe, but it was the most intense damn climax she'd ever had. She felt it in every nerve ending, exploding throughout her body, bringing tears to her eyes as the waves pounded her over and over again.

She collapsed on the chair. Mick draped himself over her back, both of them panting like they'd just completed a marathon.

"Care for a dip in the ocean?" Mick asked, sliding his tongue along her neck.

"I think that's a great idea."

They swam and played in the water for the better part of the day, then came in, took a shower, and Mick called for Simon, their butler, who appeared within the hour to prepare them an amazing seafood dinner, which meant they actually had to put clothes on. Tara didn't really mind since she'd brought a few fun sundresses to wear and she hadn't had the chance to put much on. Mick had thrown on a pair of shorts and a short-sleeved tropical shirt for dinner.

After Simon prepared their food, he disappeared for the night, advising them he'd be back in the morning to fix them breakfast whenever they were ready, but to call if they needed anything before.

She could use a Simon in her life.

They ate out on the terrace overlooking the water. The sun had set, the moon rising and casting a silver glow across the water. And it was still warm outside. Tara lifted her glass of wine and took a sip.

"Does it bother you when I have a drink?"

Mick lifted his glass of mineral water. "No. Why should it?"

"Just wondered if you miss it."

"Alcohol? Not really. It's not good for me and I can't handle it. But it doesn't bother me to see other people drink it."

"I can drink water or tea."

He laughed and picked up her hand, kissed the back of it. "Thanks, babe. But there's no reason you can't enjoy a glass of wine. To be honest, I don't even think about what you're drinking. I'm too busy looking at your hair or your mouth or your tits or thinking about how great it was to fuck your ass today."

She shook her head. "Such a guy."

He waggled his brows. "Would you have me any other way?"

"No."

"Okay then. Quit worrying about it."

She did. They finished their meal and Tara stopped worrying about doing dishes. Though she still insisted on taking them inside and putting them in the sink, even though Mick laughed at her when she did.

"How about a walk on the beach?" Mick suggested.

"Great idea. That dinner was fabulous. I need to walk it off."

Mick took her hand and led her out onto the beach. Tara inhaled the salty air and wondered how she was ever going to go back to the reality that was her life after spending a weekend at this idyllic paradise with a man like Mick.

"Tomorrow I thought we'd play some football on the beach."

She snorted and leaned against him. "Trying to put me on the disabled list so I can't work?"

"The thought crossed my mind. I'd have to keep you here on the island until you were well enough to travel."

"I'd be at your mercy, day and night. I'm a slow healer, too."

"How convenient. So how long do you think we could hold out here? A few months?"

She nodded. "At least."

"That'd be tough."

"You'd miss the start of the season."

"Someone would have to do your job for you and handle all those headaches."

She laughed. "Yeah, that would be a hardship."

He put his arm around her and tugged her close. "Nice to dream, isn't it?"

"This is paradise, Mick. I don't know how people ever leave it."

"Some might miss television and phones and Internet."

"I don't watch that much television anyway. I'm always on the phone at work, and it drives me crazy. And the only time I'm on the Internet is for work purposes. Getting away from it all here has been wonderful." She stopped and stepped in front of him, the ocean waves sifting sand and water over her feet and ankles. "Thank you for this. It's been the most amazing trip."

He tipped her chin with his fingers. "I thought you might enjoy it. And it's a nice break for me, too, before the craziness of the season starts up. I've never done the whole tropical island getaway, and when I saw it on the bid list, I thought of you and me and knew I had to win it."

"Did you?" She couldn't hide her grin.

"Yeah."

He kissed her, a slow, sensual kiss that made her slide her toes into the sand and lean against him to hold on because she was getting dizzy. With Mick, she lost her senses, which was both a good and a bad thing.

She moved beside him again and they walked, not talking. She found she could be comfortable just being with him and not saying a word, though that tended to get her mind to working, and she thought about being here with him this weekend and what it all meant.

Total fantasy. Nothing real about it. Everything with Mick since the beginning had been built on fantasy. Dream dates and wishes and over-the-top fantasies come true. He was everything she'd ever dreamed of in a man, and everything she'd never dreamed was real. But what scared her about the two of them was the possibility that, like the fantasy of this weekend, there was no reality involved in it, nothing tangible to hold on to once the fantasy wore off.

Soon his football season would start, and he'd be so intensely involved in playing that he wouldn't have time for her. And her business was taking off. She was getting more and more involved, her bookings were picking up, and she barely had time to see to Nathan's needs. Once fall came he'd have games she'd need to attend, plus making sure he handled his schoolwork.

Where was there going to be time for a romantic relationship in both their schedules?

Maybe it was time to start seeing the reality of what she and Mick had together. It was a fun summer fling, and that's all it was ever going to be. The sooner she came to grips with that, the better off she'd be. Before something stupid happened and she fell madly in love with him and started thinking they'd have a future together.

She'd had her heart broken once, and she wasn't going to let it happen again.

Mick seemed to enjoy spending time with her, and okay, he seemed to like spending time with *only* her. But that didn't mean anything. Men's thought processes were utterly different from women's. And men were inherently lazy, which meant that she was just easy to be with for the summer.

Wow, Tara, could you insult yourself any more with this thought process?

She hadn't meant to, and she knew what she was thinking sounded bad, but it wasn't what she meant. She and Mick got along great, they had fun together, their chemistry was smoking-hot, so why wouldn't they be together? She wasn't a demanding actress or model who needed to be seen and photographed and taken to events. She was fine doing whatever he wanted to do, and Nathan hero worshipped him, so there wasn't even a problem with her kid.

Yeah, right. There'd been a huge problem when her kid had gotten drunk. And Mick had stepped in like a champion. How could a guy who wanted nothing more than sex from her have gotten so involved like he had with Nathan?

Maybe he was just a nice guy. No reason to read any more into it than what it was.

She was kind of the best summer fling he could have, right? And she'd made it pretty clear she wasn't trying to put hooks into him, which would make leaving when his season started easy enough for him to do.

There was nothing holding him to her. Nothing holding her to him.

It was the perfect relationship.

So why didn't it feel so perfect right now?

"You've been quiet."

She lifted her gaze to his and offered up a smile. "Just enjoying the remarkable scenery."

"You're remarkable scenery. To hell with the ocean, the palm trees, and the sand."

He drew them away from the water and dropped to the sand, pulling her down on top of him.

She laughed. "You're pretty good for my ego."

"Yeah, they're paying me to boost you up a little."

She arched a brow. "They? Who are they?"

He put his fingers to his lips. "I can't tell you. It's a secret. But trust me, they have your best interests in mind by hiring me on to give you a little lift."

She laughed and pushed on his chest, lifting herself up to a sitting position. She slid her fingers under his shirt, loving the warmth she found when her skin met his. "So how much will I have to torture you to get the truth out of you?"

He laced his fingers behind his head. "Give it your best shot."

She unbuttoned his shirt, pulled it aside, and splayed her fingers out over his chest.

"Holding me down to get the truth out of me?" he asked.

She didn't answer and instead let her fingers drift over his ribs, down his stomach and even lower, dipping into his shorts to search for his cock. He lifted when she tugged on his shorts and removed them, tossing them to the side.

"Now I'm at your mercy."

"So you are," she said, taking his cock between her hands. She stroked him from base to tip, a slow slide of her hands, enjoying the feel of his cock hardening as she touched him.

"That's torture."

She smiled down at him. "Ready to give up your secrets?"

"No."

She swirled her thumb over the crest of his cock, using the fluid that had gathered there to lubricate her movements. His eyes were locked onto what she was doing, but she was watching his face, his sharp breaths when she gripped him hard, the way his nostrils flared when she rolled both hands over his cock. She kept her gaze focused on his face as she bent down and licked his cock head, curling her tongue around his shaft, then dragging it down the underside. She licked his balls and he lifted, moaned, and sat up, spread his legs.

"Christ, that's good, Tara."

She rolled her tongue over the sac, putting each in her mouth, wanting to taste him everywhere before putting his cock in her mouth and drawing his shaft deep inside. She went down on him, letting him watch his cock disappear between her lips. She felt him shudder, loved that she made him weak the way he made her weak when he made love to her, wanted to take him right to the brink and over it. She held on to the base of his shaft and increased the suction as she brought him to the back of her throat, then eased up on the pressure, establishing a rhythm that had him grasping her hair and thrusting into her mouth with swift, hard strokes.

She laid her hand on his thigh and felt the dampness of perspiration, knew he held back, so she swept her hand along his shaft and fluttered her tongue across the soft head.

"Yeah. Oh, yeah. Dammit, that's going to make me come. I'm going to come in your mouth, Tara."

She hummed against his shaft, needing him to let her have it all.

He arched into her mouth and groaned, then tightened his hold on her hair as he let go, spurting hot come into her mouth. She held him there, swallowing what he gave her as he rocked against her, his entire body quaking with the force of his orgasm. She finally released his cock when he fell back against the sand.

"Damn," was all he said.

Tara laid her head on his stomach, listening to the wild beat of his pulse, the upward rise and fall of his breaths while he smoothed his hand over her hair.

She lifted her head and gazed up at him. "Ready to give up your secrets to me?"

He laughed, raised his head. "Secrets? What secrets?"

"Damn you." She picked up sand and rubbed it in his stomach. He lunged for her, but she screamed, jumped up, and ran, Mick on her heels. She knew she didn't have a chance, and he was on her in seconds, tossing her to the ground. She squealed with laughter when he tackled her.

"Not fair," she yelled as he pulled her under him, the top of her dress now around her waist. She didn't care. "Your profession gives you an advantage."

"Quit whining." He grabbed sand and rubbed it between her breasts. She fisted a handful of sand and rubbed it in his hair. By the time they were through rolling around in the wet sand, Tara was convinced there was more of it on them than on the beach.

"Okay, enough," Mick said, spitting sand out of his mouth.

Tara giggled and Mick pulled her up, threw her over his shoulder, and headed for their bungalow.

He turned on the shower while Tara stripped off her dress. They stepped into the oversized shower together and she laughed as Mick turned around. He had sand on his face, in his hair, and chunks of it hung on various parts of his body.

"Do I look as bad as you do?"

He brushed sand off her shoulders. "Probably."

They lathered up and washed—rather thoroughly, since sand had gotten everywhere. Tara was thankful for the jets on both sides of the shower, and for the removable shower head, since she ended up with sand in uncomfortable spots of her body.

"Well, that was like a spa treatment," she said once she'd rinsed the sand out of every possible crevice. "But my skin is utterly smooth now."

Mick rinsed his face and turned to her. "Is that right? I think I should double-check to make sure you got all the sand out."

Tara arched a brow, then held her arms out. "Inspect away."

He turned her around and smoothed his hands over her shoulders and arms, then down her back. "Looks good here. Turn around."

She did, and he locked his gaze with hers as he swept his fingers through her wet hair, letting his fingertips trail over her nose and across her lips. He bent and brushed his lips across hers. "Tastes sand-free."

She sighed when he ran his tongue over her lips, slid between her teeth to taste her tongue before pulling away.

"No sand on your tongue."

She laughed.

Her breath caught when he rolled his thumbs over her breasts, then caught her hips with his hands. "Yes, very smooth here, but I need to take a closer look down here."

He dropped to his knees. "Spread your legs, honey."

She did, bracing against the side of the shower when he leaned forward, his tongue snaking out to lick along the folds of her pussy. She tilted her head back and let the water fall over her face and hair, the heat and steam only adding to the pressure building deep inside her as Mick sucked on her clit.

She gasped when he slid his tongue inside her. He raised her leg and rested it over his shoulder, opening her further to him.

"Smooth, sweet, so soft here. He slipped a finger inside her, fucking her with gentle strokes while he lazily drew circles around her clit with his tongue.

It was the soft and easy that took her right to the edge—and over, shocking her that it was so quick. She gasped when she came, rocking against him while he held tight to her, making sure she wouldn't fall as she rode out a delicious orgasm.

Mick stood and reached outside the door for a condom, then wrapped her leg around his hip as he shoved inside her, pushing her against the wall of the shower. He raised her hands above her head and bent to lick at her nipples.

Now it was a matter of passionate hunger, and she reveled in it.

"Kiss me," she demanded, and he lifted his head, took her mouth in a blistering kiss, ratcheting up her desire to unbearable levels as he shoved into her with deep, penetrating thrusts.

He rolled his hips over her, grinding against her over and over until she was coming again, crying out as she exploded with sensation. He let go of her arms and lifted her, kissing her with everything he had as he let go with an intimate look that melted her. She drank in his groans and held tight to him while he shuddered against her, his fingers digging so hard into her buttocks she knew they'd leave marks, but she didn't care.

The water had started to cool by the time he released her, and she was still quaking inside from the force of both her orgasm and his.

Mick reached over and turned the water off, grabbed towels for both of them. They dried off and climbed into bed. Mick pulled her against him, sweeping her damp hair to the side to kiss the nape of her neck.

Tara closed her eyes and tried to shut off the emotion that being with Mick always brought forth.

It was just sex. Just sex and nothing more.

Maybe if she kept telling herself that over and over and over again, she'd buy into it and keep the realization that she had fallen head over heels love with him at bay. Because that notion kept cropping up all the damn time, and the more she tried to push it away, the more it appeared.

She was afraid it was too late to make it disappear, despite her best intentions to talk herself out of it happening.

SEVENTEEN

"I NEED YOU TO GO TO A MOVIE PREMIERE."

Mick had just had one of the most grueling workouts of his life. The last thing he needed to see when he walked off the field was Liz, looking fresh-faced, not a hair out of place, and like a tiger ready to pounce.

He wheezed in a breath of oxygen and blew it out, then sat on the bench and grabbed one of the bottles from the assistants passing by. "Why?"

She cocked her head to the side and gave him a look. "You know why. Season will be starting up soon. I need your face front and center on magazine covers."

He gulped down half the bottle, then lifted his gaze to her. "What's the movie?"

She grinned. "It's an action flick. The new one with Matt Larson."

"When?"

"Wednesday night."

Mick nodded and grabbed for his towel. "I'll check with Tara and see what her schedule looks like."

"Whoa. I don't think so."

He looked up at her. "What?"

"You'll be attending the premiere with Valisha Staniskowa, the hot beauty gracing the cover of the swimsuit edition."

He stood and faced her. "No."

She arched a brow. "Excuse me?"

"I said, no. I'll try to get to the movie premiere if you think it'll help PR. But I'll be going with Tara. And any future events you want to plan will be with Tara as my date."

Liz let out a laugh. "You've got to be kidding me. She's a nobody."

"She's not a nobody to me, Elizabeth. She's someone I care about."

"What does that have to do with anything? I'm only talking about promotional appearances that are a benefit to your career. Appearing with Tara at these events is of no benefit to you."

He was in no mood for this, and Liz either didn't get it or was too stubborn to see things his way. Either way he wasn't going to budge. "I'm only going to say this one more time, so be sure to listen. I'm not going to do these events without Tara anymore. I care about her, and I don't want to be seen in public with other women. Got it?"

She raised her hands. "Got it. Geez, you don't have to bop me over the head with it. We'll do something different then. You have a game this weekend, and the team barbecue is after the game. Invite Tara. She can meet the wives and girlfriends. And it's a nice photo op. We'll play that up and make sure cameras are in place to take your picture."

When he gave her a look, she added, "With Tara."

"Fine. Whatever you want." He grabbed his helmet and headed off to the shower, wondering when his life had gotten so damn complicated. He had enough to worry about with his first preseason game coming up this weekend. He used to ease into these games with the zeal of a kid—no worries. But since he turned thirty and the bloodthirsty wolves of youth and vigor had started hounding his heels, every step he took had to be a careful calculation, and this time he had to put it all on the field. Management told him he was on solid footing and he was still their franchise player, but he knew that didn't mean shit if he got hurt or his performance this season didn't rack up the numbers.

And then there was Tara. How could something that had started out so lighthearted and fun and had just been sex turn into something serious?

He stood in front of his locker to get dressed and wondered what the hell he was going to do about that. He didn't do serious relationships. Hell, he didn't do relationships with women. He dated them. He fucked them. He had fun with them. Then they went one way and he went another. His career—the love of his life—was football. Always had been, and he assumed it always would be. Oh, he figured he might settle down one of these days, after his football career was over and he had the time and attention to focus on a woman.

What he hadn't expected was for Tara to come into his life and knock him back on his ass and turn his world upside down.

He wasn't ready for a relationship and commitment yet. He had to focus on this season, and that meant everything else had to go away once the season started.

He pulled the shirt over his head and sat down on the bench to shove stuff in his gym bag, then dragged his fingers through his hair.

So what was he supposed to do about Tara? Dump her? Walk away and tell her the summer had been fun, but he was done now that the season was starting up? With the other women that had breezed in and out of his life, they'd known how it was going to be.

Fun trips, fun photo ops, great sex, but when the season started, it was over. They knew it and he knew it, and they'd been fine with it, because they hadn't wanted permanence any more than he had.

They'd known the score, they'd played the game, and both sides had won.

Yet on the field today he'd read the riot act to Elizabeth for suggesting he go to a movie premiere with another woman. He'd told Liz he wasn't seeing anyone else, that Tara was the only woman in his life.

Shit.

Did he even know what the fuck he wanted?

He'd better figure it out before he led Tara on.

Or maybe he'd better figure out what she wanted. She might not want anything other than a summer with him. She was busy building her career. She had a kid to think about. It wasn't like she was the sort of woman who was out there trying to land a husband. She was fiercely independent, protective of Nathan, and hadn't wanted to get involved in his lifestyle in the first place. So it wasn't like she was all in about becoming a permanent fixture in his life.

Did he want her in his life permanently?

He sat and laid his head in his hands. Jesus, he didn't know. Could he handle that? He'd been chasing after her from the first night he met her, not even thinking about where it might lead. He'd operated on blind instinct. The chase had been fun because he'd never had to chase a woman before.

Now that the season was going to start, it was time to make some decisions, because it looked like his relationship with Tara was headed somewhere. His feelings for her were headed somewhere.

And he had no fucking idea how he felt about that or if he could even handle it. The thought of just walking away from her wasn't acceptable. He wanted her in his life. But what did that mean, both for him and for her?

Christ. If he ever needed a drink, it was now. Alcohol had always been good for making him forget things he didn't want to think about. And this was a great topic not to think about.

He grabbed his bag and fished for his keys, then pushed through the doors of the locker room, needing fresh air to clear his head. He hit the parking lot and sucked in a huge lungful of it, realizing he'd been breathing too hard, damn near hyperventilating. He popped the lock on his car, tossed his bag in back, and climbed in, forcing his breaths to calm before he started up the car.

Breathe. Settle. God, what was wrong with him? He had a great life, an amazing, successful career, an awesome woman who seemed to care a lot about him, and for the first time in years he was craving a drink.

What kind of motherfucking weak-willed asshole did that make him?

He had a lot of thinking to do. It was time to go home, change clothes, and take a long run before he did something stupid like stop at the nearest bar and get a drink.

MICK AND HIS BROTHER WEREN'T THE CLOSEST AS FAR as siblings went, but Gavin knew what he'd been through. He needed someone to talk to, and since Gavin was in town for a game, he figured this was a good time to take his brother out for a late-night meal.

They met at a bar overlooking the city. Mick walked in and surveyed the panoramic view of the Bay Bridge and downtown San Francisco before skirting his gaze to the bar. He located his brother, who was surrounded by three women. It figured.

As soon as Gavin spotted Mick, he signaled him over.

"Sorry, ladies," Gavin said. "I have some business to do with my brother tonight."

"Oh. My. God," the tall blonde said. "It's Mick Riley the football player."

The brunette standing next to the blonde sized Mick up with a head-to-toe glance, then offered up a sexy smile that said she was all his for the taking. A couple months ago he might have been interested. Now . . . not so much.

"See you later," Gavin said, taking his beer and moving to the other end of the bar, much to the disappointment of all the women, who pouted and flounced off.

"Hearts are breaking," Mick said.

"Yeah, yeah." Gavin took a seat. "Didn't figure you for the sightseeing type, but the view is nice, both outside and inside the bar."

"What? You don't want me to take you down the world's crookedest street?"

Gavin smirked. "I'll pass."

"Good game today."

"I would have sent you tickets."

Mick laughed. "I see you play plenty. Caught some of the game on TV, though. Nice homer."

Gavin grinned and tipped the bottle of beer to his lips. "Thanks. Your hometown fans didn't seem to care too much for it, since it was the winning run."

"San Francisco will get you next time."

"I wouldn't bet on it."

The hostess called them to their table, so they headed into the restaurant. Mick had asked for a booth with some privacy, so Casey had given them the small private room. After their waiter took their orders, he shut the door.

"We having a party here tonight? And if we are, please tell me those three gorgeous women we met in the bar earlier are somehow involved."

Mick shook his head. "No, I just didn't want to be overheard."

"Oh, yeah?" Gavin laid his beer on the table and leaned forward. "If it's illegal, immoral, and naked women are involved, I'm all in."

"It's kind of serious, Gavin."

His smile died. "Okay. What do you want to talk about?

"A few things. I really didn't know who to talk to about this stuff."

"Look, I realize I'm full of shit most of the time, Mick, but you know if you ever need me, I'm here to listen. No judgment."

And that's what he needed to hear. "It's a lot of things. Tara and me, Liz, football."

Gavin leaned back. "Start talkin'. You have me all night."

Mick inhaled and blew out a breath. "I told Tara I was an alcoholic."

Gavin's eyebrows rose. "Really. So you trust her that much?"

"I do. Something happened with Nathan, and I wanted to show her, and him, what could happen if a kid got too involved with alcohol."

Gavin leaned forward. "So wait. The kid knows, too?"

"Yeah. I took him to a meeting with me."

"Jesus, Gavin. I can maybe understand you telling Tara. But the kid? You know how volatile they are. What if he spills? You've taken a lot of care to keep your secret out of the hands of the media."

"I know. I don't think Nathan will say anything. He understands it's important to me to keep it a secret."

Gavin snorted and took a long pull of his beer. "Yeah. Best intentions and all that. What if you dump his mother or hurt her in some way? You know the first thing he's going to do is spread the word across the Internet that you're a drunk."

Mick shrugged. "I took the gamble. Now I have to trust them both."

"Well, that's your risk to take, I guess. Me, I don't trust anybody. All my skeletons stay in the closet where they belong."

"Hell, Gavin, you publicize all your skeletons. You're the bad boy of baseball, and you love it that way. That's why women flock to you like you've been sprayed with some kind of goddamned aphrodisiac."

Gavin waggled his eyebrows. "What can I say? I'm irresistible."

"Don't make me sick before dinner, okay?"

"Hey, you're the one who's gone all one woman, so don't blame me if you're jealous."

Mick rolled his eyes. "I can't believe I invited you to dinner."

"You can read all about me in the magazines, brother. And remember the good times you used to have." Gavin grabbed his bottle and leaned back in his chair.

Mick laughed and shook his head. This was just what he needed. The playful teasing of his brother to help lighten his mood and lift some of the seriousness.

"Okay, so tell me what else, besides you vomiting up all your secrets to Tara and her kid. So things are serious between you two?"

"I don't know. I think so. I might want them to be. I thought that's where things were going."

"But she pulled back?"

"No."

"You pulled back?"

"No."

Gavin laughed. "What the fuck, man? What's going on then? Sounds like it's all goin' good. What's the problem?"

"I don't know." He leaned forward, clasped his hands together. "I'm scared, Gavin. What if I can't do this?"

"You're asking me about love and relationships? Maybe you should talk to Mom about that. I've never had a real relationship with a woman in my entire life. I don't do girlfriends. You're way ahead of the game as far as women and the commitment thing."

Mick leaned back in his chair. "It's just that I don't know if I'm good long-term material. And then with the new season starting, I'm worried about my career."

Gavin lifted his beer. "Aren't we all. But I thought you were locked in to a contract?"

"I am. But that's only as good as the last season and the current season. They've drafted a young hotshot with a rocket for an arm. And the kid they brought in a year ago is hungry."

"So? That keeps you on your toes. And a team always has to have backup. I face the same thing in baseball. The farm clubs have kick-ass first basemen with stellar averages just waiting for me to fuck up or pull an injury. In sports you're up one day and down the next. You know there are no guarantees and you can't ride the high forever. At least you have the smarts and the business sense for backup when you're done with the game, so you're ahead of me on that."

"If you'd paid attention in school, you'd have had the same thing."

Gavin took a long pull of his beer. "Yeah, yeah. Now you sound like Mom."

"You can still invest, start some business on the side, prepare for your own retirement. You aren't getting any younger, you know."

"Uh-huh. And we aren't here to talk about me and my failings, are we?"

Mick sighed. "Fine."

Gavin waved the bottle at him. "Look, Mick. You just have to enjoy the game while you have it. Play the best game you can, and stop worrying about the other shit you have no control over."

"You're right. I don't know why I'm so messed up over all this bullshit. It just hit me all of a sudden. And then there's Liz bombarding me by trying to throw women at me."

"You say that like it's a bad thing."

Mick laughed. "Right now it is a bad thing. She's fighting me over Tara. She wants me to be seen with the latest actress or model and isn't happy I'm with Tara."

"Who gives a shit what Liz thinks?" Gavin finished his beer and set it aside, then signaled for their waiter, who brought him another beer and Mick another mineral water. After the waiter shut the door, Gavin leaned forward. "Look, Liz is great for our careers and rarely steers us wrong, but she's a giant pain in the ass. A smokin'-hot pain in the ass with the best damn legs I've ever seen, and she makes us a ton of money. But if Tara's who you want, then set Liz straight and don't let her push you into doing something you don't want to do.

"I've never known you to let anyone push you around, so what's going on inside your head?"

"I don't know." Mick pulled a piece of bread from the basket in the center of the table and slathered it with butter, waving it around in his hand. "It's like my whole life has changed in the past couple months, and I'm suddenly at a crossroads. I used to know exactly where my life was headed, and now I'm not sure anymore."

Gavin grabbed the bread from Mick's hands and shoved a bite into his mouth. He chewed for a few seconds, then said, "You're in love, brother. It's obvious. That has to be the only thing to mess you up this bad, because I've never seen you like this."

Mick took a sip of water to coat his dry throat. "You think?"

"Well, I don't know anything about love, but you're all over the place with your thoughts and feelings. So yeah, you're in love. And if this is what love does to a guy? I hope to hell it never happens to me, because dude, you are one fucked-up son of a bitch."

"So what do I do?"

"Man up, suck it up, and deal with it. Look what you've been through in your life, Mick. You went through college as a drunk but still managed to fight it and get an NFL contract. You've been sober for all these years, and not once have you touched a drop of alcohol, right?"

"Right."

"Okay, so if you love Tara, then do something about it. If you decide you don't, then cut her loose. Tell Liz to butt the hell out of your personal life and start telling her how to manage your god-damned career the way you want it managed. Just because you're at a crossroads and some things in your life are changing doesn't mean you need a drink to get through it. You haven't needed one all these years, and you sure as hell don't need one now.

"Sure, you're thirty years old now. But I've never seen a guy work harder than you to stay in shape, so go out there, play football, and continue to enjoy the game. And don't worry about losing your stamina or your mojo or whatever the fuck it is you're worried about losing. When the time comes to step away, you'll know it, and you'll deal with it just like you've always dealt with things—head-on. A drink isn't going to help you escape from the realities of your life, and you know that. You went down that road once, and you know how well that worked. Or didn't work. But only you can make that choice. I can't make it for you. So the decision is yours."

The waiter brought their food, and Mick dug in and ate, ponder-ing all Gavin had said to him.

"You sure grew up while I wasn't looking."

Gavin lifted his gaze from his plate. "No, I haven't. I still party my ass off and see a different woman every week, just like I've been doing since I was sixteen years old."

"You handle it. You have your career right where you want it and your priorities straight. You didn't end up a drunk like me."

"I had the benefit of an older brother who fucked things up in a major way, so I got to learn from his mistakes."

Gavin winked, and Mick laughed.

"I love you, asshole."

Then Gavin laughed. "Right back at you, dickhead."

EIGHTEEN

TARA WIGGLED IN HER SEAT, CAUGHT UP IN THE EX-citement of the sold-out crowd. The stadium was packed, even though it was only the first preseason game. But San Francisco had come so close to winning the division championship last season, and the team looked to be even stronger this season with a few free agent signings that would bump up their defense.

And if she was thrilled to be there tonight, Nathan's enthusiasm was off the charts, especially since Mick had gotten them seats on the fifty-yard line where the rest of the families of players sat. Nathan had been wide-eyed and taking it all in since they'd arrived a couple hours before game time, and he hadn't been able to sit still, taking pictures and texting all his friends with the new phone he'd gotten for his birthday. Mick had gotten them an extra ticket so Nathan could bring his new friend, Bobby, another freshman football player and a really nice kid who was also thrilled to be at the game. The two of them had their heads huddled together pointing fingers, talking player stats and pretty much ignoring the fact that Tara was there.

Just as it should be.

She'd settled in, feeling somewhat conspicuous in the Riley number fourteen jersey Mick had given her, but also a little possessive and okay, just a touch warmed to be wearing his name and number on her back, especially since she was sitting with all the wives and girlfriends of the players.

"So, you're Mick's girl."

She turned around and smiled at a cute brunette. "I don't know about that, but yes, we're dating."

The woman held out her hand. "I'm Roseanne Lewis. My husband is Tommy Lewis, number seventy-two. He's right tackle, offensive, and he'll be protecting Mick's butt tonight."

Tara laughed and shook her hand. "Then thank you in advance for Tommy's work." Tara introduced Roseanne to Nathan and Bobby. Roseanne introduced her to the other women seated nearby.

"How long have you and Mick been together?"

That question had come from Sue Shore, a very pregnant adorable woman seated next to her, whose husband Derek was the kicker.

"We met earlier this summer."

"We love Mick. He's great with all our kids. He's never seated a girl here with us before. His mom and dad have been here, and his brother a couple times, but never a girlfriend, so you're a first."

"Is that right?"

"Yeah. You must be special."

She felt that way, and admittedly it felt really good. "When's your baby due?"

"In a month. He feels like any minute though the way he's kicking. Going to be like his daddy."

Tara let out a short laugh, remembering having Nathan inside her and all the nights she couldn't sleep because of his kicks to her ribs. "I think they all feel that way toward the end, don't they?"

"Our daughter was more mellow than this little guy. He's a born kicker."

"I hope he follows in your husband's footsteps then."

Sue giggled. "That would be amazing."

"Kickoff!" one of the women screamed.

Tara had been so busy chatting it up with the ladies that she'd barely noticed the game had started. She put her full attention on it, though, especially since San Francisco's offense was up first, which meant after the kickoff Mick took the field.

And oh, what a spectacular figure he was in his uniform, which fit snugly across his fine ass, and the pads on his shoulders and chest, which made him look impossibly huge.

Tara tensed as he took the first snap from center, handing off to one of his receivers, who ran the ball for four yards. She let out a breath when the tacklers ran right past Mick.

Second down, Mick was under center again, and this time took the snap and dashed several steps directly back, stood there and looked for receivers, then shoveled a quick pass to the running back at his left, who ran for a gain of only two yards.

She knew what was coming with third down and four yards to go. First possession of the game was always a big deal, and Arizona would want to make a statement to San Francisco by making sure they didn't get a first down. Tara could feel the pressure as surely as if she were the one responsible for getting the ball into the hands of a receiver.

Arizona was going to blitz.

Tara gripped the arms of the seat as Mick broke from the huddle and got in the shotgun position, took the snap, and rolled back. The blitz came, and his offensive line held. Mick fired off a long pass toward a receiver downfield.

He caught it! Twenty-two-yard gain.

"Breathe, honey," Roseanne said, rubbing Tara's shoulders. "It's going to be a long game."

Tara laughed. Then exhaled.

The first quarter was tense, with the Sabers putting seven points on the board in their first possession, and Arizona answering with a touchdown of their own right after. But then things settled down a bit, and by halftime the game was tied ten to ten. In the second half Mick came out and threw completion after completion, and the running game looked solid. The defense held, and the Sabers put points on the board. The game ended up being one-sided, with San Francisco coming out victorious. Being preseason, Mick didn't play the entire game, so by the end of the third quarter Tara could relax, though she still rooted for the team.

After the game was over and the crowds had filed out of the stadium, the team gathered with wives and families for a barbecue right on the field, something Nathan was very excited about.

Tara was just happy to get the nail-biting tension of the game over with. Now she could relax.

Or so she thought, since they'd no more gotten down to the field when she saw Elizabeth heading her way, though how the woman could maneuver the turf in those four-inch heels was something Tara just couldn't fathom. Elizabeth clearly did not know the meaning of the word casual. Meanwhile, Tara was quite comfortable in her team jersey, jeans, and tennis shoes, and her lips lifted when she saw Elizabeth's disapproval.

"Tailgating today, Tara?"

Tara was so glad Nathan had met some of the other players' kids around his own age and he and Bobby had already run off to hang with them so he didn't have to put up with Elizabeth's disdain.

"As a matter of fact, I am. Right now. You seem a little over-dressed for it. Be careful you don't break an ankle sinking into the turf."

"I can walk just fine. I'm surprised to see you here."

"Really? Why is that?"

Elizabeth shrugged. "Just figured you'd be out of your league by now. Or Mick would be bored with you. Trust me, honey. It's only a matter of time. I'll keep luring him in with beautiful women, and sooner or later he's going to bite."

Tara crossed her arms. "If you think he's that shallow, have fun fishing."

Tara spotted Mick coming onto the field, so thankfully she moved away from Liz and headed over to him, put her arms around him, and hugged him. "Great game today."

He grinned. "Not bad. We have some things to work on, but it's promising."

"I thought you looked awesome. Your arm is strong, and your pass percentage was top-of-the-line."

He arched a brow, then kissed the tip of her nose. "Keeping track of my stats now?"

"Only in my head."

"Where's Nathan?"

"He's hanging out with D'Juan and Anthony's sons. They play football, too, so Nathan and Bobby have made some new friends."

Mick nodded. "Good. I'm starving. Let's go find food."

The barbecue was wonderful, as were the people, who welcomed her as if she and Mick were a permanent couple. Tara couldn't have asked for a better night for her or for Nathan, though she was still a little worried about Nathan getting attached to everyone.

At this point there was nothing much she could do about it. Her relationship with Mick was either going to work out or it wasn't, and she couldn't shield Nathan from the fallout if it didn't. At this point she had two choices. She could fling herself headlong into whatever she had with Mick and hope for the best, or she could cut and run.

She was scared of option one because the chances of her and Nathan both getting hurt were so great. But option two just wasn't acceptable to her. Mick was part of her life now, and walking away from him would devastate her.

So what the hell was she supposed to do?

For tonight, she ate dinner and tried to enjoy herself, which was damned hard to do, considering her gaze kept drifting to Elizabeth, who seemed to be having a major talk with team owner Irvin Stokes. And in the middle of that conversation, Liz kept pointing to her, then whispering to Mr. Stokes.

Great. Just great. Tara could only imagine what lies Elizabeth was making up about her. Was she putting words in Mr. Stokes's ear about what a bad influence Tara was on Mick? Would she tell the team owner that getting Tara out of Mick's life would be the best thing he could do for the future of the team?

Panic set in when Elizabeth hooked her arm in Mr. Stokes's and both of them headed their way.

"Damn," Tara whispered.

"What's wrong?"

"Liz is bringing Irvin Stokes over here."

"Why is that a problem?" Mick shoved the remnants of his cheeseburger in his mouth, then wiped his hands with his napkin and grinned. "Hey, Irvin."

Irvin Stokes was a billionaire who'd made his money in the financial markets. He was a shrewd businessman, and even though he was creeping up close to eighty years old, he still looked fit, with a head filled with silvery hair and a suit that probably cost more than Tara made in a year.

"Excellent start to the season, Mick."

Stokes stuck out his hand, and Mick shook it. "Thanks. The team looks strong. You managed to bring in some solid players to the defense."

Stokes nodded. "Our free agent signings seemed to shore up our only weaknesses, so I expect great things this year." He turned to Tara. "And this is your new lady? Elizabeth has been telling me about you."

She didn't even want to know what Liz had been saying. Tara shook his hand. "Tara Lincoln."

"Oh, yes. You did our party a couple months ago. Very nice. I was pleased with how it turned out."

"Thank you, Mr. Stokes."

Elizabeth leaned against Stokes like he was gold. "I was telling Irvin that you were an event planner. The wives and girlfriends of the players always put on a charity fund-raiser before the kickoff to the regular season, and I was thinking since this is right up your alley, you'd want to spearhead it this year."

"Oh." Tara turned to Irvin. "Of course. I'd be delighted."

Stokes took her hand between both of his. "Excellent. It's good exposure for the team and for a good cause. This year it's for the summer camps for underprivileged children in the area."

"I'll be happy to help out."

"Your work would be gratis, of course."

"I have no problem with that. I'm always willing to do charity work."

"I'm happy to hear that. Still, it's promotion for your company. I'll have our people get in touch with you. The event will be held the Saturday before the last home preseason game."

"Thank you, Mr. Stokes." She nodded at Elizabeth, who winked at her and walked away with Irvin.

"That was . . . interesting."

"Why?" Mick asked.

"Because Elizabeth doesn't like me. Why would she do that?"

Mick put his arm around her and kissed the top of her head. "Babe, I long ago gave up trying to figure out what the hell motivates Liz to do anything. Don't even try."

She shrugged and leaned against him. "You're right. It's point-less."

But still, something nagged at her. Tara didn't think Liz had suggested her because she liked her or thought Tara was a great event planner. Maybe Liz had done it for Mick because she'd finally figured out that Tara could be of benefit to Mick's career.

Though she doubted it, since Liz had made it clear that getting Tara out of Mick's life would be the best thing for Mick's career.

But it was done now, and Tara was going to be in charge of plan-ning this event. Now she just had to do a kick-ass job and impress the hell out of Irvin Stokes again.

Mick followed Tara home afterward. Nathan had made plans to spend the night at Bobby's house, so Tara dropped them off first. Mick was already in her driveway when she got there.

"Tired?" she asked when she opened the door. He shut and locked the door, then pulled her into his arms.

"Not at all. A game always revs me up."

She slid into his embrace. "Is that right? So what do you do when you don't have a willing female in your arms to help you out with all that excess energy?"

He picked her up in his arms and carried her upstairs. "Jack off."

The visual of it made her tingle all over. "I'd like to see that."

"Would you." He set her on her feet at the side of her bed.

"Are you serious?"

"Yes. Sit down."

She sat on the edge of the bed, her fingers curling into the bed-spread as Mick pulled his shirt off. The sight of his body never failed to arouse her, and especially so after watching him play tonight. She'd always been a football fan, but now that she knew Mick, knew his work ethic, and had seen him play, she knew what went into how he took care of his body. It was his job to make sure he stayed healthy, and he took it seriously. And boy howdy, did it ever show.

He was muscled in all the right places, lean in all the spots he should be, and she had to resist going to him just to run her hands over the planes and angles that had been so perfectly sculpted by all the hours he spent running and working out at the gym.

She leaned back on her hands as he undid his pants, toed off his shoes, and shrugged out of his briefs and pants, kicking them to the side. His cock was already erect, and he fisted it in his hand, sliding it slow and easy.

"What do you think about when you do that?" she asked.

"Women."

"Women you've had already, or women you'd like to have?"

"Both."

He kept his gaze on her as he slid his hand up and down the shaft. The room grew warmer, so she kicked off her shoes and pulled her top over her head. "And what do you imagine about these women? Do you think about them just . . . standing around?"

"Not really."

"So you think about having sex with them." She popped the button open on her jeans, then slowly drew the zipper down, her gaze fixated on the lazy up-and-down movements of his hand on his cock, the way his thumb circled the wide head. Her breathing quickened as she shed her pants, leaving her in only her panties and bra.

"Sometimes I think about having sex with them." He squeezed his cock in his fist. "Sometimes I picture them lying on the bed, naked and touching themselves."

Tara got up on her knees and reached for the clasp of her bra, popped it open, and pulled the bra off, casting it onto the bed. "So you think about these women masturbating."

"Yeah." He gripped his cock harder.

She swept her hands over her breasts. "Seeing a woman touch herself turns you on."

"Hell, yes, it does."

She grasped her nipples between her thumbs and forefingers, plucking them, the sensation rocketing to her pussy. Caressing herself like this, watching Mick touch his own cock, was the most arousing thing she'd ever experienced. She continued to touch her breasts with one hand, but let the other slide down her rib cage and belly, enjoying the tease as she made her way to her panties. She slid her fingers around the edge of her panties, while Mick wrapped a strangled grip on his cock and upped the pace a little faster.

"I like watching you," she whispered, then tucked her hand inside her panties and cupped her sex.

"How does it feel?"

"Hot. Steamy hot. And wet."

"Let me see."

She swallowed to coat her parched throat and drew her panties down, adjusting herself with her legs dangling over the side of the bed. She grabbed a pillow to prop her head up so she could still watch Mick, then laid her palm over her sex, letting her fingers tap along the outside of her pussy lips.

"Your pussy is wet," he said, moving closer to the bed.

"Yes."

"Tell me what you think about when you get yourself off."

"I think about someone coming into the room unexpectedly and finding me doing this."

He curled his fingers around his cock and drove his hand to the tip, using his thumb to slide over the head. "Yeah? And what happens when he finds you?"

"He stands there for a while and watches me." She rubbed her fingers up and over her clit, coating the bud with her juices, then slid her hand back down, palming her clit and lifting up as she experienced an explosion of sensation. "But then he undresses, begins to stroke his cock just like you're doing."

"And then what?"

"He comes over to the side of the bed." Tara slid two fingers inside her pussy and began to fuck herself.

Mick leaned over the bed and rubbed his cock head against her thigh.

"Can you hear it?" she asked.

"Yeah." He was panting.

"Don't you wish that was your cock inside me, fucking me?"

"Yes. Is that what the guy in your fantasies does?"

She lifted her gaze to his. "Yes. He pulls me to the edge of the bed and plunges his cock in me, then fucks me hard until I scream because I'm coming so hard I can't stand it, until he's coming so hard he can't help himself and he yells out my name."

Mick grabbed her ankles and pulled her ass to the edge of the bed, ripped a condom from the pocket of his discarded pants, and put it on. Tara braced her feet on the side of the bed and lifted as Mick thrust inside her with one hard push.

And she did cry out, because she'd been waiting for it, anticipating it, and it was so damn good she raked her nails across his arm. He held tight to her hips and fucked his cock inside her, his balls slapping her ass in a hard and fast rhythm that made her whimper and cry out his name as she demanded more and more.

He reached down and began to rub her clit, furiously taking her to the edge, but this time not letting her even stop to drag in a ragged breath. She went over in a hurry, screaming and digging her nails into his arm as she came.

"Mick! I'm coming. Oh, God, Mick, I'm coming."

"Fuck, yes. I'm coming. Tara!"

He did yell out her name as he dropped her legs and pulled her hips against his. He shouted with his orgasm, pumping against her time and time again with his release, then dragged them both onto the bed as he curled into her and buried his face against her neck.

Tara tangled her fingers in Mick's hair, and he lifted, kissing her with a deep, intense kiss that warmed and comforted her in the aftermath of such incredible bliss.

"Am I crushing you?" he asked.

"No. This just feels good."

He inhaled and let it out, then gathered her close. "I love being with you, babe. A lot."

"I love being with you, too."

"You're the best thing that's come into my life in a long time, Tara. Thank you."

She swept her arm across his back and smiled, hoping it could always be this good between them.

Maybe this was what falling in love was supposed to feel like. Scary and exhilarating at the same time.

And maybe it was okay to let it happen.

NINETEEN

TARA HAD NEVER WORKED HARDER IN HER LIFE FOR something she wasn't getting paid for. The few weeks of preseason had flown by, and she'd actually been grateful for the games Mick had out of town. Because when Mick was around she wanted to be with him. And he wanted to be with her, which admittedly she liked an awful lot. It kind of reminded her of being a teenager again, this need to be with someone so much it hurt. But that kind of longing didn't lend itself to focusing on the job at hand, so Mick leaving town for the weekend was timely. It had given her time to work with the wives, girlfriends, and volunteers who were helping her put this charity event together.

They had decided on a carnival for the kids, complete with rides and games. The venue had been selected, the weather was thankfully going to be perfect, and donations and volunteers had been pouring in. Amazing what people were willing to do for both a worthy cause and to be associated with a prominent, successful football

team. Since the last preseason game was tomorrow, many of the team members would be present. They were going to sign footballs for the kids, which would bring the media in for photo opportunities and hopefully bring attention to the charity.

The past few weeks had given Tara the opportunity to get to know the women from the team a lot better. She was quickly becoming friends with the majority of them, which meant if she and Mick broke up, she was going to miss them all. Then again, who was to say she couldn't remain friends with them?

Sue Shore had gone into labor and had her baby last week. Tara and several of the other team ladies had gone to Sue's house a few days after she'd had little Timmy, all nine pounds ten ounces of him. At twenty-three inches long it was no wonder he'd been keeping her up all night kicking her. But Sue was thrilled despite being exhausted after eighteen hours of labor. And the baby was adorable. Tara had held him for a brief few moments, and those pangs of female hormones had kicked into overdrive. It had been a long time since Nathan had been a baby.

"You planning on having any more?" Sue had asked her.

Tara's head had shot up. "I've never even thought about it."

"Well, you know, Mick does love kids." Marvella, one of the player's wives, had given her a knowing smile.

Good Lord. Her and Mick having babies? The thought had never occurred to her. "Mick and I are just dating."

"Uh-huh. He seems to like your son."

"Nathan's a teenager."

"So?" Heather Swanson scooped up little Timmy and sighed. "Mick's been around all our kids, from infant to high school age. And he's great with all sizes. He's going to be a wonderful father someday."

"Yes, I'm sure he will be."

"And since you're the only woman he's ever brought around . . ."

Tara rolled her eyes. "It doesn't mean he intends to marry me and have babies with me."

But the thought lingered all through the week. Silly thought. Marriage and babies and a family with her and Mick and Nathan and a child they created together.

Really dumb thought. Mick had his life, which was football and beautiful young women. Her life was her career and her son, who was now fifteen. The last thing she wanted was to start over again. She was thirty years old. In a few short years Nathan would be off to college, and she'd be free to focus on her business, unencumbered. She'd sacrificed so much to raise Nathan, to put herself through school, to climb the ladder, and get her business off the ground.

She didn't need a husband, and she sure as hell didn't need to start over at ground zero again, saddled with a child.

A child with Mick's deep blue eyes and dark hair. A daughter, maybe. Or another boy. Someone for Mick to watch grow, to toss a football with.

Good Lord. Put a baby in her arms, and her hormones got all whacked out. That's all it was. She and Mick were dating, and she was suddenly having babies with him?

Right, like that was going to happen. Her baby days were long over.

Focus, Tara, focus.

With effort, she regrouped and turned her full attention to the charity event. The rides had all been set up, the booths were in place, there was plenty of food, and all the players had arrived. The kids were pouring in, and the media was spread throughout the fairgrounds. Having the venue in one of the East Bay cities allowed for easy transportation, the chance for great attendance, plenty of parking, and great weather.

She'd put all the wives and girlfriends working the carnival in pink team jerseys today so she'd be able to spot them. She'd given

Nathan a red and white team jersey to wear since Mick had told her Nathan could hang next to him today, something Nathan had no problem with for obvious reasons. Nathan would be helping out the team by running for drinks, pens, opening up boxes of footballs and whatever else they might need, and assisting the team staffers. He was ecstatic just to be hanging out with the team today, so she was sure he'd act the gofer for anything they wanted, and Tara was happy Mick would be keeping an eye on him so she wouldn't have to worry about where he was or what he was doing. One thing off her list.

Now she could focus on the charity's kids, who were so excited about the carnival she could see it on their faces. They were all troubled youth ranging from elementary school age all the way to middle school and early high school age, so having a free day to just have some fun, ride the Tilt-A-Whirl or the Scrambler or the roller coaster, walk through the fun house, play skee ball or try to hit the ducks in the shooting booth would be a great way to decompress from their everyday lives. And they'd have the bonus of some one-on-one time with the team players. The kids had brought their parents or foster parents and siblings along, so it wasn't long before the fairground was full, plus the charity organizers and staffers were there, too. Tara was running from activity to activity to make sure everyone was having a good time.

She stopped off at the players' booth, which had a huge line of kids waiting to have their pictures taken and footballs autographed. Mick was hanging out with some of the guys.

"Hey," she said. "Everything going okay?"

He kissed her and put his arm around her. "Going great here. How about you? You look hot and sweaty."

She laughed and pushed her hair away from her damp face. "Busy. Do you all need anything?"

"Quit worrying about us. We have team staffers here to take care of us. And try to relax. I wandered around a little, and everything looks perfect."

She inhaled, let it out. "I'll relax when it's over." Her phone buzzed. She grabbed it from her pocket, listened, and laid her hand on Mick's chest. "Gotta go and take care of something."

"Try not to kill yourself over this."

She laughed and darted off, met up with Roseanne and a few of the other wives, and they took care of the food serving issue. Once that was resolved, she wandered through the fairgrounds to make sure the kids were being entertained. Everyone seemed happy.

"Miss Lincoln?"

She whirled around, and a microphone was shoved in her face.

"Alan Terlin, Channel 8 news. We'd like to interview you for the local broadcast."

"Oh. You don't want to interview me. Why don't you go talk to the team."

His lips lifted. "Already did that. They pointed me in your direction, said you put this event together."

"I'm just the event planner. You should really talk to the head of the foundation and the people who work there. They are the heart and soul behind making sure these kids lead a balanced life—education, social, and family." She looked around, hoping like hell she could find someone from the charity, nearly crying with relief when she spotted Carmen Sanchez. "Here, let me get Carmen for you."

She hurried over to Carmen and dragged the newspeople to her. Carmen, not a hair out of place despite running around even more than Tara was, graciously agreed to say a few words about the foundation and what they offered kids who'd had a rough start and disadvantages. Tara backed away and let Carmen have the face time on camera.

"Smooth escape."

Tara turned and faced Elizabeth, who managed to look unruffled and cool in her sleeveless top and Capri pants and kitten heels.

"What? No power suit today?"

"I have causal clothes, Tara."

"Could have fooled me. I thought you always dressed like a shark on the attack." Even in casual attire—which looked designer and expensive—Liz was still put together impeccably.

"You should have done the interview. It would be good for the team. For Mick."

"You do the interview. I'm hot and sweaty and look like hell. And the foundation can make the team look good."

"The foundation will make the foundation look good."

Tara shook her head. "Not my area. I'll let you find someone to make the team look good."

Liz shrugged her shoulders. "If you insist."

"I do."

Glad to be rid of Liz, Tara moved off to the midway where she found a group of kids trying to best the carnies in games of water balloon darts, ring toss, and milk bottle throw. She eyed the vendors carefully, stopping at each one for long enough to be sure there was a decent percentage of the kids winning. Mr. Stokes was funding these vendors nicely, and the kids should have a good chance of winning.

They were. Satisfied, she moved on.

Food was plentiful in the eating area, and there was enough to drink there as well as at all the drink stops throughout the fairgrounds. Everything seemed to be under control, so Tara figured she'd take a minute or two and stop in at the players' area, which was still filled to bursting with kids, players, and media.

Liz was there, giving some face time to reporters. She had a group of kids hanging with Mick. Tara was about to think the woman had a nice bone in her body, then thought twice. She was pushing Mick, making sure Mick looked good. Tara rolled her eyes and decided to come back later, but then stopped when she realized that behind Liz were the kids she was talking about while she was being interviewed, and that Nathan stood next to Mick.

Nathan was being photographed along with several other kids as Liz gave that interview.

"These kids come from less than positive backgrounds," Liz said, motioning behind her, deliberately inclining her head toward Nathan. "Some have been abused, some have parents who've been involved in drugs. Some live in foster care, and some are just economically disadvantaged. The foundation and the team have set up this event to give these kids something positive in their lives, when they haven't had many positive things to look forward to."

Liz turned to Nathan and motioned him over. Nathan, obviously not knowing what the hell was going on, grinned back at Liz and came over. The cameras focused on him.

"Are you having a good time today?" Liz asked.

Nathan, looking utterly bashful and camera struck, nodded. "Uh, yeah. Having a great time."

And then Liz motioned Mick over, and Mick put his arm around Nathan's shoulders. The entire thing made Nathan look like one of the troubled kids, and Mick was offering up the hero's helping hand.

Tara's blood boiled. That fucking bitch. She stood there, her feet rooted to the asphalt, not knowing what to do. Ripping Nathan out of there would cause a scene and would only make matters worse, embarrassing Nathan and herself in the process. She refused to give Liz the satisfaction. And Mick seemed oblivious to the entire thing, playing to Nathan and the cameras as if he knew exactly what was going on.

Maybe he did know what was going on. Or maybe he just didn't care.

Surely the man wasn't that clueless. Had he been in on it the en-

tire time? He and Liz worked closely together. He knew every time there was a promo op. Surely Liz had cleared this with Mick, so he had to have known.

Nausea bubbled up, and she palmed her stomach. The sun and the knowledge that Mick would use Nathan like that made her dizzy. She needed to sit down, but she refused to walk away, not when Nathan was so vulnerable.

Fortunately, the cameras soon moved away, and Tara could breathe again. She wanted nothing more than to grab her son and run like hell, but she was responsible for this event, and she wouldn't let the foundation down. So she swallowed her anger and kept her focus for the remainder of the afternoon, making sure the rest of the event went off without a hitch.

When the last of the kids had piled back into the buses and everything was wrapped up, she grabbed Nathan.

"We're leaving."

Nathan frowned. "What? Why? Mick said we'd go out to eat."

"Don't ask questions. We need to go. Now."

Mick was next to her in a second. "What's wrong?"

She couldn't even look at him. "I have to go. We have to go."

He grasped her arm. "Tara. What's the matter?"

She shook her head. "I need to get Nathan out of here."

"Is something wrong?"

Her head shot up, and she could barely meet his gaze. "You know what's wrong," she whispered. "How could you do this?"

His eyes widened. "What the hell are you talking about?"

She shook her head. "I don't want to talk about this."

She moved away from the crowd of players and wives and girl-friends, taking Nathan with her. "Mom, what's the matter with you? Why are we leaving?"

"We're done here." She was done here. She was done with Mick.

She passed by Elizabeth and saw the look of triumph on her face.

Yes. Liz had won. Finally. Tara was finished with Mick. With all of this.

MICK THREW HIS KEYS ON TOP OF THE TABLE NEAR THE front door, flopped into the chair, and grabbed the remote. He turned on the TV, needing background noise to drown out his own thoughts, because all he'd been able to think about for the past several hours had been Tara.

She'd been upset. Even more than upset. She was mad as hell. At him. And he had no idea why. He'd tried calling her cell. She wouldn't answer, despite repeated attempts.

He drove by her house and rang her bell, but she wouldn't answer, even though he knew damn well she was inside. Short of busting down the door, which he didn't think was a very good idea, there wasn't much he could do.

So now he sat here like a dumb-ass, flipping through channels and trying to figure out what the fuck he'd done to make her so mad.

They'd barely even had any time together today. She'd been busy all day with the event, and she'd done an incredible job. He'd been so proud of her, and so had Irvin Stokes, who'd come looking for her. Mick had made up an excuse for her, saying she was probably wrapping things up. Earlier in the day she'd been a little harried, but smiling and happy. And then boom—disaster. But he hadn't said anything or done anything to make her mad at him. Not mad enough to storm off without an explanation or refuse to take his calls or answer the door.

He didn't get it.

The news was on, and they had a report about the event. Mick clicked up the volume to hear Liz talking up the foundation. Mick saw himself, Nathan, and a few other kids behind Elizabeth while she talked about the kids. He leaned forward when Liz motioned toward Nathan, looked at him, then described the problems kids in the foundation had, from abuse to drugs to everything in between. And then Liz brought Nathan forward, then Mick.

What. The. Fuck. Liz might as well have hung a sign on Nathan and used him as a poster child for damaged children. And there Mick was, smiling and slinging his arm around Nathan, totally clueless about what Elizabeth had just done.

Son of a bitch. She'd used Nathan. Hell, she'd used him, too. And Mick would wager a year's salary that Tara had seen it and thought he and Liz had cooked it all up as a promotion and even planned to use Nathan in it.

Fuck! He threw the remote across the room and stood, shoving his hand through his hair. He knew Liz was a master manipulator, but he'd never known her to go this far. He never minded her using him or an actress or model to get a good promo shot, but a kid? Oh, hell no.

He grabbed his cell phone and dialed Liz's number. Even though it was late, he knew she would answer.

"What's up?"

"Get over here. Now."

She laughed. "I'm kind of busy here, Mick."

"I don't give a shit how busy you are. Get your ass over here."

There was a pause. "Here being your place?"

"Yeah."

"A problem?"

"You have less than an hour."

"I'll be right there."

He continued to pace the living room, then decided he should fix himself something to drink, realizing he'd really like a shot of whiskey. His gut churned, and the need for alcohol made his hands shake.

He clenched his fists and took a deep breath, then went to fix a glass of iced tea.

He was on his second glass when Elizabeth knocked at the door. Glass in hand, he went to the door and opened it. She strolled in, hair pulled up, earrings sparkling in the overhead light of his living room. She had on some fancy dress and heels.

"You tore me away from a very important business dinner, honey. Now what's wrong?"

"What the hell were you doing at the carnival today?"

She arched a brow. "I have no idea what you're talking about. Care to be more specific?"

He hit play on the news spot he'd recorded. Liz watched, then turned back to him. "Okay. So?"

"So? Are you kidding me? You used Nathan."

She shrugged. "He was there. With you. It was convenient. One kid is just as good as another."

Mick sucked in a deep breath, never as close to wanting to punch a woman in the face as he was right then. "Elizabeth. Listen very closely to me. You hurt Tara. And in doing so, you hurt Nathan. You put his face erroneously on national television without her permission and used him to promote me and the team. She's furious. At me."

"So? I've been telling you—and her—for months that it's never going to work between the two of you. She just doesn't get it." She pointed at the television. "That was great promo. You with underprivileged kids. Great emotional angle. Come on, Mick. Awesome bonus points."

He finally grabbed her arms, wanting to shake her so badly he had to grit his teeth to keep from doing so. "No, you don't get it. She's important to me. What you think—or want—isn't. I love her. And if I lose her over this, you'll regret it. Do you understand that, Elizabeth? Do you have any idea how much I hate you for what you've done? Right now you are about two seconds away from having your *ass fired*."

He'd said the last two words loud enough to get her attention, because her eyes widened. "What?"

"Fucking fix this, Elizabeth, or you're history. I've had it with you deciding what's best for me and my career. You haven't known what's best for me for a long time now. If you had really known what was good for me, you'd have had your goddamn eyes open over the past couple months and seen what I needed." He shoved her away from him. "You want to know what's best for me? Tara is best for me. Nathan is best for me. They make me happy, something you obviously don't understand, since you don't have a goddamn heart."

She'd gone pale, her normal snobbish bearing seeming to shrink. Good. He didn't give a shit how she felt.

"Get your ass out of my house right now. You have until tomorrow to figure out a way to fix this massive fuckup, or I will fire you. Do you understand?"

She nodded, rapidly blinking back tears as she grabbed her bag and headed for the door. "I got it. I'll fix this, Mick. Don't worry."

He held the door open for her, and she hurried through it. He slammed it behind her with so much force the pictures on the wall rattled.

God, he'd never wanted to hurt someone more than he wanted to hurt Elizabeth. And he'd never once in his life laid a hand on a woman. But she'd infuriated him and messed with his life. And no one did that and got away unscathed.

Now he had to do something to repair the damage she'd caused. Considerable damage. Maybe irreparable damage.

TWENTY

TARA SAT IN THE COOL DARKNESS OF HER LIVING ROOM, her knees pulled up to her chest, trying to keep the headache that had started last night from turning into a full-blown migraine.

Nathan, her thankfully oblivious son, had no idea what had set her off yesterday. And she wasn't about to burst his bubble about Mick. Not just yet. Later, when she was stronger, when she'd shored up her defenses, she'd sit him down and explain to him that people sometimes weren't who you thought they were, that sometimes they couldn't live up to your expectations.

She would have to break her son's heart. But her job as his mother was to hit him with the cold slap of reality and force him to step outside the bubble of fantasy that he—that they—had been living in for the past couple months. It was her own fault for trying to grab the brass ring, for thinking she could have it all—

great career, great kid, great guy. She should have known it wasn't possible.

Nathan had gone to the last preseason football game tonight. No reason to deny him the enjoyment of it, at least one last time. She'd given up her seat to one of Nathan's friends, and the friend's dad had taken them. He was spending the night at his friend's house, so she had a reprieve. She hadn't watched the game, didn't even want to think about football right now.

She just wanted to hide out in the dark and not think. Unfortunately, all she'd been doing was thinking, and her mind was on overload. Was it too much to ask for a few hours of peace?

The knock at the door said that it apparently *was* too much to ask. She pushed off the chair and inched over to the door, determined not to open it if Mick was there.

No one was there. Huh. She pulled the door open and reached down to pick up the box that lay on her doorstep. It was too late at night for a delivery service, so someone must have hand delivered it. There was no name on the box other than hers. She closed and locked the door, brought the box into the living room, and grabbed her scissors to rip it open.

Inside was a DVD with an envelope on top. Scrawled across the top of the envelope in lovely penmanship was—*Tara, Please Read Before Viewing.*

She opened the envelope and pulled out a sheet of linen paper, opened it, and read the handwritten note.

Tara,

Sorry seems like such an inadequate word, but I hope the video helps. My humblest apologies for what I did to harm your son and you. I have no excuse for my behavior. I let my goals and ambitions blind me,

*and I hope someday you can forgive me. Please view the video. This will
be on all the news channels tomorrow at the six and eleven broadcasts,
as well as all the prime sports broadcasts. Print media will be given the
story as well with photos and write-up.*

    Again, I'm deeply sorry.

Elizabeth

Tara gritted her teeth, dropped the note, and shoved the box to
the side. She stood and walked into the kitchen to pour a glass of
wine, her heart ramming double time against her chest.

The sheer balls on that woman to think she could send some
flimsy apology and expect Tara would be fine with it. She didn't care
what was on that video. Nothing could erase what Elizabeth had
done to Nathan and to her. She'd done it deliberately to embarrass
Tara. Tara could handle anything Elizabeth dished out. She was an
adult and could hold her own. But to bring her child into it was un-
derhanded, dirty and uncalled-for, and utterly unforgivable.

Another knock on the door, and Tara slammed her wine goblet
down on the kitchen counter. She'd bet anything it was Elizabeth.
Hell, she hoped it was Elizabeth. She'd love to tell the woman exactly what she thought of her.

She flung the door open, and her words caught in her throat as
she saw Mick standing there.

"What do you want?"

"Five minutes."

Dammit. She stood in front of the door, blocking his entrance.
"There's nothing you can say I want to hear."

He laid his hand against the brick. "Five minutes. That's all I
want, Tara."

He looked as miserable as she felt. God, she wanted to believe
that look was sincere. "Five minutes."

She moved aside, and he came in while she closed the door.

She stood near the door, her arms wrapped around her middle. "Start talking."

He turned. "I didn't know what Elizabeth was doing until I saw it on the news last night."

"How could you not know what she was doing? She was right in front of you. You pulled Nathan next to you when she pointed to you."

"I know how it looked, but it was so noisy there. Nathan and I were busy grabbing T-shirts and footballs, goofing off, and talking to the kids and the other guys, mugging for pictures. We weren't paying any attention to the cameras or what Liz was doing. I thought she was promoting the foundation. I had no idea until I saw it on the news. I was sick after I saw that news clip. And I was fucking furious with Elizabeth." He moved toward her. "I've never wanted to lay hands on a woman in anger until I saw that, Tara. I had to pull myself back because I wanted to hurt her. I'm so sorry."

He was hurting as badly as she was. "She sent me a video."

"What?"

"She sent me a video and a note. Said she was sorry. It's over on the chair."

He went over and grabbed the note, read it, then panned his gaze over to her again. "What's on the video?"

She shrugged. "I don't know. I haven't looked at it yet."

"Do you want to?"

"I guess so."

Mick put the video in her DVD player. It was scenes cut from the carnival, with a voice-over from a very prominent sportscaster talking about how the Sabers—and Mick—gave tirelessly to the foundation, and how much the charity stood to benefit from the carnival.

It was the same thing, with Nathan and Mick highlighted in the video.

Nothing had changed. What was her point?

Except then it did change, with the sportscaster talking about Mick, his girlfriend Tara Lincoln, and Tara's son Nathan and how they unselfishly gave of their time planning this event. He went on to say Tara was a local event planner and donated her time in preparing the event. He talked about Nathan being a sophomore at a local high school, briefly described the school, and showed a picture of the school and the team. He explained Nathan was a quarterback, and mentioned how Mick had started out as a quarterback, and he went on to make comparisons between the two.

Dear God. Nathan would love that.

Tara moved into the living room and sat on the sofa, watching how Liz had completely turned around a negative spot into something positive and beneficial. Nathan would come out of this looking like a hero. Tears filled her eyes, and she swept her gaze to Mick.

"You did this?"

"I told Liz she fucked things up. Bad. I told her to fix it."

"Looks like she did."

"I told her I'd fire her if she didn't make it right."

Tara lifted her hand to her mouth. "You threatened to fire her?"

"I did."

"Mick, what she did . . . that's amazing."

"She damn well owed it to you and Nathan to make it amazing. She had no right to manipulate you and Nathan that way. I won't tolerate anyone who works for me treating the people I love that way."

"People you . . . what did you say?"

He stood, went over to her, and grabbed her hands, pulling her to stand. "Come on, Tara. Surely by now you've figured out how I feel about you."

"No, I had no idea. We've never talked about it."

"Well, let's talk about it." His lips lifted in a hopeful smile.

Oh, God. Her mind was awash in all the pain, in what this could mean. In what she'd hoped for. And in the agony she'd been through today. All she could think about was the pain and the fear. She pushed against him. "No, don't. I . . . can't, Mick."

His smile died. "What? Why? I just told you I loved you."

"Don't." She shook her head. "I can't do this. Please. You have to leave."

He frowned, tried to hold her, but she stepped back, needing distance, needing him to go.

"Tara. It's going to be okay, I promise. I'll make sure that video is run everywhere."

"It's not that, Mick. You don't understand. Tell Liz I appreciate her making amends, but you and me? I can't do this anymore."

She backed farther away, but he wouldn't allow it, kept following her.

"What do you mean, you can't do this? I say I love you, and you push me away? I don't get it."

"We've had a great time this summer, Mick. But it's over. Your life and mine just don't mesh. I have my career and Nathan. You have your career. And the two just don't fit well."

She'd hit the front door, and he was in front of her now. She had nowhere else to go. He didn't touch her, but his body was inches from hers. "We fit. Perfectly."

She shook her head. "No, we don't. I can't live in your world, and neither can my son. Your life is parties and trips and magazine covers and the news and it's just not what I want for Nathan."

"It doesn't have to be that way, Tara. That was just Liz building up my image."

"And you need that for your career. But I need a little breathing room. I appreciate everything you've done for me and for Nathan. Now I just need some space. Nathan will be starting school soon, and he needs to focus on that, not on your crazy lifestyle."

"It can be like that."

The tears stung her eyes and she blinked them back. "Please go."

"Do you love me, Tara?"

Her heart wrenched as she lied to him. "No. I had fun with you this summer, but I don't love you, Mick."

He gave her a curt nod. "Okay."

She opened the door for him, and he walked away without looking at her. She shut the door and locked it, then rested her head on it, listening to the sound of his car starting up and driving away.

She let the tears come then. She was doing the right thing. For Nathan and for herself.

But why did it hurt so much?

MICK SAT IN THE VISITOR'S LOCKER ROOM AFTER THE opening game. He'd mentally and physically prepared and given his all for his team today. And they'd won, thirty-seven to seventeen over Saint Louis. He'd given postgame interviews to the media, put his best winning swagger on, rehashed the great plays, talked with optimism about the upcoming season and his thoughts on how well he thought his team would do. He'd done everything required of him, and when the players and media left, he'd let it all crumble around him.

A week after Tara had thrown him out of her life he still couldn't let her go.

He loved her. And goddamn it, she loved him, too. He knew she did, and he wasn't going to let her toss it all away just because she was scared.

"What the hell are you doing in here all by yourself?"

He smiled and turned to see Gavin leaning against the wall inside the door.

"Shouldn't you be playing baseball?"

"My game was earlier today in Kansas City, so I got in a while ago. Heard about you and Tara. Sorry."

"Mom blabs."

Gavin pushed off the wall and sat down on the bench next to him. "She cares. You know how she is with us. If we're hurting, she hurts."

Mick didn't say anything.

"You love her?"

"I do."

"But she doesn't love you."

Mick tilted his head toward Gavin. "She does love me. She's scared. This whole thing has freaked her out."

"Man, I don't know jack about this love thing. She loves you, so she kicked you to the curb?"

"I hurt her."

"Liz hurt her."

"No, that's on me. I should have put some reins on Elizabeth. She thought any PR was good for me. I should have been monitoring what she was doing. Plus I knew Liz didn't like Tara. I wasn't focused, wasn't paying attention. When you love someone, it's your job to protect them. And I didn't do my job."

"It's not all your fault, man. You can't be everything to everybody."

"That's where you're wrong, Gavin. I should have seen this coming, and I didn't. I have to own it. I just have to figure out how to make it right. And I don't know if I can."

Gavin laid his arm over Mick's shoulders. "I've never seen you give up on anything. You've fucked up a lot of things in your life."

Mick laughed. "Thanks."

Gavin gave him a wry grin. "You know what I mean. You've dug yourself up from below the dirt before, Mick. And if you love Tara, then don't give up on her. If she's scared or hurt, then make it right."

"I'll try. I have to try. She means everything to me."

"Then quit sitting here like a whiny pussy and go do something about it."

Mick laughed. "Thanks for the pep talk."

"That's why I'm here."

The door opened. Mick and Gavin both lifted their heads as Elizabeth walked through.

"I assume you're decent."

Mick clenched his fists at the sound of Elizabeth's voice. She hadn't tried to contact him since that night when he'd threatened to fire her. Wise move on her part.

Gavin turned to Mick and lifted his brows.

"Gavin, I didn't know you'd be here."

"Just came by to say hi to Mick."

Elizabeth strolled in, looking calm and beautiful as usual in a gray business suit, high heels, her hair pulled back, and two diamond earrings sparkling in the lights of the locker room.

"Need a ride to the hotel? Bus will be leaving for the airport soon."

He turned to face her. "No."

"I need to talk to you."

"This isn't a good time."

"It's as good a time as any." She looked over at Gavin. "Can I have a word with your brother alone?"

"Anything you have to say to me you can say in front of Gavin."

Gavin stood, leaned against the lockers, and crossed his arms, looking amused.

Elizabeth looked from Gavin to Mick. Her easy demeanor vanished.

"Okay, fine." She turned her attention on Mick. "Look, I know I screwed up. I'm sorry. Did you see the sportscast? I fixed things."

"You did. Tara appreciated it."

She inhaled, blew out a breath. "I'm glad. I'm sorry, Mick. It won't happen again. I've always been interested in doing what's best for your career, in seeing you rise to the top."

He zipped up his bag, then lifted his gaze to her. "You've always been interested in making sure your clients earn top dollar, so in return you can earn top dollar. You want your clients to be cream of the crop because it makes you look good. Frankly, Liz, I'm not sure if you're more interested in making us look good, or yourself."

She blanched. "That's not true. I only want what's best for you."

"If you cared about what was best for me, you would have known Tara was good for me. You would have cared about how I felt about her. You would have cared about Nathan's welfare. All you cared about was getting Tara and Nathan out of my life so you could shove the next actress or model on my arm for a photo op."

She lifted her hand to her chest. "No. I do care about you, Mick. I always have. I might not have done this right, but I do care about you. And Gavin. And all my clients."

"Bullshit. You love the money, the prestige, and the power. You don't give a shit about your clients. And you sure as hell don't give a shit about me, Elizabeth."

Mick picked up his bag and shifted his gaze to Gavin. "Give me a ride to Mom and Dad's? I'll take a later plane home. Figure I should stop by and visit."

Gavin nodded. "Sure."

He headed toward the door, stopped in front of Elizabeth.

"According to my contract I have to give you thirty days' notice. Consider it given. You're fired, Elizabeth."

Liz gasped.

Mick walked out, leaving Gavin alone with Liz.

She sat on the bench, her chin at her chest.

Gavin didn't know what to say to make her feel better. Hell, she probably didn't deserve to feel better. She'd screwed over his brother and Tara and Nathan. She deserved this.

She lifted her head, and tears shimmered in her eyes.

Elizabeth was the toughest woman he'd ever known. Nothing rocked her. In all the years he'd known her, he'd never seen her cry.

"I didn't mean for this to happen," she said, her voice barely a whisper. Gavin wasn't sure she was even talking to him.

"No, I imagine you didn't. You're going to take a hit losing Mick as a client."

She shook her head. "Not that. I didn't mean to hurt him, Gavin. He's not just a client. He's my friend and has been for a very long time. Or . . . was my friend. He isn't now. I've lost clients before. Losing his friendship will hurt me more than anything."

She lifted her gaze to his, the shimmer of tears making his gut clench.

"I don't have many friends." She let out a soft laugh. "I think I'm beginning to understand why."

She stood and came over to him, her eyes liquid pools of blue. Her body came so close to his her breasts brushed against his chest. She lifted a shaky hand to his face and swept her fingers across his jaw, then traced his bottom lip with the tip of her finger.

"Just in case," she whispered, then lifted up on her toes and brushed her lips to his. Her mouth was soft, and the tip of her tongue touched against his. It was a light kiss, with the promise of more.

He had to resist the urge to pull her against him and crush her to him, to deepen the kiss. A sudden need to have her, to fully taste her, rocked him back on his heels.

Oh, yeah. He wanted more. He reached for her, but she stepped back and her lips lifted.

"I've always wanted to do that," she said, then turned and walked out the door.

Well, hell. What was that about?

And why did he want to go after her? Why did he want to pull her into his arms and take that kiss a step farther?

Why did he care?

He blew out a breath and went to catch up to Mick.

MICK FIGURED HIS PARENTS WOULD BE IN BED WHEN HE and Gavin came in.

The house was quiet and dark.

"You staying?" he asked Gavin as he used his key to open the front door.

Gavin shrugged. "Maybe. For moral support."

Mick arched a brow. "You never stay here. You have your own place."

"Didn't say I was spending the night in my old room or anything. You know how it is. Too much hearth and home is smothering." Gavin pushed past him and headed down the hall. "I need a beer."

Mick shook his head and followed Gavin into the kitchen. "What do you want? Soda or water?"

"Soda."

Gavin tossed him a can.

Mick tapped on the top of the can while Gavin twisted the top off a bottle of beer and took a couple long swallows.

"So you fired Elizabeth. You'd better get the word out that you need a new agent pronto."

Mick popped the top off his soda can and sipped it. "No hurry. I'm good for awhile. I don't need any vultures knocking down my door while I'm busy trying to play football. Besides, I need to get my personal life sorted out first. The agent thing can wait."

"I guess it can. Liz looked devastated."

Mick shrugged. "She'll get over it."

"Want me to fire her, too?"

"Not unless she pisses you off."

Gavin took a long swallow of his beer, then a smile lifted his lips. "Pissed-off isn't the description I'd use."

"I thought I heard voices down here. Oh and look, it's both my boys."

"Hi, Mom." Mick stood and wrapped his mother up in a bear hug.

She went over and hugged and kissed Gavin, then sat at the table. "What are you doing here? I thought you'd have to fly back to San Francisco right after your game."

"Girl trouble," Gavin said.

Mick shot him a scathing look.

"Well, it's true, isn't it?"

"Oh, dear. Haven't patched things up with Tara yet?"

"And he fired Liz, too."

Mick rolled his eyes. "What are you—eight?"

Gavin gave him a smug grin. Mick's mother's eyes widened. "You fired Elizabeth? Why?"

Gavin opened his mouth, but Mick raised his hand. "Shut up. Let me talk." Gavin clamped his lips closed.

"She did something I didn't like. Something that hurt Tara and Nathan. It was the last straw."

"I see." His mother crossed her arms. "Want to talk about it?"

Mick looked up at Gavin, who made no move to leave.

"Gavin, let me talk to Michael alone."

"Oh, fine. I miss all the good stuff." He kissed his mother on the cheek. "I'm heading home."

She snatched the bottle of beer from his hands. "How much beer have you had?"

"Jesus, Mom, I'm twenty-nine now, not sixteen. Just a few sips."

"Then you can go. Love you."

"Love you, too." Gavin slugged Mick's arm on the way by. "Call me if you need me."

"Thanks, Gavin."

"So what happened with Tara?"

Mick filled his mother in on the details of what went down at the carnival and what happened with Tara after.

"Do you think she loves you?"

"Yes."

She laid her hand on top of his. "She's afraid."

"I know."

"What are you going to do about it?"

"I can't make her accept my lifestyle, Mom. It's a pretty heavy commitment. And she does have her own career. And Nathan."

"She's a strong woman. She can handle it. You need to give her some time."

"I'm not big on leaving things be. I'm proactive. I like to go after what I want."

Her lips twitched. "I know. You've always been the one to get things done. This time I think you need to sit back and let her stew for a while. If she loves you like you say she does, she'll come to you."

"But—"

She squeezed his hand. "Let her come to you, Michael. Don't push her, or she'll feel cornered. She knows she loves you. And she knows you love her. Now let her come to realize it."

"I'll try."

His mother gave him a knowing smile. "You do that."

TARA PUT THE FINISHING TOUCHES ON HER PROPOSAL, saved the file, loaded it up in the e-mail, and pressed send, offering up a fervent prayer to the business gods that the proposal would be accepted.

It was a big client and would mean a lot of money for her business if accepted. Now she just had to keep her fingers crossed.

She grabbed the prospective client's file, along with other files that littered her desk, and went to the cabinet to do some much needed filing. She'd been working nonstop for the past two weeks, trying to get back in the groove of work. Nothing but work. That and Nathan starting school, which fortunately kept him busy with football practices and team meetings and getting his schedule.

He wasn't happy with her at all, had taken her breakup with Mick personally, and had reverted to his old sullen attitude, though he and his coach and team had loved the revised televised and print piece on him and his team. His coach had personally thanked her for putting the team on the map, even though she'd had nothing to do with it. Coach had asked if Mick would be able to attend any of the Friday night games, and had looked crestfallen when she told him she and Mick were no longer seeing each other.

She was the one who had been dating Mick. Not Nathan, not his friends, not his coach or his team. So they were all just going to have to deal with it. Mick was out of her life. Out of their lives. They'd all get over it eventually.

Even she might get over it. Eventually.

After she finished filing, she went back to her desk to pay a few of the bills she'd been steadily ignoring for the past few days.

Her door opened and Karie, Ellen, and Maggie walked in, their expressions determined.

"Get out," Maggie said.

Tara's brows lifted. "Excuse me?"

"You heard me. It's Thursday night, six o'clock, and Nathan's first game is in an hour. Go home, change clothes, and go to his game."

She lifted her gaze to the clock on the wall. "I'll make the game. I just have a few things left to do here."

"Whatever those things are, they can wait," Ellen said.

"Bills can never wait, and I've been putting them off because I was busy with other stuff."

Maggie marched over and snatched the bills from her desk. "I'll pay the damn bills. Now go. You've been working yourself nonstop since you dumped Mick. You can't hide in here forever."

"I am not hiding. I am focusing my attention on this company. Which, I might add, pays your salaries."

Karie went behind her and pulled her chair back. "We're profoundly grateful. Go home."

"I'm the boss. I could have you all fired."

Ellen held out her purse. "You wouldn't fire us. We're the life-blood of this company. You'd crumple into the fetal position and suck your thumb without us."

Tara snorted. "You're probably right."

She walked out of her office, turned around, and all three of her employees—her friends—guarded the door to her office. "Good night."

"Bye," they all said.

Tara rolled her eyes and left the office, drove home, and hurriedly changed into her jeans and Nathan's team T-shirt. She grabbed a sweater, knowing it would get cool once the sun went down, then drove to the high school stadium, parked, and headed toward the junior varsity field.

Nathan was starting the game tonight and he was nervous and excited. Even though they'd been at odds the past few weeks, he still searched the stands for her, gave her a tilt of his lips when he saw her sitting in the third row at the forty-yard line. She gave him a little wave, and then he was off to warm up on the field with his team.

It was just like the first game she'd seen Mick play. Tara's fingers curled into her palms and she had to force herself to relax when, after the kickoff, her son took his place behind the center and counted off the numbers to the play. The center hiked the ball into Nathan's hands, and, instead of shifting the ball off to a running back or throwing it to a receiver, Nathan saw the hole the offensive line had opened up in the middle and ran through it.

Oh, God. *Run, Nathan, run!*

Tara held her breath for the entire nine yards until Nathan slid and was piled on by three tacklers. She didn't breathe until he jumped up, grinned, and headed to the huddle. Only then did she exhale amid the wild cheers.

Smart-ass. Thought he was a scrambler, did he? She'd never seen him do that before.

By midway through the fourth quarter the score was close. The team they were playing had made the playoffs last year, so they were good. But Nathan's team had showed a lot of improvement so they were playing tough, but were behind by six points. Tara had to shift her attention from the game to the scoreboard, chewing on a ragged hangnail and hoping time wouldn't run out before Nathan could march his team down the field and score again, and that the defense could keep the opposing team from putting more points up.

There were two and a half minutes left when the defense held and Nathan got the ball back in his hands. Tara could only imagine the pressure he felt to keep his team in the game. Was this what Mick went through every game? It must drive his mother crazy.

Stop thinking about Mick. And about his family.

She missed Kathleen, wished they could have stayed close. She could have used her counsel through all of this, but it would hardly be appropriate to call Kathleen to talk to her about her own son. The son Tara had dumped.

She shook off thoughts of Mick and concentrated on Nathan. First down was a run and they picked up five yards. Tara breathed in, then out, trying to calm down her raging heartbeat.

Second down was a short pass to the wide receiver, who ran for a first down. She jumped up and down and hugged one of the other moms. They were on their own forty-yard line now, and a third down twenty-five-yard run by the team's running back put them in their opponent's territory.

Tara's heart was pounding. She couldn't imagine what Nathan felt. He looked steady and calm as he threw a long pass to his wide receiver, who ran all the way to the fifteen-yard line before being tackled. Her heart was in her throat as the next two downs got them nowhere. Third down and forty-five seconds on the clock. Nathan was in the shotgun, took the ball from center, rolled back to his left—nothing. He stayed in the pocket, turned to his right, spotted his tight end in the middle of the field, and fired off a rocket pass to the tight end, who sprinted into the end zone for a touchdown.

Oh my God. They'd scored. Screaming erupted. Tara shouted, yelled Nathan's name, and burst into tears. It was the best game ever. The extra point put them ahead, and though the other team got the ball back, time ran out, and Nathan's team won.

No victory could have been sweeter. Tara didn't even care that it was only the first game of the season; it had still been the best game she'd ever seen him play.

After the game and all the celebrations, Tara went down on the field. She hung back while he talked with some of the students, including a young girl—a JV cheerleader. Very cute, with dark hair pulled into a high ponytail. When Nathan saw her, he smiled, and her heart clenched, because he looked just like a little boy again.

He'd never be her little boy anymore though. He was growing up, and it was time to give him his space. She went over to him and hugged him. "You played an amazing game."

He grinned. "Thanks, Mom. This is Carla."

"Hi, Mrs. Lincoln."

"Not Mrs. And you can call me Tara. Nice to meet you, Carla."

"Oh. Okay. Nathan played great, didn't he?"

"He did."

"Um, some of us are going to Coach's for an after the game pizza party," Nathan said. "Is it okay? And I'd like to spend the night at Bobby's house. His parents said it was fine."

Tara shifted her gaze to Bobby's parents, who waved and nodded. She waved back. "It sounds fine to me. I'll go talk to his parents. You have a good time."

"Thanks, Mom."

Tara had a brief conversation with Bobby's parents, who assured her they'd pick up Bobby and Nathan from Coach's house after the party. Tara would pick up Nathan tomorrow afternoon, so it was all set.

She turned around to head home but stopped in the middle of the field, her heart slamming against her chest when she saw Mick. Or at least she thought she saw him. He'd be pretty difficult to miss, since he was so damn tall, and she'd committed his face to memory until she died. And even though it was dark, the stadium lights were still on. He'd ducked to the west side of the bleachers and disappeared into the crowds leaving the stadium. She followed, quickening her step as she moved off the turf and onto the sidewalk, passing the bleachers where she'd seen him standing and out to the parking lot where a score of people where getting into their cars and taking off.

She climbed onto the brick planting area and scanned the crowds, thought she spotted his black SUV pulling out of the parking lot.

She was obviously imagining things. Why would Mick be here?

She'd told him she never wanted to see him again. He'd made no contact with her in over two weeks. He had a game Sunday. This was a local high school game. No media attention. He'd have no reason to be here.

She was an idiot. She'd worked so hard to push Mick out of her mind.

"Mom?"

She looked down to see Nathan, Carly, Bobby, and Bobby's parents gaping up at her while she stood like some idiot on the brick wall.

"Oh. Hi there."

"What are you doing up there, Mom?"

"Uh, just though I saw someone I knew."

The side of Nathan's mouth curled. "Mick, maybe?"

He held her hand while she jumped down. "No. Why would you think that?"

"Duh, Mom. Because he was here."

"He was? How would you know that?"

"Because I invited him to the game." Nathan turned to Carly and Bobby. "I'll meet up with you guys in a sec."

Nathan looked at the ground after his friends left. There was something he wasn't telling her.

"Nathan?"

He finally lifted his gaze to hers. "Look, I didn't want you to go all batshit . . . uh . . . crazy on me about it. I called him and asked if he wanted to watch my first game. He said he'd love to. I left a ticket for him. He came to the locker room before the game, talked to the guys. No big deal, okay?"

"You missed him."

Nathan shrugged. "Just thought he might want to see me play."

Tears pricked her eyes. God, this kid needed a man in his life. "I'm sorry, Nathan. This is why I don't date."

"Bullshit. Stop using me."

Her eyes widened. "What?"

"You've kept your life on hold because of me. You don't let anyone get close to you because of me."

"That's not true."

"You love Mick. Don't you?"

She opened her mouth to deny it but then stopped herself.

"Don't bother saying a word. It's obvious you're practically crying yourself to sleep every night. I don't know why you're being such a big baby about this, Mom. You love him. He loves you. Simple, right?"

She rubbed her temple. "No, Nathan. It's not simple."

"Then tell me what the problem is."

"The problem is between Mick and me and is none of your business."

"Why don't you quit treating me like I'm a little kid and start treating me like maybe I can handle some grown-up problems? I'm always going to be here for you when sh— when stuff happens that's bad. You don't have to make life perfect for me. I know bad things happen. I know you had a shitty—fine I'll just say it—a shitty life when you were younger. That doesn't mean you have to look for the bad in every thing and every person. Not everyone is like that. Mick isn't like that."

She held up her hand. "Okay, wait a minute."

"No. I'm not going to wait. And I don't think you should wait anymore either. You put your life on hold for me. And really, I get that. I appreciate it. But I'm not a baby anymore. Let go, Mom."

She stood there, speechless, looking at her little boy who had grown up and was now giving her advice. "I guess you have grown up. I'm sorry."

"Don't be sorry. Just stop using me as an excuse for not doing what you really want."

She inhaled, let it out. "Do you think I've been doing that?"

"Not always. But with Mick? Yeah. And stop it."

She nodded, flabbergasted at her son, who had somehow grown up when she wasn't looking. "Okay. I will."

"I like him, too, Mom."

She sucked in a breath, realized she hadn't been the only one to love Mick.

"I know you do."

"He's not a bad guy."

"No, he's not."

"Even if you don't get back with him, I want to be friends with him. Would that be okay?"

She sat on the brick wall and held her son's hands. Surprisingly, he let her. "That would be fine. I can't think of anyone who's a better person to be in your life than Mick."

Nathan grabbed her up into a fierce hug that brought a rush of tears to her eyes.

"I love you. Gotta go. Bye."

"Bye." She laughed through the tears as he ran off with his friends.

"Go find Mick and tell him you love him," Nathan yelled when he was halfway down the parking lot.

Tara was mortified, but the kids all laughed, and Bobby's parents just waved and shook their heads.

Oh sure, her kid dropped this epic pronouncement about maturity and love on her, then ran off for pizza. He'd understood it all so easily, when she clearly hadn't.

Youth. She certainly hadn't been that smart when she was his age.

She got into her car and started it up, then made the turn for home, got a block down the road, and abruptly pulled onto the freeway.

Nathan was right. It was time to stop being scared and stop making excuses.

She knew what she wanted, and it was time to go get it.

TWENTY-ONE

MICK HAD JUST FINISHED TAKING A SHOWER WHEN HE heard the doorbell.

"Shit." He grabbed a pair of pants and shrugged into them, throwing the zipper up while flying down the stairs. He'd ordered the pizza, figuring it would be at least an hour before it arrived.

He grabbed his wallet and pulled the door open.

It wasn't the pizza guy. It was Tara.

"Oh. I thought you were pizza delivery."

She swallowed, her throat working as she did it again. "No pizza here. Sorry. Can I come in?"

"Sure." He stepped out of the way and closed the door behind her. "I was in the shower."

"I can see that." Her gaze raked over his chest and lower, and damn his dick for noticing her lingering where he hadn't bothered buttoning his pants. "Want something to drink?"

"Water would be good."

He went to the kitchen and filled up glasses with water for both of them, dragging his fingers through his still-wet hair before carrying the water out.

"Thanks."

"Sit down."

She did, took a couple swallows of water, and set the glass on the coffee table. "You were at Nathan's game tonight."

"He invited me. I tried to stay out of your line of sight, figured you wouldn't be happy if you knew I was there."

"About that . . ."

"Look, I stayed hidden. There was no media. I fired Liz, so she won't be getting in your way."

Her gaze snapped to his. "You fired Elizabeth?"

"Yeah."

"Why?"

"You know why."

"Mick. I hope you didn't do that because of me."

He took a seat in the chair. "Partly because of you. Partly because of me and what I want from my career. And what I don't want anymore."

"What don't you want?"

"I don't want all the media attention, all the models and actresses and movie premieres and the other stuff."

"What do you want?"

"I want to play football for as long as my body will let me, and for as long as I can do a good job at it. And I want a wife. A son. Maybe another kid."

She swallowed. "Ready-made family, huh?"

Her voice had gone hoarse. There were tears in her eyes. He moved to the couch. "I've known what I wanted since that night several months ago when I met this beautiful woman in a ballroom. She was perfect for me."

She blinked, and her eyes went soft and dark. "Is that right?"

"Yes. I knew then there was something special about her. I didn't exactly know then that I wanted to marry her, but I know that now. I love you, Tara."

Tara lifted her gaze to his. "I knew that night there was something special about you, too. But I was scared. I've never been lucky in love."

He tipped her chin with his fingers. "Time for your luck to change."

He brushed his lips against hers, and she sighed. He gathered her against him, so damn happy she'd come to him that his heart felt like it was swelling inside his chest.

He wasn't a guy who was used to emotion, but he felt tears pricking his eyes. He shut them out and concentrated on the way Tara made him feel. Happy. Perfect.

And when her body touched his, all he felt was heat. Her hair brushed against his arm, and he lifted his hand to sweep along its length, tangle his fingers in it, and tug on it a little. She moaned against him and pulled her lips from his.

"I love you. I've missed you. I've been so stupid."

He put his finger against her lips. "That's over now. The past is always over. You only have to think about the future." He pulled her onto his lap. "I'm going to make love to you, then we're going to talk about that future. I've missed being inside you."

She held on to his arms. "God, I've missed that, too."

He pulled her sweater off and dragged her T-shirt over her head, laid her on the couch, and licked over the swell of her breasts. The taste of her set him on fire, the need to feel her hard nipples against his tongue overruling his desire to take things slow. He unclasped her bra and pulled it away, then took her nipples in his mouth, rolling his tongue over the hard buds until she arched and fed them to him. He sucked and licked her, and she

THE PERFECT PLAY   297

writhed against him until his cock was about to bust the zipper on his pants.

He drew her jeans off, already inhaling the sweet smell of her desire.

"You wet for me?"

She looked up at him. "All I've been doing is thinking about you, dreaming about you. All I want is for you to fuck me until I come."

He left her only long enough to get a condom, tossed it onto the table, but first he needed to taste her. He drew her panties off, her moisture glistening in the overhead lights. He used his thumb to trace the seam of her pussy lips, loving that she shuddered at his touch. When he slid his finger inside her and bent down to capture her clit between his lips, she cried out, bucking against him.

"Oh, God, Mick, I won't last long."

He didn't want her to wait. He wanted her to come, wanted to taste her as she let go and came against his mouth and tongue. He pressed down with his tongue against her clit and dragged it across her soft lips, keeping his finger inside her pumping away, then brought his lips over her clit and sucked.

"Oh, God, oh, God, Mick." She rocked against his mouth while he lapped up her come, removing his fingers to suck up all her juices while she shuddered against him. Then he pulled away only long enough to drop his pants and put on the condom. He spread her legs apart and inched inside her, needing to fuck her hard but needing to savor this moment, because he loved her now, and it was like the very first time.

With Tara, it would always be like the first time.

It was perfect.

TARA WATCHED THE PLAY OF EMOTIONS ON MICK'S FACE, from passion to near pain as he entered her. She was so filled with love for this man she could barely contain her joy. The pleasure he brought her held no bounds. She lifted against him, still pulsing inside from the orgasm he'd given her. Her pussy tightened around him, gripping him as he swelled inside her and dragged impossible sensations from her with every thrust.

She held on to his arms as he moved slow and easy at first, then quickened the pace, rolling his hips over her clit and grinding against her until she climbed that precipice again. He took her right to the edge, then pulled back, giving her that wicked smile that told her he knew exactly where she'd been, but wouldn't let her go just yet.

"Bastard."

"You love me."

"Yes, I do. Now let me come."

He dropped down on top of her and kissed her, a bone-melting kiss, his tongue sliding over hers, his fingers buried in her hair, his body connected to hers in the most intimate way. There wasn't a part of him that wasn't touching her, from his cock to his mouth to his heart.

It was perfect.

And when she came, she cried out against his lips, and he groaned against hers, and it was the sweetest sound of love that left her laughing and crying and thinking life was just so damn good, and she'd almost thrown it all away.

After, they ate pizza and curled up together on the sofa.

"You want a big wedding?"

She turned to look at him. "I have no idea. I've never thought about it."

He arched a brow. "You're a woman. All women think about stuff like this. And besides, you're an event planner."

She shrugged. "I just never thought I'd get married."

"You're getting married. Plan a big wedding."

"I don't have any family. Except Nathan, of course."

"You have my family. They're now your family. And they're huge. And then there's the team. Also huge. And lots of friends."

"Guess I should start a guest list."

He kissed the tip of her nose. "Guess you should." He grabbed his drink and took a long swallow.

"Do you really want a baby?"

He shifted his gaze to her. "Do you?"

She smiled at him, remembering the feel of the baby she held. "I've thought about it."

"I'd love another kid like Nathan. Or maybe a little girl like you."

Her heart warmed, and she snuggled against him. "I have no idea what I did to deserve someone like you."

"Just lucky, I guess."

She shoved her shoulder into him, and he laughed.

"I'm the lucky one, Tara. I have you; I have Nathan. I have the perfect life. Thank you."

She lifted up and kissed him, a long, lingering kiss.

"Mmmmm, pepperoni. Perfect, indeed."

KEEP READING FOR A SPECIAL PREVIEW OF
THE NEXT BOOK BY JACI BURTON,

CHANGING THE GAME

GAVIN RILEY KNEW ELIZABETH DARNELL HAD BEEN
avoiding him for the past several months. And he knew why.

She was afraid he was going to fire her just like his brother
Mick had.

Oh, sure, Mick played in the NFL and Gavin played Major
League Baseball, so in a lot of ways they were similar. And since
Mick was Gavin's big brother, many people thought Gavin followed
Mick's lead, especially in business matters. After all, Mick had hired
Elizabeth first and Gavin had followed suit.

But people would assume wrong. Gavin made his own decisions
about business and didn't do everything his brother did. Even if Liz
had messed with Mick's personal life, hurt Mick's girlfriend and her
son, and had done just about everything humanly possible to piss
his brother off. And she might have apologized and set things right
with Mick, Tara, and Tara's son, Nathan, but it had been a case of
too little, too late.

There were things a sports agent did that were valuable to an athlete's career. But screwing with an athlete's love life could be the kiss of death for an agent.

Liz had never once touched Gavin's love life. In fact, Liz threw women at him like a pimp. Beautiful women. Actresses, models, the kind of women that made Gavin look good. Gavin had no complaints. In fact, Liz had done the same thing for Mick until he had fallen in love with Tara Lincoln and put an end to Liz coupling Mick with the latest and greatest starlet on the cover of whatever magazine would get him the most exposure. But Liz had tried to get Tara and her son out of Mick's life, which had resulted in Liz getting fired.

And that's why she'd been avoiding Gavin, no doubt afraid Gavin had sided with Mick and was ready to do the same—which Gavin found pretty damned amusing. Elizabeth watched over her clients like a hawk, and for her to go to complete radio silence was like giving up and letting the vultures swoop in and take over her prime real estate.

Not that Gavin was the best player around, but she'd sat on him since she signed him, not letting any other agents get within talking—or signing—distance.

Maybe it had something to do with that night Mick had fired her.

Mick had walked out of the locker room, leaving Elizabeth alone with Gavin.

Liz had come up to him looking all teary-eyed and vulnerable, two things that were totally uncharacteristic of her.

Then she'd kissed him. And walked away.

Not that he'd thought about that kiss much over the past months. Much.

Except she'd avoided him, which was also uncharacteristic of her. So had it been the kiss that had sent her into hiding, or the fear he'd fire her?

It was time for her to come out and face the music.

She couldn't avoid him forever, and especially not at this sports banquet where she had several clients, Gavin included, though she was doing her best to steer clear of him.

He'd laid low most of the night, letting her flit around and focus on a few of his baseball peers. He always enjoyed watching her work a room full of hotshot jocks. Elizabeth commanded attention. It didn't matter whether a room was filled with the hottest females around—a guy would have to be either limp dicked or dead not to notice her. Hair the color of his favorite red sports car; incredible blue eyes; creamy, soft skin; and legs a man could only hope to some day have wrapped around him. And she showed it all off with practiced precision. She was a walking sex bomb with a wicked brain. Lethal combination.

Gavin would be lying if he didn't admit to being tempted by Liz. But he never mixed business with pleasure, and he took his opportunities elsewhere. Liz had been a great agent, had locked him up tight with the St. Louis Rivers Major League Baseball team right out of college, and she'd worked her ass off to make him rich, get him product endorsements, and keep him in his position at first base. He never wanted to do anything to change that.

Besides, he doubted Elizabeth was his type.

Gavin was pretty damned particular about the women he chose. And ballbusting women like Elizabeth? Definitely not his type.

But they needed to get a few things straight, and she could only avoid him for so long.

The banquet was winding down and most everyone was leaving. Liz was with Radell James and his wife, walking with them toward the main ballroom doors. Gavin shot out a side door and hung back, unobserved, while she said her good-byes.

She looked good tonight in one of her usual business suits. Black, which seemed to be one of her favorite colors, and tailored to within an inch of its life. The skirt hung just above her knee, and those shoes she wore played up her toned calves, too. She walked through the front doors of the hotel and outside with Radell and his wife.

Gavin stepped outside unnoticed while Liz talked with Radell. He stood in the background and watched until Radell and Teesha's taxi arrived.

After they left, Liz leaned against the brick wall and closed her eyes. She looked tired. Or defeated. Her guard was down.

Time for Gavin to make his move. He stepped in front of her.

"You've been avoiding me, Elizabeth."

Her eyelids shot up and her eyes widened with shock. She started to push off the wall but he pinned her there by placing his hand on the wall by her shoulder. There was a planter on the other side, so she had nowhere to go.

"Gavin. What are you doing here?"

"It's the sports banquet. You knew I was here. In fact, I'd say you danced around tables doing your best to not see me tonight."

She blinked. Her sweetly painted mouth worked, but nothing came out for a few seconds. He didn't think he'd ever seen her at a loss for words. Her eyes darted from side to side like a cornered animal looking for escape.

But she finally relaxed, her gaze warmed and the old Elizabeth was back. She tipped her finger down the lapel of his jacket.

"I wasn't avoiding you, sugar. I picked up a new client so I had to babysit him a bit and introduce him to all the right media people. Then there was Radell and we had a few things to discuss that were important. I'm so sorry we haven't had a chance to catch up. Did you need me for something?"

"Yeah. We need to talk."

In an instant, the warmth fled. Her expression narrowed. "About what?"

"You and me."

Something flashed in her eyes, something hot he'd never seen before.

Or maybe never noticed before. As soon as it was there, it was gone.

Maybe he'd just imagined it. But Gavin didn't imagine things, and what he'd seen caused a tightening in his balls. It was like the kiss that night, throwing him for a loop and making him second guess everything he thought about her. He'd always maintained his distance from Liz because they had a professional relationship. Besides, she didn't pay much attention to him. She never fawned over him in the same way she did with Mick and a lot of her other clients. She'd always maintained her distance. He figured she never had any interest in him, which suited him just fine since he had no problem finding women, and women had no problem finding him.

But what he'd just seen in her eyes had been . . . interesting.

"You and me? What about you and me?" she asked.

"You finished with all your client stuff?"

She nodded.

"Let's go somewhere and . . ." He skimmed his gaze down her body, lingering where her silk blouse lay against her breasts. He dragged his gaze back to her face, searching for a reaction.

She swallowed and the muscles of her throat moved with the effort.

Elizabeth was nervous. Gavin didn't think he'd ever seen her nervous before.

This was perfect.

"Talk."

"Talk?"

"Yeah." He pushed off the wall and signaled for the valet, gave him his ticket, and grabbed Elizabeth's hand, bringing her with him to the curb while he waited for the valet to bring his car.

Fortunately the sports banquet was in the city where he was in spring training. Damned convenient and no travel time biting into his schedule. He traveled enough on season, and having to add one more event where he had to hop on a plane would have been a drag.

He tipped the valet when he brought his car. He and Elizabeth got in and he zipped onto the highway.

"Where are we going?"

"My house."

She arched a brow. "You have a house? Why not one of the hotels?"

"I stay in enough hotels during the season. I want a place to myself during spring training."

They drove in silence. Gavin made the turn north toward the beach.

"You rented a house on the beach?"

"Yeah. It's remote and I can run in the mornings."

She half turned in her seat. "Dammit, Gavin. Are you going to fire me? Because if you are, I'd rather you just do it right away. Don't drag me out here to your house, then expect me to take a cab back to the hotel."

Gavin fought back a laugh. "We'll talk when we get inside."

"Shit," she whispered, then folded her arms in front of her and propped her head against the window for the remainder of the drive.

He pulled off the highway and took the beachfront road, pulling into the garage. Elizabeth let herself out of the car and followed him inside, looking like a prisoner on her way to an execution.

He flipped the lights on and opened the sliding door leading out to the back porch.

"Nice place."

He shrugged. "It'll do for now. Want a beer or some wine?"

"Why? Trying to soften the blow?"

He slipped his hands into the pockets of his slacks. Ignoring her question, he asked again. "Wine, beer, something else?"

She inhaled and let out an audible sigh. "Glass of wine would be nice, I guess."

He opened a bottle of wine, poured a glass for her, then grabbed a beer from the fridge.

"Let's go outside."

The house had a great back porch, though he supposed out here it was called a veranda, or balcony, or something. Hell, he didn't know what it was called, only that it overlooked the ocean and he liked sitting out here at night to listen to the waves crash against the beach.

There was a long cushioned swing for two, and a couple chairs. Liz sat in the chair and Gavin took the other one.

She took the glass he offered and tipped it to her lips, taking several deep swallows of wine. "Is there a particular reason you dragged me out here to your beach haven instead of telling me what you needed to at the hotel?"

Yeah. He wanted to set her off balance. Liz was always in control. Besides, he didn't want her to stalk off or find an excuse to leave.

And . . . hell, he really didn't know why he'd brought her here, other than he wanted to know why he hadn't seen her in months. Typically she was on his tail constantly, until the thing happened with his brother. Since then she'd all but fallen off the face of the earth.

"You usually call me twice a week and I see you at least once a month."

She shrugged. "You were busy with the end of your season. I was busy, too. Then there were the holidays."

"You always make it a point to be wherever I am so we can have dinner. And when was the last time you missed holidays with my family?"

She snorted. "Your brother fired me. His fiancée hates me. I hardly think it would have been appropriate to spend the holidays with your family."

"It wouldn't have mattered to my mother. She loves you and thinks of you as family. Personal is different from business."

"Not to me, it isn't. And I'm sure it isn't to Mick and Tara, either. I wouldn't have wanted to interfere in your family celebrations. I know I'm not welcome there anymore."

She looked hurt.

This was a new side to her. Gavin looked closer, suspected she was full of shit since he knew she had no feelings. She was just bitter about losing Mick as a client.

"You could have arranged to see me outside of family gatherings."

She studied her nails. "My schedule has been kind of full."

"Bullshit. You went into hiding after Mick fired you."

Her head shot up. "I don't hide. Losing Mick was a giant financial hit. I had to scramble to sign clients to lessen the burden."

Gavin laughed. "You've made a ton of money off Mick, off me and the other guys. I don't think you're hurting."

"Fine." She set her wineglass down and stood, moving toward the railing to stare out over the ocean. "You can believe whatever you want to, since you've already made up your mind. And if you're going to fire me, then get it over with so I can get out of here."

Gavin stood and came over to her. "You think I brought you here to fire you?"

She faced him. "Didn't you?"

This whole "vulnerable Elizabeth" thing was a new side to her he'd never seen before.

Maybe it wasn't an act after all. He'd been convinced Elizabeth wasn't capable of actual emotions.

It would appear she was capable of hurting, and he didn't know what the hell to do about that.

Moonlight danced across her hair, making her look like a goddess lit by silver fire. For the second time tonight Gavin realized that Elizabeth was a beautiful, desirable woman. He'd always thought of her as a vicious shark, which was a great place to file her in his head because she was the business side of his life. Oh sure, she was always great to look at, and he had to admit he'd admired her body more than a few times, but he'd never thought of her as someone who had . . . feelings or emotions.

But as the light played with her eyes, he thought he saw tears welling up in them. And something else lit up her eyes when she looked at him, something he'd seen in many women's eyes before.

Desire. Need. Hunger.

Couldn't be. Liz was cold. He'd seen her drive a three-hundred-pound lineman into the ground with her sharp tongue, take a cold-hearted team owner by the tie and squeeze millions from him without so much as blinking. Liz was ruthless and had no soul. She would cut your heart out before she ever showed you she was vulnerable.

He'd seen what she'd done to Tara and her son, Nathan, and how she hadn't once thought about how it would affect them. She'd wanted to cut them out of Mick's life. Emotion and how they felt hadn't entered the picture. They were an inconvenience and needed to be removed.

Whatever act she was putting on for him now was just that—an act, a way to gain his sympathy or distract him so he wouldn't toss her out on her ass. Losing clients was bad for business. And Liz was all about business, all the time. As far as he knew, she didn't have a personal life. She ate, breathed, and slept business twenty-four hours a day, seven days a week.

So yeah, Elizabeth vulnerable? That was a freakin' laugh. Those tears were manufactured and he wasn't buying it. And the idea of her wanting him? No way. She'd usually been straightforward with him, so he didn't understand what game she was trying to play.

"Liz, what are you doing?"

She frowned. "Excuse me?"

"What are you trying to do here?"

She rolled her eyes. "I have no idea what you're talking about, Gavin. You brought *me* here, remember?"

She drained her glass of wine and held it out to him. "Either get on with the reason why you brought me here, or refill my glass. You're making me crazy."

Ditto. He grabbed her glass and took it into the kitchen, finishing his beer along the way.

When he came back outside he found she'd kicked off her shoes and taken off her jacket. Wind whipped strands of perfect hair loose. They flew in the breeze, wild and untamed.

He'd like to see Liz wild and untamed, but he'd bet she gave orders in bed, too.

He never thought about Elizabeth and sex in the same sentence, preferred to keep the two topics separate.

So why now? Was it the look she'd given him earlier?

Dammit. He didn't want to think of her that way.

She shivered and rubbed her arms.

"Want your jacket?

"No. I'm just cold by nature."

He could make a remark about that, but decided to let it slide. He handed her the wine and poured himself a whiskey from the bottle he'd brought outside with him. Beer just wasn't cutting it.

It was time to get down to business and tell her why he'd brought her out here tonight.

"I screwed up with Mick," she said, staring at the water, not looking at him. "I thought I could control him, that I knew what was best for him. Turns out I had no idea. I wasn't listening to him when he told me he wanted Tara. I thought it was a fling. But he was in love with her and I didn't want him to be in love with her."

This was new. Liz opening up to him? They talked business, and sometimes had a few drinks and laughs when they were together, but mostly talked sports. Nothing personal. Ever.

"Why didn't you want him to be in love with her?"

"Because if he was, things would change."

"What things?"

"Mick was so easygoing. I could fix him up with an actress or model for promo and he'd go along with whatever I suggested. His face was on the cover of so many magazines, his name was everywhere. I made him famous."

He moved up next to her. "His arm made him famous, Liz."

Her lips curled in a wistful smile. "That was part of it. You guys don't understand PR at all. You think all you have to do is what you do out on the field, when it's so much more than that." She emptied her glass again, then set it on the table. "Being good at your sport is only a small part of making you into an icon. The gossip magazines, the media, your pictures and your endorsement deals . . . everything else is what makes you."

She turned to face him. "You could be the best goddamn first baseman in all of baseball, but if I don't get you the deals to hawk deodorant or razors or underwear, if the public doesn't find out who you are, doesn't see your face eight times a day on commercials and in print media and online during your season? No one's going to care, Gavin. No one's going to care that you had a three seventy-eight batting average with forty-eight home runs; that you won your sixth consecutive Golden Glove and that you were the National League's MVP. No one's going to care. They care because the media tells them to care. And the media cares because I tell the media to care.

"All you guys want to do is play your sports, have your parties with your women, or buy your expensive cars and make sure you look good. You want those endorsement deals so you're financially secure, but you don't realize how cutthroat it is out there, how hard it is to get those deals. Because for every one of you there are forty other guys clamoring for the same spot. That's what you pay me for. Not just to negotiate your contract, but to get all those deals for you, and to put your face on the cover of *Sports Illustrated*, and to make sure you end up in *People* magazine. That's what you pay me for. That's why you need me."

She pushed off the railing and stumbled into the kitchen.

Hell. He had no idea what *that* was all about. He knew damn well what she did for him. She was on a roll, wasn't she?

But he liked the feisty Elizabeth much more than vulnerable, sad Elizabeth. He was just going to let this play out and see where she went with it.

SHIT. LIZ LEANED AGAINST THE COUNTER AND TOOK a long swallow of wine, wishing she'd never agreed to come here with Gavin.

Spilling her guts like that had been stupid. She never talked to Gavin like that. Everything with him was always superficial. She told him how great he was, or she set him up for a photo shoot. And she renegotiated his contract and got him the best deal. That was it. That was all they ever discussed.

She always kept her distance from him, usually met him in crowds and at public events where she'd be safe.

And she had a damn good reason for it.

One, she was four years older than him. She didn't date younger guys. Ever.

Two, she was in love with him and had been for years.

Three, he was totally, utterly and completely oblivious to it, and she intended to keep it that way.

Oh sure, she flirted with him, just like she did with all her clients. Surface stuff, nothing but fluff. She never wanted Gavin to think she treated him any differently than she did any of her other clients. And he was mostly clueless because he paid very little attention to her except when it came to business, thankfully.

But she did treat him differently, because she felt differently about him. She kept her distance because of how he made her feel.

When it had happened, she couldn't say. God knows she'd tried to keep it from happening. But there was just something about him. Maybe it was his dark good looks, his mesmerizing green eyes, the way his dark brown hair fell over his brow, or the sexiness of his goatee. Maybe it was his lean body that he honed into shape with daily workouts at the gym and playing noncompetitive sports outside his own sport of baseball. Maybe it was the way he catered to kids on the field, always taking the time to sign autographs or stop and talk to them. He was a big jock and worth millions, but he'd never developed a giant-sized ego about it like many of her clients did. He was a genuinely nice guy.

But what she really loved about him was his smile. There was something wickedly devilish about Gavin's smile. It was a secret, mature kind of smile, the kind of smile that made a woman want to know what he was thinking about.

She'd been curious about his smile when she'd first met him and he'd looked her over in the way a man looks at a woman. But as soon as she'd signed him, that had been the end of it. He'd never looked at her that way again. Oh, she'd seen him look at other women with that smile, and in many ways she'd regretted signing him on as a client, even though she'd given him one hundred percent of herself as an agent.

But she'd woefully, wistfully, regretted not having him direct that wicked smile at her.

Until tonight. Tonight, outside the hotel, he'd looked at her that way for the first time. He'd looked at her like a man looks at a woman he's interested in having sex with. Her breath caught and for one brief moment she'd wondered . . .

"You hiding in here?"

She jerked around to face Gavin, her fingers clutching tight to the empty glass of wine.

"Refilling my wineglass."

His gaze shifted. "Glass is empty."

"So it is." She lifted the wine bottle. "And so is the bottle."

Gavin went to the wine cooler and pulled out another bottle, grabbed the opener and popped the cork out. His warm fingers slid over her chilled ones as he held the glass steady and refilled her glass, his gaze never leaving hers.

"Your fingers are still cold."

There was that look again, that smile he'd given her outside the hotel earlier tonight, the one he'd never let her see before. Her belly tumbled and, oh, God, her nipples hardened. She wondered if Gavin could tell through her flimsy bra and silk blouse.

"I'm fine."

"Okay." He held on to her hand and she tucked her bottom lip between her teeth.

"You'll have to spend the night."

She swallowed. "What?"

"I've had three whiskeys. I'm not driving. You'll have to stay here tonight."

"Oh. Uh . . . I could call a cab."

He smirked. "You could. But you don't want to, do you?"

What? What the hell was he talking about? Was he hitting on her?

Oh, no. Oh, hell no.

She went for her bag and dragged out her cell phone. "I'm calling a cab."

He grasped her wrist and leaned into her. "We're not done talking, Liz."

He wasn't referring to having a conversation. She knew it, and so did he.

"Why now, Gavin? Why, after all these years, are you doing this now?"

"Why do we have to dissect it?"

Her heart pounded so loud she wondered if Gavin could hear it.

He directed her phone to the counter, pulled her fingers away from it.

Call a cab. Go home. Get out of here now before you do something incredibly stupid, Elizabeth.

"I don't have sex with my clients, Gavin."

His lips quirked. "You want me to fire you so I can fuck you?"

Her body was going up in flames. Why was he doing this to her?

"Not particularly."

"Do you want me to fuck you?"

She couldn't breathe. How was she supposed to answer that?

Lie, you idiot, just like you've been lying for the past five years.

He moved to the center island like a predator, caging her between it and him by placing his hands on either side of her hips.

"You're panting, Liz. Do I scare you?"

"No."

He leaned in closer, his hips brushing hers. And then she felt the hard ridge of his cock and every ounce of common sense fled.

He bent and pressed his lips her neck, his hair brushing her cheek. She inhaled, breathing him in, realizing this was the closest she'd ever been to him. His smelled like fresh soap and everything she'd ever dreamed of. She gripped the granite counter so tight her fingers hurt.

She tried swallowing again, but she'd gone dry. At least her throat had gone dry. Below her waist she was wet, primed and ready for him to slide inside her and give her what she'd fantasized about for the past five years. Her pussy throbbed with anticipation, her breasts hot and swollen. Her clit tingled, and if he rubbed against her just the smallest bit, she could come, just thinking about how good it could be between them.

"Gavin," she squeaked.

"Touch me, Elizabeth," he murmured, sliding his tongue across her neck. "Put your hands on me and tell me this is what you want."

Damn him. Damn, damn, damn. How could she not give him what he asked for? How could she not take what *she* wanted?

But this would change everything between them. And would undoubtedly cost her Gavin as a client.

Gavin pushed his hips against her, and she melted, slid her arms up and tangled her fingers into his hair. She pulled on his hair to bring his face up, and the wild need she saw in his eyes matched her own.

His mouth was on hers in seconds, lighting the fire that she'd banked for all these years. It exploded when his tongue slid between her teeth.

She'd dreamed of his lips, the taste of him. He tasted like whisky and hot sex. He licked her bottom lip, nibbled at it. Her fingers were lost in the soft thickness of his hair, the only thing soft about him, as his mouth ravaged her. She knew there'd be nothing easy about Gavin. He was hardness and pain and she reveled in it as he drove his tongue inside her mouth and tangled with hers, sucking her tongue hard until tears sprang into her eyes.

She let out a ragged moan. Gavin grabbed her hips and lifted her onto the counter, settling between her legs, grabbing her butt to draw her heated center against him. He pulled her blouse out of the waistband of her skirt, lifting it off her head in one jerky motion.

He skimmed his hand along her throat and between her breasts. Elizabeth leaned back and watched as he laid his tanned, dark hand across the cup of her bra.

"Sexy, Elizabeth." He lifted his gaze to hers, then back to her bra as he pulled the cup aside, revealing her nipple, which was hard and puckered. "Such a pretty nipple, too."

She held her breath when he bent and put his lips over her nipple. The second she felt the hot suction, she gasped, her fingers moving into his hair again. She couldn't believe this was happening. All the hot fantasies she'd stored up of her and Gavin together were coming to life.

She'd never believed her dreams could become reality. She might be a little drunk tonight, and she knew he was, too, and this would probably never happen again. So she was committing every moment of it to memory so she'd never forget it. The pull of his lips on the tight bud of her nipple, the sight of his dark head against her pale breast, the scent of him as she inhaled in a deep breath and simply the way she felt—totally consumed by him.

It was her every fantasy to be taken by him. She'd known it was going to be like this.

And she'd never, ever tell him how much it meant to her. She had to keep herself under control, didn't want him to know how much power he held over her.

Never give a man power over you, or he'll destroy you.

She lived by those words, and yet right now she was in languorous splendor.

She'd take back control later. Now she gave it up willingly as Gavin dragged the other bra cup aside and lavished attention on her other nipple, using his fingers on the nipple he'd made wet with his mouth. And when he looked up at her, his eyes now filled with a darkness that melted her to the countertop, she waved the white flag in surrender.

He pushed her skirt up over her hips and laid the palm of his hand over her sex, smiling up at her in the way she'd always wanted him to—that secret smile he'd always reserved for other women, never her.

"You wear some very sexy underwear, Elizabeth. Do you always dress this way, or did you wear these tonight with the intent to seduce someone?"

She fought to find her voice. "I always dress this way."

"When was the last time you fucked someone?"

Her eyes narrowed. "None of your business."

He swept his hand up across her sex and she gasped. "Answer me."

"No."

Pleasure shot through her as his fingers teased her, then stopped. "When was the last time you fucked a man, Elizabeth?"

She knew better than to give him that kind of control. She'd already given up too much. "When was the last time you fucked a woman, Gavin?"

He swept his fingers along the side of her panties, and she swore if he got anywhere near her clit, she'd come. "You want me to lick your pussy, don't you? You want me to make you come, don't you?"

Her sex throbbed, her mind awash with the visuals of his head buried between her legs, his soft tongue lashing her pussy until she screamed in orgasm. "Yes. Make me come, Gavin."

"Then answer me. "

"Why do you need to know?"

He shrugged, his fingers lightly teasing the satin material of her panties. It was a breath, a whisper of touch across her sex. Enough for her to feel it, yet . . . not enough. "I want to know. Tell me. How long has it been?"

"Two years."

He frowned. "Is that the truth?"

"Yes."

"Damn, Liz. Look at me."

She dragged her gaze to his. He grabbed the tiny wisps of material at her hips, and ripped. She gasped. He smiled, then dragged the remnants of her very expensive panties away. Her naked butt hit the granite counter and she shivered.

"Cold?"

"A little."

He swept his hand under her butt and lifted her, then planted his mouth on her sex.

Oh, God. Oh, God. Oh, God. It was so good. She lifted, watching him as he slid his tongue in a wide arc across her clit, then dragged his tongue down her pussy lips, shoving it inside her.

"Gavin," she whispered, trembling at the sensations of his tongue rolling along her flesh.

It had been so long since a man had touched her. She didn't allow it, for so many reasons. Sex was so complicated, and often she got so little out of it.

Thoughts fled as she gave up and allowed herself to feel, to experience the magic as he sucked her clit, ran his tongue up and down her pussy, licked her until she fought for every ragged breath.

He grasped her wrists and held her, his fingers digging into her skin, the pain only intensifying the sensations as he took her to the edge of control.

And embarrassingly, she wasn't going to last. She wanted to because this was the sweetest pleasure she'd ever felt. It was magic and she was only going to have it once. But the rushing tide of orgasm wouldn't hold, and she lifted, cried out, and came, her climax a shockwave of sensation that zapped her nerve endings with unbearable pleasure. Gavin tightened his hold on her while he lapped up everything she had to give.

Her muscles quivered and he helped her sit up, his face wet from her. Her hand shaking, she used her thumb to swipe across his chin. He grabbed her thumb and sucked it, his gaze still dark with unquenched desire. He handed her wineglass to her and she took a couple long swallows to quench the raw thirst in her throat, but it didn't quench her thirst for him.

She was afraid it would take a long time for that thirst to be slaked.

He lifted her into his arms and placed her on her feet. All she wore was her skirt and bra, which was off kilter. He was still completely dressed, his hard cock visible against his dark slacks.

He grabbed her hand. "Come on."

He led her down the hall, her bare feet padding along the wood floor toward the master bedroom that was all burgundy and cream and wide windows overlooking the ocean. She wished it was daylight so she could see outside, but there were open French doors leading to the terrace, a soft breeze blowing inside, and a lazy fan circling over the . . .

Oh, my God.

A bed that could sleep at least six people.

Now she understood the appeal of this house for Gavin.

It was the bed. Had to be the bed.

She wondered how many people he'd had in that bed at one time.

"You rent this house before?"

"I own this house, Elizabeth."

Yes, it definitely made sense.

"Plan many orgies?" she asked as she wandered into the room and stopped at the foot of the massive four poster.

He frowned. "Huh?"

"That bed is not made for one, or two, people to sleep in."

He continued to give her a confused look, then glanced at the bed and back at her. "Oh. I sprawl. I like a big bed."

"Gavin, that goes beyond big bed. That's the kind of bed a polygamist would covet."

"I don't have orgies, Elizabeth." He grabbed a remote off one of the nightstands, pushed a button, and the drapes started to close.

"Oh, please, don't shut all the night out. I like it open and breezy. It's not like you have peeping neighbors or anything."

He clicked the button and reopened them.

"Thank you."

He tossed the remote to the table. "Undress."

She put her hands on her hips. "You like giving orders."

He moved in front of the bed and casually leaned against the footboard. "Don't make me tell you again."

She tilted her head back and laughed. "Or, what? You'll spank me? You want my clothes off, Gavin, get your ass over here and undress me."

His eyes went dark, and oh, God. There it was. That not-quite-there smile, the one that screamed secrets.

Except his smile fled, and he stared her down, the heat swirling in his eyes. And then he advanced on her.

For a second, she trembled.

And she never trembled.

Whether it was excitement or raw desire, she didn't know, but he was on her in seconds, her bra ripped and tossed to the ground. He grabbed her skirt and she felt the strength of his hands at her zipper.

"Wait. Fine, I'll do it."

He stopped and stepped back, a smirk on his face as she drew the zipper down and let the skirt fall to the floor.

"Asshole," she said as she stepped out of it. "That underwear cost a fortune."

He didn't apologize, instead raked his gaze over her naked body, and any anger she felt fled in the face of the heated, hungry look on his face.

He unbuttoned his shirt, pulled it off, and tossed it on top of her skirt, then undid the button on his pants and jerked the zipper down. He kicked off his shoes and dropped his pants, then his boxer briefs, his erection bobbing up and making her lick her lips and crave the feel of his cock in her hands and mouth.

He was magnificent and everything she could have imagined. Lean, with muscled abs and thick biceps, tan and sexy, and as he jerked her into his arms, she couldn't think of any place she'd rather be, even though she knew there were a thousand reasons they shouldn't be doing this.

And a million reasons why she wanted to.